FROM THE ASHES

LAUREN JANKOWSKI

Crimson Fox
PUBLISHING

TURNER, OREGON

FROM THE ASHES: Book Three of the Shape Shifter
Chronicles
Copyright © 2013-2017 by Lauren Jankowski.

Published by Crimson Fox Publishing
www.crimsonfoxpublishing.com

Cover art by Najla Qamber Designs.

This is a work of fiction. Names, characters, places, and
incidents either are the product of the author's imagination
or are used fictitiously. Any resemblance to actual events,
locales, organizations, or persons, living or dead, is entirely
coincidental and beyond the intent of either the author or
the publisher.

All rights reserved, which includes the right to reproduce
this book or portions thereof in any form whatsoever
except as provided by the U.S. Copyright Law.

ISBN: 978-1-946202-46-8

Second Edition.

DEDICATION

For survivors. For anyone who has ever been knocked
down by life and gotten back up again.

PROLOGUE

Night coated the land above the laboratory. The moon and stars were absent as a storm raged. Gnarled tree branches whipped wildly about in the violent gusts of wind that howled like a wounded animal, screaming through the thick forest, stripping the few dying leaves from their branches. The grasses in the open field were flattened as the storm continued its destructive tantrum. Lightning cracked, splitting open the dark sky just long enough to bathe the land in a colorless glow. Rain flooded everything from the tops of the trees to the roots of the plants and the air was heavy with water. The roar of thunder shook the landscape as another bolt of lightning tore off a thick limb from an ancient oak, exposing the paler wood beneath the rough bark.

Oblivious to the fury above were the few who worked the night shift in the Grenich Corporation's laboratory. It was deep underground, a windowless warren lit only by the harsh glow of the many florescent lights throughout the vast facility.

A long day of experimentation had come to a close. The barracks were full of meditating experiments, unable to sleep due to the procedures they underwent during their first year inside. The scientists who performed most of the medical testing had retired to their living quarters on one of the lower levels, and so had the handlers who worked on the intensive combat training. The only ones still awake were the guards in the entrance rotunda; a large circular white room that oozed cold sterility, like every area in the laboratory.

There were fourteen guards in all, two before each door in the rotunda which held the only entrance to the Grenich facility. Toward the center of the room was an enormous stairway leading up to the exit. The guards were all dressed identically: a plain white uniform covered them from head to toe, including a helmet complete with a reflective visor that concealed their features. To the average person, they would look like some kind of alien from a distant galaxy or futuristic soldiers, somehow defying the laws of time. The Grenich Corporation tried to erase any form of individuality, which they believed disrupted harmony. To them, harmony was the key to order and peace.

The men stood completely still and could have easily been mistaken for marble or stone statues. They carried a short sword on their left hip, more for decorative purposes than anything else, and their preferred weapon of choice, a submachine gun, sat to their right. For six hours, from midnight until six o'clock, the guards were the only ones awake in the facility. Six o'clock marked the beginning of each day: the employees arrived in their uniforms and the experiments would come out of their meditative states. Everything was on a strict schedule in the Grenich Corporation and everything was monitored to make sure the regimen was kept. There was no room for deviation of any kind.

"How do you guys *stand* like this for six hours?" One of the guards suddenly spoke, causing all heads to simultaneously swivel sharply in his direction in a smooth mechanical motion. "I mean, I can do it, but in this bland place with all the hospital fumes? Tricky, very tricky."

Another guard approached the one who dared break their silent watch. The first guard tilted his head and clicked his tongue.

"Well, you're not a welcoming bunch," he remarked as he reached into one of his uniform pockets. Automatically, thirteen guns pointed at him. The man raised his other hand, a placating gesture, and slowly removed his hand from his pocket. In a movement quicker than the eye could see, he hurled a glass ball to the ground. It shattered and the space was instantly engulfed in thick billowing smoke. A few of the newer guards began firing in the general direction of the intruder, hitting the walls and occasionally other guards. The more experienced guards shouted at their newer counterparts to stop firing.

The mysterious intruder carefully made his way through the smoke, searching for a particular door. He ducked under one guard, feeling around in the smoke, pausing in a crouch when a bullet hit the wall above him. He continued on, sidestepping a falling guard, and kept his hand along the wall until he finally brushed against a heavy door handle. One of the guards, groping around in the poor visibility, found his arm and latched on. The false guard pulled back his fist and smashed it through the face visor of the man holding him. The visor shattered and when the intruder pulled back his fist, bits of flesh, blood, and reflective glass clung to it. The strong grip on his arm vanished as the guard fell backward. The invader shook most of the gore off his once pristine white glove, and turned his attention back to the door he wanted to go through. Bullets riddled the wall beside him, causing him to flinch.

He pulled out a slick white plastic card with a single black strip down the side. The intruder swiped the card through the slot where employees slid their identification cards and glanced over his shoulder. The smoke was still thick and visibility was nonexistent. The other guards were trying to keep the gunfire down to a minimum, while also trying to locate the intruder. The man allowed himself a small smile: guards could be so dense sometimes and he knew how to exploit even the smallest weakness. The gunfire was starting to die down, much quicker than he had anticipated. He turned back to the sophisticated locking system.

"Please enter your five digit code," a pleasant feminine voice stated. The intruder spun around and struck another guard with a high roundhouse kick that broke the man's helmet in half. The mysterious man quickly entered five completely random numbers, hoping the woman who had given him the special key card knew what she was doing. If she didn't, things would get most unpleasant. The key pad went from red to green and the door unlocked. The man pulled open the heavy metal door, slipped inside, and dragged it closed behind him. He swiped the card through the key pad on the other side and locked the guards in their smoky hell. The intruder stripped off the white uniform, revealing the midnight blue ninja garb he wore underneath, and tossed the uniform to the side. Pulling off his helmet and tossing it away, the man enjoyed the sensation of air on his skin even if it was only around his eyes. He removed the white gloves from his hands to reveal tight black ones underneath. He adjusted the gloves and took off down the dimly lit hall.

The man moved with a stealth that only came from years of intense and dedicated training. He was an invisible phantom moving through the halls and his soft black shoes made no sound on carpet or tile. He paused in the cubicle room and allowed his body to melt into the small shape of a charcoal gray cat with bright golden eyes. This form allowed for easy passage to the barracks; it was much simpler to elude the guards who would now be roaming the different levels. By that logic, he probably should have been a fly, but he was not a huge fan of turning into insects. There were just too many drawbacks to such small forms. Feline was the way to go if you wanted stealth, speed, and silence.

The mysterious man continued toward the stairwell, pausing again at the door to allow his body to take on its usual human form. For all the advantages a feline form had, it also had its fair share of drawbacks — paws being a big one. Again, he swiped the plain white keycard through another scanner. The door unlocked for him almost immediately. He stepped out into the gray stairwell and shut the door behind him. The lights in the stairwells had a sickly green hue and made an irritating buzzing noise constantly.

The man slid the keycard back into a hidden pocket. He had no idea who made the card he was using, but whoever it was, was a damn genius or a wizard or both. The thing was like a psychic identification card. His mentor had given him the tool when he agreed to help her and her other protégé with a particularly dangerous set of missions.

Halfway down the stairs, the man heard the boots of more guards coming up and rolled his eyes. He sped up until he was running and when the two of them came into view, he took full advantage of the element of surprise. Grabbing a hold of each railing, the man launched his feet out, striking them both squarely in the chest. They sailed backward and collided with the wall on the next level down. Before they had a chance to recover, he pounced on them. Stomping on the visor of one, his foot easily went through the plastic and into the skull within. He grabbed the head of the second one and slammed it against the wall a couple times before striking out with a well-aimed kick to the throat, shattering the hyoid bone. The mysterious man stepped around the bodies and the growing pool of blood, continuing down to the bottom level.

He finally reached his destination and swiped his key card through the slot, bouncing impatiently on his heels for the split second it took for the heavy door to unlock.

The barracks were in their own branch of the main laboratories, an area the guards frequently referred to as "the kennel."

The man pulled the door open and stepped into the hallway, looking down the rows of white doors with yellow walls between them. Starting down the first row, he looked up at the red plates affixed at the top of each door. Gold numbers jutted out of each one, indicating which experiment was in the room. The shape shifters behind the doors had no names, no identities — only numbers. They were weapons, nothing more than products in the eyes of those who claimed ownership of them.

The man hurried down the hall, bringing up a map of the facility in his mind's eye. The seven series barracks were located on the east side, and the two he needed to extract were on the second level. He had hacked into the Corporation's system the previous day to make sure the three he had been asked to rescue were in the facility. He had been dismayed to find only two were. One was out on assignment.

The man had just turned down another hall when he encountered two more guards. He quickly turned back around the corner, barely escaping the hail of bullets. They had been a little too close for comfort. Thinking fast, he used the two walls to climb up high enough so his back pressed against the ceiling. The man dug a pair of throwing knives into the wall to ensure he didn't fall before he wanted to. He waited patiently, his sharp eyes never moving from the space beneath him. Sure enough, the guards came around the corner to investigate, guns pointed in front of them. Without giving them a chance to look up, he yanked the knives out of the wall and dropped down like a giant spider. He buried the blades in the vulnerable spot at the base of their necks, easily killing them. The man yanked his knives free, wiping the blood off on the white uniforms. He spun them once and put them back in their sheaths. Reaching down again, he examined the guards' weapons. Both guns had about half a clip left, so he removed them and slung one over his shoulder and the other over his back. They were heavy, but he took no notice.

The man turned back to the hall, watching the numbers. He stopped when he saw the first number he was searching for. The faint sound of small mechanical gears turning drew his attention a little further down the hall. Behind his mask, a bitter grin began to grow. There was a security camera out in the open. Most of the cameras were hidden, but a few were in plain sight. There wasn't an inch of the facility that wasn't under constant surveillance. The higher-ups in Grenich saw all.

The man swaggered toward the camera, his pace smooth and deliberate. The thought of what Grenich did and strove to do, made him see red. He had dedicated his life to taking Grenich and all its subsidiaries down, making sure those responsible for the heinous crimes would be held accountable. The man stopped a few feet away from the camera. The dark-colored eye turned toward him, locking onto the intruder in midnight blue.

~~*~*~*

A few nights later, a meeting took place in a dark room. Three desks sat in front of an enormous plasma screen, two slightly shorter desks sat behind the first row, and one long table sat in the back of the room. On one side of the room was a single chair, occupied by a petite woman with short blonde hair and dark brown eyes.

On each desk, a small reading lamp illuminated the face of the occupant with a dim glow. There were also two fancy fountain pens and a folder of each individual's business. Off to the side, the woman in the chair remained a silent figure, patiently waiting for further instruction. Everyone in the room was dressed in business clothing, finely made and expensive.

The plasma screen cast a dirty gray glow across the room as the attendees, nine in the room and two on video feed, watched security footage from the main laboratory. On the grainy film, the mysterious man in midnight blue approached the camera and paused, waiting until he was front and center in the image. He gave the camera a one-fingered salute, then raised his gun and shot the camera out. When the screen turned to gray and white static, the footage disappeared and was replaced with the image of an older man: Set. To the untrained eye, he looked ordinary. He wore a plain caramel-colored suit, had thinning white hair, and intense dark blue eyes. He usually chose to wear his older appearance when he met with investors and potential clients. He sat on a small couch made of rich reddish brown leather with a plaintive expression on his face and folded his hands in his lap. On his right sat a striking woman. She had curly hair the color of gold, perfect features, and a curvy build. Her looks were accentuated by a bright red dress that revealed her perfect body and her nails and lips had been painted to compliment the fiery shade. She held her head high with the confidence of a queen.

"Well. That was certainly . . . interesting," Set stated in a pleasant tone. Everyone stared at him blankly, doing their best to conceal their reaction to the comment. It didn't matter, not when dealing with a telepath. Set smiled and ran his index finger over the smooth couch arm he leaned against, the very portrait of calm and collected.

"The two he removed from our facility, were they survivors of the project?" he asked as his dark eyes once again rose to observe the people in the room. The man in the middle cleared his throat.

"Yes sir, that is correct," he replied as he folded his large hands in front of him. "We believe he would have taken the third had that one not been out on assignment."

"You want to explain how someone walked into one of our laboratories practically unimpeded, Mr. Carding?" the man to Carding's left demanded calmly. He had dark hair and dark brown eyes. He held himself with the self-assurance of a prince, his head high and his shoulders back. Gripping the arms of his chair, the man leaned back, dark eyes narrowing at Carding.

"Now Vladimir, that is not important right now," Set stated in a placating tone. There was nevertheless a hint of ice in his amiable words, reminding Vladimir of his place.

"Yes sir, I apologize," Vladimir said as he returned his attention to the screen in front of him.

"I already know who our mysterious visitor was. I believe he uses the alias Anubis nowadays. However, there are two things I'm having some difficulty figuring out. I do not understand his motivation and I do not know who could possibly be the brains behind this operation," Set continued as he smoothed his tie. "Tracy, my dear, please report your findings."

The blonde woman who sat off to the side smiled and nodded as she stood. She smoothed the front of her pastel blue business suit. A pair of specially made silver pistols sat in tan holsters about her slim waist.

"Yes sir," she addressed the screen, respectfully bowing her head before turning her attention to the room in general. "There is no trace of the intruder or of the stolen products, but I am confident if I check up regularly on our recruitment teams that I will be able to capture at least one of them. Our experiments are concerned with self-preservation and 7-299 has shown a heightened retaliation response during simulations and training sessions. Once I capture that one, the experiment will lead us to the other one as well as the thieves behind this burglary."

"A wise course of action, Tracy," Set stated. "Let me know if you require anything."

"I will, sir. Thank you," Tracy addressed the screen and then took her seat again.

"Lord Set?" The man to Carding's right, a tall scarecrow of a man, with hair a shade lighter than wheat, raised his hand. He looked concerned.

"Yes, Vincent," Set spoke as if he were calling on a pupil.

"What if Tracy's plan doesn't work? What if these two don't act the way you predict they will?" Vincent asked. Set smiled, chuckling a little. The room's occupants all shifted uncomfortably, knowing Set's laughter foreshadowed unpleasantness. The woman to his right smiled maliciously as she looked down at her subjects.

"Ladies and gentlemen," Set began, inching forward on the couch. "Experiments are not shape shifters. They are not individuals. They are weapons, worth billions. They are property, animals incapable of complex thought or feeling."

He leaned forward even more, his expression becoming colder. "More than that, they belong to me. That is my property, possibly my Key, and I want it back. *You* lost it. So in the unlikely event Tracy's plan doesn't work, you will dedicate every last second of your insignificant lives figuring out one that will, or your incompetent heads will adorn my wall. No one is to rest until *my* weapons are back in *my* possession. Is that understood?"

His tone, though calm, was icy and chilled the occupants in the room. They had displeased him and he would not hesitate to execute each and every one if they failed, family or not. Everyone in the room nodded. They understood and they would follow their orders without question. Set blinked and his usual pleasant smile and demeanor fell easily back into place.

"All right, good," he said, sitting back again. "Meeting dismissed."

The image on the enormous plasma screen disappeared.

CHAPTER ONE

The whisperings about the mysterious woman — Blitz as she would eventually come to be known — began to surface more than a year after the secret meeting. The rebels believed she was one of the legendary glowing-eyes. Others believed her to be a normal woman, but accounts couldn't agree on exactly which race she was. Some believed her to be fey, others thought she was a shape shifter. A few stories even suggested she was a human. Most stories agreed she was a woman, but there were conflicting accounts of where she had come from and who she was. Some insisted she was an escaped prisoner. There were stories casting her in the role of a woman scorned, by a lover or family member. One legend told of a mysterious woman in black looking for her murdered children, who would devour anyone who crossed her path.

No one knew the identity of the first witness, which was common for urban legends. One thing the stories had in common was what the woman wore: a black reflective catsuit made of some material like vinyl — only much nicer and more flexible. The sheen on the smooth material was so clean that if you were close to her in a well-lit area, you'd be able to see your reflection as clearly as if you were looking into a dark mirror. The catsuit was skin-tight and slinky, like something a heroine in a sci-fi movie would wear. It accentuated her body perfectly, molding to her like a second skin. She also wore driving gloves made of the same material and combat boots, which seemed to be attached to the catsuit. No one had ever seen her eyes. She concealed them behind small black sunglasses. She was so perfect she looked as though she had been specially designed. According to a few stories, the mysterious woman wore a silver charm at her throat: a circle around a leaping cat with a lightning bolt carved into its side.

Some storytellers told of a woman who needed no weapons. Others believed the woman to be armed and her weapons left a lasting impression on them. There were some who claimed she carried bladed weapons so sharp they could slice through concrete in a single stroke as easily as a hot knife through a stick of warm butter. A few even insisted the weapons had the same engraved symbol as the one she wore at her throat.

No one had ever seen her move. Some believed she was a phantom, a ghost, or even a wraith. A few theorized she was a personified curse. Witnesses only caught brief glimpses of her in the darkness of night, a pale face from a distance or a rippling shadow. Some began insisting she was a kind of vampire since she was never seen in daylight.

Another thing agreed on was what the silent warrior was doing. She was stalking her prey, like a lioness watching a herd and waiting for the opportune moment. It was only a matter of time before she pounced and the first blood was spilled. None believed her quarry stood a chance.

~~*~*~*

At a popular new nightclub, the bouncer out front tried to remain in control of a line of impatient clubbers. The city's lights pierced the night and the asphalt glimmered with the residue of a recent rain. It had stormed all morning and only let up once the moon rose. The blinking multicolored lights from the club seemed to add to the annoyance of the young twenty-somethings waiting to get into the already overcrowded club. Most of the women were dressed in skimpy clothing, their faces glittering along with their clothes. The men were dressed in nice casual clothes.

Humidity hung heavy in the air. Most businesses were closed; only a few restaurants and the clubs were open. This club — already the most popular one in the city — sat between two hulking buildings, sleeping giants in the night. Though it appeared small from the outside, the club was rather large, able to fit two hundred and fifteen people inside, not that the owners, the Pinkerton sisters, cared about fire codes. On a given night, the club probably had more than three hundred people crammed inside.

"Folks, if you could just stay behind the line," the large, bald bouncer said again. He had an earpiece in place, which Lindsey and Danielle frequently screeched instructions through. He was waiting for them to tell him when to allow more people entry, unaware of the danger lurking just across the street.

A woman stood in the empty street. She was leaning against a nice blue car that was not hers, arms crossed over her chest. A silver charm glistened at her throat. From the base of her neck down, she was concealed in what looked like black vinyl. In actuality, it was a more valuable and flexible material, one that would repair itself if damaged. The suit fit her like a glove. Her pale face was flawless, even in the dirty yellow glow cast by the street lamp above her and she was remarkably slender. Her black hair was short so no opponent could grab hold of it and sunglasses concealed her eyes.

She straightened up to her full height, only a little taller than average. The muscles in her legs tensed in preparation for the sprint across the street. At her top speed, she could move so fast she would be invisible to the naked eye, although a flaw of the modifications meant she would only be able to hold that speed for a very short amount of time. If her estimates were correct, and they usually were, she would have just enough time to get into the club without being noticed by the people in line or the large bouncer. The woman hadn't brought her weapons with her. The six guards would be armed and therefore, her own weapons were unnecessary.

The woman stiffened, digging her combat boots into the asphalt. She waited patiently for the right moment. Her perfect hearing took in the sounds all around her, a sensory overload that would have overwhelmed anyone who had not undergone the modifications she had. She took off her sunglasses, keeping her eyes shut as she tossed them over to the small patch of grass where she would retrieve them later. Her ears picked up the sound of someone pushing the door to the club open, exiting after a night of drinking and dancing. She opened her unnaturally luminous green eyes and pushed off the asphalt. Her surroundings became an abstract blur of color as she sped inside, effortlessly weaving around the couple leaving the club, locked in a kiss. The breeze that swept over the people outside was ignored. Cool breezes were pleasant and a welcome relief on a warm autumn night.

Blitz stood inside the club, her back pressed against the wall. In her mind, she brought up the blueprints she had found during her research. There was a curved hallway in front of her. A few couples were passionately kissing and groping each other. She could smell the pheromones they gave off. The hall would lead her to a flight of mesh stairs, which wound around to the ground level of the club. There would be a bar to her immediate right. Throbbing music poured down from the speakers, suspended high above the club. She tilted her head as she identified the current track that was playing. It was a little less than halfway through.

Blitz moved unnoticed past the people in the hall, navigating her way through the twists and turns to the stairs. Perfume, cologne, aftershave, and sweat lingered in the air. She stepped onto the first gray mesh stair. The noise of the club's patrons was covered up by the loud music that blasted from the speakers. Blitz moved weightlessly and was completely silent as she strode down the staircase. She focused on the sea of bodies writhing and swaying to the music on the ground floor, spotting the six bodyguards almost immediately. The ones she was after — the owners of the club — would be at the bar serving alcohol and flirting with the more attractive male patrons.

"Nice eyes," a girl with fiery orange hair dressed in punk fashion complimented as she walked past Blitz with her friend, pausing to look the beautiful woman up and down suggestively. Blitz ignored them. Until she executed her plan, normals would think her just another clubber. To them, her eyes would be nothing more than costume contact lenses.

One of the guards on the ground floor straightened up when he noticed her on the staircase and watched her suspiciously, his hand hovering over his gun. She recognized him as a Grenich guard. The Corporation always protected its own when it benefited them. Blitz could handle their guards. They were just humans with superior training. They had some vague idea of what she was capable of, but there was no way they could ever match her speed, agility, and skill, despite what the Corporation had told them. Six normals weren't a challenge, not even close.

She continued descending the stairs, not surprised when the guard began to cross the floor. He watched her every move as he pushed his way through the crowd. Blitz suddenly turned and leapt off the stairs, soaring through the air like a bird of prey. She landed and rolled forward into a section of high tables and chairs. People stared at her in amazement, unsure whether to be impressed or frightened.

With an incredibly powerful and accurate leaping kick, she used the top of her foot to send the nearest table hurtling at the guard who was running for her. The large table smashed into him and two other patrons, sending them all crashing to the floor, spilling shattered glass and alcohol. Blitz dropped down into a sweeping kick and knocked another guard off his feet. The man had come at her with his gun drawn, probably hoping to get a better shot. When he fell, the gun went off.

The club became a scene of chaos as people began screaming and scrambling for the exit. Blitz knew how to use the frenzy to her advantage and was unaffected by the melee. The guards weren't as lucky and became lost in the midst of it. The music and dark blue lighting added to the disorientation, creating a blind panic. Blitz moved easily through the terrified patrons, scanning the crowd for the guards. She spotted a guard and spun around in a high roundhouse kick, striking him in the temple. His skull fractured against her foot and he fell into the crowd, taking a few people down with him. She ran to a wall, pushed off it with her foot, and punched another guard in the face, sending him crashing to the floor. He screamed as he disappeared under a multitude of feet.

Blitz continued moving smoothly through the swarming people when she encountered a terrified patron wielding a beer bottle. He swung at her head once and she effortlessly ducked under the wild swing. He tried to catch her on the back swing, but she lifted her long leg in a side kick and shattered the bottle with her boot. She struck out with another side kick, this one much more vicious, and knocked him sideways. The side of his head bounced against the edge of a table and he fell.

The sound of a gun rustling against the tight gray shirt of a guard drew her attention to the left. She back flipped into the swarm as one of the guards opened fire. Three different people fell, red seeping through their expensive clothing and pooling on the floor around them. A man who was hit in the leg started shrieking when people began to trample him. He dragged himself under a table, hoping for sanctuary. The music cut out and the regular lights came on. Screaming and thundering footsteps were now the only sounds in the club.

Blitz ran through the crowd, focusing on the shooter who had paused to reload. She reached him just as he slid a new magazine into place. Grabbing his wrist, she forced him to shoot wildly into the crowd, hitting more panicking patrons. Maneuvering his arm backward at a painful angle, she slammed her palm flat against his elbow, breaking it. He fell to his knees, yelling in pain. She followed through with an elbow to the face that broke his nose. Blood gushed from it, mingling with sweat. Blitz forced his arm to stay down and twisted his wrist, making him shoot himself in the gut. The gun was hers. She spun around, kicking high and bringing her leg down, breaking his collarbone with her heel. Her sharp eyes darted about as she looked for another guard. She heard one behind her.

Beefy arms wrapped around her thin body as a guard grabbed hold of her. She could see his comrade approaching her from the front with a cattle prod. The guard pressed a button on the base and electricity ran up to the two prongs at the top of the weapon. Blitz could hear the crackling sound, even in the din of panic surrounding them.

"Drop the fuckin' gun," the guard holding her growled, his hot breath reeking of beer, meat, and cheese.

Her face was completely blank as Blitz released her grip on the firearm. It clattered to the floor, the sound lost amid the sounds of utter terror. She remained still, as though resigned to her fate, making them let their guard down. Blitz waited patiently for the right moment. When it came, she pushed off the ground, forcing the guard holding her to arch backward slightly. Blitz struck out with both feet, catching the man with the cattle prod directly in the face. He fell under the feet of the stampeding crowd. She leaned forward and landed a vicious scorpion kick to the back of the beefy guard's head. He grunted but stubbornly refused to let her go. It was a bad strategy. Her arms were still somewhat free. Blitz thrust her hand back and grabbed a hold of his testicles, squeezing until his grip loosened enough to allow her to ram an elbow into his nose, easily breaking it. She spun out of the now non-existent grip and kicked him in the ribs, a couple breaking under the sudden impact. A leaping roundhouse kick to the head finished him off.

Blitz ran toward the bar. Two guards attacked her at once, as she had anticipated. She fluidly evaded their punches and deflected their kicks. Blitz punched one in the gut, doubling him over, and backhanded the second one, knocking him away. Using his comrade to brace herself, she leapt up and side kicked the guard even further away to collide with a nearby table. In the short time it took for him to recover, she had grabbed the gun from the first guard in a single fluid move. She pulled the trigger twice. Blood sprayed everywhere as he became unidentifiable. She spun around and kicked the other guard in the face, knocking him backward and into merciful darkness.

Most of the patrons had made it up the stairs and out of the club. It was just her, the bodies of a few guards, some unlucky bystanders who had been trampled or wounded in the pandemonium, and the two stunned bartenders. The few who had survived the chaos were crawling on the floor, moaning and crying, or unconscious. Blood, alcohol, and shattered glass covered the floor in a giant river. There wasn't an inch of the club that hadn't been affected by the mayhem.

Blitz hadn't even broken a sweat. Her eyes flicked over toward the bar. The bartenders, Lindsey and Danielle Pinkerton, stood behind the counter as if that would protect them. They stared at the woman standing in the midst of the carnage. She still had a gun in her hand and her glowing green eyes fixed on them. Blitz could read the terror in their wide eyes and uncertain stances. They were afraid.

At the sound of distant footsteps, Blitz spun around and pointed her gun toward a lone figure near the top of the stairs. The large bouncer from outside had come to investigate what the hell was going on. He stood completely still, staring at the gruesome scene before him.

"Leave now," Blitz commanded in her emotionless but still authoritative voice. The bouncer hesitated, unsure if he had heard her correctly.

"The offer expires in five seconds," she stated. "One …"

The bouncer turned and ran as fast as he could.

Blitz heard Lindsey Pinkerton pull out the shotgun she kept under the bar and spun away, out of the path of the deadly slug. She aimed her own gun and pulled the trigger, only to hear it click. It was empty. She tossed the useless weapon to the side.

"Aw, poor little guinea pig out of bullets?" Lindsey taunted with more confidence than she felt. "Whatever will it do now?"

She pumped the foregrip of the shotgun and fired again, but Blitz became a blur and disappeared. The slug slammed into the wall, leaving a large ragged hole. The two sisters stood in silence, looking around nervously as Blitz remained crouched behind the bar. Carefully avoiding the broken glass, she began to creep around the front of the bar, listening to the conversation between the two women.

"What the—? Where the fuck did it go?" Lindsey asked as she reloaded the shotgun. Blitz moved over to the opposite end of the bar, peering up to make sure they were facing the other way. They were distracted by a groan off to the side, providing Blitz with the perfect opportunity to leap over the bar and creep up on them.

"I don't—" Danielle began as she turned around only to find herself eye-to-eye with glowing green. Before she could react, Blitz had struck out with her hand. She dug her fingers into Danielle's bare throat, grabbed a hold of her windpipe and tore it out. Blood sprayed all over her face, warm droplets getting in her short hair and rolling off her catsuit like raindrops. A gurgling rattle came out of the mess that had once been Danielle's throat as her body sank to the ground, toppling to the side.

"Oh shit!" Lindsey exclaimed as she glanced over her shoulder and doubled her efforts to reload the shotgun. Blitz hurled the lump of Danielle's throat she still held in her strong hand. It splattered in Lindsey's face, causing her to scream. Blitz executed an effortless crescent kick, knocking the shotgun out of Lindsey's loosened grip. She sprang forward and thrust the palm of her hand straight at Lindsey's nose, breaking it. Blood poured from the woman's nostrils, staining her animal print halter top. Before she could recover, Blitz grabbed a hold of her straw-colored hair and viciously slammed her head down on the bar a few times, just enough to stop the woman's screaming. She threw the woman into the shelves of alcohol behind the bar, smashing dozens of bottles and breaking the shelves. Glass rained down to the floor in a symphony of delicate shattering.

Though the glass tore into her skin, Lindsey managed to grasp a larger shard of glass. She spun around, desperately trying to stab the mysterious woman. Blitz grabbed hold of her wrist, maneuvered so she was behind Lindsey again, and once again slammed her face into the bar. She squeezed the bones of her wrist until she heard the loud pop of snapping bone, effectively disarming her opponent. She forced the hysterical Lindsey over to the flap. Raising the rich mahogany wood top, Blitz forced Lindsey's head in the empty gap, ignoring the barely comprehensible pleas and threats she hissed at her. Before the club owner could finish another shaky threat, Blitz slammed the top down with as much force as she could. She broke Lindsey's skull open like a grapefruit. Almost immediately, pink brain matter and copious amounts of thick dark red blood began oozing out of the large split in her skull, staining the once blonde hair crimson. Lindsey's corpse began to gruesomely twitch and spasm in Blitz's grasp. She dropped it.

Blitz spotted a rag under the bar and grabbed it, using it to wipe most of the blood off her face and out of her short hair. Grabbing a bottle of vodka from under the counter, she started to make her way around the bar, pouring a bit of the alcohol on the rag. Stuffing the rag partway into the bottle, she found the body of the guard who smelled faintly of tobacco. Rifling through his pockets, Blitz found his lighter and lit the alcohol-soaked rag as she continued on her way to the stairs, tossing the bottle down onto the ground. She heard the crackle of flame spreading through the club as she continued up the stairs.

The distant wail of sirens reached her hypersensitive ears, but she was unconcerned. They were still some distance away. The police station was at least a ten-minute drive from the nightclub, even without the normal city traffic. The Corporation would sanitize the scene before tomorrow.

Blitz moved out of the club soundlessly, stepping out into the street and crossing the damp asphalt. The car she had been leaning against earlier was gone, most likely belonging to one of the panicked patrons. Her sunglasses were still right where she had thrown them. Blitz calmly picked them up and placed them over her glowing eyes. She looked back at the club one last time and then walked away, allowing the night to swallow her.

~~*~*~*

In a secluded cabin, located deep within a wilderness, a doctor made his residence. It was a decent-sized home with five bedrooms and two baths. He enjoyed the peace and solitude of the wilderness. It was a nice vacation from his reality: warring with a powerful evil hidden just below the world most would call "normal." He often spent a few minutes sitting on the porch that wrapped around his home, just listening to the sounds of the forest and pretending he didn't know the dark secret that was the Grenich Corporation. Beautiful birdsong and the distant sound of rushing water from the nearby river served as a reminder of what he fought for. On better days, it almost seemed worth all the pain and misery.

As he sat on the porch, taking a short break to watch the sun rise over the hills, the doctor mused on the two experiments who shared his home. It was difficult to teach them about the concept of freedom. In the Corporation, their identities had been ripped away from them. They didn't even have names, only numbers: 7-299, known as Blitz, and 7-295, who was originally called Jack.

The doctor sighed and ran a hand through his scruffy, light brown hair, briefly resting his hand atop his head. Another experiment he knew — Coop — had an easier time adjusting to the outside world when he had escaped, decades ago. *Easy isn't the correct term*, the doctor thought with a smile that more resembled a grimace. Rehabilitating an experiment was a risky and unpredictable ordeal. First, they had to survive an intense withdrawal from the heavy doses of drugs the Corporation pumped into them daily.

If they survived the withdrawal, they next had to be introduced to a world they had only read of in Corporation books and seen in footage shown in lessons. The doctor tried exposing them to things they had either never experienced or had just forgotten in the hopes it would wake them up to the lies of the Corporation.

Some small part of him knew they would never recover fully. The doctor didn't know how to go about explaining emotions to them. The two sharing his home were still cold and distant; the woman more so. They were both still highly dangerous due to a few knee-jerk reactions they would probably never lose, but they were capable of leading nearly normal lives.

Of course, this was based solely on two cases from years ago. Although hundreds of experiments were released, only two actually escaped from the Corporation. Only those two still managed to evade the Corporation's many eyes, mostly by using the skills learned in the Corporation, ironically.

The doctor pushed off the wicker chair he had been sitting on, frowning when he heard the television in the main room of his home. He opened the screen door that allowed the nice cool wind into the cabin. The heavier door, the one he closed and bolted at night, was open. The morning mists were already concealing the forest ground, snaking around the trees. The doctor shivered and pulled his dark blue jacket a little tighter.

He wandered into the main room and saw Jack sitting on the dull tan couch, glowing brown eyes fixed on the television screen. He had short dark brown hair, an olive complexion, and a medium build. He tended to favor darker colors, like the other experiment. Blitz had disappeared a couple nights ago and the doctor could only hope she wasn't doing what he feared she was.

Jack had an epiphany a few months back, and now he had an insatiable hunger for knowledge. He had a voracious curiosity about nearly everything. It was one thing to know something, it was quite another to actually enjoy it.

Jack studied every book he could get his hands on. The doctor had a small library and books could be found everywhere in his house. Jack had devoured every one within a week. The doctor had to rely on Perrin, his old mentor, to send new things. Jack had also become fascinated with music, puzzles, and food. Compared to the flavorless gruel that was served at the Corporation, everything was a delicious new experience.

It was rare to see Jack sitting in front of the television.

The experiment glanced at the doctor before returning his attention back to the set. The room was still dull as fog continued to obscure the sun. The doctor's own father and grandfather had built the cabin by hand centuries ago. The more recent additions, such as indoor plumbing and electricity, were something he had put in himself. The doctor was sure he had said every known curse word at least twice in every room. He was not an electrician or plumber by trade, but he had no other choice and forced himself to learn enough to install what he needed to.

"What are you watching, Jack?" the doctor asked as he pulled up a stool from the small bar behind the couch, taking a seat beside Jack — careful to stay well out of his personal space — and focusing on the screen in front of them. It was coverage of some kind of protest, judging by the signs being waved about.

"They, the normals, they're protesting the death penalty," Jack replied, frowning as he leaned forward a little. "I do not understand. This man, he raped and killed young girls, most of whom had only reached their teenage years, and still they want him to live. Why? Surely the punishment fits the crime. Why would they want such a man to live?"

The doctor scrubbed a hand over his face, the stubble on his unshaven face roughly scraping against his palm. "They don't condone his actions, but some are morally opposed to the idea of a death penalty. They feel justice can be done without taking a life."

"But isn't death a form of justice?" Jack asked as he turned to look at the doctor.

"Some believe so," the doctor replied. "Others don't agree. The problem with the death penalty is that it doesn't really discourage criminals like the ones they execute. Most people are either born sociopaths or they're not. And there is always the chance of executing the wrong person. Some feel it's not worth the risk of killing an innocent person. It's a very complex issue, Jack. There have been some good books and papers written about it. I could try to find some if you like."

Jack nodded and then went quiet, thinking over the doctor's response. "What about experiments? There is blood on our hands — more than enough to warrant the death penalty."

"What was done to you in the Corporation was reprehensible and you were brainwashed to an extent. However, now that you are out and free, you are responsible for your actions. It is what you do now that matters," the doctor explained, trying to keep the weariness out of his voice. It was too early in the morning to be tackling tough moral issues.

"Where do you stand on the death penalty?" Jack asked as he looked back to the television.

"I think killing is wrong unless you're defending yourself or others and have no other options. If it's matter of life or death," the doctor replied as he continued to watch the screen. The footage of the protestors was replaced by the image of a plastic-looking news anchor attempting to look somber as he announced the killer had been executed. The doctor glanced at the scroll toward the bottom. It was something about war. To his relief, Jack turned off the television. He turned back toward the doctor, one elbow resting on the back of the couch while one knee rested up on the cushions. His glowing brown eyes studied the doctor.

"You plan on defeating the Corporation?" he asked.

The doctor nodded. "Yes, and we're going to do it."

"And you plan to kill the Corporation mouthpiece, Carding?" Jack pressed as he continued looking into the doctor's bloodshot blue eyes. The doctor was taken aback by the simple question. He swallowed, knowing he had brought the inquiry on himself. He didn't know how to answer. Carding had ruined his life and he'd be lying to Jack as well as himself if he said he had never thought of killing the man. The doctor knew he had enough blood on his hands already after working for the Corporation for years, oblivious to their true purpose. He still carried the guilt of not noticing what seemed so obvious in hindsight.

The doctor was saved from having to answer. Looking up at the silent television set, he nearly jumped out of his skin when he saw a reflection in the dark glass. Blitz stood in the hallway leading to the two rooms she and Jack occupied.

She had abandoned her catsuit for her house clothes: tight pants and a tank top that were made of the same material. Her arms were crossed and she was leaning with one shoulder against the wall. Her feet were bare, as they usually were when she was in the cabin, and she wasn't wearing her sunglasses. The doctor hadn't heard her come in. Though he was an expert on experiments, he was not one and so he was susceptible to their skills and abilities. He never heard Jack or Blitz when they moved.

She wasn't looking at them. Her gaze was out the bay windows off to the side across from the entrance hall.

The doctor turned in his seat. "Where have you been the past couple days?"

Her thin shoulders lifted in a small shrug. "Reconnaissance."

"You smell like blood," Jack mentioned as he looked her up and down.

"I slipped," Blitz answered. The grace with which the experiments moved made it near impossible for them to fall or even slip. She was lying and it made the doctor more than a little uneasy.

Jack turned back to the silent TV, quietly clarifying, "Not your own blood."

"Unless it's yours, it's none of your concern," she was quick to respond.

"Blitz." The doctor waited until she was looking at him. "What did you do?"

She remained calm and unaffected. "I neutralized a threat."

"Tell me you didn't kill somebody, Blitz. Please, tell me you didn't kill somebody," the doctor almost pleaded with her. She continued to stare at him with her piercing green eyes. A cold knot formed in the doctor's stomach as he realized his biggest fear had just happened. When it came right down to it, he could do nothing to stop her from going out and slaughtering people.

"They were Grenich employees," she explained. "By now, the Corporation has erased them."

"That's worse!" the doctor snapped furiously as he stood up. "How could you be so reckless, Blitz? Do you want to be captured and brought back to the Corporation?"

Blitz shrugged again with infuriating disinterest. "There are worse scenarios."

A moment of tense silence followed, during which Jack just sat on the couch watching the reflection of Blitz and the doctor on the screen.

"Who were they?" the doctor finally managed to get out, rubbing his brow.

"Danielle and Lindsey Pinkerton," she answered. The names surprised the doctor. He blinked and fell quiet, studying her. Jack glanced out the window when the cabin became a little darker. It was going to be an overcast day.

"So it was revenge?" the doctor asked, confused.

Blitz looked off to the side briefly before turning her gaze back to him. "I do not engage in such petty irrational acts. They posed a significant threat to us. I neutralized the threat."

Blitz turned and disappeared down the hall that led to her room.

The doctor looked back at Jack, a puzzled expression on his scruffy face. He glanced toward where Blitz had been and then made his way to his own room, closing his door gently.

Jack reached for a book he had left on the coffee table in front of the couch. *The Count of Monte Cristo* by

Alexandre Dumas, the newest book Perrin had sent. It was a thick book, worn from repeated readings. He had just started it the previous night, but was already halfway through it. At the rate he read, he would most likely finish it by dinnertime.

~~*~*~*

Blitz knelt on the tiled floor of the bathroom, which was painted a shade of yellow so light it could easily be mistaken for white. She finished vomiting and noticed the small amount of blood that she had brought up along with the bile. She flushed the toilet and sat back, leaning against the pleasantly cool porcelain tub. Her skin was noticeably warmer than usual.

"Murder most foul, as in the best it is, but this most foul, strange and unnatural," a familiar voice quoted, drawing Blitz's attention. Sitting on the edge of the small sink was a ghost who had been haunting her for the past year or so. The ghost looked almost exactly like her, but her hair was longer and her eyes didn't glow. She was wearing a plain white dress that was borderline cliché for a spirit. She was nearly transparent yet contained enough substance to convince Blitz she was actually there. Blitz theorized she was hallucinating, knowing a virus was working within her system. There was no such thing as an afterlife and therefore ghosts couldn't exist.

"Gotta love the Bard," the ghost continued, glancing at her nails before looking back to Blitz. "Now there's a guy who knew what he was talking about. Think he was a shape shifter?"

Blitz didn't respond, only watched the ghost. The ghost seemed to grow tired of her silence. She drummed her nails on the smooth countertop, making a quiet clicking sound, and swung her long legs back and forth.

"A couple low level retrievers were significant threats? Really?" she asked, her voice dripping with skepticism as she looked at Blitz. "Your logic seems rather flimsy. The Pinkerton sisters were no threat to anyone, certainly not to you. You can't possibly expect to kill anyone and everyone connected with the Corporation."

Blitz pushed herself up to her feet and stared at the ghost, who grinned.

"I was created to function in adverse situations. I will do what I must," she muttered before moving to the bathroom door. She glanced back over her shoulder, but the spirit had vanished. There was nothing in the bathroom but the faint odor of vomit. Blitz switched off the light and continued to her room.

CHAPTER TWO

On the grounds of the mansion, a thick mist lazily rolled down from the surrounding hills and settled over the vibrant green grass, dulling the few colorful leaves that remained on the trees. The haze obscured the normally beautiful land, giving everything a smoky dreamlike appearance while clouds obscured the brilliant sun. The dreary gray reflected the melancholy mood of the inhabitants of the breathtaking estate. A few shape shifters in wolf form milled about a dry marble fountain in the front yard. Everything was silent except for the occasional breeze rustling the leaves of a tree or bush.

Shae stood on the stone balcony outside Isis' old room, leaning against the weathered brown stones behind her, her arms crossed over her old cranberry-colored sweater. Her auburn hair was done up in a tight ponytail and dark green eyes surveyed the land before her. She thought back on the five years that had passed since Isis' death. Each year seemed to get a little easier, though she still missed her cousin. In the beginning, she and Steve had tried to spend a little time each week on the balcony outside Isis' old room, but the visits became less and less frequent over the years. Steve's lover, Justin, would be back in a couple weeks and the two would be able to spend a short time together before the other protector had to leave again.

Shae and Steve had broken the news to Isis' adopted family together, which didn't go as expected. Her own parents didn't remember her and there was no evidence to suggest Isis had ever existed. Like so many shape shifters over the years, she seemed to have been completely erased from reality. Talking to them had been the hardest thing to do, because Shae knew the truth and yet had to act ignorant. Were it not for Steve, Shae was not sure she would've been able to do it. He kept reminding her it was for their safety.

She received occasional updates from Jensen, her late cousin's lover. Those were almost all the same: he and Electra had found nothing; they had hit another dead end, and so on and so forth. Though the findings were discouraging, Jensen somehow managed to give Shae hope he would find Isis' killers. He had a determination no one could break. Jensen sometimes came off as a cocky bastard, but he had a heart of gold and was a noble protector.

Shae glanced behind her when she heard someone open the glass door leading out to the balcony. She wasn't surprised when Steve's head poked out, offering a sad smile.

"You want some company?" he asked gently.

"It's a shitty day," Shae warned, looking back out to the dreary land in front of her. Steve stepped out onto the stone balcony and leaned on the railing near her, sticking his hands in his pockets.

"Thought you'd be on shift," Shae mentioned.

"Just finished it. What about you? I'm sure Loman has a cold case you could take a crack at."

"Needed a break from people being awful to each other."

Steve nodded, looking down at his feet. "Jet mentioned the Deverells are following up on another lead."

"Yeah. Probably another dead end."

Steve looked out across the land, following Shae's gaze. Shae didn't want to become a pessimist, but it was hard not to be. Five years and nothing but dead ends. It was enough to make anyone lose hope.

~~*~*~*

Jade toyed with her beer bottle at a table in the Lair. Alex sat next to her and Hunter sat across from them, her gaze traveling over the large dance floor as she moved her shoulders to the music. Cassidy had gone to the bar a few minutes earlier to get them another round of drinks. In the main part of the club, music pounded over the speakers. Strobe lights blinked furiously. The dark blue lights mounted into the ceiling bathed the sea of pulsating bodies in a strange glow, giving paler flesh an odd green tint. Rebels stuck out with their bright neon hair, but everyone else just kind of blurred together. The air smelled of sweat and body odor, and a peculiar scent that was an odd mix of smoke and plastic. It was a disorienting scene to anyone unfamiliar with clubs.

The four at the table had been coming to the Lair frequently, mainly when Alex and Jade weren't out playing cops. Originally, Alpha had offered sanctuary to any grieving protector who desired it, going so far as to extend the offer to Jet. Jade and Alex continued to regularly frequent the rebel Lair to unwind after long days. Since the Four were temporarily incomplete after Isis' death, Jet and Lilly had been sending the surviving members out to help Detective Loman with his more difficult cases. The cases sometimes became repetitive and Jade found herself wondering how Steve could stand it. It was all people lusting for power or pissed off at their cheating lovers. The usual shit Jade couldn't care less about. She rubbed her forehead with one hand. Just thinking about it was so damn frustrating that it was giving her the beginning of what promised to be a massive headache. She felt Alex nudge her shoulder.

"You all right?" Alex asked, concerned. Jade nodded and took a sip of her beer, which was now unpleasantly warm and flat. She rubbed the back of her sore neck, hoping she would be able to talk Sly into giving her a neck rub. Sly was spending tonight with Alpha, but she and Jade had a date the following evening. Sly's long fingers were known to perform miracles when it came to tense muscles.

"Where the hell is my twin brother?" Hunter yelled over the pounding music. Jade started to shake her head when something caught her eye out on the dance floor. Briefly, out of the corner of her eye, Jade could have sworn she saw sparks of electricity. She squinted as she tried to see through the dim blue lighting that covered everything in an eerie glow. *Damn club lights,* she thought as she turned her attention back to Hunter and Alex.

"What is it?" Alex asked as she glanced over toward where Jade was looking.

"Nothing," Jade replied, just loud enough to be heard over the music. "Oh look, the wayward Lothario returns."

Cassidy was making his way back to them, dragging a young shape shifter woman with him. Hunter and Alex both shot Jade a look. She had been particularly bitter the past few years. The older protector briefly held up her hands before lowering them again and wrapping them about the beer bottle, rolling it between her fingers and staring intently at the glass in an attempt to block out the loud music.

Cassidy reached the table, breathless. He had obviously forgotten the drinks in his hurry. He was sweating profusely. The Lair was usually sweltering and they had all begun to sweat shortly after sitting down. Jade was still trying to figure out how the many humans who frequented the Lair didn't pass out from heatstroke.

"Okay, you are not going to believe what Chloe here just told me," Cassidy yelled over the music. Jade winced and glared at him. He seemed to think they were all hard of hearing as he shouted way louder than he needed to. The younger protector pushed the longhaired brunette forward, nodding at her to repeat whatever story she had told him. She was cute and obviously a magazine reader. Everything about her was trendy from her hairstyle to her designer shoes. She had gray-blue eyes and was about ten pounds underweight with little muscle definition. Mousy was the first word that popped into Jade's head when she saw the girl. She was very nervous and fidgeted uncomfortably under the gaze of the three women at the table, gnawing on her lower lip. Jade's patience had been low before Cassidy brought Chloe over, but now it was entering the dangerously low levels. The girl reminded her of one of those annoying yappy dogs some rich human women carried in their overpriced purses.

"Go on, they don't bite," Cassidy urged the nervous young woman. *Yet,* Jade thought as she ran a fingernail over her beer bottle. Luckily for her, both Hunter and Alex had much more patience and managed to be reassuring.

"Well, last night, I went to this hot nightclub a couple states over," she began in a cartoonish nasal voice that made Jade cringe. "This place was run by these two sisters and it was *the* place to go. It had everything—"

"Is your story going anywhere?" Jade asked irritably, causing Chloe to jump. Alex kicked her under the table, clearly telling her to shut up.

Chloe swallowed, building up her nerve again. "You've heard all those stories of that woman the rebels have been calling Blitz, right?"

"Guardians have mercy," Jade muttered under her breath as she ran her hands over her face. That damn urban legend had been circulating for a while, and everyone had a different tale about this supposed Super Woman, or whatever the hell she was, and what she did. Jade had grown weary of the legend as soon as it began. It was some horny teenage boy's fantasy: a femme fatale vampire stalking the shadows in a skin-tight vinyl costume. It sounded more like dominatrix porn to her. If she had to hear one more graphic description of what the supposedly flawless woman looked like, Jade was going to lose her mind.

"I know. I didn't believe the stories either. I mean, who would walk around in a catsuit? Unless it's like Halloween or something," Chloe continued as she started to twirl her dark hair around her index finger. "But that was before last night."

Jade closed her eyes briefly before turning her attention back to Chloe. "Let me guess, you saw her stalking around the club?"

Chloe shook her head. "I saw her massacre it."

Alex and Hunter exchanged a look, but Jade was far from convinced. Chloe began gnawing on her bottom lip again. Jade resisted the urge to take her by the bony shoulders and just shake the damn story out of her.

"She came in and just started killing people. It created a panic. I nearly got trampled in the chaos." Chloe brushed her hair aside, revealing a large bruise that she had tried to cover up with makeup. Jade raised an eyebrow and leaned over Alex for a closer look. It was quite a large bruise, probably from crashing into a wall or some other hard surface.

"I don't know what happened after we got away. My friends and I were lucky to get out of there. I don't know how many were killed in the rush to get out or were killed by her," Chloe hesitated, shifting her weight. "She wasn't a normal shape shifter. Her eyes glowed, like the stories rebels tell. And the things she did . . . I saw her kick a table, like the ones over there, clean across the club into one of the bouncers or guards, whatever the hell they were. And the way she moved, that kind of speed and accuracy, it was faster than anything I've ever seen, except for in movies maybe."

Alex pointed over at one of the empty tables. "The table she kicked, you said it was like that one?"

Chloe glanced over her shoulder and nodded. "Yeah, exactly like that, same height and everything."

Alex got up and moved over to the empty table, examining it. Jade quickly forgot the annoyances in the club as she focused her attention on Chloe.

"Why didn't we hear about this massacre on the news or anywhere else?" she asked as Cassidy sat down next to Hunter.

"That's the bizarre thing," Chloe replied, flipping her hair behind her shoulder. "When I didn't hear anything about it today, I went down there just to see if there was any kind of investigation happening. The place was empty and available to rent. It looked like nobody had been there in years. I called up the friends I was with, two humans and another shape shifter. The humans don't even remember going out last night, but my other friend, Sarah, remembers it clear as day just like me. Sarah had managed to snap a picture of the woman as we were running out, not a great one, but it had vanished from her phone."

"You said this was a couple states over?" Hunter asked.

Chloe nodded. "We shifted into birds and flew home. I don't know what happened and truthfully, I really don't want to know."

Hunter and Cassidy thanked her and she eventually walked away. Jade turned her attention to where Alex was still examining the table. She carefully lifted an edge of the medium-sized circle and couldn't lift it very much. Placing it back down, Alex approached their small table again, shaking her head.

"There is no way you could kick that thing the way Chloe described," she reported as she leaned down, placing her hands on their table. "It's sturdy and pretty heavy. The base is weighted. You could tilt it over, but you'd have to be pretty damn strong to actually get any distance on it."

"Okay, if I stay here another minute, my ears are going to start gushing blood. Let's head back to the mansion and talk about it there," Jade said as she got up from the table. She needed a quieter atmosphere to think, not a rave. Alex, Hunter, and Cassidy were quick to follow her.

The walk back to the car was silent until they reached the dark blue sedan. It was much cooler outside than it had been in the club. A breeze swept over them as they approached the car. Jade pressed the button on the keys and the car chirped.

"What are we going to tell Mom and Dad?" Cassidy asked, playfully shoulder checking his twin sister. Hunter smiled and punched his upper arm.

Jade shrugged. "Same thing Chloe told us."

"Think there's anything to her story?" Hunter sank down into the car's cream-colored interior. Jade opened the driver's door. She lifted her face to the sky, smelling the crispness of the air around her. She loved the autumn season.

"Don't know. But we know the rebels have been telling stories about similar shape shifters for years. The woman Chloe described sounds a lot like one of the glowing eyes," she replied as she got into the car. "It's worth looking into."

~~*~*~*

He was sitting on the couch in his apartment. The warm sun illuminated everything in a pristine glow. It was the perfect temperature and a breeze drifted by at just the right time. The couch was cool and smooth beneath him, his feet rested on a coffee table. Everything around him was bright and alive.

Out of the corner of his eye, he caught a glimpse of movement. He rose out of his comfortable position and moved toward the balcony doors. He drew open the curtains to reveal her, his lover. Isis.

She was a vision of magnificence in a slinky silver dress that fell to her ankles, so tastefully simple and yet it somehow enhanced her beauty. Her dark hair brushed against her jaw line and when she looked over her shoulder at him, he saw her eyes were currently sparkling blue. The same shade of blue as the ocean. Her slender arms were crossed over her chest. She turned to face him, a playful smile dancing across her face the moment their eyes met. He put a hand on the clean glass and she mirrored his action.

Then the doors suddenly turned into blood. Dark crimson rivers showered both of them. Their surroundings became a scarlet haze.

She fell to her knees, the blood creeping up to her midsection. He lunged forward, grabbing her arms and holding her tightly, as much for his sake as for hers. The blood was so hot, so fresh. The smell was a horrible overwhelming coppery scent and the matching taste made him gag. He held tight to her, because he refused to lose her again. He couldn't, he wouldn't.

He took her face in his hands, forcing her eyes to lock with his. He begged her to stay, pleaded with her over the roaring of the river surrounding them. It soaked through their clothing, splashed up on their faces, splattering them with crimson droplets. She looked into his eyes with a haunted gaze, one that pierced right through him. Her mouth moved, yet didn't make a sound, as it formed a two-word plea.

"Kill me."

Jensen jerked awake violently, smothering a yell as he sat straight up in the dirty motel bed, his body bathed in a cool sweat. The taste and scent of blood still lingered faintly. The nightmare happened on a regular basis. It took him by surprise the first time. After experiencing it a few more times, he soon learned it was nothing more than an illusion.

He looked around the pitifully small room. It was the cheapest place he could find, and he definitely got what he paid for. Everything had a layer of grime on it and the place reeked of stale tobacco smoke from countless cigarettes and cigars. They hadn't updated anything since the early seventies and Jensen ventured to guess they didn't clean very often judging from the countless stains. He wouldn't have been surprised if the filthy yellow walls had been white at one time. As it was, he and Electra slept in their clothes to avoid any unnecessary contact with the surfaces in the room.

Neither of them slept very much, maybe two or three hours a night if they were lucky. Both guardians and shape shifters could go a little longer without rest than humans, but they still felt the effects of exhaustion. Jensen rubbed his eyes with his thumb and index finger. He glanced over to where Electra was sleeping. She was on her side, facing away from him, using one arm as a pillow. That didn't surprise him, considering they fought regularly. He had warned her he wasn't going to be cuddly on this mission. Still, deep down, Jensen knew he was using more force than was necessary when talking to his shadier contacts. Electra was currently annoyed at him because he had broken a man's jaw earlier that day. Jensen had gotten fed up with the man sniffing around for more money and wound up decking him before storming off, taking mild satisfaction in the sharp snap of bone when the jaw broke. He knew Electra was tired. She had lost her twin sister; the last thing she wanted to do was play babysitter to a grown protector. Sleeping in disgusting, rundown, decrepit rooms probably wasn't high on the list either.

"Your sleep is troubled."

The soft voice behind him caused Jensen to reach under his pillow and wrap his hand around the handle of his knife. He gripped it tightly and spun around to face the direction of the voice. He couldn't see much in the darkness, but he assumed it came from over by the rickety table on his other side. Jensen got out of bed and put himself between where the voice was and Electra.

"Who are you?"

A pair of glowing dark blue eyes appeared in the darkness in front of him. Jensen swallowed nervously but kept his knife pointed in front of him. With his other hand, he reached for the drawer.

"You needn't retrieve your gun. I am not here to harm you. I apologize for approaching you in the middle of the night. I arrived a couple hours ago and you were both sleeping. I had no wish to disturb your rest. However, if you wish, I shall turn on the lights."

Jensen was already on edge. When he spotted movement to his side, he lunged at the intruder. He wasn't taking any chances. The intruder tossed Jensen over his shoulder, slamming him to the ground. Jensen responded by burying the knife in the stranger's leg. The man leapt away from him and Jensen scrambled to his feet. He heard his knife land with a dull thud on the dirty carpet, somewhere in the shadows. Jensen lashed out with a powerful side kick, pleased that his kickboxing was finally being put to good use again. The stranger easily blocked him, spun out of his sight, and struck him in the back with a powerful elbow jab. Jensen crashed into the wall, spinning back around to face whomever it was, ignoring the ache from the strike.

The unnaturally luminous eyes were a few feet in front of him. The irises were dark blue, but they glowed as if they were made from the liquid found in glowsticks. It was the only part of his opponent that Jensen could see in the shadows, and it freaked him out.

"Jensen, I have no desire to injure you. Please hear me out."

Jensen pushed the hesitance to the back of his mind and lunged at his attacker again, this time with a series of jabs. The glowing eyes weaved to the left and right, easily dodging his strikes with a fluid grace and an unnatural speed. Jensen had an excellent reaction time, but he knew he would never be able to move like his attacker did. What the hell was this thing?

A side kick to the abdomen doubled him over and a sweeping kick knocked him on his back. His attacker casually crouched down next to him. Jensen could just barely make out his silhouette. Jensen subtly reached down to one of the pockets in his pants. He found the pen he was looking for and removed the cap with his thumb, making sure he was soundless. He continued gasping, pretending to be winded.

"You need to stop," his attacker said. "You will wake your travelling companion."

"And I should just trust you? You're the one who broke into my room," Jensen gasped out.

"I'm sure you can appreciate the need to operate off the grid, Aldridge," the man replied, his calmness never wavering. "I need to be as invisible as possible, so yes, I often enter places without knocking or announcing myself."

Jensen struck out blindly with the pen, aiming at what he hoped was his attacker's femoral artery. The glowing eyes jerked backward. Jensen flipped back up to his feet and lunged forward with a knee strike, knocking the attacker away from Electra's bed and toward the front door, hoping to get the fight out into the hall and away from the young guardian. The attacker disappeared momentarily, right before Jensen felt an elbow slam into his nose and mouth. He tasted blood as he stumbled back, his vision swimming.

"Jensen, turn the lights on," Electra calmly ordered in the darkness. Jensen felt around the wall until his fingers brushed over a switch. He flipped it on and looked over to the stranger, now illuminated in the light.

Electra stood directly behind a strange man, the barrel of the gun pressed against the back of his neck. She was a decent shot, but at so close a range, it didn't really matter. The man in front of her stood stiffly, his hands held up. His hair was dark brown and he was wearing a long tan trench coat, similar to the kind favored by detectives in old noir movies. Jensen could just see a light-colored top beneath the coat and he couldn't help but feel some satisfaction when he saw the pen jutting out of his assailant's shin, dark red blood dribbling up around it. There was also a small gash where Jensen assumed he had stabbed the man. It was strange. The gash should have been much larger and deeper. It seemed to be rapidly healing. Jensen watched in disbelief as the wound sealed itself up and disappeared.

"Now, who the hell are you and what do you want?" Electra growled, taking a small step back so he couldn't strike at her. The man slowly turned around, keeping his hands up. Electra looked surprised and pointed the gun toward the floor, switching the safety back on.

"Coop?" Electra whispered in disbelief. Jensen glanced between her and the man's back, moving around so he could get a better look at the stranger's face.

"You're not serious," Jensen stated, letting out a quiet laugh. "Unbelievable."

The strange man, Coop, reached down and jerked the bloody pen out of his leg. He tossed it into the garbage can across the room. He walked over to the dresser and sat down, pulling his leg up to assess the damage done by the pen. In a matter of seconds, the wound was gone, leaving nothing but flawless skin. There was no mark to indicate he had been stabbed just minutes earlier.

"Bloody hell," Jensen muttered, his eyes widening. Electra approached Coop. She was also marveling at his rapid healing abilities. She jumped when he looked over at her, taken aback by his eyes.

"You can relax. As I tried to tell Jensen, I didn't come here to hurt either of you. Jensen overreacted," Coop said. "It was an unwise strategy."

"May I remind you that you were the one who broke into our room," Jensen responded as he dropped onto the uncomfortable lumpy mattress he had been sleeping on earlier. Coop looked at him and stood up.

"And as I tried to explain earlier, it is of the utmost importance that I remain unseen when I travel. I'm taking enough of a risk approaching you like this," Coop replied, unbothered.

Electra observed Coop. He strode across the room and pushed aside the curtains, peering outside.

"Your eyes," she began.

"Are unimportant," Coop interrupted as he dropped the curtains and sank down in one of the rickety chairs. "I have the information the two of you have been looking for."

Jensen got up and moved over to where his knife lay on the floor. He picked it up, grabbed a rag from the dresser and cleaned off the blade, then placed it on the dresser. Coop watched his every move.

"What are you, Coop?" Electra pressed, her voice gentle and patient. "The rebels have stories about a group of shape shifters they refer to as 'glowing-eyes.' Are you one of them?"

Coop looked down at his hands briefly before raising his eyes to meet hers again.

"Perhaps. I am not entirely sure," he replied quietly, a hint of weariness creeping into his flat voice. "As for what I am, that is a little more complicated. In another life, I was known as Mark Waterson. I had a family, whom you met briefly, years ago. What I am now is a shape shifter who has undergone intensive experimentation, traded to a Corporation in payment for a debt. I was modified to fight and kill, to win wars and reduce human casualties. You are looking for Grenich? I am from one of the main laboratories. The glowing eyes? That's the brand of the Corporation, a trademark found on all of their finished products."

Coop paused, glancing down at his feet and closing his eyes. To Electra and Jensen, it looked as though he were in pain. He didn't speak for a long while, just let his breath out slowly.

"Coop, what are you talking about?" Electra asked. Jensen continued looking at the man in front of him with a certain amount of curiosity. Normally, he would have dismissed Coop's story as ludicrous. After fighting him and experiencing his extraordinary ability firsthand, Jensen wasn't so sure. There was also the matter of his eyes and apparent self-healing. Shape shifters healed fast, but not instantly the way Coop had.

Coop looked up again, glanced to the side, and then back at Jensen and Electra. "I know you've been searching for me. I planted that envelope in your apartment. I regret the destruction within your residence. I was ambushed by another experiment and we fought."

"You trashed my place?" Jensen asked incredulously, anger creeping back into his voice. Electra looked over at him with an expression of pure annoyance.

"Really, Jensen? *That's* what's important right now?" She turned her attention back to Coop. "How did you get Isis' necklace? And how did you know where Jensen lived?"

"Reconnaissance work, a necessary skill for soldiers and spies," Coop answered as he reached into a pocket of his trench coat. "As I mentioned earlier, I have the information you have been searching for, a list of names. I would have brought it sooner, but the information took a while to obtain. Your constant movement also proved to be an inconvenience."

He pulled out a small piece of paper, creased from being folded multiple times. He handed it to Electra who took it, unfolded it, and read the names. She passed it to Jensen and he hesitantly took his eyes off Coop to read the names on the list. They were neatly written in blue ink.

"Those are the people responsible for Isis' death," Coop continued. "Most of them were employees of Grenich at one time or another so they won't be easy to track down. You're going to have to work with the Monroes and the others. Combining your resources is the only way you'll find them, and you do not have much time. Someone else is hunting them, and that individual is going to move fast. Some of the names on the list are going to vanish without a trace. The Corporation is very skilled at cleaning up, as you will find out."

Coop took a pair of sunglasses out of the pocket of his

coat and placed them over his eyes, effectively hiding the unnatural glow. He jammed his hands in his pockets and began to move toward the door.

"Wait. You're not coming with us?" Electra called after him, turning to look at the strange man. Coop paused, his hand on the filthy door lever. He turned back to face them.

"No, not yet. There are things that need my attention and this journey is one you must go on alone," he said, leaning against the door briefly, a thoughtful expression crossing his face. "Experiments don't experience emotions like normals. When I first escaped Grenich, I learned to mirror other people's feelings in order to blend in. One thing that really eluded me was this silly concept of hope that normals — non-experiments — have had since who knows when. Do you know that for every tyrant the Earth has had, there has been a resistance? For every evil witnessed, someone stood up and said 'no.' They may not have been successful or even widely known. They may have been tortured, killed, or simply forgotten. Still, no matter what the adversity, normals never lose that hope. When things are at their absolute worse, you make a stand because you believe in a better world. You may not truly understand freedom, you may debate what it means, but you're willing to fight for it. I admit that even now I still do not fully understand why, but it holds some meaning."

Coop fell silent again for a moment. "To me, that's what's worth fighting for in this twisted world."

He opened the door, but hesitated. "It is customary to wish you luck on a particularly difficult and dangerous journey. I don't believe in relying completely on such a notion, but I wish it to you nonetheless."

He silently slipped out of the grimy little motel room, closing the door behind him. Both Jensen and Electra were still for a moment.

"Something tells me we haven't seen the last of him," Electra said as she turned to Jensen. He sat on the mattress again and folded his hands in front of him, resting his chin on the backs of his hands.

"We should head back to the mansion tomorrow," he mentioned.

Electra nodded her consent.

~~*~*~*

Ajax frowned as he looked out the windshield of the car. Ominous dark clouds were beginning to cover up the moon and stars. It was already starting to drizzle and he could only hope his two younger brothers would come out of the club before a downpour began. Like all other rebel clubs, this one was smaller than the Lair and that much was a blessing.

"Looks like rain," Malone observed from the passenger seat. The top half of his seat was reclined back so he was almost lying down. He had pulled his dark blue baseball cap over his eyes so he could doze for a few minutes. The dark interior of the car had been silent until he spoke. Ajax wasn't in the mood to listen to music, preferring silence so he could lose himself in his thoughts. Nero and Devin had gone into the club to ask around, see if anyone knew of an Ace. Five years and they still hadn't found any trace of Orion's daughter. Ajax wasn't surprised. Roan was a liar; he had always known that. But Jet and Lilly had requested they look into any leads and they had promised to help the leaders of the protectors. The Deverells had always done so and always would.

If Orion did have a daughter, then he definitely knew how to hide her. Ajax couldn't count the number of leads they had investigated. Nero would go into the rebel clubs with one of his brothers, normally Malone or Devin since the rebels weren't huge fans of Ajax. He was a protector to the bone and loyal to Jet and Lilly — vile conformity in their eyes. He didn't fit in with rebels at all. Malone and Devin, though they were also loyal to the Monroes, could at least blend in for a while. Nero, the youngest and by far the wildest brother, easily fit in with the rebels. He loved them and, for the most part, the feeling seemed to be mutual.

"They've been in there a while," Ajax commented. The car's interior was cool. Ajax had turned the air conditioning off not too long ago. He gazed in the direction of the club's entrance.

"They'll be out soon," Malone said as he pushed his hat up so he could look out the window on his side. Ajax grunted in response as he watched the small droplets of rain trail down the clean panes of glass. The interior of the car retained a new car smell. The Monroes' cars were all well taken care of and few showed any sign of their age. *Well, except for the few Sly has borrowed,* Ajax remembered, almost smiling at the thought. The informant didn't really understand the point of taking care of vehicles and frequently brought them back with scratches and dings.

"Dare we hope?" Malone asked jokingly, attempting to lighten the mood in the car. The frown of concern remained on Ajax's face as he continued to stare out the window. Worry had been gnawing at his insides like a parasite for the past fifteen or so minutes. His brothers had been in there for almost two hours. It hadn't taken that long at the countless other rebel clubs they had investigated. Malone's weary groan brought Ajax out of his thoughts.

"Do you want me to go in there?" he offered. His dark blue eyes held a tired look, but Ajax knew that he would do whatever he requested without hesitation. Ajax shook his head, offering his brother a grateful smile.

"Nah. We'll give them another few minutes," Ajax responded as shifted his weight, attempting to get more comfortable. He crossed his long legs in front of him. Malone looked back out the windshield at the mostly empty parking lot. It was almost four in the morning.

The sudden sound of a thump on the passenger side of

the car caused both brothers to look behind them, each instinctively reaching for the weapon they wore. The back door opened and Nero fell into the back seat on top of a rebel with neon green hair. They were locked in a passionate kiss. One of Nero's hands was groping her large breast over her skimpy halter-top and her legs wrapped around his waist as she kissed him just as amorously.

"What are you doing?" Ajax yelled. Nero pulled out of the kiss just long enough to glare at his oldest brother. The rebel seemed unbothered by the audience as she began to strip off Nero's clothes. Malone was trying to smother his laughter as he got out of the car. He had no desire to be caught up in the inevitable argument.

"What does it look like?" Nero snapped as the rebel made fast work of his belt and began working on his jeans. "We'll be done in an hour or so, nothing kinky, I promise. I'll clean up. Now get out, big ears!"

"You are not having sex in this car!" Ajax stated, trying to regain some control of the situation. "And I do not have big ears!"

"Ajax, do you know how long it's been since I've had the chance to fool around? Not sex, just fooled around? Long enough for me not to care you're in here. I swear, we'll do it right in front of you," Nero said before turning his attention back to the woman who was still working on his jeans. "And you do have big ears, they match your nose."

Ajax stepped out of the car and let out a frustrated growl as the two shared a chuckle at his expense, making sure to slam the door loudly behind him. He knew Nero wasn't modest when it came to anything relating to sex. No shape shifter was, but Nero lacked any form of inhibition. He'd do it anytime, anywhere.

Ajax ran a hand over his face as he moved around to the front of the car. He closed his eyes and turned his face to the cool drizzle, allowing it to wash away some of the tension that had built up in his lean body. It had been a long few years and everything seemed to be going wrong. He opened his bright blue eyes, searching out Malone and Devin. They were standing under a lone streetlamp, bathed in a bright glow. They both looked at their older brother as he approached them.

"Well, we've lost the car for the time being," he reported irritably. "Remind me to invest in a leash for him so you two can keep him under control."

"I'm sorry, Ajax," Devin apologized. "I really tried to keep an eye on him, but you know how he is."

"He called me big ears," Ajax complained, ignoring his younger brother's excuse. Malone had to turn away and bite his tongue hard. Tears began to form in his eyes as he tried desperately not to laugh.

"Well you do have big ears, but at least they match your nose," Devin deadpanned, cracking at the last word. Malone burst out laughing. Ajax shot his brothers a look of pure loathing as they practically fell over laughing.

"I hate the three of you," he grumbled sourly. He looked around the parking lot and back toward the rebel club when he saw the door open out of the corner of his eye. A young rebel with short platinum blonde hair stepped out with a trash bag. She was dressed in a black shirt and dark denim jeans. Her clothing was so baggy that it was difficult to tell her gender, particularly from a distance. Ajax tilted his head and started toward the solitary rebel.

"Ajax?" Malone asked, breathless from laughing. The eldest Deverell ignored him as he jogged across the lot. He checked his pace so as not to startle the young rebel when he approached. He knew she was a shape shifter, but there was something else about her.

"Excuse me?" Ajax called out when he was a few feet away from the young woman. The rebel glanced over her shoulder then turned around so she was facing Ajax, giving him a once over. Even close up she was incredibly androgynous and could have easily passed for any gender.

The resemblance to her father was almost uncanny. She had his eyes, nose, and mouth.

"Yeah?" she replied.

"What's your name?" Ajax asked as he stopped in front of the woman. The rain had lightened to a mist, which was pleasantly cool.

The young woman frowned suspiciously. "Sorry, buddy. I'm not lookin' and you're not my type anyway."

Ajax smiled, knowing he had walked right into that one. "Does the name Orion Deverell mean anything to you?"

She crossed her arms over her chest. "The only Orion I know of is the constellation."

"You're Ace, aren't you?" Ajax pressed as he took his hands out of his pockets.

"Depends," the woman replied with a casual shrug. "Who wants to know?"

"My name is Ajax Deverell. Orion was my older brother," Ajax began. "I know this is quite sudden, but the Monroes need your help."

Ace snorted and shook her head, moving over to a nearby dumpster. "I'm a rebel. The problems of protectors don't concern me."

"They should," Ajax continued, glancing out toward the dark night and glimmering asphalt. "They concern Alpha enough that she's agreed to a temporary alliance."

Ace tossed the bag into the dumpster, glancing over at Ajax again. "Heard about that. What's going on?"

"Tell me," Ajax began after a moment, unable to hide the grin that crept across his face. "What do you know about the prophecy of the Four?"

CHAPTER THREE

Blitz stood in the middle of her plain room, twirling her kali sticks. She was working on her left side, twirling the stick up and down in a repetitive motion. Up to her shoulder, down to her knee, and repeat. Her room was bare: nothing decorative adorned the walls or any other surface. She had a dresser with a mirror on top of it, a desk, and a bed. The drawers in the dresser and desk were empty. Her sunglasses sat on the bare wooden surface of the desk next to a small lamp. Even the bed looked unused. She preferred to meditate sitting on the floor. Blitz really only used the walk-in closet, where she stored her clothing and weapons.

She glanced toward the window behind her, checking the position of the sun. It was exactly 5:36 in the evening. A sudden tremor in her right hand drew her attention to the side. Blitz tested the hand, twirling the stick in the same repetitive motion. She did it with no trouble. She twirled both sticks up once more and then walked into her closet, placing them in their proper place, a velvet-lined drawer. The drawers near the bottom of the closet were all lined with black velvet. She kept her weapons in perfect condition and tended to them daily.

Closing the drawer, Blitz walked to the very back of the closet where her catsuit hung. She stripped off her tank top and pants, tossed them aside, and took the catsuit off the hanger. Blitz easily slid it on over her svelte body, pulling up the zipper in front. Once zipped, the pull seemed to melt away and become part of the material. The silver charm she always wore about her throat seemed to shimmer even more radiantly against the black of the catsuit.

Blitz reached down to where her light combat boots sat on the floor and slipped them on over her feet. She grabbed her motorcycle gloves from the top shelf in the closet, standing on the tips of her toes in order to reach them, and pulled them on over her slender hands.

Blitz picked up the pants and tank top she had been wearing and grabbed two empty hangers, hanging them up in the closet so they wouldn't be wrinkled. She doubted the material could actually wrinkle, but she hated leaving any kind of disorder. Blitz glanced around at the drawers of weapons, debating whether to take something. She reached down to the drawer just under the kali sticks and withdrew her weapon of choice: her sais. She doubted she'd need them, but she decided to take them anyway. If nothing else, they added to the intimidating aura she exuded. Blitz tied the black belt about her waist, watching as it melted into the catsuit. She walked out of the closet and moved over to the desk, grabbing her sunglasses and slipping them over her luminous eyes as she made her way across the room to the door.

Blitz closed the door quietly behind her as she stepped out of her room. The doctor wouldn't be up for at least another two hours and she didn't want to wake him. He didn't get enough sleep and she knew he'd try to stop her. The last thing she wanted was one of his lectures meant to elicit emotions she didn't possess. He was an expert on experiments, but every once in a while he seemed to forget what she was. She felt nothing, not guilt or sadness or regret. Blitz continued down the narrow hall and made a right turn, entering the kitchen.

Jack sat at the table, his nose buried in a book. He glanced up at her when she entered but immediately turned back to his book. Blitz stepped up into the main part of the kitchen where the refrigerator, stove, oven, and sink were located. Even wearing boots, her footsteps were silent on the hardwood floor. She opened the refrigerator's large stainless steel door, reached into the cool interior, and retrieved a bottle of water.

Blitz moved into the part of the kitchen where the table was, pulled out the wooden chair next to Jack, and sat down, cracking open the cap on the bottle of water. Jack remained engrossed in his book. Blitz craned her neck to see the title.

"*Night Watch* by Stephen King," he said without looking up. She glanced off to the side again. Jack closed the book, raising his glowing eyes to meet her concealed gaze.

"Are you going out again tonight?" he asked.

Blitz took a sip of her water, but didn't respond. The cool liquid slid down her aching throat. The doctor had left the air conditioning on even though none of them really needed it. Jack and Blitz could only feel the extremes in temperature and both were trained to survive in such climates. She glanced at the worn paperback. It had a green binding with black lettering. On the cover, there was a shadow around a skeleton, something that normals found eerie for reasons that eluded her. She looked back toward Jack, who was still watching her.

"Blitz, you have to stop," he spoke gently. That was something Blitz couldn't help but notice about him when they were first extracted. She had no memory of Jack's tone being anything other than gentle, even when they had been in the main laboratory.

"No," she replied, screwing the white cap on top of the transparent plastic bottle. She put it on the table and watched as water began to condense on the side.

"Everything I've read involving revenge—" Jack began after a brief pause.

"You and the doctor are making the same mistaken assumption. This is not revenge. It is neutralizing a serious threat to our continued survival," Blitz responded flatly as she rose out of the chair in one boneless motion. She had no interest in what was fast becoming an unimportant and frivolous discussion.

"You are going to force the Corporation's hand, Blitz," Jack insisted as he rose with identical fluidity. "You're going to make things worse. You may not believe it to be revenge, but that's exactly what it looks like and revenge is an endless cycle. It isn't just a fictional concept. It's all around us. People fighting each other, killing each other, dying in wars, arguments about insignificant things becoming blood feuds, it's everywhere."

"We saw the same things, Jack," Blitz reminded him as she moved around the table. "It is what we were created for."

"But we do not have to contribute to it, not anymore," Jack protested. Blitz paused at the doorway to the kitchen, turning to face him.

"You and I both know that is not true. This is Grenich's world. They can erase a person from the face of the planet with just a snap of their fingers. Killing is what we were created to do. I know that you are experiencing the same instincts, faint though they may be. You're bored being sedentary. You can't fight your nature forever," she stated. "I will probably be back tomorrow night, maybe early the day after."

She didn't give Jack a chance to respond as she turned and was lost in the last rays of the sun.

~~*~*~*

Mel White was alone in his private car on the train,

lying on his bed in the lavishly decorated bedroom while his six guards remained out in the main part of the car. It consisted of a table, a few chairs, and a fully stocked bar. The bedroom was a bit smaller, just a large bed and a plasma screen television. The dull red sheets of the bed had been overly starched. The cream-colored lamp was on beside the bed. The shade on the window was drawn, blocking out the navy blue of the dark night outside. The plasma screen engrossed Mel. It was alive with vibrant colors, a scene of murder and mayhem lighting up the otherwise dark room. In his cold brown eyes was the reflection of a woman cutting her way through numerous foes. He felt faintly aroused watching her bounce around on the screen.

Mel swore when his cell phone began ringing. He fumbled for the remote and quickly put the movie on pause. He turned to the nightstand and felt around until he found the smooth silver surface of his cell phone. He looked at the number on the screen and groaned in annoyance. Tracy: of all the people he didn't want to speak to at the moment, she was high on the list. *Best not to keep the frigid bitch waiting,* Mel thought as he flipped open the small phone.

"I'm so sorry to interrupt your onanism, love," a soft voice filtered through the small speaker right as Mel raised it to his ear, mock sincerity in her overly sweet and polite tone.

Mel froze, terrified when he realized the mistake he had made. Tracy was a telepath, and a damn good one. She could hear every thought from everybody attached to the Corporation and she had just heard him call her a bitch. Blatant disrespect was an offense punishable by death. *She could probably make my head explode right now if she wanted,* Mel thought fearfully.

"My apologies, ma'am," he managed to stammer. He could practically hear a smirk spread across her features. She loved fear, gobbled it up like kids did candy. Right now, Mel knew he reeked of it.

"Relax, Mr. White. There will be no exploding heads this evening," she said in what should have been a reassuring tone. "I call on behalf of the heads of Grenich. It seems we may have a bit of a situation on our hands. As you are undoubtedly aware, two of our more valuable commodities were stolen more than a year ago. We have reason to believe one of them may be stalking the recruitment team of which you were a part."

Mel swallowed. Those goddamn experiments. Though they were animals, they were probably the most dangerous creatures on the planet. Now that two were on the outside, no longer under the control of handlers, it did not sit well with Mel White.

"I have been assigned to return them to the facility," Tracy continued. "I just missed one at the Pinkertons' nightclub—"

"Did it kill Lindsey and Danielle?" Mel interrupted, inwardly cringing at his second mistake.

"Yes," Tracy replied in a moderately terse tone. "As well as their guards."

"Jesus," Mel breathed in disbelief. "How the hell did one experiment take them out?"

Tracy chuckled, a bone-chilling sound. "Mr. White, our products are top of the line, billion dollar weapons. You think six large men are going to stop one?"

"So basically the guards you give your recruitment teams are just for our peace of mind and not worth jack?" Mel asked.

"Your words not mine, love," Tracy replied lightly. "I have a hunch our seven series will be after you next, so I will be boarding your train at the next stop. I won't be long. I'm just going to have a look around."

She hung up before he had a chance to reply. Mel glanced briefly at his cell phone before closing it and placing it on the nightstand. He looked at the screen, frozen on the image of a blonde woman leaping into the air. Fear began to creep over him, slithering beneath his pale skin and burrowing in his stomach like a tapeworm. He sat up and draped his legs over the side of the uncomfortably stiff mattress. He ran his large hands over his face, covering the bottom half so only his eyes showed.

"Okay, they have been experimenting on these things for who knows how long," he tried to reassure himself as he reached over and switched off the lamp. "They know them inside and out, meaning they can predict every last move. I'm perfectly safe. Just another few minutes to the next station. Tracy will come on board and trap the damn thing, and everything will be fine. I've got six guards out there and I have a gun in here. It's not going to get into this car without alerting someone."

"Your logic is flawed," a calm voice whispered from the shadows. With a little yelp, Mel White spun around. In the dim light of the television set, he could just make out a silhouette on the opposite side of the bed. He groped around the wall behind him, searching desperately for the light switch to illuminate the small room. It seemed like his large hand traveled over miles of well-polished paneling before finally finding the goddamn switch. He flicked it up, illuminating the room in a bright glow from the overhead light.

The creature stood on the opposite side of the room, leaning against the small sink. The seven series obviously knew she controlled the situation. She was clothed all in black, from the base of her neck down to the tips of her toes. The pale face resembled a ghost's and the glowing eyes were concealed behind small black sunglasses. The short-cropped hair was different. The last time he had seen the seven series, her hair had been bleached blonde. Now it was as black as the creature's clothing. He glanced sideways, trying to control the annoying tremors that were wracking his body. His gun was in the nightstand, but he would never reach it in time. Even if he did, it was about as useful as a popgun. The seven series could avoid bullets and he wasn't a great shot anyway.

She walked, slowly and deliberately, over to the television set. Without taking her eyes off him, she reached down and pressed the power button. The picture on the screen, the silhouette of a sword-wielding woman in the dark surrounded by foes, vanished. The entire space was silent. Sweat began to trickle down Mel's bald head as he tried to remember the seven series' identification number.

"I've got six guys out there. All I have to do is yell," Mel began, attempting to threaten her. He knew the experiments were heavily motivated by self-preservation instincts. His eyes were drawn to the charm about her throat, the cat and the lightning.

She shrugged, unconcerned. "Go ahead."

Mel stared at her, trying to read her. Was the seven series calling his bluff? No, experiments never did that. He closed his eyes briefly as realization poured over him.

"They're dead, aren't they?" he asked, already knowing her answer.

"Yes," she answered. "An enjoyment of alcohol is easy to exploit. They have been dead for a while now, ever since the last stop."

"What?" Mel backed up to the small window in his bedroom. He opened the shade and saw the train was no longer moving. He turned and nearly jumped out of his skin when he saw her face inches from his own.

"Look, I have nothing to do with experimentations. I'm just a glorified security guard. Killing me won't hurt the Corporation. They'll just get someone else. I'm a nobody," he tried desperately. She shook her head once, her face a blank mask.

"You help with recruitment. You take shape shifters off the street and are paid for it. You provide the Corporation with stock. Your connection with Grenich makes you dangerous," she stated softly. Mel knew he only had one shot at getting away and he was prepared to take it. While he had been talking to the seven series, he had been fumbling around the nightstand behind him. His meaty hand found the small lamp.

He gripped it and swung it around from behind his back, hoping to catch her with the wild swing. With one deft flick of her hand, the seven series had shattered the lamp within his grip while thrusting forward with her other palm. The blow struck him square in the nose, shattering it. He stumbled backwards, dazed from the powerful blow, tasting the coppery tang of blood that now flowed freely from his nostrils.

He felt the lamp's cord jerk out of his hand and wrap around his throat, tightening mercilessly like a noose. She kicked his knees out from under him as his large hands pulled desperately at the fatal circle about his neck. He kicked and thrashed, but she sat securely with her knee digging into his back.

Blitz heard Mel White's last gurgling breath as she choked it out of him. She gave the cord an extra yank and snapped his neck. Dropping the two ends of the cord, Blitz stood up in one fluid move, and began to walk out of the private car. When she opened the door to where the dead guards lay motionless in the main part of the car, she was suddenly struck by a wave of dizziness. Blitz latched onto the doorway and gritted her teeth as she waited for the spell to pass, pressing a hand against her forehead to quell the sudden dull throbbing.

Blitz looked up when she heard someone clicking their tongue. Her blood froze when she saw the petite figure in the far doorway: Tracy, one of the top Grenich enforcers and the one most favored by the head of the Corporation. Immediately Blitz straightened up, studying her opponent. Tracy was dressed in a modest gray business suit. Her specially-made handguns sat in holsters on her slender waist. No one knew exactly what Tracy was, but every experiment knew she was someone to be feared.

"7-299, you have been one *bad* little guinea pig," she chastised almost playfully. Blitz stared at Tracy, her hands twitching in anticipation. Tracy reached for her gun. Blitz was at her side in a flash, kicking the gun out of her hand and hit her with a powerful right hook. Tracy spun around and slammed her elbow into Blitz's back, knocking her into one of the walls. Blitz winced when she felt a dull ache, indicating a bruised or possibly cracked rib. She spun around to face her skilled opponent.

Tracy used her thumb to rub away the blood from her split lip. Experiments were fast and skilled, but she was one of the few people who could predict them. Her boss wanted the seven series alive, so Tracy could not rely on her guns. Blitz started forward as did Tracy. They both front kicked, both found their mark on the other's sternum. They knocked each other to the ground, winded.

"Come on, 7-299, be a good soldier and come home," Tracy managed to pant out, chuckling. "I promise the disciplinary action taken will not be unreasonable. I will oversee it myself, you have my word."

There was nothing but silence in response. Tracy pushed herself up on her elbows, staring at the empty space where Blitz should have been.

"God dammit!" she snapped as she smacked the floor with her palm. She pushed herself to her feet and brushed herself off, looking around at the carnage in the private car. Tracy sighed, knowing her boss would tire of cleaning up after the rogue seven series. It was bad for employee morale if the heads of the Corporation couldn't keep their own products under control, to say nothing of their clients. Tracy took a small cell phone out of the inside breast pocket of her suit as she made her way to the room, taking in the scene. Quickly scrolling through the few numbers in her address book, she found the one she wanted and hit the speed dial as she stepped back out into the main part of the car.

"It's me, sir," Tracy said when the man on the other end picked up. "The experiment got away, but I can now confirm that the hunter is 7-299, as you suspected. I need a team out here to sanitize this most recent mess … If I had to guess, I'd say she hopped on in one of the major stations, most likely posing as an employee. There's probably a body and a uniform somewhere — either on board or at one of the stations. The seven series got into the private car and poisoned the liquor, knowing full well Mr. White wouldn't drink any. The scene resembles one of the Corporation's simulations."

Tracy paused and glanced out one of the small windows when the train slowly began to move forward. "The train has just started again. Could you send a cleanup crew to the next stop? Thank you, sir. I shall see you soon."

Tracy hung up and looked at one of the still bodies in a chair. She pushed the corpse aside, sinking into the chair as it fell to the ground with a thump. Drumming her fingers on the felt-covered table, she tried to figure out who the seven series would target next.

~~*~*~*

Jack had been meditating when he heard the back door to the cabin open. He blinked once and glanced toward the window in his room. It was quite early in the morning, only 5:48. The doctor was still asleep, having found no trace of Blitz since she had left the previous day. Jack continued to listen as the door closed and someone entered. He got up and moved to the door of his room, opening it and looking down the long hallway to the sitting room in the very back of the cabin. Nothing but the muted glow of the fading night. Jack padded down the hallway. The hardwood floor was pleasantly cool against the soles of his bare feet. He entered the large room.

Directly in front of him was a stone fireplace that hadn't been used since the doctor had brought them there. He didn't say anything, but both Blitz and Jack knew he was afraid fire would trigger unpleasant memories of the years they spent in the Corporation. A few chairs were scattered about the room as well as a couple of couches and a futon. On the windowsills, there were purple flowers. The doctor enjoyed plants and gardening, which he did every day.

The sitting room was peaceful and one of Jack's favorites. He often came here to read and practice sparring with Blitz. The sparring matches had ended when she suddenly became withdrawn, shortly before she had attacked the Pinkertons' club. Jack placed his hands on his hips, closed his eyes, and lifted his face to the ceiling above, imagining the sun was warming his face. He turned around, already having heard her breathing when he entered.

Blitz lay on one of the sofas against the wall, her willowy body stretched out across the three red cushions. Her head was propped up on a pillow resting against one of the wooden arms of the couch. She was still clad in her catsuit, but had shed the sunglasses, gloves, and boots. Blitz wasn't looking at him but rather at the picture over the fireplace: a large black and white photograph of a nude woman's back. Black lines on her sides made her back resemble a violin. Ever since arriving at the cabin, Blitz regularly studied the portrait. Neither the doctor nor Jack knew why.

Jack glanced down at his nightclothes, which consisted of a plain dark T-shirt and matching pants. He looked back at Blitz. She was paler than usual.

"Are you all right?" he asked as he approached her.

"I am," she replied, her eyes never moving from the picture. "I saw Tracy last night."

Jack stared at her, his eyes widening. He had a faint sense of fear, which was still a somewhat alien feeling to him. He wasn't used to emotions yet and Jack wasn't sure he ever would be.

"It's okay. She didn't follow me, I made sure she wouldn't be able to," Blitz said, her voice a little stronger.

"We fought. Briefly. She damaged a few ribs."

"You're lucky it wasn't worse," Jack mentioned as he sat on the coffee table across from her. "She is one of the only non-experiments who can kill us with her bare hands. We're not invincible, Blitz. Our abilities make us superior to normals, but we can still be killed."

"I am fully aware of that. I was not looking to fight her, which is why I retreated at the first opportunity I had," Blitz stated. Jack clasped his hands in front of him, going quiet as he thought over his words. He sometimes found he had trouble expressing things, which he was sure would become easier with practice.

"They want us back, Blitz. We're important to them for some reason. They'll never stop hunting us. And I," he paused before softly adding, "I don't want to go back."

Silence fell over them for a long while, heavy and stony. Blitz looked up at the immaculate wooden ceiling.

Jack unclasped his hands and placed them on his knees. "The doctor will be—"

"I killed a man who wasn't attached to Grenich," Blitz interrupted. Jack studied her with his luminous brown eyes. She met his gaze, her expression blank and unreadable as it always was. He tilted his head and spread his hands, waiting for her to elaborate.

Blitz swung her legs down, rising to her feet, and walked to the set of double glass doors. Her eyes were fixed in the distance, past the murky shadows that still lurked throughout the woods.

"At the train station, before we left. I was in a room and he came up behind me. I heard him breathing as he came down the hall. Elderly, at least seventy-two. I was hiding in one of the rooms . . ." Blitz trailed off and turned to face Jack who had also gotten up and stood a few feet behind her. "I needed some kind of uniform to blend in."

She went quiet again so Jack pressed, "What happened?"

"I snapped his neck," she answered simply with a

shrug. "It was sloppy and not something I had anticipated doing."

Blitz looked back out the windows. Jack came up beside her and hesitantly reached out, laying a hand on her tense upper arm. She instantly jerked away and stared at him. He shrugged.

"I don't know. The doctor says sometimes physical contact is comforting. You sounded . . . I think normals term it 'upset.'"

She continued to stare at him, perplexed by the random act. Physical contact was prohibited at the Corporation, except for during sparring practice. The experiments were taught the hard way that any sign of affection or reassurance would result in unimaginable pain. Jack was still trying to get over his aversion to physical touch. It could set off a knee-jerk reaction in experiments that caused them to grab the person's arm and twist it almost to the point of breaking it. It was one of their less dangerous instinctual reactions.

"There was also a young girl on the train," Blitz continued on after a moment. "Humans were fawning over her, calling her 'cute' and 'adorable.'"

Jack shrugged. "Normals like the innocence of the very young."

"Innocence is weakness," Blitz said, repeating one of the daily lessons that had been drilled into their skulls at the Corporation.

Jack shook his head. "I don't believe that's true."

Blitz twisted her body toward Jack. For a minute, Jack thought she would strike him and his body went rigid. It was another automatic response to a perceived threat: an experiment's body would tense up when preparing for a fight.

"I don't understand you, Jack. I don't understand your desire to live in a state of delusion." She gestured out to the dark land. "Don't you see reality anymore?"

"Whose reality?" Jack asked. She shook her head,

walking past him and disappearing into her room. Jack looked out the window and somehow Blitz's answer was clear to him. When she looked out at the world, all she saw was Grenich.

~~*~*~*

In her room, Blitz stood with her back to the door. The lights were off and the blinds were drawn. Normally, she kept at least one light on. It was another behavior she couldn't quite figure out. She could see just as perfectly in the dark as she could in the light. Right now though, Blitz wanted to be surrounded by blackness. She wanted to feel solitude and darkness made it easier. The coming day, however, had other plans for her.

Her glowing green eyes snapped open when she heard a sigh of boredom. Blitz glanced over to the dresser and saw the ghost, who was perched on the edge with her hands resting on either side of her. Her attire had changed — she now wore a white blouse and dark blue jeans. A soft aura glowed about her, enhanced by the shadows. She shook her head. The glistening strands of her dark brown hair shimmered radiantly and her eyes fixed on Blitz, a small smile on her rose-colored lips.

"Why are you *so* troubled by the little girl?" the ghost asked in an innocuous tone.

"Who are you and what do you want?" Blitz asked as she took a step toward the ghost. The ghost continued to smile coyly as she slowly swung her long legs, which were crossed at the ankle.

"That little girl approached you on the train and asked for directions to the observation car," the ghost continued. "She was completely unafraid. Now why would that bother you, hmm? Could it be perhaps there is just a small part of you that remembers a time before Grenich?"

Blitz kept her expression blank as she watched the radiant specter before her. "Even if that were accurate, which it is not, it does not matter. What I am now is what I will always be."

There was a brief silence in the room. The rising sun cast the shadows from pitch black to a muted gray. The ghost continued to glow, unaffected by the change in light.

"But soft, methinks I scent the morning air. Brief let me be."

The ghost raised one leg and crossed it over the other, folding her hands over her knee. Blitz watched the ghost warily. The ghost leaned toward her as if she were going to tell Blitz a secret.

"Death is not the solution," the ghost stated before vanishing. Blitz was once again alone in her dark room with nothing but her thoughts.

CHAPTER FOUR

It was dawn when Jensen pulled his sleek silver Jaguar up to the mansion's garage. He shifted into park and glanced over at Electra. In the few days it had taken them to return to the mansion, she had said nothing. They had driven straight through, neither wanting to make any unnecessary stops on the way. She would keep watch the few times he had to pull off the road in order to get some brief shut eye. He could go a couple days without sleep, but even he needed some rest in order to not doze off on the road. Electra, being a guardian, didn't know how to drive.

Jensen observed Electra. She was identical to her sister and it had taken him some time to get used to that. Sometimes it still seemed like he was driving with an apparition. She was resting her head against the window, staring at nothing. Jensen looked out her window, taking in the mists that snaked over the grounds.

"We're here," he said softly. Electra swallowed and nodded, closing her eyes briefly. He had suggested a few times that she just Appear back at the Meadows, but for some reason, Electra had refused. She wanted to accompany him back to the mansion, perhaps just to have some mild sense of closure, a conclusion to the journey. Jensen wasn't entirely sure. He never was quite sure what the young guardian was thinking.

Jensen stared out the windshield, turning off the engine. He had a feeling they were going to be there for a while and he didn't want to use up any more gas than necessary. He wouldn't force Electra out of the car before she was ready to leave. They had formed an odd sort of bond, a weird kind of friendship. They both loved Isis, both had been grieving for her, and both needed answers. Jensen admired Electra's strength. For the past five years, she had kept him from spiraling out of control.

As if sensing him looking at her, Electra blinked and spoke. "She's gone."

Jensen sighed. "Electra—"

"I don't know why, but I just realized now that we'll probably never get answers," she continued, ignoring him. "Even with the list, how many of those people are we really going to find, with someone else hunting them? Will we ever really know what happened or why? We probably won't ever find her body. I found my twin only to lose her before I really even got a chance to know her. She's just gone."

Jensen looked back out the windshield. "I won't accept that, Electra. As long as there is breath in my body, I will hunt the names on that list. Neither the Monroes, nor the Deverells, nor I will rest until we get answers. We may not find out exactly what happened, but we're not going to stop until we get some acceptable form of closure and justice. All right?"

Electra looked over at him, studying his face. After a moment, she nodded.

"Okay," Jensen said, pausing as he carefully chose his next words. "You're not going to like this, but I think you should stay in the Meadows. You are a guardian and after what happened … we just don't know enough right now. I shouldn't have let you travel with me this long."

"Yeah," Electra agreed. Jensen could tell she wanted to do more to help, but understood his reasoning. She had probably been homesick anyway.

Electra opened the car door. A cool autumn breeze caressed her skin, gently lifting and dropping some strands of her shoulder-length hair. It ruffled the purple blouse she was wearing. She grabbed her bag from the backseat of the car and looked at Jensen again.

"Thanks for . . ." she paused, unsure of how to sum up their trip. Jensen waved her off, indicating he understood what she meant.

"Don't mention it. You're good company," he said as he kept his blue eyes on the gravel driveway. "Sorry we didn't have time for souvenir shopping."

Electra smiled a little. "Maybe next time."

Jensen laughed at her response. The young guardian straightened up and closed the door. The car started again, a gentle purr that had become almost comforting over the years. He watched as she disappeared in a flash of brilliant silver light.

Jensen pulled up to the garage. He paused long enough to press the garage door opener and then smoothly drove inside. Jensen spotted the Deverells' Porsche and pulled into the empty space next to it. He turned off the engine again, grabbed the garage door opener, and closed the door he had driven through. When the door started to swing shut, Jensen tossed the opener onto the passenger seat. He massaged his brow and let out a breath.

The garage was quiet. Everything was parked in its proper space; no vehicles were missing. The bright lights that hung from the ceiling were all on, bathing the garage in a clean incandescent glow. The light tan tiles on the floor glimmered. The cars and motorcycles all sparkled like new. Each one was well taken care of.

Jensen shifted his weight and leaned back so his head was resting on the headrest, his face turned toward the roof of his car. The protector closed his eyes and tried to will the tension out of his body. Under his closed lids, all he saw was her. Jensen opened his eyes and snapped. He began beating his hands against the black steering wheel in front of him, muttering curses under his breath. The side of his hand brushed against the horn a couple times, creating a cut-off honk, but he didn't care. The past few years had yielded pretty much nothing until Coop had shown up and the more Jensen thought about it, the more frustrated he became with his inability to find anything of worth.

After a minute of beating the hell out of the steering wheel and swearing, Jensen put his head against the top of it. Suddenly, the whole situation struck him as hilarious and he began to laugh. He leaned back as he continued to laugh loudly. Anyone passing by the car probably would have thought they were witnessing an unhinged man having a meltdown. As his manic laughter died down to snickering, his eyes closed again.

"Witness the breakdown of a cursed man, the last of his line," he muttered to himself, chuckling sadly.

The feeling of being watched caused Jensen to glance out the window. No one. He was still completely alone in the garage. Jensen glanced to the other side and nearly jumped out of his skin.

Isis was sitting in the passenger's seat. Her body was turned toward him and she rested her head between her thumb and index finger, studying him. She was wearing the same clothes she had worn when he had brought her back to his apartment. The first time they had made love. The last time they had made love. Jensen swallowed, his mouth very dry. There was a lump in his throat and tears burned his eyes. She lowered the hand that had been supporting her head as she continued to look at him, a sad smile dancing across her beautiful face. Jensen yearned to touch her skin or to run a hand through her silky hair. He wanted to take her in his arms and never let go, but he resisted the temptation for fear she would disappear the second he got too close.

As if reading his mind, Isis reached out and laid her slender hand over his. Jensen stared in amazement, wondering how a touch could be so warm and yet so cold at the same time. Though it was a simple caress, it felt so intimate. Jensen hesitantly turned his hand over and laced his fingers with hers, smiling when she didn't disappear. He began to massage her hand with his thumb, almost forgetting that she was supposed to be dead. Isis scooted forward so most of her weight rested on her knees. Jensen had to tilt his head up to maintain eye contact. She put another cold hand on the side of his face. Her eyes were a stormy blue color and they locked with his.

"Kill me." Her rose-colored lips moved without sound, just like in his dream. Jensen frowned and shook his head, confused by the plea.

A sudden knocking on his window caused Jensen to jerk awake. He looked around, momentarily disorientated. Looking to the window, he was face to face with Nero, who stood just outside his car. The youngest Deverell looked concerned.

"You okay?" his friend asked. Jensen swallowed and looked back to the passenger side, already knowing she would be gone. He rubbed his eyes, shaking his head once to rid himself of any remaining grogginess. *Definitely need more sleep,* Jensen thought as he flexed the hand that had held the apparition's. He turned back to Nero and nodded, offering his friend a weak smile. Jensen opened the car door, allowing Nero to step back first, and got out, shutting the door behind him. He stuck his hands in his jacket pockets, a force of habit.

~~*~*~*

Electra Appeared in her room in the castle that had always been her home. Her room was still tidy. The messengers had obviously kept it clean in the time she had been gone. She had made sure to straighten up the already clean room before leaving with Jensen. As she dropped her bag on the bed and kicked off her shoes, Electra noticed a shadow passing under her door and hurried across her room. She opened the door and looked out, spotting her mother walking down the hall. Electra swallowed and stepped out of her room, closing her door. Passion froze when she heard the door click shut. She turned around as Electra approached her.

"Mom, listen, I—"

Electra was cut off when Passion slapped her across the face. She raised a hand to her stinging cheek and looked at her mother in shock. Passion had never struck her before. Her mother rarely even yelled at her. Then again, Electra had never run off before. Tears welled up in Passion's eyes as she glared at her daughter.

"Your sister is murdered and your response is to vanish for five years without even leaving a note?" Passion growled in a dangerously quiet voice. "What were you thinking, Electra? If it weren't for Jet and Lilly, I wouldn't even know if you were alive."

Electra's mouth opened and closed as she struggled to find the words. She knew what she had done was wrong and thoughtless, but she had not been thinking at the time. She had just needed to escape from the grief that haunted her home. The castle seemed unusually quiet. Even the portraits seemed to be glaring accusingly at Electra.

When Electra didn't respond, Passion shook her head in disappointment and continued down the hall. She disappeared around a corner, leaving Electra alone in the cold hall. Electra stood in silence for a few minutes. She turned and went back into her room, quickly closing the door once she was inside. The young guardian put her back against the cool wood and slid down so that she was sitting on the floor, weeping the tears she had been holding back for so many years.

~~*~*~*

"So, did you find anything?" Nero asked as he and Jensen made their way into the mansion, looking his friend over. Jensen knew he had lost some weight. He had always been lean, but now he probably looked unhealthy. He didn't care, especially not when there were more pressing issues.

"We got a visit from Frankenstein, also known as the mysterious Coop," Jensen began as he produced Coop's list from his left pocket. "He gave us a list of names: the people responsible for Isis' death."

"Frankenstein's monster," Nero corrected as he took the list from Jensen. Jensen stared at him, confused.

"Pardon?"

"Frankenstein was the doctor who created the monster, but people got confused and started calling the monster Frankenstein," Nero explained as he read the list.

Jensen shook his head. "I'm tired, Nero. I don't really feel like discussing the minutiae of classic novels."

"Just want to make sure you don't sound as dumb as you look," Nero taunted with a playful smile. Jensen snickered and shook his head as he stepped up to the door that led inside the mansion. The two walked down the dark tiles of the hall.

"Did I miss anything?" Jensen asked.

"My brothers and I finally found Ace a couple days ago," Nero said as they turned into the main hallway, his attention focused on the list. "Jet and Lilly have called a meeting tonight, can't wait to see the look on their faces when they see you're — huh."

Nero stopped, staring at the list and frowning.

"What is it?" Jensen asked as he moved beside Nero so that he could see the list. In the back of his mind, Jensen noticed how quiet the mansion was. It was dawn so most shape shifters were probably asleep, but there was usually some kind of noise to indicate someone was home.

Nero glanced at his friend. "Have you heard that urban legend about Blitz?"

Jensen paused and thought for a moment. "A few of my contacts mentioned it. She's some sort of vampire dressed in black vinyl who stalks around at night, right? Supposedly hunting for a guy she's got a blood feud with or a lover who did her wrong? Some cliché nonsense like that. Why?"

"Well, Cassidy was talking to some chick at the Lair who claimed to have survived a massacre by this mystery woman a few states over. The club was supposedly a hot new thing in that town, owned by the Pinkerton sisters." Nero turned and began walking again with Jensen following. Jensen scowled. Shortly before Coop's unexpected visitation, he had read a story about the Pinkertons' new club a few states over and that had been his next destination. What he would have done once he arrived, Jensen didn't know but he expected it probably would have involved violence.

"From fake paramedics to nightclub owners, you do know how to pick them," Jensen responded.

"Bitter much?" Nero pointed out, unbothered. "Anyway, Jet and Lilly had Sly try to track them down, see if there was any merit to the story. There is absolutely no evidence that Lindsey and Danielle Pinkerton ever existed. The occurrences of vanishing people seems to have gone up recently though. It's downright unsettling if you ask me."

"So? They probably created new identities and went underground," Jensen replied with a dismissive shrug. It was fairly easy to create a new identity if you knew the right people. Nero shook his head as he handed the list back to Jensen.

"Using false names doesn't mean disappearing off the face of the Earth without a trace," Nero said. "You going to see Jet and Lilly?"

"I am and then I'm going to drop by Shae's room, see

how she's doing, and afterward I'm going to sleep for at least a day and a half," Jensen replied as he paused by the main stairwell. Nero nodded in the direction of the Monroe's study, indicating the protector leaders were still awake. Jensen started off in that direction.

"Good, you need it. You look like shit," Nero mentioned as he followed his friend.

"Thank you, Nero. Always good to know you're there to kick me when I'm down," Jensen said as they finally reached the oak wood door to the main study. Nero smiled as he raised his hand and began incessantly knocking. A few moments later, the door was yanked open to reveal a haggard Jet who looked less than thrilled with Nero's annoying gesture. The annoyance gave way to surprise when he saw Jensen. Lilly, who had been sitting on the lounge, closed the folder she had been looking over and placed it to the side.

"Jensen," she greeted warmly, smiling.

"You're back," Jet said softly as he opened the door further to allow the two men entrance. Jensen nodded, offering Jet a small smile of greeting before crossing the space to embrace Lilly.

"Welcome back," she whispered.

"You were greatly missed and I thank you for keeping us up to date," Jet mentioned as Jensen stepped out of Lilly's embrace. "We worried nonetheless."

"I know, and I do apologize for that," Jensen mentioned. "Though I am grateful for your concern as well."

Jet smiled as he tightly gripped Jensen's shoulder, an affectionate gesture. Jensen was like a son to the Monroes and their home had always been a safe place, the closest thing he had to a home after the decimation of his family.

Jet gestured to the chairs in front of the large desk in the room. Jet sat down in the chair behind the large desk while Jensen and Nero sat in the two chairs across from him. Lilly smoothed the front of her dark green dress as she leaned against the desk, smiling as she looked between the two men.

"Electra went back to the Meadows," Jensen began. "We didn't find much, but we did get a visit from Coop."

Jet's eyebrows rose and he exchanged a look with his wife. "Oh?"

Jensen nodded and handed Lilly the list Coop had given them, which she took between her fingers. Her dark blue eyes scanned the writing on the folded paper. The day was bright, chasing away the creeping fog that had snaked about the mansion's grounds. It warmed the study with its comforting glow. None of the occupants in the room took notice.

"Those are the people responsible for Isis' death, according to him. I already knew about the first two so I think it's probably legit," Jensen said as he leaned back in his chair, running a thumb over his bottom lip. "I thought about going after them myself, but I don't think I have all the resources I'd need to track them down. Coop also mentioned we aren't the only ones after those people. I think we should probably act fast."

"It was wise of you to not follow up on this alone," Lilly mentioned as she handed Jet the list. The protector studied the names, his brow furrowing. After a moment, he put the list down on the desk and looked back to the two men.

"I agree we should act fast," Jet said. "We're meeting tonight and we can discuss what to do then. I imagine you're tired from traveling, Jensen. Your room is still available."

Jensen nodded, offering the Monroes another smile of gratitude, and pushed out of his chair, heading back to the still open door. He was exhausted, but he had one more thing to do before calling it a day.

~~*~*~*

Isis' room was solemn and hushed. Even though the dawn sparkled outside, the light was muted in the room. Silky curtains shielded the windows. No one had occupied the room since the previous tenant's death.

The bed was freshly made, the curtains around it were drawn and the comforter was smoothed. The furniture inside the room was free of any dust. The wood was polished on the wardrobe, dresser, and nightstand. The carpet was soft and clean. The ferns in the washroom were healthy and dark green, well cared for like the rest of the room. The few lights were always off. The room appeared to be waiting for an occupant to take up residence. Everything was immaculate, including the lilies that adorned the stone balustrade that ran around the small balcony outside. On the opposite side of the room, the door opened as a visitor hesitantly entered.

Jensen swallowed the lump that sprang up in his throat when he saw the interior of the room. Nero and he had parted a short time earlier and Jensen had made his way to the second floor, hoping to speak with Shae. At the last minute, he changed his direction and headed for Isis' old room. Jensen paused just inside the room and inhaled the fresh air. He could almost smell the faint lavender scent of her soap.

The weary protector crossed the room to the balcony doors and moved aside one of the curtains, looking out across the land surrounding the mansion. There were few clouds in the clear autumn sky. The leaves remaining on the trees were brilliant shades of red, yellow, and orange. Jensen closed his eyes and felt the sun on his face, allowing the peaceful atmosphere to wash away some of the tension that had built up in his body.

"Hello, stranger."

Jensen opened his eyes and looked over his shoulder. Shae stood in the doorway and Steve was behind her. A small, but mischievous, smile played on Shae's face.

"We were coming down the hall and noticed light

coming out of this door," Steve explained as Jensen crossed the room. "Welcome back."

"It's good to be back," Jensen responded. Shae wrapped her arms around him in a friendly hug, which he returned with one arm. They hadn't known each other very long, but through his updates, they had become close.

"Got worried about you when you didn't check in for a month," Shae mentioned as she stepped out of the hug.

"My apologies," Jensen said sincerely as he shook Steve's hand, smiling at the other protector.

"Did you find anything?" Steve asked, his dark brown eyes hopeful.

"I did," Jensen replied, sliding his hands in his pockets. "Coop found Electra and me. He gave us a list of people responsible for Isis' death. I just gave it to Jet and Lilly."

"Good," Shae stated, her tone abruptly becoming cold. Jensen looked over at her, his heart breaking at the amount of hatred he heard from the normally compassionate and upbeat protector.

"Word of advice: don't go down the vengeance path," he said, sounding world-weary. "It won't bring her back and it'll only leave you feeling empty."

Steve and Shae exchanged a look. Jensen smiled bitterly and shook his head. Neither of them had known him during the years he had sought vengeance for his family. The only reason he had survived was because the Deverells managed to pull him out of situations where he got in over his head. Jensen still bore quite a few scars from those years.

"If you'll excuse me, I need to catch up on some sleep," Jensen mentioned as he stepped around them, back into the hallway. He had reached his socializing quota for the day.

"Good. You look like shit," Shae teased.

"That's what they tell me," Jensen replied over his shoulder as he headed toward his own room. He stopped when he reached his door and opened it, smiling when he saw that the room had been made up. *Thank you, Lilly*, he thought, knowing the wise former guardian had probably made sure his room was kept tidy for his return. She and Jet had always gone out of their way to make sure the Aldridges felt at home in the mansion. Jensen walked over to the large mattress and sat down, kicking off his nice shoes before lying down on his side.

"Oh damn," he muttered when he realized he had forgotten his stuff in the car. *I'll get it later,* Jensen resolved as his eyelids slid shut, almost on their own accord. His last conscious thought was a prayer to the guardians that his sleep would be dreamless.

~~*~*~*

Roan lay on his back, staring up at the bland ceiling above him. The dungeons were peaceful, as they usually were. The tan bricks surrounding him were almost calming. The guardian glass was so clean it gave the illusion there was no wall in front of him and he could just waltz out whenever he felt like it. The mattress beneath him was also comfortable. The guardians were against all forms of torture and so they treated their few prisoners with more kindness than they deserved. They were served three meals a day and the cells were kept cozy and clean.

However, it was the solitary environment that could threaten a prisoner's sanity. Roan only saw others when Astrea, the guardian in charge of the dungeons, came three times a day to supervise the messenger bringing his meals. He had no physical contact with anyone, but he didn't really mind. Atonement was not something that could be achieved overnight. It was something he had to earn, and Roan knew it would probably take him centuries. The assassin's history was long and bloody, unforgivable in the eyes of most guardians and shape shifters.

Roan's hands were behind his head. His green eyes were fixed on the ceiling and he appeared to be in a trancelike state. He had been worried about Passion for the past few years, but he didn't dare ask how she was. Roan knew she was shattered. She would recover, she had always been strong, but she would probably never be the same. He thought about his ally and what he was up to. He frequently wondered if the doctor was any closer to achieving his goal, which he thought highly unlikely. Roan wished they had some way to communicate. He wanted to know if Set was any closer to finding the elusive Key he had been seeking for so many centuries.

A sudden pounding on the glass wall pulled him out of his thoughts. Roan turned his gaze to the side, a little annoyed by the obnoxious interruption. His breath caught in his throat when he saw who was there.

Electra, his surviving daughter, stood in front of the glass. The soft red of her shirt seemed to enhance her pale complexion. Her hair was loosely pulled back. Her hands were on her hips and her eyes were a dark stormy gray color. Roan swung his long legs off the bed so he was sitting on the edge and he opened his mouth to greet her.

"No pleasantries, Roan," she warned coldly, her eyes never leaving his. "I just came to ask you a question."

Roan nodded once. "Okay."

"When you were an assassin, did you know of anyone named Blitz?"

Roan frowned, puzzled. "Who?"

Electra shook her head impatiently. "It's an urban legend among shape shifters, fairly recent as best I can tell. Since assassins usually stick to the shadows and try to remain anonymous, I want to know if she has been around longer than the legends. If there's any truth to them. According to the stories, she's a killer, so I figured it would be best to ask another killer."

Roan stared at her, still confused. "I honestly don't know. The name isn't ringing any bells. Could you give me the gist of the legends concerning this Blitz?"

Electra shrugged. "There are a lot of different stories

about her. The only thing they have in common is what she wears: a skin-tight reflective black catsuit with gloves and combat boots. She has a silver charm at her throat, a cat with a lightning bolt shape on its side. She only comes out at night, but she is always wearing sunglasses—"

Roan went rigid at the last detail. "Wait, back up. You said she always wears sunglasses? Do they say why?"

Electra shook her head. "Not really. Some people say that she is hiding her identity and others say she has no eyes. I even heard a rebel suggest it was because her eyes glowed."

"It sounds like an experiment, Electra," Roan interrupted her again. "If this story has any truth to it, I would bet Blitz is an experiment from Grenich."

Electra opened her mouth, probably to make a smartass comment, but closed it again. A thoughtful expression crossed her face and she looked a little disturbed.

"But . . . I thought Coop was the only experiment who escaped from the Corporation," Electra mentioned.

Roan rubbed his palms together. "Just because she was out in public doesn't mean she's an escapee. Think about it, Electra. What do assassins do?"

"Are you saying experiments are assassins?"

"They're whatever Carding and the Corporation needs them to be and yes, frequently they are assassins. One night an experiment could be an assassin, the next he could be a thief, and then protecting a Corporation asset the next week. It all depends on their assignment."

"Great," Electra muttered as she turned to leave, finished with her interrogation. She stopped when Roan called her name as he approached the glass wall. She turned back.

"Tell Jet and Lilly that experiments are not normal shape shifters. They have no emotions and no concept of mercy. They are only concerned with completing whatever their assignment or mission is and then returning to the facility they're being kept in. They will do whatever it takes to complete their task and killing is often the easiest and most effective way to ensure success. Don't try capturing them and don't touch them," Roan warned. The seriousness in his voice and eyes unnerved Electra slightly.

"Is that all?" she asked. Roan nodded and she left, leaving him alone again. *Please, please, let her tell them,* Roan thought as he lay down once again. His green eyes returned to the ceiling above him. The former assassin sat up suddenly as he remembered something important from his years working in the Corporation.

"Black is forbidden," he whispered to himself. Black was a strictly forbidden color at the Grenich Corporation. Anyone caught wearing or carrying anything black would be eliminated on sight. Carding and the other higher-ups abhorred the color for some reason and would not tolerate it. If an experiment was wearing black, it could only mean one thing: he or she *had* escaped from the Corporation. But it was impossible.

Roan smiled and lay down again, berating himself for getting so worked up over some meaningless urban legend. Still, he could not help but wonder about the mysterious Blitz. Another thought was nagging at him. *If* she had somehow escaped, when did she learn the concept of rebelling? Coop had been out for years and still had an aversion to the color black. It was a deeply ingrained fear.

Roan shook his head, trying to push the thoughts out of his mind. *It's an urban legend, nothing more,* he thought, almost convincing himself the legend was nothing more than a story. Almost, but not quite.

~~*~*~*

Night fell on the grounds of the mansion, engulfing the land in inky shadows. The mansion was lit with a warm glow from the many lights throughout the home. It was still very quiet, but this was a more pleasant silence. Most of the occupants were out by now; only a few remained at home.

Ace continued down the long hallway, admiring the architecture on the way to the meeting room. She was in no real rush. Jet and Lilly had given her the grand tour when she first arrived and Ace had a great memory. She paused at an abstract sculpture, reaching out a hand and running it over the smooth curves of the cool stone — marble from the looks of it.

"Don't steal that," a stern voice came from behind her as a woman passed by without looking at her. Ace recognized her as Jade and blushed shyly. Jade was an incredibly beautiful woman. She wore a tight dark green tank top and matching pants, which hugged her long legs. Her hair fell just below her shoulders in a single neat braid and she had dark tan skin.

"I'm a rebel, not a thief," Ace replied a little defensively.

"Same thing," Jade called back as she turned a corner, disappearing from Ace's sight. Ace rolled her eyes, already annoyed with protectors. She had been raised by the rebels since she was almost six years old and knew very little about her parents, other than they had both been protectors.

"Don't mind her," a pleasant feminine voice came from behind her. "Jade will warm up to you eventually."

Ace turned around and smiled at the attractive woman who stood behind her. She had shoulder-length hair, which was sleek and black, and brown eyes. She was only slightly taller than Ace.

"Ace, right?" she asked, smiling when Ace nodded. "I'm Alex. You looking for the meeting room or just dilly-dallying for the hell of it?"

Ace snorted. "I'm not known for being timely."

Alex laughed at the response and gestured for her to follow. They walked down the remainder of the hall toward the corner Jade had turned. Both walked at a brisk pace. Ace matched Alex's stride as they went down the hall. She still didn't feel the need to rush, but decided to keep up with Alex so they could continue their conversation.

"Why no neon?" Alex inquired as they reached the middle of the hall, looking pointedly to her hair. Ace chuckled at the question.

"Cause I got no patience," Ace answered. "I tried it once, but I got a headache every time I looked in the mirror. When my hair was much longer, I dyed it a couple different colors. I think I might grow it out again, play around with some different colors."

"I see," Alex said as they walked down the main hallway. She turned about partway and walked a short distance down another hall, stopping at a dark wood door. She turned the silver doorknob and entered, Ace following close behind. There was a long table in the center of the medium-sized room with a white dry-erase board at the front. Computer chairs were set up all around the table and the entire room was brightly lit. There were a few windows toward the ceiling on the wall opposite the door where Alex and Ace had just entered. As Ace had expected, most of the shape shifters were already present.

Jet and Lilly sat at the head of the long meeting table, listening intently to something Ajax was saying. Remington sat next to Jet, also listening to Ace's oldest uncle. Nero and Devin were playing a game of football using nothing but their thumbs and index fingers and a small white piece of paper folded into a triangle. Malone sat next to Devin and flipped through a newspaper. He licked his index finger and slowly turned the page, every action slow and methodical. Nero, ever the immature prankster, flicked the small paper right at Malone. He hit his older brother right in the center of his forehead, causing Malone to look up in irritation. Malone shook his head and muttered something that Ace didn't catch, though she imagined it was something quite colorful.

Jade was sitting in a small group that consisted of Shae, Steve, and a man Ace had yet to meet. The man was tall and debonair with a lean build. He stood by Jade's chair. His clothing was immaculate and not a dark brown hair was out of place. He had an attractive face and his blue eyes held an intense look as he listened to something Jade was saying. He didn't appear to notice anyone else had entered the room.

Ace glanced behind her, surprised to see the enigmatic and gorgeous Sly. Her short black hair was smooth and shone in the light. Her emerald-colored eyes regarded Ace for a moment before turning back to where Jet and Ajax were talking. Ace liked Sly, who she knew was Alpha's lover as well as Jade's. Sly was the nearest one to a rebel in the mansion. *Well, not exactly. Hunter and Cassidy are definitely rebels*, Ace thought as she smiled and nodded at Sly.

"Okay, I believe everyone is here," Jet stated as Ace took the empty seat between Malone and Alex. Everyone was sitting except for Sly and the stranger Ace didn't recognize. Malone closed his newspaper and folded it, laying it in front of him.

"First thing's first," Jet began. "Everyone's met Ace, correct?"

"Almost," Nero replied, turning to the stranger. "Jensen, this is Orion's daughter, Ace. Ace, this is our good friend Jensen. Ace the rebel meet Jensen, the last Aldridge and former thief."

Jensen nodded at Ace before turning to Nero. "That's nice. Thank you."

"Anyway," Jet interrupted before the two could begin their friendly bickering. "This meeting is going to be brief. There are two things we're concerned about and want to focus on."

"As most of you are aware, Jensen and Electra returned with a list of names from Coop, who claims they're the ones responsible for Isis' death," Lilly continued.

Ajax had told Ace about her cousin and what had

happened to her. The topic of Isis was sensitive and she knew well enough to be respectful. Ace remained quiet and kept her eyes on Jet and Lilly.

"Second," Jet continued after the brief pause. "There is some evidence connecting the urban legends about a woman called Blitz to the possible massacre at the Pinkertons' nightclub. Electra spoke to Roan about it and he thinks *if* the stories are true, emphasis on if, they may be about an experiment. He warned us not to engage this woman if we spot her. Generally, we take whatever Roan says with a grain of salt, but we are taking this particular warning seriously. Don't go looking for trouble. I'm sure it's just an urban legend, but I would rather be safe than sorry."

Lilly nodded in agreement with her husband's statement.

"It would make a kind of sense if they were true. What if this experiment is targeting people connected to this corporation?" Sly's quiet voice came from behind the Monroes. Jet glanced over his shoulder at her and she just shrugged as she hooked her thumbs into the pockets of her jeans.

"What about the names?" Jade spoke up. Jet gestured toward Steve, who cleared his throat and folded his hands in front of him.

"I called Loman and he's going to help me run a trace on the names," Steve replied.

"We're also requesting Sly and Jensen go through their channels to see what they can find," Lilly continued as Jet spun his chair around to the small cabinet behind them. On the smooth top, he had placed two sheets of paper. He handed one to Sly and the other one to Remington to pass down to Jensen.

Sly glanced at the paper, arching an eyebrow. "You're not waiting for Loman and Steve?"

"Loman's a good detective, so is Steve, but their resources are limited through no fault of their own," Jet responded. "Coop implied time was of the essence and we know you and Jensen can get the fastest results."

Jensen looked down at the list again. He flipped the paper over and looked over at Jet and Lilly, his charming smile slipping into place.

"Jensen, you take the first three and I'll take the last," Sly said as she moved toward the door. "I can probably find them by tomorrow night, night after that at the latest."

She closed the door and Jet sighed heavily. Lilly placed her hand over his, offering him a supportive smile. Ace could tell he was uncomfortable with Sly's methods. She was reliable, but also known to use morally questionable tactics to get information — at least, as far as the protectors were concerned. Jet turned his attention back to the shape shifters still in the room and then nodded to Lilly. She squeezed his hand once before turning her attention to the other shape shifters.

"I don't think I need to say this, but I'm going to anyway. Losing Isis was hard on all of us. However, that doesn't mean we compromise what we've always stood for: protecting the innocent and doing as little harm as possible," Lilly stated.

"Lilly and I will not tolerate any mission of revenge or vigilantism. We're going to catch those responsible and bring them to the dungeons in the Meadows. That's it. If we hear of any unnecessary force or torture, there will be severe repercussions. Are we clear?" Jet finished.

Most of the people nodded immediately, but there was some reluctance in a few shape shifters. Jensen was silent, his eyes remaining on Jet and Lilly. Shae also seemed to hesitate before nodding her acquiescence.

"All right. Meeting dismissed," Jet stated.

CHAPTER FIVE

Naomi Green sat at a small table set for two on the outdoor terrace of a swanky restaurant. Simple light pink tablecloths covered the wooden tables, which were set with custom-made flatware. The terrace had a little iron fence surrounding it and the floor was made of beige wood. Trees grew outside the fence, shading the patrons who sat near the railing. The air was buzzing with chatter as people discussed the many aspects of their lives over lunch.

Naomi was looking at her untouched glass of expensive wine. She began fidgeting with the gold symbol she wore at her neck, running a long finger over the backward curvature of the "P" and the sharp points of the arrows. As she glanced out over the crowded restaurant again, she slipped her right heel in and out of the pricey white shoe holding it prisoner. Naomi looked down at her gold watch and shook her head. It was a little after one o'clock. Her eyes were drawn to a young girl sitting with her mother at a nearby table. She smiled when the little girl waved at her.

A slender form in a long brown skirt stepped in front of Naomi, blocking her view of the young girl.

"Miss Green," a pleasant voice came from above her.

Naomi looked up to the angelic face of the blonde woman she had been waiting for. Tracy smiled, exposing her perfect white teeth. She stepped over to the opposite side of the table and folded her petite frame into the white wrought iron chair. The thin shadows of the tree fell upon her face — the silhouettes of the leaves drifting over her features.

Tracy glanced over at the girl, her lips curling up into a smile. "It seems as though the maternal instinct never quite dissipates."

Naomi had never heard an accent like Tracy's before. It was so subtle almost no one noticed it. It was only after years of working with her that Naomi had picked up on it. The last lingering remnants of a long dead language. Tracy's eyes turned back to her.

"Thinking of little Adeline?"

"No," Naomi replied softly.

"You're a horrible liar, love. When did you get in from London?" Tracy asked, crossing her slim legs at the ankle. Many of the men at the restaurant, both patrons and waiters, had been glancing at Tracy. She knew it, but paid them no heed.

"Night before last," Naomi responded as she pushed her wine away. "I'm attending the ball tonight like you requested. I will speak with Mr. Derringer about his investments in the Corporation. I'm certain his loyalty still lies with you. Lord knows Grenich has made him more than enough money."

Waiters rushed around, delivering garish dishes to the people who ordered them. One young man approached Tracy and Naomi's table, but Tracy waved him away.

"The heads of Grenich are concerned. Your work has been less than stellar of late, which is why they sent me to have a little chat with you. Make sure all is well," Tracy explained as her posture relaxed even more. Naomi was quiet for a moment.

"My loyalty is with Grenich, as it always has been," she

said. Tracy raised her eyebrows, observing her.

"I was not suggesting otherwise. Still, the past couple retrieval missions have been rather messy."

"Is it my fault you send me on missions with incompetent novices?" Naomi hissed. Tracy leaned forward, her eyes narrowing.

"You dare to speak to me like that? Let me remind you, love, what the Grenich Corporation has done for you. Your eldest is alive because of our cutting-edge research. Do not forget the bargain you made: your life for your daughter's."

Naomi went quiet and looked down at her lap. "My apologies, ma'am. I meant no disrespect."

Tracy sat back, still glaring at the woman. "A disrespectful revenant. Now I have seen everything."

Another soft breeze wrapped through the terrace, ruffling a few cloth napkins. The temperature seemed to drop a few degrees, but Naomi chalked it up to the approaching winter.

"The Four, whatever's left of them, might be at this ball tonight. We have evidence they might know about our recruitment team. If they do, they will undoubtedly want to question you. Rest assured, Grenich will be there to ensure your safety. We take care of our own," Tracy said as she stood up, looking sideways at Naomi as she bowed her head respectfully.

"Thank you, ma'am. The heads of the Corporation are very kind."

Tracy smiled as she leaned forward and lifted Naomi's symbol with her immaculately manicured, flawless hand. She let the symbol rest on the flats of her four fingers.

"I do love these, so pretty and so powerful."

Naomi tried to swallow her nervousness. She disliked having Tracy's hands that close to her throat. Tracy laughed lightly and let the symbol drop back into place at the base of Naomi's throat. Naomi suppressed a shudder at the sudden iciness of the gold.

"Enjoy the ball, Miss Green," Tracy said. "Worry not, all shall be well."

Tracy smoothed her skirt and strode confidently back toward the restaurant, disappearing into the dark shadows inside the open glass doors. The symbol at Naomi's throat remained unnaturally cold.

~~*~*~*

Night fell on the grounds of the huge estate where the charity ball was being held. The large home was modeled after a Spanish hacienda. Guests would drive up a long, straight gravel driveway and hand their keys to one of the valets dressed in red. The moon lit up the dark sky, turning it from black to navy blue. The wonderfully soothing sound of Bach drifted out of the open entrance doors. Inviting golden light spilled out, illuminating the expensive clothing of the wealthy guests. The ball had started promptly at seven o'clock, but the staff had been preparing since dawn. Inside, the many workers rushed around the enormous house, making sure none of the guests were uncomfortable for even a moment.

Outside, the few valets were taking it easy. Many had retreated to what had once been servants' quarters; a glorified shed that had room for one table and a few chairs. In the small building, a poker game was currently being played between most of the valets. It was the job of the rookies to remain out in front of the hacienda, waiting for any late arrivals. The two younger-looking men were tasked with parking cars for the duration of the ball. The company had sent them that day. They had references of course — great ones — but they were new to the town and so they were at the bottom of the metaphorical food chain. It didn't matter though. They had actually volunteered to remain outside the entire evening.

Jensen leaned against one of the huge white pillars marking the entrance to the hacienda, looking out at the long drive leading up to the enormous property. The front of the hacienda had four gigantic columns and three short white steps leading up to the beautifully tiled walkway in front of the double doors. Jensen had complained most of the afternoon about the hideous uniform. He felt naked without his usual nice clothes. He only stopped when they arrived at the hacienda.

"The things humans do with money," he scoffed. "Unbelievable."

Nero glanced over his shoulder from where he stood at the bottom of the steps. "Says the guy who hasn't lived in anything smaller than a mansion for most of his life. By the way, do you know what they're raising money for?"

Nero tossed a smooth stone over the drive at the multi-tiered ornate fountain in the center of the small roundabout, raising his hands up in victory when the stone splashed in the water on the top tier. Jensen approached him, accepting a small handful of gravel. He whipped a pebble at the fountain.

"They say to feed some starving nation, but I wouldn't be surprised if it were actually for a new golf course or some other pointless endeavor. They should raise it for the large man whose face I'm going to rearrange," Jensen grumbled. Nero snickered, throwing another pebble. Jensen had a run in with one of the guests earlier. A large man had pulled up in a Rolls-Royce, with a woman who appeared to be at least twenty-five years younger than him sitting in the passenger seat. He stepped out of the car and almost immediately lit a fat Cuban cigar. He proceeded to blow smoke in Jensen's face as he dropped the keys in Jensen's hand, demeaning him further by inquiring whether or not Jensen knew how to drive his particular car. Jensen responded politely, but only because Ajax had been yelling in his earpiece not to do anything stupid. They were in constant communication, as they always were. The Four were inside, mingling, and Ajax was in a truck with Malone just outside the property. Sly had found out that a

Ms. Naomi Green was going to be in attendance at this ball. She was going back to London tomorrow, so they only had one shot at grabbing her.

"Where is this freaking woman?" Nero groused. "I can only wear this monkey suit for so long."

Jensen tossed another pebble. The fountain was quite large, towering over the drive. It was illuminated with bright lights. A few white lights were also scattered about the driveway to ensure the valets could see where the gravel started and ended.

The purr of another expensive vehicle drew Nero and Jensen's attention to an approaching car. They watched as a sleek dark red convertible pulled up the driveway, stopping once it was next to them. Every muscle in Jensen's body tightened when he saw a middle-aged woman in a fancy pastel blue gown sitting behind the wheel. Jensen's eyes hardened as he realized this woman was one of the names from Coop's list. Sly's scouting dossier had included a picture from a charity gala in London and Jet had identified her as the woman he had seen in the morgue the night of Isis' death. Suddenly, Jensen was very aware of the handgun he had stuffed in the back of his pants. It pressed up against his lower back, so warm and inviting. He could almost hear it calling—

"'Ello Miss," the strange Cockney accent Nero adopted took Jensen's mind off the gun. He stared at Nero, completely taken off guard by the comic intonation. He thought it was Cockney, but with Nero, it could have been almost anything.

"I'll be takin' care of your car tonight," Nero said as he took the keys from the now perplexed Naomi Green. She gave him a small polite smile that clearly showed how crazy she thought he was and hurried inside, never noticing the other valet who stood stiffly off to the side. Jensen watched her walk up to the front door and down the short main hall. She disappeared around the corner, heading for the large ballroom. Jensen turned back to

Nero, who had just confirmed with Ajax and the Four that Naomi Green had entered the hacienda.

"What the hell was that?" Jensen whispered, keeping his voice quiet so he wouldn't be overheard.

"That was me stopping you from doing something incredibly fucking stupid," Nero replied in his normal voice. "I saw your hand twitch and I know you've got a gun behind your back. Remember what Jet and Lilly said? No vigilantism. Besides that, you've got how many witnesses in there? This woman is low-level, but she still could have valuable information on Grenich. You putting a bullet in her head would do more harm than good."

Jensen looked off into the night. "I don't know what you're talking about."

"Yeah, right," Nero replied as he walked over to the driver's side of the convertible. "Jensen, don't be that guy. You got to put your personal feelings aside for this one. I loved my niece too, but I know she wouldn't want me going Edmond Dantès on everyone with a connection to this corporation."

Jensen went quiet, staring at Nero in disbelief. Nero looked at him expectantly.

"What?" he finally asked. Jensen shook his head.

"I'm sorry, I'm just trying to wrap my mind around the fact that you actually read a book as long as *The Count of Monte Cristo*," he teased.

"You and my brothers, all of you continually underestimate me. I do have layers, you know," Nero said, pretending to be offended. Jensen managed a quiet laugh as he glanced out into the night.

"I'm going to take a walk around the property, clear my head."

Nero gave him a sympathetic smile and then, without warning, dug the keys along the side of the car. Jensen looked at him in surprise. Nero shrugged as he opened the deeply scratched door and dropped into the driver's side.

"I'm petty. Sue me," Nero stated as he slid the key in

the ignition, turning it and starting up the car again. "I was kinda hoping she'd drive up in a Lamborghini, but this baby will do just fine."

Jensen couldn't help but smile as Nero pulled away, spraying up a few pebbles of gravel as he sped toward the designated parking area. Jensen began walking in the opposite direction, heading for the back of the estate.

~~*~*~*

The trees on the estate were enormous, providing decent cover. The thick branches nearly touched the heavens. Lush foliage, which was nevertheless starting to thin in the fast approaching winter, concealed the many birds that called the trees home. In one particularly large oak tree, an owl was metamorphosing. Its wings elongated and slimmed down until they were human arms. The stocky head stretched out until it became a head with an elegant neck. The feathers shrunk and molded together, first becoming skin and then a slinky skin-tight black material. The clawed feet grew until they became long slender legs. The owl's ears disappeared, becoming cropped black hair instead. Behind a set of black sunglasses, the round glowing yellow eyes blinked once and became glowing green eyes.

Blitz crouched down on a branch, near the trunk. She leapt down, landing on the soft ground beneath the tree. Her face was wrapped so only her eyes were showing, leaving open a little space under her nose so she could breathe. She had been watching the movements of the guards and valets closely, waiting for an opportunity to present itself. The security guards were changing shift and the valets had all but vanished. The windows on the first floor would not be a good way to enter. There were too many people at the ball and the servers would be constantly moving between the ballroom and the kitchen. Many of the windows on the second floor were open, it being a warm night.

Blitz sprinted across the lawn toward the back of the hacienda. Reaching the flight of stone steps, she leapt up on the railing and ran up. She dropped off at the top onto the stone porch. Blitz ran toward an enormous clay vase, jumped up on it and pushed off with her feet, soaring straight up and grabbing hold of an outcropping. She pulled herself up and ran across it toward a balcony. She jumped up toward the balcony and managed to grab it.

Pulling herself up, Blitz climbed onto the balcony and rolled across the rough stone. Pushing herself to her feet, she moved toward the glass double doors. Testing the handles, she found them locked. Using her elbow, she broke the window and reached inside, unlocking the door. Pushing it open, she stepped inside the dark room. Blitz pulled the heavy drapes over the broken shards of glass, just in case a guard checked the room on his rounds.

Her eyes darted about the space, which appeared to be a guest room. Blitz strode across the soft carpeting to the door, opening it a crack to peer out. The hallway was clear, but she needed to get down to the basement. The guests were mostly staying in the ballroom, but a few would wander out into the hall to socialize. Then there were the constantly moving staff. There was nowhere near enough cover in the long hall to just run through it.

A soft meowing drew her attention down. A small black cat rubbed against her legs. Crouching down, Blitz picked up the cat and tossed it inside the room. She closed the room door behind her as she stepped out into the hall. The cat stuck its paw out under the door, mewing. Blitz closed her eyes and allowed her body to melt down into the small form of a black cat. She took off toward the steps, bounding down them.

She ran through the hall, dodging around the legs of servers and other workers, ignoring the few who cursed at her, and made her way to the basement door, hidden down one of the long halls. Once she reached it, Blitz allowed her body to melt back into its normal human form. She straightened up and shook the dizziness from her senses. Soon shape shifting wouldn't be quite so easy.

Blitz opened the basement door and slipped inside. Descending the steps to the large basement, she made her way to the back where she knew the fuse box was. She removed a small rectangular object from the belt around her waist. Yanking open the box, she identified the wires and began her work.

~~*~*~*

In the main ballroom, beneath two enormous crystal chandeliers, a sea of color danced and spun to merry tunes. A healthy glow illuminated the lovely people on the hardwood floor, smiling at their dancing partners. All the men were dressed in black tie, while the women stood out in their unique designer gowns. There was no talk of unpleasantness in the ballroom, only the usual innocuous chatter and gossip. The musicians continued to play Bach and Beethoven, Mozart and Tchaikovsky, on their expensive string and woodwind instruments.

Naomi Green stood off to the side mingling with some friends of hers. She wasn't listening to their conversation, only nodding whenever it seemed appropriate. She played with the charm at her neck as her eyes wandered over the dance floor. Naomi excused herself from the group and made her way across the floor, intending to get a flute of champagne. There was no way she was going to get through the night without alcohol.

When she had almost reached the table, her arm was captured in a tight grip. She quickly turned her head to see who would dare touch her, unable to hide her surprise when she saw it was one of the Four. The woman was medium height with dark hair, which was done up quite nicely. She wore a pastel blue gown that actually looked flattering on her, considering it was on the cheaper side.

Her dark eyes were blazing with something akin to hatred. Her immaculately manicured nails, which were a pearly pink color, were dangerously close to cutting Naomi's skin.

"Jesus fucking Christ," Naomi grumbled under her breath, more irritated than scared. She had already deduced it was Alex. She had seen Jade a couple times in the past and knew she was Latina, and the other one was white.

"You have two choices, Ms. Green," Alex growled threateningly. "You can come with me to some place a little more private or I can interrogate you right here in front of all these nice high-society people."

"Mr. Derringer has a nice library just a short ways down the hall," Naomi offered, still annoyed. "We wouldn't be disturbed there. You could Appear without worrying about detection."

"Fine," Alex said as she shoved Naomi with a bit more force than was necessary. "Lead the way."

Naomi smiled and waved reassuringly to the few people who had noticed the rough treatment. "You know, a little less brashness might be wise."

"Shutting your mouth would be a lot wiser," Alex responded without missing a beat as she followed Naomi across the ballroom toward the door. They stayed off to the side, avoiding the dancers. Naomi opened one of the glass double doors and stepped out, followed closely by Alex. The door clicked shut behind them, muting the quiet chatter and pleasant music. They began to walk straight down the long hallway, fashionably painted in neutral colors. A few portraits decorated the walls, mostly grim-looking bearded men. Naomi adjusted one of her gloves, slipping out the throwing knife she kept hidden in it.

"I've got Naomi with me," Alex reported in her earpiece. "We're heading to the library. I'll—"

Naomi suddenly spun around, lashing out with the small knife. Alex barely had time to dodge the arc of the blade. She ducked under another swing, grabbing Naomi's arm and twisting it behind her, attempting to get the woman in a joint lock. Naomi struck her in the throat with her elbow and Alex stumbled back, colliding with a decorative table. Naomi thrust forward with the knife, cutting deeply into Alex's side. She then kicked at Alex's wounded side, causing the shape shifter to gasp in pain. Alex grabbed a decorative plant on the table, throwing it at Naomi, who ducked.

The lights in the hacienda went out, plunging everything into blackness. The visibility was almost nonexistent. Some light came from the windows near the front door.

"Dammit," Alex grumbled, looking around. She heard a strange sound from the kitchen, an odd hissing noise followed moments later by thumping. The music in the ballroom had stopped, adding to the heavy quiet. The only sound was the faint murmurings of the guests in the ballroom.

Naomi came from out of nowhere, punching Alex in her wounded side, causing the shape shifter to shout in pain. The woman shoved Alex against the wall, pushing her small knife against her throat. Alex tried to shove the woman away, but Naomi Green was surprisingly strong. She pressed the knife down even harder, drawing a thin line of blood.

"How are Jet and Lilly these days?" she asked the wounded protector. "Still poking their noses where they have no business being? The young ones never learn."

Alex swallowed, wincing in pain. Naomi put more pressure on the knife preparing to slit the protector's throat when she was violently yanked away even deeper into the shadows. Alex dropped to the floor, coughing and massaging her throat. She felt the wound in her ribs, which was much deeper than she had originally thought. Raising her eyes, Alex tried to find Naomi. There was a soft whistle somewhere nearby. The sound of the mirror shattering as a dark form collided with it caused Alex to swiftly crawl away. She felt exposed in the dark main hall, especially with there being a potential hostile that she couldn't see.

Another form leapt on top of the one that had crashed into the mirror. After a brief struggle, one figure stood up and moved away. Alex could barely make out the form anymore — it seemed to be melting into the darkness. She cautiously crawled across the floor toward the stairway and pulled herself to her feet using the banister.

The mysterious figure stopped abruptly and twisted halfway to look back, as if sensing Alex watching. Alex felt her breath catch in her throat when she saw luminous green eyes. The two stared at each other for a beat. Alex remained completely still, trying to quell the fear she felt. After a moment, the mysterious Blitz turned and continued on her way, disappearing in the shadows.

Alex carefully lowered herself down to the stairs, feeling lightheaded. She could smell blood and wondered whether it was her own. She wasn't sure how much time passed, but the next thing Alex was aware of was the lights coming back on and Jade insistently shaking her shoulder. The younger protector frowned, noticing that she was lying on the steps.

"Come on," Jade whispered. "We've got to get out of here."

Alex let Jade help her to her feet, leaning on the other protector for support. Remembering the brief fight, she glanced over to where she had heard the shattering glass, noticing the empty mirror frame. Naomi's body was a few feet away, a large puddle of blood surrounding her head. Her throat had been slit so deeply, it looked like she had almost been decapitated. There were dozens of cuts on her arms from where the glass of the mirror had sliced open her flesh and the reflective shards were scattered about the floor. One large shard of glass was jutting out of the woman's eye, blood lazily dripping to the floor around the glass.

"Guardians have mercy," Alex breathed, stunned at the

brutality of the kill. She quickly followed Jade outside.

~~*~*~*

Blitz Appeared on a small road behind the estate. She fell to her hands and knees, panting and shaking. There was not a single part of her body that did not ache fiercely. The night was cool and calm around her, but she didn't notice. Blitz made a mental note not to Appear again. It was too risky and sapped up too much of her rapidly deteriorating energy. She hadn't even Appeared where she had planned. Blood pounded in her ears and she struggled not to vomit.

After a moment, the pain had gone down to a tolerable level. It was enough for Blitz to shakily climb to her feet. She stumbled over to the side of the road where there was a white picket fence in front of a field of crops — corn from the scent and look of it. Blitz leaned her weight against the sturdy fence post and took a few deep breaths as she attempted to rid herself of the dizziness she felt. Tremors continued to wrack her frame.

When the shaking ceased, Blitz put her sunglasses over her luminous eyes, pushed off the fence and turned to leave. She had a day's journey back to the isolated cabin and her sleek black motorcycle was hidden in the brush about an hour up the road.

Blitz froze when she saw the man standing a short way behind her. He looked just as surprised to see her. The man looked her up and down, curious.

"You're Blitz, aren't you?" he asked. She didn't respond and remained out of the pools of bright light, allowing the thin shadows to shroud her. The man took a step forward and she took a stiff step back, her body rigid as she prepared to fight him off. To her shock, he stopped and raised his hands. He reached up to one ear and pulled out an earpiece, switching it off.

"I just want to ask you something," the man explained,

reaching into an inner pocket of his uniform. She heard the faint trace of a British accent in his voice. Blitz glanced behind her, checking for any backup the man might have, but remained still. The wiser strategy would have been to leave, but she didn't. She didn't know why, but some small part of her wondered what he wanted.

As he pulled a folded bit of paper out of his pocket, she observed him. His dark brown hair was short and a little wavy. He had a very attractive face and a lean build. He wore a valet's uniform. Blitz glanced at the gold nametag: Jensen. It jogged her memory where she had seen him before: he was the last Aldridge — a high-priority target at Grenich. Blitz watched as he unfolded the paper.

He held it out. "Are these the people you're targeting?"

She remained quiet, gazing at him suspiciously. He wasn't intimidated by her, which meant he was either very brave or very foolish. In Blitz's experience, the two weren't mutually exclusive. Jensen was confident with his words; obviously a highly-educated man. There was a haunted look in his expressive blue eyes. He shook the paper a little.

"Look, I'm not going to hurt you or try to capture you. Will you please just look at the names?" he said, insistently. There was a hint of desperation in his voice. Blitz took a hesitant step forward and read the names.

"Those are your targets, right?"

She looked back at him, but gave no indication either way. Jensen folded the paper and put it back in his pocket. He glanced behind him, back toward the hacienda.

"I already know you're targeting them. You killed Naomi Green. I heard before I switched off my earpiece," he explained, looking back at her. "The protectors are going to be looking for you."

He studied her for a moment. "I'll look the other way and try to keep them off your back."

Blitz stared at him, trying to figure out what his angle

was. The Aldridges were protectors, loyal to the Monroe family. He couldn't just let her go. It went against his oath as a protector. Jensen stuck his hands in the pockets of his pants, kicking at a small rock on the ground.

"They killed someone whom I cared for," he mentioned, his voice soft. "As far as I'm concerned, the people on that list are getting what they deserve."

Blitz looked somewhere beyond him and he twisted his body a little, looking over his shoulder. His moment of inattention presented her with the perfect opportunity to knock him out. A chokehold would do it, it wouldn't take very long and it would give her the chance to escape. But Blitz hesitated.

"They'll be coming soon," Jensen mentioned, looking back at her again. "If I were you, I'd get out of here."

Blitz hesitantly turned away and started making her way down the road. She glanced back at him once more before taking off.

Jensen watched her disappear into the night. He switched his earpiece back on and put it in his ear again as he started walking toward the hacienda.

~~*~*~*

"You had a run in with an experiment, didn't you?"

Jet closed his eyes in annoyance at Roan's question. After they made sure Alex would be all right, Lilly had gotten permission to speak with the legendary assassin about the events of the night. The guardians had granted the Monroes more access to Roan after Isis' demise. Jet glanced over at Lilly, who stood next to him with her arms crossed over her chest.

Roan sat cross-legged on the small bed in his cell, looking at the protector leaders. There was no sign of taunting in his serious gaze, just awareness.

Passion stood just behind the Monroes, her arms crossed over her chest and her eyes fixed firmly off to the side. The protectors needed a guardian to accompany them in the dungeons. Passion had already warned Roan she was only there to supervise and had no interest in speaking to him further. She just wanted to know what was going on. Roan respected her wishes, though he could not help but glance over at her occasionally.

Jet cleared his throat. "We don't know. The team had an encounter with Blitz on a mission last night. They had infiltrated a ball to apprehend Naomi Green, but Blitz managed to get the drop on them. I'm sending Jensen out to do some research, but I have a feeling he won't find anything."

"Probably not," Roan smiled bitterly, although it looked more like a grimace. "People attached to Grenich have the tendency to cease existing, especially when an experiment is deployed. Don't ask me how. I honestly don't know."

Jet nodded. "Okay. The woman who killed Naomi Green—"

"How'd she do it?" Roan interrupted as he uncrossed his legs and put his feet on the ground, leaned forward, and folded his large hands over one another. He turned his face toward the ground, closing his eyes and massaging the knuckles of the bottom hand with the long fingers of the one on top. He was absorbing the facts and arranging them in his mind until they made some kind of sense.

"Alex and Ms. Green got into a fight in the main hall. The power went out and Blitz ambushed them. There was a struggle and she slit Ms. Green's throat," Lilly explained.

Roan smirked briefly but didn't open his eyes or look up. "Sounds like an experiment. Quick and efficient, in and out."

"That's reassuring," Passion muttered dryly.

"There are a couple things that don't fit into what you've told us about experiments," Jet began.

"Go on," Roan responded, still looking toward the floor even though his eyes were closed. A story was beginning to take shape in his mind.

"Ms. Green had gotten the better of Alex, probably would have killed her," Jet continued and Roan could hear he was puzzled. "Alex couldn't see much in the dark, but she did see Blitz's eyes. Blitz saw Alex but she didn't kill her and she didn't even threaten her."

Odd, Roan thought. "Really?"

Jet nodded and a confused look crept onto Roan's face as he glanced to the side, his thoughts now racing. There was no doubt in his mind she was an escapee. Experiments didn't show mercy and they certainly didn't leave witnesses. But if she was an escapee, why was she killing people? They were dangerous when they got out, but it was mostly due to muscle memory. This one was actually *hunting* her victims down, as if she were on a mission.

"And Jensen managed to sneak up behind her," Lilly added. "He said she looked unsteady when he first arrived. She ran off into the night before he could approach her."

"She's sick," Roan said, almost to himself. He got up and began to pace around his cell.

"Sick?" Jet asked and Lilly's expression reflected concern. Behind them, Passion pushed off the wall she had been leaning against.

"I just had a very unpleasant thought," Roan began as he approached the glass wall, resting one of his hands against it. He looked to Jet and Lilly again.

"Go on," Jet said.

"There were different branches of the Corporation, different areas of research. It was all about the experiments and how to make them better, more efficient weapons. A small sector was concerned with viral research and bio-warfare. Because of their modifications, experiments are immune to practically every kind of poison and disease imaginable except for ones made by the Corporation designed specifically to kill them," Roan explained. "I'm not entirely sure if they ever tested experiments as carriers for viruses. The virus demonstrations that I saw killed the experiments within minutes, putting them down like animals that have outlived their use. However, using experiments as carriers isn't completely out of the question for Set."

"Are you saying he may have released an infected experiment for the sole purpose of testing some sort of contagion?" Lilly asked, horrified at the implication. Though the protectors were still leery about Roan's tale of Grenich, they couldn't deny what they had seen with their own eyes. If there really was some sort of madman out there using shape shifters as guinea pigs, viral testing seemed frighteningly plausible.

The color left Passion's face as she stepped up beside the Monroes, glancing between Roan and them. Roan remained leaning against the glass. He turned his eyes to her and she met his gaze for the first time in what seemed like an eternity. The guardian looked back to the Monroes.

"If no one has shown any symptoms, I think you're all right," Roan said reassuringly, his smoky voice calm as ever. Jet and Lilly exchanged a look. They would keep a close eye on the ones who possibly could have been exposed to any virus, but it did seem unlikely no one would have symptoms hours after contact.

"Thank you, Roan. That's all we needed," Jet said, grudgingly sincere. Roan nodded once, accepting the protector's reluctant gratitude. He watched Passion and the Monroes until they were out of sight, then went back to his bed. He lay down, folding his hands behind his head.

"So you're sick. Poor girl," he said to himself, speaking as though the mysterious experiment were with him. "I imagine you have quite a story to tell. The question is will you have a chance to tell it?"

~~*~*~*

At the secluded cabin, the doctor stepped out onto his

porch. He carefully sipped hot Chamomile tea from his evergreen-colored mug. The sun was just beginning to rise, gradually turning the sky into a dreamy shade of purple. It was pleasantly cool outside. The summer had been unusually hot, almost unnaturally so, and the heat had carried over into the autumn. The past few days had been a relief.

The doctor turned toward the comfortable wicker rocking chair where he usually sat. Blitz was sitting there, her long legs folded under her. She was wearing her sunglasses and full regalia. One elbow rested on the chair's round arm, her gloved palm supported her head. Her gaze was distant, but she was aware of the doctor. She had heard him pouring the tea and predicted the exact time he would emerge from the large home.

"Beautiful isn't it?" The doctor gestured with his mug toward where the sun was rising. Her gaze remained on the horizon. She had been deprived of sunrises and sunsets at the Corporation, being kept underground in the barracks for the most part. Even when she had been sent out on missions, her mind was fixed only on the objective and disregarded "insignificant" matters like the sun rising. She kept track of it in order to tell the time, but she had never "enjoyed" one as the doctor frequently seemed to.

This particular day seemed no different from her Corporation days. Her sharp mind was buzzing with too many thoughts and too much information. A cool wind swept the fallen brown leaves up before gently wrapping about the two people on the porch. Blitz stood from the chair and started to move to the door the doctor had come out of.

"Blitz," the doctor called. She paused at the door, resting her hand on the doorframe.

"You can stop," he said gently. "You don't belong to Carding or anyone else for that matter. You don't have to kill people."

Blitz didn't respond. After a moment, she stepped

inside the cabin and closed the door behind her. She glanced to the side when she entered the main room and saw Jack stretched out on the couch, nose in a book — *Nightmares and Dreamscapes* by Stephen King. He had only read a few pages, but she knew he would be done by the afternoon, evening at the latest. Blitz turned and stepped up the one step into the hall leading to their quarters. When she reached her room at the end of the hall, she entered and shut the door behind her. Taking off her sunglasses, she rubbed her eyes with her thumb and index finger.

Blitz crossed the room and lay her sunglasses down on the desk. She took off her gloves, tossing them onto the bed. She unzipped her catsuit partway, enough to expose her warm chest to the cool air. She coughed quietly, which made her throat feel as though it were on fire.

"Soon you'll go completely colorblind," a familiar voice came from behind her. "That's when you know you have forty-eight hours left, maybe less."

Blitz turned and saw the ghost in her mirror. At one time the mysterious specter had been a source of irritation, but now Blitz looked at her with indifference. The ghost had a white lily tucked behind one ear, standing out in stark contrast to her dark brown hair.

"Don't forget: once the colors fade, only two days remain," the apparition continued. "Unless of course you tell the doctor what's going on. Though we both know you won't."

Blitz approached and laid her palms on the cool dresser. "I don't understand what you're referencing."

The specter smiled and leaned down, resting her weight on her elbows. "Yes you do. You believe you're a soulless monster who exists only to kill and yet you continue to act contrary to that. You're quite a dichotomy, Blitz."

"You're a hallucination," Blitz replied, her voice faint and scratchy.

The ghost straightened up and shrugged. "That's

certainly possible, but it doesn't make my words any less true. You proved it by not killing the woman who saw you kill Green."

"She was no threat to me," Blitz responded easily with the answer she had been telling herself ever since the previous night.

The ghost laughed. "Oh please. Even *you* don't believe that. What about the man who approached you on the street? Jensen Aldridge? He had a gun, which made him a significant threat. You had every reason to kill him and you didn't. Why?"

"I had no quarrel with him."

"You were taught at Grenich to show no mercy, especially not to an armed foe," the ghost countered. "You see how you just continue talking in circles? You have no logical explanation for why you act the way you do."

Blitz turned her back to the mirror, attempting to tune the ghost out. The ghost, however, was never one to be ignored.

"To die, to sleep — to sleep, perchance to dream. Ay, there's the rub, for in that sleep of death what dreams may come, when we have shuffled off this mortal coil, must give us pause," the ghost's soft voice took on a haunting quality. Blitz turned around, but the ghost had vanished from the mirror. Blitz stared into the clean reflective pane of glass for a few moments, examining her drawn face. She struck out, punching the mirror with her powerful fist. The glass shattered into tiny pieces, raining silver shards down upon the once bare dresser.

Blitz looked down at her fist, which was gushing bright red blood from the many lacerations in the pale skin. She watched as the skin repaired itself, expelling the shards of glass that had been embedded in her flesh. In a matter of seconds, her skin was flawless once again.

CHAPTER SIX

Caleb Brown took an expensive crystal bottle of quality cognac from its place on the shelf behind the bar. The room was dark except for the small lights illuminating the bar and the flickering amber glow from the fire in his fireplace. Caleb popped out the decorative top of the crystal bottle with one large hand. He was wearing a tailored dark blue suit and plum-colored shirt. His brown hair was still damp from swimming fifteen minutes earlier. He lifted his gaze to his unexpected guest who quietly observed him.

Across from him, sitting on one of the tall red bar stools, was Tracy. Her short blonde hair was brushed to one side as it always was. She was wearing her casual clothes, jeans and a pastel yellow blouse, which told Caleb she had been out in public for one reason or another. Her brown eyes watched as he poured the brandy into the glasses already waiting on the bar. She was resting her chin on the back of her folded hands as she watched him. Caleb pushed one of the snifters toward her. She accepted it with a polite smile, gently swirling the amber liquid around the smooth glass. She lifted it to just below her nose and inhaled the scent. It smelled faintly of caramelized peaches, almonds, and candied fruit.

"Quite expensive tastes you have, love," she commented before taking a sip of the pleasant-tasting brandy. Caleb smiled and sipped from his own snifter.

"What do you expect me to drink? Box wine?" he asked.

"No, I suppose not," Tracy replied as she stood from her seat, snifter in one hand. She approached the large windows at the back of the room. She swirled the liquid around as she looked outside. The lights about Caleb's multi-million dollar home pooled on the stone walkway that traveled around the property. Tracy sipped the brandy again and glanced at the liquid. She did enjoy imported alcohol. It made putting up with a shape shifter somewhat more bearable. In the fireplace, one of the logs popped loudly as the fire consumed it. The crackling of burning wood was pleasant ambient noise.

Caleb approached Tracy from behind, swirling his own drink. He looked over her bony shoulder, chancing a quick glance down her blouse first. *White lace, what a tease,* he thought as he turned his gaze outside. Tracy shook her head as she sipped the cognac, enjoying the pleasantly warm air of the large room.

Caleb had a seductive personality and the atmosphere in his property matched it. He had been a well-known seducer before joining the Grenich Corporation. He made his living charming wealthy women. He had classic good looks, as though he had been carved from some exquisite stone. There were few people who could resist his gorgeous face and body, and his charm was just the cherry on top. His tall frame and muscular build also gave him an incredibly intimidating presence. Like most seducers, Caleb was all about money. He fit in perfectly at Grenich and had proven himself to be a valuable asset.

"So, those things aren't going to attack me?" Caleb asked.

"No, they've been programmed to only neutralize her," Tracy reassured him as she finished her cognac. She turned around and handed him the empty snifter. He finished his own, turned his broad back to her, and strode over to the bar, setting the empty glasses on the smooth finish.

"The new product from Transylvania arrives and I get to be the lucky guinea pig," he commented as he turned back, leaning so his elbows rested on the bar. The faint firelight sparkled on the gold Rolex on his right wrist.

"They're not what you should worry about, love," Tracy replied as she approached him. Her hips swayed ever so slightly, just enough to entice him. Caleb smiled and met her eyes again, enjoying their little dance.

"And what should I be worried about?" he asked softly.

"The seven series," she answered seriously. Caleb studied her for a moment.

"You know, Tracy, I'm not some naïve school boy. I know Grenich thinks of shape shifters as mindless animals. The Corporation sees me as expendable," he said, looking over at the windows. "Perhaps I would have better luck with the protectors."

"That would be a very grave mistake, love," Tracy said as she leaned forward over him, drawing his eyes back to her.

"And why is that?" Caleb asked, unbothered.

"Protectors are helpless against a seven series. Jet and Lilly have no idea what they're up against. If the seven series didn't kill you, Grenich most certainly would," she explained. "This life of luxury you are enjoying is thanks to the Corporation. You betray us, you lose everything. A seducer couldn't live a protector's life, even if he or she wished to. As a group, you're much too materialistic."

Caleb smiled and shook his head. "You always were good at pillow talk."

"I have places to be," Tracy said as she straightened up again. "I'll be back tomorrow afternoon, hopefully to pick up the products and retrieve our wayward weapon, or whatever's left of her. This new product is still learning the difference between a kill order and a disable order, so there may be a bit of a mess tomorrow. Thank you for the brandy."

Caleb nodded and waved at her retreating back. Tracy stepped up into the kitchen and disappeared around a corner. A few moments later, Caleb heard a door shut. He pushed off the bar so he was standing. He buttoned up the bottom of his suit, ran a hand through his damp brown hair, and moved out of the room. He also had some matters to attend to.

~~*~*~*

The clouds drifted away from the gibbous moon. A breeze rustled by Caleb Brown's enormous house, making the brightly-colored leaves whisper in the trees. It was the dead of night and everyone in the gated community was fast asleep. Everyone except for the woman who stood across the street from the wealthy man's property.

Blitz crossed her smooth arms over her chest, her shaded eyes fixed on the estate in the distance. Her brow furrowed as she observed the scene before her. It appeared to be empty and all indications pointed to the same conclusion. The house was dark and there was no movement or sound in it or the surrounding property. Still, something didn't feel right about the scene before her. It was too peaceful, too perfect. There was a scent on the wind Blitz couldn't identify. She didn't see any wires or thin laser beams that would indicate a state-of-the-art security system and there were no guards. Caleb was arrogant, but he was far from stupid. In fact, he was one of the more dangerous targets on her list. She knew Grenich wanted her back and would go to any means necessary to retrieve her. By now, the Corporation had figured out her pattern and would be laying traps at each victim's residence. She now had to anticipate their countermoves as well as the target's.

Blitz glanced to the side while moving over to the sidewalk across the street. There were no cars parked on the street. All the expensive vehicles would be safely tucked away in the huge garages next to the large homes. There were two huge green bins parked out in front of each house, waiting to be picked up by the garbage men who would arrive at dawn like clockwork.

Blitz moved over to the nearest bin and lifted the lid, turning her face away for an instant when the stench of combined rotting and rancid food violated her ultra-sensitive sense of smell. Her mind immediately identified every last scrap of what was in the bin and the one thing she was looking for wasn't in it. She silently shut it, glancing about the street again just to make sure she was alone. Blitz moved over to the next one and lifted the lid. She reached in and retrieved two empty cans.

She walked back across the street and moved to one side of Caleb's driveway, striding along the high brick wall surrounding it. Blitz glanced to her left, her eyes carefully scanning the street to be sure it was empty. Her sharp ears had already told her that, but she was always cautious. Bending her knees slightly, Blitz sprang up, landing silently atop the brick wall. If anyone witnessed the feat, they would have known immediately she wasn't human.

The hairs on the back of her neck bristled when she saw the dark grounds before her. Something was definitely not right. Blitz shifted her hold on the blue and red can and tossed it out, watching as it arced and then hit the grass. It rolled a few times and stopped. Blitz crouched down and waited for a few moments, watching to see if anyone or anything would come to investigate the can. Nothing.

She rolled the yellow can in her hand a couple times. Blitz twisted her position slightly so she was facing the driveway. Blitz pulled her arm back and launched the can into the night. The yellow can arced over the driveway and landed on the opposite side of the property. Again, Blitz waited and watched for a few moments. Again, nothing came to investigate the can.

The comforting feeling of the flawless sword on her back and the guns at her thighs reminded her she had come prepared. Caleb was probably going to be her most difficult target. Not only did he hold some favor with Carding and many of the higher ups, but he was also the only member of the retrieval team who had actually been trained in fighting experiments. To the best of her knowledge, he had never gone up against a seven series. Carding would never teach a lowly employee every single trick Grenich's precious products knew. Of course, there were some abilities experiments possessed even Carding knew nothing about.

Blitz spread her arms out to the side as she silently dropped onto the property. She landed on the soft grass below her, behind a few decorative hedges, and perched on her toes and fingertips. Her willowy body was rigid as her eyes darted left and right. Empty. The unidentifiable scent was a little stronger. She straightened up, remaining alert. Blitz began to make her way toward Caleb's house, caution coloring her every step. She could feel eyes on her, tracking her progress.

The sudden sound of a deep, rumbling growl caused Blitz to freeze. She remained completely still, looking to the left where the sound had originated. Another, equally menacing growl came from behind her. She twisted and scanned the grounds again. In the darkness, Blitz could just make out some kind of movement. She squinted, unable to distinguish a form from the shadow it was hiding in. Another growl from her right — she looked and again couldn't distinguish any form. On a whim, Blitz looked down and noticed the grass was flattened, as if something large had stepped on it. She went down to one knee and held her hand just above the impression. It was a paw print belonging to some enormous animal, not a species native to the area. The print was about twice the size of her hand, much larger than any animal print she had ever seen. There was another growl, one that was much closer, and Blitz swiftly looked up.

Eyes were staring back at her from a few feet away, stormy gray in color and lacking any pupil or iris. They were glowing, the brand of the Grenich Corporation. Blitz glanced to the left and saw another pair of eyes. Behind her, a third. She got to her feet and turned around once, taking a quick count. Twelve eyes, six creatures, and they had her surrounded. She watched as the eyes in front of her slowly floated upwards as the creature stood on two legs. Whatever they were, they were much taller than her. The creature in front of her snarled and one-by-one, the other creatures echoed the sound. Blitz tensed as she carefully untied her sword from her back and held the sheathed weapon, already forming a plan in her mind. Since she had never encountered these creatures before, Blitz theorized they were a relatively new product. It gave her a small advantage: new experiments were usually not completely refined until after a few trial-and-error missions.

Blitz gripped the hilt of her sword, waiting to see what they would do. They remained still. She knew they were waiting for her to make the first move and it helped her predict how they would come at her. She would have to rely on her precision and timing. With one fluid move, she had her sword unsheathed and tossed the sheath to the ground. Just like she predicted, they all rushed at her.

Blitz spun around once, instantly calculating the angles at which they were attacking her. In a split second, she had dropped to her knee with the tip of the sword lightly touching the ground. In the next few milliseconds they were in perfect range. With one elegant lightning-quick movement, Blitz stood and spun around, this time with the blade pointing outwards. The sword easily slid through tendons, muscles, and bones as it sliced her six opponents in half. Normal steel would not have been able to cut through bone so easily, but Blitz's weapons weren't made with normal materials. The torsos fell forward and the legs fell back as blood shot up from the gaping wounds, spilling gore out across the grass.

Blitz swept the blade of her sword downward. The weapon was once again immaculate; blood slid easily off the material like water off a duck's back. Retrieving the sheath, she slid the weapon back in and then tied it to her waist. Blitz took a moment to examine the bodies of her enemies. They had dark gray fur and tufted pointed ears. The bodies faintly resembled a man in shape, but in size they were at least six-foot-eight, maybe even seven feet tall. Yellow claws protruded from the fingers and toes. The hands and feet were shaped similar to animal paws. They even had thick brownish pads on the bottom. They had muzzles too, most of which were curled in a death sneer. Blitz could see a mouth full of incredibly sharp teeth — carnivore's teeth.

The bodies began to twitch and then rapidly melted back into human form. They were young men, probably just out of their teens, with blind glowing gray eyes.

"Wereanimals," she said under her breath.

She knew the higher ups researched a lot of paranormal subjects, but she hadn't ever seen an actual wereanimal outside of books. Wereanimals had been shape shifters in the first war of the Meadows who had betrayed the guardians and been cursed for their treachery. They were unable to control when they shifted, or what animal they shifted into, and the sunlight burned their skin, forcing them to live underground. They were the rabid animals of the supernatural world and shape shifters theorized the human myths of werewolves and other monsters originated from run-ins with wereanimals. Most of them had been hunted down and eliminated by protectors. The last sighting of one had been in the early 1900s. Where had these come from?

A breeze swept through the trees again, pulling Blitz

out of her thoughts. She looked once more at the corpses. Now that they were in human form, they looked more like regular young human men, though with mutated features. She continued to the house, kicking a torso out of her way and stepping over some viscera as she moved toward the backdoors. She had already eliminated one threat.

Caleb Brown was next.

~~*~*~*

Caleb closed the top of his gray laptop. He stood up from the rigid wooden chair he had imported from Germany. The pleasant sound of Mozart played in the background, drifting out from the high-end stereo system. Opening one of the rich mahogany doors to his closet, he removed a brown silk robe, which he tossed onto the bed. He gradually removed his expensive clothing, stripping down until he was naked. He grabbed the robe again and pulled it on. Caleb gathered his clothes and stepped into the enormous second floor hallway, walking over to where a panel of the wall pulled out to reveal a laundry chute. He tossed the clothing down the chute to the basement where the laundry room was. Shutting the panel, he walked back into his room and closed the door behind him.

He moved over to his master bathroom, which was decorated entirely in neutral colors. Caleb walked over to the shower and turned the water on, fiddling with the temperature controls. When it was the perfect temperature, he stepped under the water and pulled the smoky door closed. Turning around, Caleb put his face in the stream, running his hands through his now soaked dark brown hair. Suddenly, it went dark and the stereo system went silent.

"Dammit," he groaned. He reached over to the control panel and shut the water off. Grumbling irritably to himself, Caleb stepped out of the shower and felt around for his robe. He soon found it and pulled it back on, stray droplets of water continuing to drip from his hair and body. He gave his eyes a few moments to adjust to the darkness. He had night-vision goggles, but they were at the bottom of some closet and he didn't have the patience to hunt them down.

Once he could see the outlines of furniture, Caleb moved over toward his nightstand. He opened the top drawer, removing a large silver handgun and its holster. Tying it under one shoulder, Caleb drew the gun and double-checked to make sure it was loaded. He jerked around when he thought he saw movement by the open door, squinting at the darkness. He didn't think there was an intruder, not with the pack of werewolves outside, but Caleb wasn't one for taking chances. Stepping out of his bedroom, he looked around the empty hallway and made his way to the main stairwell. Caleb jogged down the carpeted steps, sliding his hand down the smooth banister, and then made his way toward the kitchen, where the only entrance to the basement was.

Caleb padded down the hardwood flooring of the hallway, the bottom of his slippers slapping the flat wood. His eyes and ears were open, alert for any sign of movement. Everything was quiet. He was alone. At least, he thought he was. It was quite difficult to tell in the dark. His eyes would start playing tricks on him soon. Shadows would seem to move and he would catch glimpses of things that weren't there. Rubbing his eyes, Caleb continued on his way.

Most of his walls were decorated with instruments of war: swords, knives, and other such things that had long been obsolete from actual battle. Things that became archaic once humans discovered firearms and nuclear weapons. Caleb missed the days of sword fighting and archery. To him, there was a certain intimacy in fighting hand-to-hand. He wasn't a huge fan of guns but it didn't stop him from using them when he needed to. After all, those who didn't have guns could still be shot.

Caleb entered his large kitchen and crossed to the wooden door in the far corner. As he reached for the doorknob, the light sensation of something crawling across the back of his neck caused Caleb to slap at the offending sensation. The old hinges of the basement door creaked loudly, echoing in the empty house, when the door was pulled open. Caleb felt along the dark floor, searching for the doorstop. He found a box filled with something heavy — judging from the sound it was glass bottles — and dragged it over so that it was propping the door wide open. He stuck his hand into the abyss leading down to his basement. Finding a flashlight hanging on the wall, Caleb took it and turned it on, creating a large beam of bright light. He cautiously made his way down the steep steps.

The laundry room was in the basement and there was another room Caleb called the "electrical room," which was where the fuse box and hot water tanks were located. The room was filled with the guts of the big house, but Caleb only really knew about the fuse box. He made his way to the door, turned the knob, and pushed it open. Caleb moved past the monstrous shadows of the various appliances and machines, heading toward the dark gray fuse box on the opposite wall. He froze after just one step into the room.

The fuse box lay on the stone floor, torn clean off the wall. A tangled mess of wires, all different colors, snaked out from the hole where the box had once been. In the minimal light, they almost looked as though they were reaching for him.

"What the hell?" Caleb growled as he stomped across the relatively small room to the mess that was sticking out of the wall. Whatever had ripped the fuse box out had also taken a good chunk of the wall with it. Caleb frowned as he examined some of the wires, which had been cleanly severed by something sharp. His flashlight beam crossed something solid and silver sticking right out of the wall toward the bottom of the tangled wires. He felt it, smooth and finely crafted steel with a few holes in it. It was the handle to some kind of weapon. He wrapped his hand around it and pulled on it, but it was stuck tight. Caleb put the flashlight down near his foot and used both his hands to try and dislodge the object. It took him three or four good yanks before it finally came loose, nearly sending him sprawling. Once he got his balance again, Caleb bent down and picked up his flashlight. The beam of light illuminated the object, which was the finest combat knife he had ever seen. It was surprisingly light and smooth, perfectly balanced. Caleb had never felt a material like it before. It was steel and yet nicer, more refined and tougher somehow. His eyes widened when he realized what the knife had been made from. *Guardian silver, holy hell,* he thought as he twirled the knife once, testing how it handled. Guardian silver was impossible to get on the streets. Nobody but the guardians possessed weaponry such as this. Like most shape shifters, Caleb had only read about the priceless material.

Caleb flipped the knife over and smirked at the engraving he saw toward the hilt of the weapon: a leaping cat with a lightning bolt in its side. So she was here. Caleb tried to figure out how in the hell she had gotten past the pack of werewolves. If the seven series was using guardian silver, he supposed it was possible. His next thought was how pissed Carding and the rest of the higher ups would be if she had somehow managed to kill the new product. His thoughts were interrupted by the sound of billiard balls cracking against each other. Slipping the knife into one of the deep pockets of his robe, Caleb took his gun out of its holster. He made his way back out to the main part of the basement, cursing the lack of light. She had a pretty good advantage over him. *Unless,* Caleb smiled. He shoved his gun back in its holster, ready to pull it out again at a moment's notice.

He emerged into the main part of his basement, swinging the light toward the pool table. The balls, which had been in a neat and orderly triangle, were now scattered all over and a pool cue was laid across the table. Caleb threw the beam from his flashlight around a bit, knowing he wouldn't see her. *The wayward guinea pig is about to get a very unpleasant surprise,* Caleb thought as he made his way back up the stairs.

He entered the kitchen, kicked the box at the top of the stairs away from the door, and closed it once again. He still had his flashlight, and he also had a knife and the gun in case she decided to make a move. The light from the moon turned the blackness into a shade of blue, which almost seemed to glow.

Caleb entered his dining room. A crystal chandelier hung high above the large table, which was surrounded by elegantly carved chairs. It was the towering walls of the room that he was interested in. The room held most of his prized weapons. He approached the far wall where a particularly special sword was displayed in a glass case. Five years ago, when the mission to kill the hybrid went so well, his bosses were especially pleased with him. Besides the large stipend he received, they had also presented Caleb with a beautiful sword as a token of their gratitude. The sword was long and sleek, almost like a katana in shape. Instead of a smooth blade, the sword had jagged teeth on one side of it, perfect for inflicting the maximum amount of damage.

Caleb moved around to the back of the display case where a glowing number pad was. He tapped in his code and the machine beeped, unlocking. He opened the door, reaching in and removing the sword as well as its scabbard. He put the sword in the golden scabbard and then tied it around his waist. Everything around him was still. Caleb knew he wasn't alone though. He turned around and whistled as he would for a dog.

He kept his back to the wall as he inched down the hall, pulling his gun out of its holster. Approaching one doorway, Caleb peered around the corner. Empty. He continued down the circular hall, checking each and every lavishly decorated room. They were all empty. Caleb scratched his head. Maybe Tracy's warning and subsequent trap had made him paranoid. *Maybe the creature's waiting for me upstairs,* Caleb thought as he glanced up to the ceiling. In the middle of the conservatory, there was a wide-open area lit by the dome-shaped window overhead.

Caleb turned to make his way to the main staircase and jumped. There, in the middle of the conservatory, was a svelte figure standing as still as a statue. The domed window high above her head illuminated her in moonlight. Her body was covered in a form-fitting catsuit. At her throat, he could barely make out the silver charm identical to the one engraved on the knife Caleb had found. The glowing eyes were the only thing he could clearly see. A shadow on her left hip suggested she was carrying a sword. Caleb would bet his life she was also carrying a gun or two. He chuckled, laughing at the seven series' arrogance.

"You've been out of your cage too long. Should've tried sneaking up on me if you wanted a fighting chance," Caleb stated. She remained silent, just watching him. Caleb knew feminine experiments tended to be more dangerous than their masculine counterparts. The Grenich scientists didn't quite understand why, but Caleb always assumed it was due to their needing to prove more than men. Men were expected to be aggressive, women were naturally more passive. Because of this, the handlers tended to be harsher on the women and expected more from them.

Caleb reached into the pocket of his robe, removing the knife. He held it up by the hilt, waggling it slightly. Her eyes never moved from him.

"I believe this is yours," he said. He hurled it at the seven series with a precision that would have proved fatal to a normal opponent. Right as she caught the blade, he drew his handgun and fired a couple shots at her. It looked as though the seven series was moving before she had even caught the knife, spinning away from the bullets as they whizzed harmlessly past her. The seven series moved too fast for even Caleb's sharp eyes to see and he knew once she started moving, she wouldn't stop until one of them was dead.

Before he even knew what was happening she had disarmed him, stabbing him in the hand and then leaping into a strong kick to his wrist before ripping the knife free of his flesh again. The handgun clattered against the marble, disappearing in the shadows, and Caleb's scream echoed throughout his house. Blood from his hand splattered across the clean tiles. She tried to slit his throat with the small combat knife and he was barely able to move out of the way as the blade skimmed the air dangerously near his neck. He kicked out, barely hitting her side as she dodged. He used the split second to pull out his sword. The seven series placed the knife back in a sheath that was tied about her waist and drew her sword with one smooth move, twirling it so the tip pointed to the floor. Caleb swallowed when he saw the sword was also made of guardian silver. If the seven series knew how to wield it, and he was certain she did, she could probably cut his weapon in two as if it were nothing more than a twig.

She began to approach him, her stride slow and deliberate, her green eyes blazing. Caleb raised his sword so it was shoulder-high, pointing it directly at her face. He pressed the small button toward the bottom of the hilt. A cherry red flame raced down the length of his blade with a quiet roar. Some of it shot off the tip, speeding right toward the seven series' face. She ducked swiftly, narrowly avoiding getting a face full of fire. Caleb maneuvered around the seven series and brought his sword down, slicing open her shoulder before she had a chance to recover. The seven series kicked backward, landing a clumsy blow to his shin, and scrambled out of the way so she could stand.

Caleb lunged at her again and managed to bury his sword deep into her side before she had a chance to get to her feet. The seven series let out a shout, which was more in surprise than in pain. He withdrew the sword and kicked her wounded side, slamming her back into the wall behind her. The seven series was panting for air, but her eyes remained fixed on him. *This thing has to be sick or something. No way she couldn't avoid that last blow,* Caleb realized as he gripped the hilt of his sword with two hands and swung at her head. The seven series was barely able to roll out of the way. She lashed out with a kick and managed to strike his knee. It was enough to send him crashing to the ground.

Blitz leaned heavily against the wall beside her for support as she fought her way back to her feet. She could feel hot blood pouring down her side from the ragged wound and knew Caleb had hit something vital, most likely her kidney. As long as it wasn't her heart or her brain, she was in okay shape. Her body could heal the damage. It might take an extra hour or two, but it could repair it. The virus was slowing her down, working much faster than she had originally anticipated.

Caleb came at her again with a yell, but this time she was prepared. Every move was excruciating and made spots dance in her normally sharp vision, but her instinctive self-preservation drove her on. She swung her sword and easily chopped his wicked-looking weapon in half, successfully extinguishing the flame. Before he could register what had happened, Blitz leapt up in a snap kick and knocked the hilt right out of his hands. He was weaponless now.

Caleb began to back away from the foe advancing on him again, leaking blood the entire way. Normally, a wound like hers would have been a death blow, but it only motivated her to fight harder. He dove toward the handgun that lay a few feet away, trying not to lose sight of her. Blitz launched herself right at him and stabbed her sword straight through the back of his neck, severing his spinal cord. His body crumpled to the floor. She stood over the corpse, raised her sword, and brought it down on his neck, severing the head from the body. He was already dead, but she preferred to be sure.

For a long while, it was quiet except for Blitz's harsh panting. She felt much more worn out than she should. Her sword glimmered faintly in the moonlight, blood still dripping off it. Her hand seemed to go limp as she dropped it. Distantly, she heard it clatter against the tiles. She sank to her knees, sweat pouring off her face and the tip of her nose. She reached a slender hand up and gingerly touched the back of her shoulder, hissing at the pull on the wound. It was healing, but at an unusually slow rate. For the first time she could remember, blood loss was a real concern. Her stomach lurched and she fell forward onto her hands, wincing at the pull on her wounds, and vomited. She hadn't eaten much so it was mostly bile and a little blood. Once she was done, Blitz carefully lowered herself to the floor and rolled onto her back. The coolness of the tile soothed her throbbing wounds. The taste of vomit in her mouth threatened to bring on another retching fit.

Groaning and rolling onto her side, Blitz tried to will herself to her feet. She had to get up. She refused to die on the floor next to a Grenich underling. At first, her hurting body refused to comply with her wishes. Her hands shook wildly as tremors went through them.

A hazy memory of being electrocuted in a tub of ice water flashed through her mind. On random days the Corporation would subject the experiments to electric baths, just to test their limits as well as to see how they would hold up if they were ever captured and tortured. If an experiment wasn't walking in a straight line thirty seconds after the electric bath, they were eliminated. Blitz growled and shook her head, ridding it of the memory. She fought to repress the pain radiating from her wounds. That was what was most important at present.

"You can run from the past, but it always manages to

catch up to you," a familiar voice caressed her ears. Blitz's head snapped to the side, causing her vision to swim for a moment. The mysterious specter who seemed to follow her everywhere was standing over Caleb's head, surrounded by a glowing aura. After a moment, she looked back to the wounded woman. Blitz could swear the ghost was disappointed in her. Her expression was similar to the doctor's every time Blitz went out to eliminate a threat. She rolled to her side and dragged her body over to the railing surrounding the conservatory. When she was in a sitting position, Blitz turned and was surprised to see the specter leaning against the railing right next to her.

"Caleb Brown was a shape shifter. He had no sway within the Corporation, no power," the ghost stated, drumming her fingers on the rail. "They might still retaliate. Violence begets violence in one unending cycle. If I were you, I would be rather worried about that."

"It is of little concern to me," Blitz muttered as she closed her eyes.

"It should be, because Grenich won't just go after you. Set is not known for being discriminatory in a fight and Jack is also valuable to him," the ghost reminded her. "That's your problem. You don't think about the consequences of your actions. What you do doesn't just affect you. It affects those close to you as well. What about Jack and the doctor? You might lead Set right to them, unintentionally. Combining all your resources, you could stand a fighting chance against the Grenich Corporation. Go after them on your own and you doom not only yourself but also those close to you."

"When I'm dead it'll be pointless to go after them. Grenich never does anything without purpose," Blitz replied as she ran a hand through her sweaty hair. The ghost was quiet for a moment.

"Remind me exactly how your death will make Jack and the doctor any less dangerous," she said. Blitz shrugged as she looked up to the ghost again. She had been tempted to do some research into specters, until she realized the apparition was most likely a hallucination, a figment created in her own mind.

"What exactly are you trying to achieve? You kill one recruitment team and you think it will hurt the Corporation? They'll just use one of their countless others. Set gains power every day. Preying on the weak and creating more revenants to do his bidding is just business to him," the ghost said. Blitz looked down and used her foot to push her sword over so it was in reaching distance. She leaned forward and grabbed it, barely registering the pull on her wounds. Cleaning off the blade, she pushed the sword back into its sheath with noticeably less grace than before. Blitz leaned back and took a few deep breaths before attempting to get to her feet again.

By the time she managed to get up and steady her tired body against the railing that encircled the plant life in the center of the conservatory, Blitz realized something was different.

"No," she breathed as she stumbled around the railing and made her way down to the plant area. She moved toward one of the ferns and looked at the fronds. The tremors in her hand had stopped, but Blitz didn't notice. The fronds were gray instead of green. She was colorblind. Blitz closed her eyes and ran a hand down her soaked face. She glanced over at the shadowy lump of Caleb Brown's corpse. A cold feeling wrapped around her stomach like a parasite and in her mind, she could hear the ominous ticking of a clock.

"Only forty-eight hours left," the ghost stated as she approached Blitz from the left. "Unless you talk to the doctor. It isn't too late for you. You can put an end to all of this. All the carnage, all the suffering, it can all be over if you just talk to the doctor."

Blitz swallowed and winced at the pain in her raw throat. She had known her health was deteriorating, but she thought she would have just enough time. Only two threats left to neutralize. She was so close. Blitz tried to sort out the problem in her mind, ignoring the ache from her healing wounds. The solution suddenly hit her.

"I'll have to Appear again," Blitz mumbled as she glanced back to the ghost. The mysterious spirit shook her head. Her short brown hair lightly brushed her chin.

"You're too weak. Your body would shut down the moment it materialized," the ghost responded softly. "Remember what happened last time you Appeared?"

"I can manage at least one more time, maybe even twice," Blitz stated as she began to make her way out of the conservatory, still trailing a little blood. "That's all I need. I can finish this."

"You really think this is worth your life?" the ghost asked, sounding similar to Jack and the doctor. The only response she received was the front door closing. She looked up to the dome-shaped window and a few moments later, a large bird soared across the night sky.

"That is the question: whether tis nobler in the mind to suffer the slings and arrows of outrageous fortune, or to take arms against a sea of troubles, and, by opposing, end them," the ghost said faintly as she faded away.

CHAPTER SEVEN

Sunlight illuminated the mansion's ground, chasing away the fog that had settled over the lands. Various kinds of animals playfully chased each other about the lawn. The bright light streamed in through the many windows while breezes rustled through the bright yellow and orange leaves of the trees. Yet the beautiful day was lost to one resident who sat hunched over a single sheet of paper at his desk.

Jet supported his head with one hand as he read the scribbled handwriting on the sheet of paper he held in his other hand. Sly had been in earlier and left him a note about what she found in the estate where Naomi Green had been murdered by the experiment. No matter how often Jet read the words with his bloodshot eyes, they just made absolutely no sense to him. How could a woman simply be erased from memory? Sly, using her considerable good looks and clever mind, had charmed her way in to see the owner. Her goal had been to find the address of Ms. Green's residence in London so Jet and Lilly could notify their allies in Europe. He would have sent the Four, but it was a relatively simple job and they were still trying to sort out the close call they'd had on their mission at the hacienda. *Well, at least they weren't shaken like Remington,* Jet thought with a humorless snort. When Alex had been getting healed, Remington had been as rattled as Jet and Lilly had ever seen him. He had snapped at Jet for the first time, but Jet was as patient as Remington had been with him countless times over the long years.

Jet glanced up when he heard a quiet knock on his office door. After a moment, the door opened and Lilly's lovely face appeared around it, her soft golden hair draped over one shoulder. She smiled slightly when she saw him, but he could see the concern in her bright sapphire eyes. He waved her in and she entered, closing the door behind her. Lilly approached the desk, her bare feet barely leaving an impression on the soft carpeting. When they had first married, Jet often wondered if she even touched the ground or if she just floated above it. He handed the sheet of paper over to her and stood up, walking around the desk so he could sit in a chair next to her.

"Sly's findings," he explained as Lilly began to read. "Apparently, the owner of the estate has never heard of a Naomi Green before. Sly even went the extra mile and contacted the people on the guest list. No one has heard of her or remembers anyone fitting her description attending the event. Another weird bit of information that she found: everyone there was human, except for the Four and Nero and Jensen."

Lilly looked over to her husband, her brows raising a little. "That's very strange."

Jet nodded in agreement. "Jensen contacted his associate who gave him the information on Ms. Green, and according to her, there is absolutely no record of Ms. Green ever existing. No birth certificate, no social security number, nothing. The house she lived in is empty and according to Jensen's informant, the realtor claims it has been on the market for over ten years now. Jensen said she's going to dig around a little more, but it's looking quite bleak."

Lilly handed the paper back to him. "Could she have used an alias?"

"I thought about that," Jet replied, shaking his head. "But it wouldn't explain how she seems to have been erased from the minds of everyone who knew her."

"You mean all the humans who knew her," Lilly corrected and Jet frowned, turning his eyes to the front of the desk.

"That's another thing bothering me," Jet commented, rubbing his palms together. Lilly twisted in her seat, leaning more on the arm as she watched him.

"Only humans forget these people. Shape shifters don't. Why? And how?" he said quietly, thinking out loud. His fingers began to drum on the stiff arm of the chair.

"I do not know," Lilly responded. "I have lived many years and I have never encountered something that affected humans but not shape shifters. Both species are usually susceptible to the types of magic or charms that would affect memory. And if that is what we're dealing with, I do not believe there has ever been such a targeted attack as we're seeing."

Jet made a noncommittal sound in response. His mind was racing as he thought about the kind of power needed to achieve something like this: erasing a person from the memories of the people they interacted with. It was a scary proposition and Jet questioned whether they would be able to counter such an ability.

"Sweetheart, when was the last time you slept?" Lilly asked as she reached over to him and gently ran a hand down the side of his face.

"I'll sleep in a few minutes," Jet mumbled, his eyes still firmly fixed on the desk in front of him as he continued trying to sort out the problem. Lilly's gentle but insistent tugging on his shirt sleeve made him look up into her loving eyes.

"Come," she urged in a gentle tone as she pulled him to his feet. "We have a long night ahead of us. We won't solve this quandary in a day. You need some sleep in order to clear your mind."

Jet opened his mouth to argue, but closed it again. He knew he was exhausted. His mind was going around in circles, but he knew Lilly was right. They both needed to be well-rested for the trying week ahead. He smiled at her and nodded, allowing her to lead him out of the room.

They walked out of the office, down the hall and into the longer hall where all the tapestries hung. When they were a little more than halfway to the main stairway, Jet abruptly stopped when he saw movement out of the corner of his eye. He turned to where he thought he had seen the motion.

"Jet?" Lilly asked when her husband moved toward one of the pillars. Jet didn't hear her as he approached one of the middle pillars and walked around it, a frown of confusion creasing his features.

"Did you see that?" he asked, looking over to his wife as she approached him.

"See what?" Lilly asked, concerned. Jet looked back to the pillar and shook his head. He was sure he was losing his mind.

"You'll think me mad. I could have sworn that I saw someone walking over here," he replied as he looked up at the tapestry in front of him and squinted. He shook his head after a moment.

"I'm losing my mind," he said, turning his gaze back toward her and smiling. Lilly glanced up at the tapestry he had been looking at briefly. It was the one of the breathtaking Selene in battle.

"I definitely need more sleep," Jet muttered, almost to himself. He turned and made his way to the winding staircase, pausing to wait for his wife. Lilly looked back to the tapestry, reaching out and laying her hand on it for a moment. Then she moved away, walking over to where Jet waited for her. She took his hand within hers and interlaced their fingers. Together, they ascended the stairs.

~~*~*~*

In her room, Alex sat on the bed. She couldn't keep still and continued to fidget on the once smooth sheets covering the queen-sized mattress. They were all wrinkled and disarrayed from her constantly shifting her position for an hour or so. The sunlight streamed through the windows.

Alex sighed and glanced at her small wristwatch. She let out a frustrated growl and began to bounce her leg, trying to find some hidden reserve of patience. *How long does it take to find one damn book?* Alex thought irritably. As soon as she finished the thought, a silver light shimmered in the middle of the room. Within seconds, Electra stood in front of her. An enormous dusty book was clutched in her hands. The brown binding was a little worn, which was to be expected. The tome was practically as old as time itself. It was a volume of the complete history of the guardians.

"Finally," Alex said excitedly as she grabbed the ancient book out of Electra's hands. She ran back to the bed and dropped the book on it, flipping it open and skimming through the thick tan pages. Electra picked a cobweb out of her hair, running her fingers through the smooth locks to brush out any remaining dust.

"Thank you, Electra, for going into the depths of the guardian library to find this book," Electra muttered as she tied her hair back with the band she wore around her wrist.

"Yeah, yeah, thanks," Alex said distractedly, not looking up from the book.

"I had to ask for Athena's help finding that book. She's not exactly the most pleasant guardian in the Meadows, especially toward other women," Electra mentioned, brushing some dust off her shoulder. "And she has made it quite clear on several occasions that she doesn't care for me in particular."

There was a knock on the door, but Alex didn't look

up from the ancient volume in front of her. "Could you get that?"

"Did I become your handmaiden and just not realize it?" Electra asked as she crossed the room to open the door. Jade stood in the doorway with Shae behind her. Neither one looked too happy to be there.

"Hey Electra," Shae greeted as she and Jade entered. They were both dressed in running pants and tight tank tops, obviously ready to go for a morning run.

"There's your book," Jade groused as she tossed a dark blue book down in front of the one Alex was reading.

"There are some pages missing," Alex suddenly exclaimed, continuing to page through the first book. There were some elaborately painted pictures on a few pages, but most of it was just words written in fancy guardian script, which resembled medieval text.

"That's impossible," Electra said as she approached Alex to look over her shoulder. It was near sacrilege to remove pages from any tome. Electra had to beg Athena, the guardian in charge of the library, to borrow the book. The library in the Meadows was practically a territory in itself. It was one of the few places where guardians were allowed to interact freely, outside of courtship and other official business arrangements.

"Look," Alex replied, pointing to a small cluster of torn pages still attached to the binding. "It doesn't matter though. It looks like some of what I'm looking for is still in here."

"That doesn't make sense," Electra said under her breath as she flipped through the book. "What are you looking for anyway?"

"An old legend Remington told me when I was younger, about things so evil the ground they walked on died," Alex responded, grabbing the small blue book Jade had brought. "Do you remember when we were investigating Cara's place? All the plants were dead, even the pines."

"Then why don't you ask Remington?" Jade pointed out. "And what does this have to do with anything?"

Electra had hopped up on the clean surface of the dresser and Shae stood near the windows, looking off in the distance. The room was warm, but not overwhelmingly so. Jade stood at the foot of the bed where Alex sat cross-legged in the center, the ancient book still open in front of her.

"I didn't ask Remington because he's still upset by what happened at the hacienda," Alex replied with a small grimace. Remington was still doing his hovering act over her, which was just plain irritating. "I think whatever caused those plants to die might also have something to do with these disappearances and the odd shape shifters — the glowing-eyes or experiments, whatever we're calling them."

"How did you come to that conclusion?" Shae asked from where she stood by the windows.

"Roan mentioned Chaos is in charge of this Corporation that's attempting to create the perfect living weapon. When he attempted to take over the Meadows, the guardians vanquished him and according to Roan, he went into hiding and became the first necromancer," Alex explained. "Necromancers have control over life and death. Chaos, or Set as he's now calling himself, had to cover his tracks pretty well to hide from the guardians for so long. The ability to erase someone would be the perfect way to do so, if he could figure out how."

She held open the small blue book, a collection of rebel legends Alpha had loaned to them. "There are rebel stories going back to colonial times about these peculiar shape shifters, whom they call glowing-eyes, and a lot of the stories also involve people vanishing without a trace."

Alex flipped through the pages of the ancient guardian tome, frowning. "There's something about the ground being burned, but then the next page is missing. The page after the missing ones is the beginning of the legend of

Selene. No mention of the plant life dying or revenants that I can see."

"I don't know if this has anything to do with what you're looking for, but Death came up from his swamp a couple days ago," Electra mentioned. "He had a closed door meeting with Adonia."

All three looked at her wearing identical expressions of shock. It was almost unheard of for Death to come up from his dwelling that lay beneath the swamps in Ocean's lands. He was one of the only guardian men who lived in the lands of the guardian women. None ever went down to his lair. Death was notoriously bitter and didn't get along with anyone, guardian or shape shifter. He was one of the last of the original guardians and since he had no heir, he was unable to travel over the mountains to retire.

"What was he up there for?" Jade asked.

Electra shrugged. "I don't know, it was a private meeting. But he looked and acted different. He was wearing a robin's egg blue zoot suit and a matching fedora hat. And he was actually … nice. Not just civil, he smiled and said hello to me. I asked Phoenix what was going on and she didn't know either. I was going to ask Mom later if she knew what was up."

"All right, so to summarize: there's a Corporation experimenting on shape shifters in an attempt to create a living weapon and they've been doing so since probably the Renaissance, if we're to believe the word of the deadliest assassin in history. This Corporation was created and is ruled over by a former guardian, who is now a necromancer. And there are likely revenants and who knows what else involved," Jade said, pausing as she looked at the three other women. "Great. So we're still in the dark. I'm going for my run. I'll be back in an hour."

Jade left the room, shutting the door behind her. Shae moved over to the bed and picked up the blue book, thumbing through a couple pages. Electra also got up and approached the bed again, running her fingers over the few torn pages in the ancient volume.

"Jade's right: this is absolutely insane," Alex shook her head. "We'll probably wind up researching the boogieman next."

She closed the ancient book in frustration and handed it back to Electra. Shae glanced at her as she continued paging through the small blue book. Electra looked concerned as she held the old tome.

"I'm going back to the Meadows. There are a couple of questions I'd like to have answered. I'll let you know if I find out anything about the missing pages," she said. Shae and Alex watched as she disappeared in a radiant shimmer of silver light. Both remained quiet for a moment, each lost in their thoughts.

"You know, there are cautionary tales told to children about creatures coming and taking them away if they're not good," Shae commented as she sat on the edge of Alex's bed. "It's kind of like stranger danger, only with a more supernatural twist. Everyone knows the stories. Humans, shape shifters, and guardians alike tell them to their kids and then the kids tell the stories to their friends. The most dangerous thing in the world lives in your closet or under your bed."

Alex shrugged. "But those are only stories."

Shae looked at her skeptically. "So are shape shifters and other supernatural creatures to humans."

She stood up, laid the book on the bed, and quietly left Alex's room. Alex picked up the small blue book and began paging through it again, her eyes darting back and forth over the small print.

~~*~*~*

Electra strode down the second floor hall toward her mother's room. Her shoes clicked on the marble floor, each click adding to her resolve. She reached her mother's quarters and shoved the door open, storming into the large room. The red satin sheets on the bed in the center of the room contrasted with the light lavender walls. No matter how many times Electra entered her mother's room, those red sheets were still the first thing her eyes fell on. She had a feeling that had been her mother's intention.

Passion spun around in her chair, which was in front of a small desk. She was holding a bright blue dip pen in her left hand.

"Electra? What's the matter?" Passion asked as she turned her body toward her daughter, revealing the sharp writing nib at the base of the glass dip pen. Electra didn't respond as she approached and dropped the heavy book down in front of her. Passion looked toward the worn binding. She lightly lifted the cover as Electra continued to flip through pages. The only sound in the room was the rustling of the paper.

"Where did you get this?" Passion asked when she read the title. "More importantly, *why* did you get this?"

Electra stopped turning the pages and flattened the book, forcing the cover Passion had been holding to the desk. "Alex was looking for an old story Remington told her. She asked for this book, but there are pages missing and they seem to be an important part of the War of the Meadows."

Passion looked at her daughter, confused. Electra pointed insistently at the book. Passion leaned forward, her eyes widening a little when she saw the torn edges of paper. She looked at the pages that preceded and followed whatever had been torn out.

"That shouldn't be," she whispered.

"Mom, what was torn out of this book and why?" Electra asked, trying not to sound like an interrogator. Passion shook her head as she continued to look at the book in front of her.

"I don't know, Electra. I didn't think any book in our library was missing pages and I don't understand why it would be," she answered. She sounded troubled. Electra sighed and pulled up the chair that sat in front of her mother's vanity mirror.

"Look, the pages are torn out right after the vanquishing of Chaos and then it goes right into the legend of Selene," Electra observed. Passion nodded, smiling for a brief moment. Even as a little girl, she always loved the story of Selene and it was Electra's favorite as well. Passion had regularly told her the story when she was younger. Of course back then, she had made the ending a lot happier than it actually was.

"Chaos had a consort, right?" Electra asked.

Passion's brow creased. "I think so. A guardian woman. I believe she was from the lands of fire. Oh, what was her name?"

"We all know most of the history about the War. So why would someone remove information we already have?"

"I don't know. It doesn't make any sense," Passion replied with a shrug as she continued flipping through pages in the book. "Perhaps something was inaccurate?"

"Is it possible we've forgotten something and someone wants to make sure it stays that way?" Electra asked. Passion looked at her daughter.

"Are you suggesting there's a traitor in the Meadows? Because that is a *very* serious accusation."

"I don't know," Electra sat back. "But if what Roan says is accurate, we're facing a very old enemy who thrives on chaos. If we're missing pages from an important part of our history, it's really not a good sign. There's an old adage on Earth: those who do not learn from history are doomed to repeat it. I don't think we're in the best shape to go to war against a guardian, much less one of the original ones."

Passion rubbed her forehead. "I'll ask Artemis about Chaos' consort. She'll know."

Electra didn't answer, but she still felt troubled. Eventually, she picked up the book from the desk and made her way across the room toward the door.

"Where are you going?" Passion asked as she lay her pen down on the desk.

"I'm going to return this book," Electra called over her shoulder as she closed the door. Passion shook her head and turned back to the page in front of her. She had been writing a report for Adonia. The wise leader of the guardian women had been concerned about something and requested each guardian report any oddities they had noticed. It didn't matter how small or insignificant it seemed to be, she just wanted to know about it. Passion hadn't known what to write. Something unusual was happening on Earth, that much was certain. Even Roan felt it, though he was in a cell within the dungeons. The few times she had seen him with Jet and Lilly, the assassin paced the cell like a caged animal.

She picked up her pen and scribbled down a quick note about what Electra had discovered. The guardians had never censored anything before. In order to do so, they would have had to gain the approval of the High Council first. Why they would feel the need to edit out parts of a war all guardians learned about from a young age was beyond Passion's understanding.

Passion laid her dip pen down and neatly folded the paper she had written on. She stuck it in a clean envelope and sketched her name across the front of it. The guardian stood up and moved out of her room to deliver it to Adonia's office.

~~*~*~*

The Deverell brothers were relaxing at Jensen's apartment, taking a break from research to watch a soccer match. Jensen paced the floor behind them. The trees were mostly bare; only a few brightly-colored leaves remained on the branches. A sudden chill invaded the air, warning of winter. The windows were now closed to keep out the cold. Devin glanced over his right shoulder before turning his attention back to the match.

"Jensen, you're going to wear a hole in the floor," Malone warned, not looking over at the pacing shape shifter. Malone sat off to the side in a chair with his feet up on Jensen's new coffee table, supporting his head between his index finger and thumb. Nero and Devin were both sitting on the couch. They had been watching the match for about an hour, while listening to Jensen walk around the apartment.

The four occupants didn't even look up when they heard a key turn in the lock. It was Ajax's turn to pick up lunch so he had said he would meet them back at the apartment. The door opened and the eldest Deverell strode in, carrying a large pizza box with a plastic bag on top. He set the food down on the coffee table before taking the plastic bag and sitting across from Malone on the opposite chair. Jensen continued to pace, rubbing his long hands together with a look of concentration, not even noticing the warm scent of the pizza.

Ajax pulled a clear carton out of the plastic bag, glancing toward Jensen and then at the TV. "What'd I miss?"

"About an hour or so of that," Malone replied as he jerked his head in Jensen's direction. He pulled a large slice of cheese pizza out of the square cardboard box that Nero and Devin were already attacking. Ajax opened the carton with his vegetable wrap in it. He had been in the mood for something light and picked up his lunch at a local deli.

"Our brother, the rabbit," Nero said. Ajax grinned at him and brought the wrap to his mouth. Nero shrugged and ate his slice of pizza.

"He gets it from his mother. Both of them always enjoyed vegetables. Orion was the same way, come to think of it," Malone replied as he got up to raid Jensen's fridge for drinks. "Jensen, the food is disappearing."

He received no reply as Jensen continued walking

about.

"It's like he's in his own world," Devin said with a shake of his head, his eyes glued to the screen. The afternoon sun was hidden behind the clouds, giving the day a sense of grayness. Ajax put his wrap down and brushed his fingers with the napkin he had been holding under the clear container. He approached Jensen, stepping in his path so the younger protector had to stop his repetitive walk. Jensen glanced up at him, annoyance swimming in his expressive blue eyes.

"What's on your mind, Jensen?" Ajax inquired.

"Nothing in particular," Jensen responded as he tried to step around Ajax. Ajax moved to block him.

"Come on," Ajax said, gesturing over his shoulder as he began making his way to the apartment door. Jensen followed, still partly lost in his thoughts.

Ajax led the younger protector out into the hall of the apartment and shut the door behind them. He stood with his arms crossed for a moment, regarding Jensen. The younger shape shifter stood ramrod straight. He was wearing his usual nice jacket and pants, both showing no sign of any creases or wrinkles. His shoes were shiny as if they had just come out of the box. To anyone else, Jensen would appear the embodiment of a dapper young gentleman from an affluent background. But Ajax could see the pain he kept hidden.

"I'll ask you again," Ajax began. "What's on your mind?"

"I told—" Jensen began, stopping when Ajax raised a hand to stop him. He should have known better than to try giving an evasive answer. The Deverells had known him for far too long.

"I know what you told me and now I want the truth," Ajax interrupted. Jensen ran his fingers over a smooth surface within his pocket, a small good luck charm that he kept close at all times. The slight motion didn't escape Ajax's sharp eyes.

"What's in your pocket?" he asked as his eyes traveled back to Jensen's. Jensen shrugged and glanced down the hallway. It was quiet, but he attributed that to it being a weekday afternoon. The other tenants were at work, their kids at school. Jensen much preferred working nights with Jet, Lilly, and the Four, but the Deverell brothers wanted to see the match they had recorded the night they went to the hacienda and it was impossible to sleep with them in his apartment. As if to add merit to the thought, a chorus of angry yells faintly traveled through the closed door.

Jensen glanced up at the single window down at the end of the hall, suddenly fascinated by the glistening particles of dust dancing about in the light. The windowpane was spotless, telling him that maintenance had probably been through no more than an hour ago.

"Jensen," Ajax's stern voice brought Jensen's attention back to him. Jensen sighed and removed his hand from his pocket, holding the item out for Ajax to see. The older protector examined what was cupped in Jensen's palm. It was a silver necklace with an emerald charm in the shape of a clover, identical to the one Electra wore. Jensen could tell Ajax recognized it from the way he shifted his weight.

"I ran into Blitz," Jensen mentioned, leaning back against the wall.

"You told—"

"I didn't tell you everything," Jensen began with a shake of his head. He put the necklace back in his pocket where he knew it would be safe. He could keep it safe. Ajax watched him, patiently waiting for him to continue.

"I let her go. When I turned off my earpiece, I asked her about her targets. She didn't give me any answers, not that I expected her to. I told her I wouldn't try to capture her and I let her go."

"Jensen," Ajax said under his breath and Jensen could hear the disappointment in his soft voice.

"Come on, Ajax. She's targeting people who are killing and experimenting on shape shifters. She's doing our job for us," Jensen argued.

"No, she's murdering people. People who might have valuable information, I might add. Who knows what Naomi Green could have told us?"

"And who's to say that information would have been useful or even accurate? It's bad enough we're listening to Roan. Now we're going to listen to some sadistic maniac's employees?"

Ajax shook his head and looked down to the window at the end of the hall.

"As far as I'm concerned, she's doing us a favor," Jensen grumbled. Ajax looked at him sharply, his eyes narrowing.

"What she's doing is just as wrong as whatever was done to her. I agree with you that the world is a fucked up place and sometimes we have to do things we don't like or agree with. However, it doesn't give us the right to kill people who have wronged us."

Jensen slumped against the wall, turning his eyes down the hall. Anger was pulsing just under his calm demeanor. He had been a loyal protector for years, but he couldn't deny the desire for revenge. Jensen had lost so many people he cared about, more than he could count, and there was a part of him that thirsted for vengeance.

"What would your sister think if she could hear you now?" Ajax asked gently. Jensen glared at him.

"That's a low blow," he responded coldly.

"She dedicated her life to justice and always tried to do the right thing," Ajax continued. "You're a protector, Jensen. Not an assassin or a vigilante. I know it's difficult, but you have to let go of some of this anger you're bottling up."

Jensen was quiet for a moment. "If I let go of the anger, what will I have left? I can't deal with emptiness anymore."

Ajax went quiet for a moment, studying the younger protector. Jensen stuck his hands in his pockets, swallowing. He knew he didn't deal with grief in the healthiest ways. There were times when he wondered if that ability had died with his family. Orion, Jet, Lilly, and Nat had managed to keep him from spiraling after the massacre of Aldridges. The Deverells had done something similar after the loss of his sister. Jensen knew they worried about him and part of him wished he could reassure them he wouldn't do something he would later regret, but he just couldn't.

"You have your memories. Nobody dies if we keep them alive within our hearts and memories," Ajax pointed out, reassuringly. "And if memories aren't enough, you have Nero."

Jensen laughed despite himself and Ajax smiled, chuckling softly.

"What if I don't want him?"

"I can't give you the other two. They're too useful."

"You're terrible," Jensen snickered.

"You haven't known Nero as long as I have," Ajax responded.

The two old friends shared a quiet laugh in the hallway. Jensen let out a breath after a moment. He had lived with the Deverell brothers most of his life and they were his family in all but blood. After being orphaned, Jensen had almost forgotten what family meant until Jet and Lilly took him and his sister in. It seemed like an eternity ago.

A soft buzzing sounded in the otherwise quiet hall. A sudden burst of extremely raucous cheering came from inside Jensen's apartment. Jensen shook his head and took his cell phone out of his pocket, glancing at the screen.

"Peyton," he told Ajax as he answered the phone.

"I'm going to head in and make sure my brothers don't trash your place," Ajax said with a slight smile. "Are you going to be okay?"

"If they don't trash my place or get me evicted, then yes," Jensen replied. Ajax laughed and made his way back into the apartment, trusting Jensen was being honest. He closed the door behind him to give Jensen some privacy. Jensen answered his phone and moved over toward the window.

"Peyton?" he said.

"I got the information you requested," her mellifluous voice stated. "It isn't much, but some of it is rather . . . unusual."

Jensen rubbed the bridge of his nose. "That's fine. I wasn't expecting much more than you already gave me. I'm just trying to tie up a few loose ends."

Peyton snorted. "Good luck with that, my friend. I'll be waiting for you at the old movie theater, house eight. It's three o'clock now, so you'll easily make the showing of *Lady Vengeance* in forty-five minutes."

Jensen bit back a groan as he looked out the window to the shrubs that ran along the fence on the right side of the building. Peyton was a strange woman. Besides being a pediatric nurse by day and thief by night, she also had a strange affection for small independent films that dealt with violence. That particular genre had never been his personal cup of tea.

"I'll see you there," Jensen said. She hung up first as she always did and he slipped his phone back in his pocket. He glanced toward his door when another chorus of cheers reached his ears. Jensen surmised that someone had just scored a goal on their team. Either that or a fight had broken out. He opened the door of his apartment and stepped inside, over to the thin coat rack. He grabbed his long black coat, pulled it on, and walked over to the counter, retrieving his keys.

"I'm going to the old movie house to meet Peyton. I'll be back in an hour or two," Jensen said, adjusting the collar of his coat. "Please don't rile up the neighbors. The last thing I need is Mary banging on my door again."

He was answered with a series of noncommittal grunts. Jensen shook his head and left, closing the door behind him.

~~*~*~*

The old movie theater stood at the edge of a quiet neighborhood. It was located next to a small pizza parlor that was the local hangout for high-school kids. The theater itself harkened back to the golden age of cinema. The elderly owner enjoyed showing movies that only received limited releases, and every Thursday he would play a movie that was already out in wide release just to give his loyal patrons a chance to see their favorite films on the big screen again. Jensen had no idea how he got the prints — not to mention the rights — to do so. Few young people came to the old theater, preferring instead to see the blockbusters at the popular glitzy theater in the more populated part of town. College kids frequented the old theater though, which kept it afloat.

Jensen wasn't a frequent moviegoer, but he had always admired the charm of the small theater. The Deverells were friends with the elderly owner of the place, who often marveled at how the brothers never aged, much like the movies he showed. It was a joke between them. A part of him was glad Peyton insisted on meeting in the old place because Jensen knew if she didn't, he wouldn't come to it at all. He walked down the quiet sidewalk, glancing up at the gloomy overcast sky. A frigid wind knifed through his coat and Jensen kept his hands protected in his pockets.

He turned under the marquee proclaiming the night's movies: *Oldboy* and *Lady Vengeance*, just like Peyton said. Jensen moved up to the ticket booth, surprised to see the ancient owner manning the cash register. A smile lit up his wrinkled face when he saw Jensen standing before the clean glass. The old man took pride in his movie house and it showed by how clean everything was. It was the only movie theater Jensen knew of that didn't have sticky floors.

"Jensen!" the owner greeted happily. "It has been too

long."

"Hello George," Jensen responded, smiling politely. "Is Peyton here?"

"Oh yes, she's already inside. That girl does love her small releases," George replied, the smile never falling from his face. Jensen passed a ten under the window, despite George's insistence it was on the house. A steady drizzle began to fall as the old theater owner printed out the small pink stub. Jensen nodded his thanks and proceeded to the red double doors, pulling one open and stepping inside.

The dim lighting illuminated the hall as Jensen walked down the freshly vacuumed carpet toward house eight. When he reached the house, Jensen grabbed one of the decorative curvy gold handles on the large black door and pulled it open. The lights were so low even his sharp eyes had difficulty distinguishing the two or three people sitting in the movie house. He moved into one of the rows toward the back, taking a seat right in the middle. Peyton liked to be the one to approach him. It meant she was in control of the situation. Since Jensen knew her, he played her little game. He still kept his knife hidden in one of the inner pockets of his coat. He knew Peyton, but that didn't mean he completely trusted her. Ever since the decimation of the Aldridge line, Jensen was armed at all times. There was one too many assassins who would enjoy taking him out. He never was one for taking chances.

Jensen soon heard the confident click of heels strike the aisle running down the theater. The clicking paused briefly before continuing down the row just behind Jensen. He heard a quiet squeak as she took a seat behind him, a little to the left. Jensen kept his eyes on the screen, surprised by how visually beautiful the movie was. Every frame could be a portrait.

"Enjoying the movie?" her pleasant voice inquired just behind his ear. The warmth of her breath tickled his lobe, but Jensen barely noticed. He glanced to the side, his patience quite low. Peyton was flirtatious by nature and he wasn't in the mood for it.

"It's all right," he replied. Peyton chuckled, brushing some of her soft blonde hair behind her ear. She leaned forward and rested her slender arms across the back of the seat next to Jensen, her eyes still glued to the screen.

"Revenge is an interesting topic, don't you think?" she asked him, getting closer so her soft lips brushed against his ear. "There's a kind of eroticism to it. I think it has to do with the artistry involved, all the careful planning and such."

"I don't get off on violence," Jensen responded indifferently. In his younger years, the two would banter playfully for a minute or two before getting down to business. Now, he didn't have the patience for it.

"No, from what I hear, you much prefer the forbidden fruit. A daughter of the Meadows, for instance," Peyton said suggestively without missing a beat. Jensen scowled and bit the inside of his cheek to keep from snapping back at her. The last thing he wanted to do was get into a public argument in a movie theater so he kept his eyes on the screen. He could hear Peyton sigh softly behind him.

"You look absolutely terrible, by the way," she whispered. Her tone could have been mistaken for concern or even compassion if the listener didn't know her.

"It's been a long few years," Jensen answered, glancing over his shoulder at her. "You look well. I'd like to know when pediatric nurses began wearing thigh-high boots."

Peyton smiled prettily and shrugged. "It's my day off. I get to wear whatever I like."

"Ah," Jensen said as he turned back to the screen. He just wanted to get this over with and continue with his hunt.

"I did find a little more information," she continued as though reading his mind. Jensen glanced over his shoulder so she was in his peripheral vision.

"And?" he whispered. The thief reached behind her and produced a large goldenrod envelope, handing it over to him.

"Short answer: absolutely nothing," Peyton replied. "Those four names, those four people, have never existed."

"That's impossible," Jensen hissed as he opened the folder, glancing at the few sheets of paper that were inside. "You saw Naomi Green. Your sources saw Naomi Green and so did Sly's. You gave me the information on the ball."

Peyton smiled again. "You want to hear the long sad story of Naomi Green?"

Jensen twisted in his seat, raising an eyebrow. "Go on."

"Back in the early 30s, there was a woman named Naomi Van Houten. She married a fairly well-to-do man who had a successful importing business. They had two daughters: Adeline and Margaret. When she was eight, Adeline became ill with a disease we now know as leukemia. She deteriorated fast and it looked like she was going to die."

Peyton took the folder from Jensen, flipping through a couple pages. "This was years before Sidney Farber came along with his research, which would eventually become chemotherapy. Adeline should have died, *but* she suddenly goes into complete remission."

"Sounds impossible," Jensen remarked, glancing up at the screen when it suddenly became bright. Peyton looked at him with a secretive grin.

"It should have been. And here's why you love me so much. I managed to track down a shape shifter who worked in that hospital at the time. It took a lot of coaxing, bribing, and a few well-placed threats, but I got him to talk to me. According to him, Naomi Van Houten was at her daughter's bedside every single day. Right up until her daughter went into remission. Then she simply vanished and no human remembered her. They remembered Adeline as the child of a widowed father."

"So how do you know it's the same woman?" Jensen asked. Peyton pulled a picture out of the file.

"Van Houten has a couple grandchildren and great-grandchildren, some of whom are very into social media. Take a gander at this picture I found online."

Jensen took the picture from her and stared. It was the spitting image of Naomi Green, albeit a little younger.

"According to humans, Naomi Van Houten died giving birth to Margaret," Peyton continued, flipping to another page in the file. "Two years after Adeline went into remission, a Grenich bank opened in London and as with many banks, a number of women worked there as secretaries. You're probably wondering what the relevance is. Take a look at this snapshot taken after the start of World War II."

Jensen looked at the picture she held out in front of him. The screen became bright again and he studied the picture of several women. It looked like they were selling war bonds. Naomi Green was off to the side.

"Here's a creepy bit of information: show humans this picture and they don't see her. Most shape shifters do, but I have encountered a couple who don't. The ones who don't tend to be younger," Peyton continued.

"Isis didn't see Bryn's body in the pictures she took," Jensen mentioned.

"Didn't she take those pictures before she found out about what she was?" Peyton asked. Jensen nodded. "She hadn't tapped into her abilities yet, probably didn't see the world the way we do."

"I suppose," Jensen replied. Peyton turned her attention back to the folder.

"Green's story got me thinking about how many other names from that list have similar stories. Grenich is highly secretive and it's next to impossible to get any information on their employees. What little I found out though seems to indicate that a lot of the people who work there have only existed for ten or so years."

She handed the file back to him and he slipped it back into the envelope, rubbing his eyes once.

"One more thing, Jensen," Peyton said, sitting back in her seat. "All the names you gave me frequently received large deposits in their Grenich accounts. Around the time the Blitz stories started, those same accounts were frozen."

"Listen, Peyton. I don't like this at all. Something isn't right. I'm grateful for the information you found, but I think this is the end of this search. I don't want you getting yourself killed over this. Or worse, erased," Jensen said.

"No worries there," Peyton replied as she stretched her arms over the two empty seats on either side of her. "I already planned to tell you I was resigning from this particular errand. We've known each other for a long time and I don't dislike you, Jensen. You don't annoy me like others do and you've gotten me out of a couple unpleasant situations, but that doesn't mean I'm willing to die or risk my wellbeing for you. This makes us even. Next time, it'll cost you and my time is quite expensive. I do have a day job, Jensen, and it's not being your errand girl."

Jensen got out of his seat and began to make his way toward the exit, grumbling, "There's not going to be a next time."

Peyton smirked as she listened to him leave, the door softly shutting behind him. "We'll see, my friend."

~~*~*~*

I should probably call Sabina, let her know I'm all right, Ace thought, feeling the pangs of homesickness. She had been experiencing it ever since arriving at the mansion. She lay on her back on her large bed inside her mostly empty room, tossing a bright green tennis ball up and down. Ace often found the need to keep her hands busy, a habit that had probably come from years of being a bartender. She sighed and glanced over toward the window, tossing the ball up and catching it without even looking. The sun was setting, which meant soon Jade would open her door and remind her they had a meeting. Jade, she was a character. Ace had never gotten along with authority types and so she frequently butted heads with Jade. She knew the older shape shifter had spent her life as a protector, but the way she confused rebels with thieves irked Ace to no end.

Ace got up and started to walk around her room, tossing the ball up and down the entire time. She had been a rebel for most of her life, ever since she was nine years old. Or was it since she was ten? She couldn't remember. Most of her memories of her father and the night he left her at the rebel club were vague at best. Ace remembered her father bursting into her room — it was the first time she had seen him look genuinely afraid. He had grabbed Ace's small backpack and stuffed as many things as he could in there before grabbing a duffle bag out of the hall closet and stuffing even more of her things inside. He wouldn't answer Ace's questions about what was wrong or where her mother was. It was the first time he had ever looked ill; his skin had been clammy and unnaturally pale. Ace paused briefly when she realized she couldn't recall the faces of her parents. Sabina had once told her that she resembled her father, especially her bright blue eyes.

Ace had never been more afraid than she was the night her father sped through a downpour to a rebel club. The drive seemed to take hours. When they arrived at the club, Ace watched as her father spoke with Sabina, the head rebel of the state. At first, Sabina looked at Orion with irritation. Ace hadn't been able to hear the entire conversation, but in the end, Orion had convinced Sabina to take his young daughter and protect her. When he brought Ace to the entrance of the rebel club, he was crying. It was the only time Ace had ever seen her father cry and it terrified her. After a brief goodbye and a promise that Orion would always watch over her, her father had gotten back into the car and drove away.

Ace stopped in front of her window and tossed the ball

from hand-to-hand, mesmerized by the sunset. That first night, she cried her eyes out in her new room, the tiny room next to Sabina's. Though some small part of her resented her father for leaving, Ace was also grateful. She couldn't think of a better friend and mentor than Sabina. She had waited her out, bringing meals to her door and then leaving her alone to eat in peace. Sabina was gentle and patient with her. She never forced Ace to do anything she didn't want to do.

Ace chuckled sadly in the darkening light as she remembered the first time she had ventured out of that room in the rebel club she now considered home. She remembered waking up, her small face still stained with tears, and hearing glasses clinking together. She was a curious child by nature, so she had to investigate. Ace had traveled down to the club level and spotted Sabina with two other women, who she later found out were bartenders. The three of them were putting away the alcohol while practicing flair bartending, a skill most rebels possessed. Ace, still being quite young, was instantly captivated. The two bartenders saw her and immediately started fawning over how cute she was. She was about to run away and hide in her room, but Sabina called her over. It had been more than a month and she thought it was about time her new charge earned her keep and asked her to help out. Her two employees, Lena and Kaylee, would teach her the ropes.

"And you are not to drink anything," Ace repeated Sabina's stern words. From that day forward, Ace was a rebel. Not in the strictest sense of the word, but she earned her keep with her wild bartending skills and adopted the lifestyle. Ace tossed the ball over to her bed. It landed on the ruffled sheets. She moved over to her nightstand and pulled open the drawer, moving aside the socks she kept in there. Underneath was a small blue handkerchief that had never been used. It was balled up and easily missed. Like her father, Ace knew how to hide things. She took it out and reverently opened it up to reveal a small silver locket in the shape of a heart. It had been her mother's, a gift from Orion on her mother's last birthday. Ace knew there was a picture of her with her parents inside, but unfortunately, her father had forgotten to pack the key when he tossed it into Ace's backpack. Either that or Ace might have lost it. She didn't want to break the locket open and she had never learned how to pick locks, so she just kept it near her at all times. She supposed her parents' faces would remain a mystery.

Ace had just put the locket back and closed the drawer when the door was flung open and the lights were switched on. Jade stood there, her smoldering brown eyes sizing up the young rebel. Ace blinked against the sudden onslaught of bright light.

"Ever hear of knocking?" she asked sourly.

"Knock, knock," Jade quipped dryly as she rapped on the door with one hand. "The meeting's going to start soon so get down there."

"Yes, mistress," Ace replied, pausing for a moment. "Jade?"

Jade had been turning to leave but stopped when Ace called her name. "What?"

Ace ran a hand over her short hair and shook her head after a moment. "Nothing."

"Okay," Jade said as she regarded the younger woman for another moment. Then she turned and left, closing the door behind her. Ace sat quietly for a minute. She was looking forward to returning to the rebel club and picking up her own life. She didn't fit in among protectors and it was isolating. Ace didn't enjoy the feelings of loneliness she frequently experienced at the mansion. She stood up and moved over toward the window in her room, glancing up to the now dark sky. The constellation Orion was clear in the heavens.

CHAPTER EIGHT

It was foolish for assassins to hold a meeting in broad daylight. They always waited for darkness to fall before meeting with each other or prospective clients. It was a simple rule and the only one they all followed religiously. Blackjack was no different, but he had no choice on this particular day. *She* was coming.

Blackjack was enjoying a luxurious life like the others on the recruitment team. Carding had backed him to the leaders in the assassin world and the Grenich representative's word held a lot of clout. Blackjack had been made head assassin of an entire state, meaning he got a little bit of whatever money assassins made while in his state. He made hundreds of thousands of dollars a year and didn't even have to lift a finger. The head assassin had made more than enough in the past five years to ensure he could live comfortably for quite some time if he wished.

It was why he needed to call a daytime meeting of some of the head assassins who worked under him. He had to put someone in charge so he could get out of town for a bit. Blackjack had already packed a bag and made transportation arrangements from Adara's former home, the Obsidian Manor, where he had taken up residence.

With any luck, Blitz would arrive to find him gone and his henchmen waiting for her. He was going to put that creature down if it was the last thing he did. Screw Grenich's orders. Nobody tried to kill him.

"Sir?"

Blackjack turned when he heard the throaty feminine voice behind him, smiling when he saw who was standing in the doorway of his private quarters: Marla, possibly the most gorgeous assassin in the world. She had long legs practically up to her neck and natural blonde hair. She had the darkest eyes Blackjack had ever seen. Marla rested one hand on the butt of the gun she wore around her waist. She was one of the fastest draws in the assassin world and rarely used any other weapon.

"Most of your associates have arrived, complete with guards," she reported as she approached him and ran her slender hands up his broad chest. "They are being shown to your meeting room and their personal guards will be situated in the main hall, just like you requested."

Blackjack captured her full lips in a passionate kiss as she wrapped her arms behind his neck, massaging the back of his head with the long fingers of one of her hands.

"Thank you, my dear," Blackjack said. Marla smiled and pulled away, ever the tease.

"We don't have time now, sir," she said, looking pointedly down at his crotch before raising her eyes to meet his again. "Perhaps afterward?"

Blackjack grinned. "Can't, sweetheart. I'm leaving on an extended vacation."

Marla almost seemed to pout. "Oh well."

He looked at her thoughtfully as he approached the bed and flopped down on his side. There was a bowl of fresh red grapes on the nightstand and he picked a couple off their vine, popping them into his mouth one at a time. "You already know I'm going to appoint you the temporary head of this state. But of course, I may change my mind if you can't find some way to repay me for this honor."

Marla arched a perfectly-shaped blonde eyebrow at him. She was quiet for a minute before slowly stripping off her holsters. "I suppose I could think of a way to show my gratitude. But it may hurt a little. I like to play rough."

Blackjack grinned as she pulled off her top, revealing her perfect breasts beneath a white lacy bra. "Oh that's perfectly fine. After all, what's pleasure without pain?"

~~*~*~*

Security precautions had been taken. It was only common sense and assassins needed to be slightly paranoid in order to survive the dangerous lives they led. There were guards patrolling outside the Obsidian Manor, all located in strategic positions so that every corner of the grounds were being watched. It should have been impossible to breech the property.

Most of the head assassins had been instructed to park their cars out in front of the Manor's garage. All except for Marla. Blackjack's lovers were allowed to park their cars inside the garage, a special privilege afforded to a select few. The garage was dark and quiet, cool in the warm afternoon.

Blitz let go of the chassis of Marla's car, dropping the few inches to the cold stone ground. She inched out from beneath the car and rolled onto all fours. Coughing softly, Blitz winced at the fire in her throat. She made her way across the garage to where a security camera was located in the corner. She leapt up, grabbed it, and yanked it down, tossing the useless camera aside. Blitz then moved over to the door leading into the garage, pressing herself against the wall next to it. Removing a throwing knife from her belt, she waited patiently.

After a couple minutes, she heard footsteps approaching the garage. There were some words of caution exchanged between the guards and then the door opened. The first one, a bald guard, stepped inside the garage, pointing his gun toward the area under where the camera had been. As he moved into the garage, a second guard, a younger man, stepped through the doorway. His gun was also pointed in front of him.

Blitz grabbed the muzzle of the gun, yanking the younger guard inside and throwing him against the nearest car. He collided with it and fell to the ground on all fours as she tossed the firearm onto the nearby workbench. She hurled the throwing knife when the bald guard spun toward the sound. The blade of the knife pierced his eye before he could even fire a shot. His body crumpled as the second guard lashed out, punching her in the gut. Blitz stumbled backward, crashing into a workbench with a grunt.

She reached behind her and grabbed a screwdriver, lunging forward toward the second guard, who had climbed to his feet. He held his fists in front of him and she advanced a couple steps. He kicked at her and Blitz blocked it with her fist before jumping forward, burying her knee into his gut. As the air rushed out of his body, she spun so that she stood beside him. With one fast strike, Blitz buried the screwdriver in his ear.

As the body fell to the ground, Blitz moved back toward the workbench, protectively holding her aching ribs. It hadn't been a powerful strike and she normally wouldn't have noticed it, but the virus was wreaking havoc with her body. She retrieved the firearm from the wooden surface. Pausing, Blitz ran a hand over her forehead, her eyes wandering over to the bald guard. She moved toward him and knelt next to the body, stripping the holsters off it. He had a handgun, some extra clips, and a switchblade. Blitz had her own guns, but she had to use her bullets sparingly and needed to save at least one. The one positive thing about attacking a manor full of assassins was they would have their own weapons. Noticing a security badge on the man's chest, attached with a thin wire, Blitz grabbed it and cut the wire with his switchblade. She got back to her feet, tucking the card and switchblade in a pouch on the back of her belt.

Blitz moved back to the door, watching the movements of the guards. Thankfully, most of them weren't looking in the direction of the garage. If there was an attempted breech, chances were it would come from the outside. Blitz looked at the Obsidian Manor as she pulled the guard's holster tightly about her waist. It was just a few feet to the door, but it was still open ground. She hated open ground. It left her vulnerable, even if she was in top condition.

Blitz carefully pulled the door open and stepped out into the afternoon sunlight. She shut the door behind her and dashed to the side door of the manor, pressing herself back against it. The guards out front remained oblivious to her presence. She turned her attention to the door. Blitz pulled the slick key card out of the back of her belt and slid it into the slot over the lever. The lock beeped, the bolt slid open, and Blitz pushed down on the lever, opening the door. She stepped inside the shadows of the manor.

~~*~*~*

Blackjack zipped up his pants and Marla pulled her shirt back on, wiping her mouth with the back of her hand. There was a knock on the door.

"Enter," Blackjack called out as he reached for his bag. He tossed it on the bed and looked up at the door when one of the younger security guards entered, holding a dark tablet in his hands.

"Sir, we may have a bit of a situation," he stated.

"Which would be?"

"One of the garage feeds went off line. Two men went to check it out and never came back," the guard stepped forward and held out the tablet. "She just entered the manor through the west door.”

Blackjack snatched the tablet away from him. He looked at the shadowy figure of the woman in black. As he stared at the security capture, the sound of gunfire began.

“Shit,” he muttered under his breath and turned back to his suitcase, tossing the tablet to the bed. The guard watched him, somewhat nervously, as he waited for orders. Marla retrieved her guns and Blackjack pulled a large shotgun from his wardrobe.

“She’s here?” Marla asked as she grabbed the tablet Blackjack tossed on the bed, staring at the shadowy figure. It wasn’t a high-quality picture and Marla could barely make out the woman.

“Yeah,” Blackjack grumbled as he retrieved a box of shells. “Let’s see: ten guards outside, five downstairs, and twenty guards came with the leaders for the meeting. Do me a favor, darling. Use the secret passageway in the next room, go downstairs, and inform our guests of the situation. Get them out of here and have the guards take care of the intruder. I don’t care what they do. Shoot her, stab her, skull fuck her to death for all I care, just make sure they put her down.”

Blackjack turned to the guard, who still looked uneasy. “What the fuck are you standing around for?”

The man glanced between the two assassins and then left the room.

“And if she gets past them?” Marla asked.

“She won’t!” Blackjack snapped defensively. She shrugged and left the room, fully-clothed and armed, to carry out his orders. Blackjack loaded the shotgun, leaned it against the closet, and retrieved another holster from the same closet. He strapped the tan holster with the handgun about his waist so it sat on his hip. The assassin looked down the hall. If she somehow made it past the guards, Blackjack would be long gone.

The sound of gunfire reached his ears and he moved out of his room, pausing just around the corner from the upstairs meeting room. There was a mirror adjacent to where the wall met the ceiling, allowing him to see around the corner without worrying about being shot in the head. He held the shotgun with the muzzle pointed in front of him and started walking backward, toward a secret staircase at the end of the hall.

~~*~*~*

Blitz had to resort to using the gun a lot sooner than she had anticipated. She wasn't able to move as quickly as she had once been able to and was only able to slit the throats of two of the five guards in the main hallway. The remaining three had opened fire, alerting the guards patrolling out front. Using her senses of smell and hearing, she estimated the number of guards both outside and inside: at least thirty-five. She hid behind a pillar, thumping her head against it, trying to figure out whether she could get through all of them.

Blitz turned her head when she saw movement out of the corner of her eye. Dashing straight at it, she slammed her body against the guard she found, knocking him back into the wall. She drew the switchblade and stabbed him twice in the throat before throwing the knife at a guard down at the opposite end of the hall. She took control of the first guard's gun, firing at a few of the others. She took a shot to the knee and fell, shielded by the dead guard's body.

Letting out a grunt of pain, Blitz fumbled with the dead guard's belt. Her fingers brushed against something spherical: a grenade. She grabbed it off the belt and threw the body off her. Pulling the pin on the weapon, Blitz hurled it toward the center of the hall and, pushing off her good leg, dove behind a marble statute. The explosion seemed to shake the enormous manor and a wave of heat swept over Blitz. She looked at her injured knee, hissing when the bullet fell from the wound. The bone healed swiftly, but the wound was taking a while to seal up. She peered out from behind the statue and noticed quite a few guards were still disoriented from the blast. Her eyes fell on a larger man and she scrambled out from behind the statue. Her movements were clumsier than usual, but she was still able to get up to a decent speed.

The large man spotted Blitz when she was a little more than halfway to him. He pulled his gun and fired but she was too quick, dodging low so she swept under the deadly path of the bullets. She didn't stop until she was behind him. Skillfully pulling the arm that held the gun toward her so it was straight out, Blitz slammed her palm down on his elbow, breaking it, and followed through by slamming her elbow into his face. He was out cold and she had his gun. Swiftly spinning around, Blitz opened fire on the other assassins running at her even as she moved across the floor. She never stopped moving. To do so would mean death.

By the time she had finished with the gun, Blitz had killed five of the remaining guards. A canister rolled toward her and she lunged behind another statue, closing her eyes. It exploded and her ears rang. It was a flash bomb. Her hearing was compromised, meaning she had to rely on her eyes and nose for the next hour or so.

A strong hand grabbed the back of her neck and lifted her off the floor. She was thrown backward and hit the ground, rolling a few times before crashing into a wall. Swallowing, Blitz turned her eyes toward the assassin who was advancing on her as she pushed herself to her feet. She let out a sharp gasp when she felt a blade sink deeply into her shoulder. Turning to the stabber, Blitz punched her in the face and kicked her in the stomach, knocking her away for the moment. Yanking the blade out of her shoulder, she spun back toward the assassin who had thrown her. With one fast swipe, Blitz had opened his jugular.

She turned her attention back to the woman who had

stabbed her, now on her feet again. Blitz quickly ducked under a shot that had been aimed at her head. There were at least three shooters on the upper landing. There were two guards in her peripheral vision, but she focused on the woman in front of her, who was beckoning her forward. The woman lashed out with a punch and Blitz ducked under it, reaching forward and yanking the taser off her weapons belt. She continued maneuvering until she was behind the guard and buried the taser deep in the flesh at the back of her neck. Blitz pressed the button and watched as she shook wildly, crying out in agony. A bullet pierced her side and Blitz let out a growl of annoyance and pain as she dove behind a couch. The assassin continued firing, bullets piercing the top of the couch. Blitz soldier-crawled behind the couch, keeping her eyes on the advancing feet. When the guard was within range, Blitz sprang up and kicked the couch at her. The woman fell over the large piece of furniture and Blitz leapt up, landing on the guard's helmeted head and snapping her neck. She pushed off with her feet, launching herself at another guard and tackling him to the floor. She quickly rolled over so he was on top, shielding her from the marksmen on the second floor. Reaching down, she yanked his handgun from its holster and threw him off her, bolting out of the open main hall and hiding behind another corner. The floor was becoming slippery with the amount of blood being spilt. Blitz leaned out from her cover and fired a few rounds at the three remaining marksmen, but only managed to kill one and wound another.

A bullet slammed into her shoulder, knocking her to the ground. She let out a grunt and rolled onto her back, pointing her gun down the hall where the bullet had come from, firing the final rounds in the firearm. She managed to shoot the assassin in the chest and the woman fell. Blitz paused to take in the scents as she clumsily climbed back to her feet, the bullet falling from her shoulder as the wound gradually began to repair itself. There were still quite a few hostiles left. They were conserving their rounds and forcing her to go on the offensive, hoping she would get out in the open and make a mistake. To her dismay, the strategy was working.

Blitz tossed the gun she had retrieved away and drew her own guns. She took a deep breath, mentally scanning her body for any other damage. She had taken a few hits, but nothing serious had been damaged. Still, she ached and was beginning to tire. Blitz glanced to the side, swallowing before spinning out into the open. Her guns, though they looked similar to Berettas, sounded nothing like most firearms. When fired, instead of a harsh report, there was a soft, almost metallic, whisper. They also had a higher round capacity. She ran forward, leaning back, and slid across the bloody floor, firing her guns at the guards on the landing. She managed to kill the remaining two marksmen and also took out another guard.

There were still quite a few guards to take care of. Blitz only had one bullet left, which she was saving. She reached the pillars beneath the stairs and sought cover again. As she did another mental check of her body Blitz found she had been grazed about a dozen times. There was a nasty gash on her temple and blood threatened to leak into her eye, which would further impair her vision. There was no denying it — she was slowing down. Blitz gritted her teeth as she slid her guns back into their holsters and drew her sais.

Blitz kept to the shadows and weaved about the edge of the main hall, cutting down whatever opponents she could find. Stab one in the head, sever the spinal cord on the next, punch, strike, dodge, deflect — her mind went into basic killing mode where she only thought about the fastest and most efficient way to take down her opponents. She didn't even recognize their differences anymore. They were armed, they were skilled, and therefore they were a threat. Blitz got behind a tall woman, grabbed the collar of her shirt, and threw her to the ground with a forceful yank.

She used her heel to viciously grind the woman's windpipe into mush before moving on.

Blitz ducked into a crouch when another guard came at her with a loud shout, swiping at her with a pair of short swords. She could feel the short blades pierce the air just above her head. As she blocked one strike with her sais, the sword-wielder kicked her in the stomach, knocking her down. Blitz rolled to the side when he attempted to stab her in the chest, narrowly dodging the strike. Lashing out with a kick, she managed to strike his knee and he stumbled. They both scrambled to their feet at the same time. He recovered faster, lunging forward and bringing one of his swords down again. Blitz was barely able to stop the weapon and felt the strike rattle her bones. She leapt back when he attempted to disembowel her with the second sword. Another guard leapt at her with a knife and she barely avoided the sharp blade aimed at her back. She spun behind the guard and used her as a shield when the sword-wielder thrust forward. He skewered the guard and as he attempted to pull the sword out, Blitz pounced on him. She slammed her elbow into his face and kneed him in the gut. She sliced his throat open with one sai and thrust the longest prong of the other one into his temple, yanking it out and letting the body drop.

Three more guards came at her, which worked to her advantage. She gracefully spun around, spending an equal amount of time killing each one. Disembowel the first, slit the second's throat, and a combination of the two for the third. Head, chest, under the armpit, throat, groin: the mantra of vulnerable areas to target continued to run through her mind in a constant hum.

A few guards had made a run for it, escaping before she could come at them. One final man came running at her and Blitz was ready for him, though she didn't look it. She spun around at the last second so she was behind him, holding his thick arm in a tight joint lock that was impossible to break. With a vicious jerk of her body, she broke his arm before stabbing the longest prong of the sai right between his legs. With one merciless move, Blitz lifted the screaming assassin off his feet using her sai and sent him into a midair somersault, spraying blood everywhere. When he crashed to the floor, she dropped to one knee and drove both sais deep into his chest. When she ripped them out, dark hot blood sprayed up at her face and hair but she paid it no heed. It wasn't the first time she had seen blood or felt it on her skin, and she knew it wouldn't be the last. She stood again and looked around.

Blitz took a few seconds to listen and make sure she had taken care of all the guards on the lower level. She heard ragged breathing and realized it was her own. Her lungs were burning and she was sweating profusely. She did a final mental check of her body, dismayed to find many of the wounds she had received had not fully healed. At some point, Blitz had taken a shot to the gut and it hurt to breathe. At least two ribs were broken and one wrist was sprained. There was a jagged gash running up her arm. Her catsuit had "healed" faster than the wounds on her body. She found she was unable to catch her breath and she continued panting. Blitz looked at the carnage around her. Even though she was colorblind, she could see everything was dark with blood. Her sweat was likely tinged red from the blood that had sprayed up in her face and short hair during the battle.

She moved swiftly and silently so she was beside the staircase, under the overhang of the second floor of the manor. Her sharpened hearing took in the faint sounds above her. Blitz moved to the staircase and saw a woman standing on the stairs. She wore two guns and was studying the slaughter in the main hall with the typical indifference of an assassin. Her eyes fell on Blitz and the two stared at each other for a moment.

"Blitz, I take it? I'm Marla. There's a secret stairway in the back of the manor. Blackjack went out to the garage. If you hurry, you can still catch him," the woman stated. Blitz glanced sideways toward the door she had originally come in. She looked back at the woman, who shrugged.

"I want this territory, you want him dead. Have at it," she said, gesturing toward the door. Blitz backed up toward the door. She didn't take her eyes off the assassin as she exited the manor.

~~*~*~*

Blackjack closed the trunk of the car. It had taken him longer than he had anticipated to find the right set of keys to the car he wanted. The assassin heard the door open and immediately retrieved the shotgun from the top of the car, pointing it at the door and firing. Blitz went down with a raspy cry. He pumped the grip on the shotgun as he approached where she had fallen. Blood had sprayed on the wall and window of the door. He thought he had hit her shoulder, but the creature went down too fast for him to be sure. Blackjack checked his pace as he stepped around the car she had fallen behind. There was some blood leading outside, but no body.

The assassin quickly slammed and locked the door, running back toward the small sporty car. Sinking into the driver's seat, he started the engine. He grabbed the garage opener and pressed the button, making sure his shotgun was within reach as the door rolled up. Blackjack pulled the car out of the garage, flooring the accelerator.

A lone shadowy figure appeared in front of the car shortly before a long wooden staff shattered the windshield, piercing the assassin's right shoulder and pinning him inside the car. He let out a shout of pain as he veered wildly across the dirt and crashed into the side of the Obsidian Manor. The airbag exploded in his face, breaking his nose. As Blackjack struggled, every movement caused agony to race through him.

He felt around wildly for his shotgun, but couldn't find it. It had probably fallen on the passenger's side when he crashed. With his one good arm, Blackjack reached into his jacket pocket and fingered the switchblade he kept in there. There was a crunching noise outside as footsteps approached the car. Pulling out the knife, he flicked it open. He turned his attention to the staff, which was still jutting out of the window. It looked like the handle of a rake. A thump on the hood of the car brought his attention to the windshield. The experiment towered above him, staring down at the trapped assassin.

"Look, why don't we deal?" he called out. "I've got—"

She grabbed the end of the wooden staff and pushed it even further into the car, causing Blackjack to scream and curse. The woman hopped off the car and moved to the driver's side window, watching him.

"So what now? Am I expected to beg for my life?" he sneered at her.

Blitz was silent as she continued to move around the car to the passenger side, watching as the man continued struggling. He knew what she was going for and attempted to reach the shotgun. It was useless. Blackjack was unable to move with the staff jutting out of his shoulder. He tried to keep his eyes on her, which proved to be impossible. She was toying with him and it was frightening.

Blitz reached in through the open window of the passenger side and retrieved Blackjack's shotgun. Pumping the grip, she observed him a moment longer as he tried to pull the makeshift spear out of his shoulder. The experiment pointed the shotgun at him and fired, watching as blood and brain matter splattered all over the car.

The shot echoed through the empty land. Blitz didn't notice as she made her way back to the garage. She tossed the shotgun onto one of the cars, no longer having any use for it. Moving toward the back of the garage, she retrieved two large red gas cans. When she had first arrived, she had noticed the smell of gasoline in the garage. Most assassins kept extra on hand. In their line of work, one never knew when they would need extra gas, either for a weapon or an unexpected trip.

Returning to the car, Blitz proceeded to empty both gas cans over and inside the car. She tossed the empty cans inside and pulled her Zippo lighter out of the back of her belt. Flicking it open, she touched the flame to the gasoline and watched it ignite.

Blitz moved back to the garage and slumped against it, sliding down so she was sitting on the ground. She knew she had to move, but needed to rest for a moment. Watching the fire was relaxing and allowed her to think about something else. She was unsure if Grenich would send a sanitization team since Blackjack wasn't officially part of the Corporation. He got paid by Carding, but to the best of her knowledge, the assassin had only worked for him once or twice. One thing she was sure of — they would be unable to make him into a revenant, even if the heads of the Corporation wanted to. Damaging or destroying the brain and/or body made it impossible to create a functioning revenant. Blitz had made sure the bodies she left in her wake would not be reanimated. The doctor would probably label the feeling she was experiencing as catharsis. Blitz neither knew nor cared. She just wanted to rest and observe the climbing flames.

She thumped her head back against the wall as she watched the fire consume the car and body inside. Exhaustion seeped into her very bones. Blitz wondered how much longer she had. She knew it wasn't much, a little less than a day by her estimate. Come tomorrow afternoon, she would be dead. Blitz had been killing for so long, so very long, but had never considered her own demise. As sick as she was, she found death to be a welcoming notion. Back before she had been infected, Blitz could have done twelve different jobs in one day without even breaking a sweat. Now she was off the drugs and dying from some virus created in the main laboratory.

As she watched the fire grow, Blitz wondered why the Corporation still employed ordinary assassins. They had countless living weapons at their disposal. To use a normal, it seemed so unnecessary and not cost-effective.

"A countenance more in sorrow then in anger."

Blitz turned and expected to see her specter. For the first time in a while, the ghost was nowhere to be found. Blitz looked around, patiently waiting for the specter to appear and lecture her on the wrongness of what she was doing, but she never came. It left Blitz with a strange sensation. Loneliness? She grimaced and held her throbbing shoulder, rotating it once. Blitz gasped at the pain that flared up and protectively held the wounded limb against her body. It was going to take a long time to heal. The shotgun blast felt like it had nearly torn her arm off. Blood was still leaking down her arm as the wound slowly sealed itself. Blitz felt a little lightheaded and she couldn't tell whether it was from the virus or blood loss or both.

Blitz looked off across the land of the Obsidian Manor. She wanted to get her last target and then die. Being sedentary felt too vulnerable. If she stopped moving, the chances of failing greatly increased. She was already dying, but she wasn't dead yet. Blitz looked up at the sky, closing her eyes and inhaling the clean air. For a moment, she wondered what it felt like to appreciate the air like Jack and the doctor seemed to be able to do. Thinking back on all the people she had killed so far, Blitz wondered what else she could do. The only thing keeping her going was a strange need, a drive she didn't entirely understand. The doctor would probably term it anger or rage. She was incapable of such inconsequential things as emotions and had no interest in what he called "introspection."

A dull throbbing raced through her already aching body. She had almost reached her expiration date. Though she could never remember feeling so before, Blitz was beginning to feel tired. It was an odd sensation and one she did not like. Her body was failing her and she really just wanted to sleep.

Blitz looked back to the crackling flames and the fire

reflected in her eyes. Taking a deep breath, she forced herself to her feet. She could smell cooking flesh and burning metal. It was nauseating, but strangely soothing. This job was finished and now she had to move on. There was one final target to kill. Blitz looked around once more for her ghost, but saw nothing. Allowing her body to melt into the form of a raven, Blitz spread her dark wings and took to the skies. She had to keep going, for just a little while longer.

CHAPTER NINE

The Four were speeding toward Caleb Brown's location. In the back seat, Ace looked out the window, watching the scenery fly by. She was sitting next to Alex in the spacious silver car that Jade had borrowed from an ally who lived in the area. Jade seemed to lack any kind of understanding when it came to speed limits.

The shape shifters had been given their missions at last night's meeting and no one had slept since. The three teams had set out at dawn to apprehend their assigned marks. Alex, Shae, Jade, and Ace had been given the task of retrieving a man named Caleb Brown. Ajax, Devin, Malone, and Nero were going to retrieve Blackjack. That left Sly, Steve, Jensen, and Alpha. The rebel leader had come in later than Ace and told Jet and Lilly she wanted to help, end of story. Both the Monroes seemed grateful for the offer and didn't question her motives. If Alpha wanted to help, they were glad for it. That particular team was going out to get Onyx.

"What should we do after wrapping up here?" Jade asked Shae without taking her eyes off the road. Shae barely acknowledged her, her gaze remaining outside. Jade glanced over at her and then turned her attention back to the road.

"Steve will be fine," Jade reassured her teammate. "He's got a good head on his shoulders and he has been a protector all his life. He's certainly been on more dangerous missions before. Anyway, he's not the one you should be worrying about."

"Who should I be worrying about, Jade?" Shae asked, unable to keep the weariness out of her voice. Ace folded her hands behind her short hair, feeling more than a little bored.

"Jensen," Jade answered, shaking her head as she made a sharp turn. "I don't know what Jet and Lilly were thinking, sending him out to get her. You know he's got a personal strife with her and he's been less than stable lately."

Shae squinted in the bright morning light, reaching forward to crank up the air conditioning a little more.

"I'm sure Jensen will be fine," Alex said from the back, continuing to look out her window. The houses began to space out more as they got into the wealthier area. Ace half expected to see a barn full of Thoroughbred stallions when she saw how much land some of the houses occupied. Everything was gated off and there were plenty of small blue signs warning of the state-of-the-art security systems.

"Alex, the woman murdered his sister *and* two of his lovers in cold blood. Jensen is a good guy, but everyone's got their limits. Hell, if the Monroes had sent us after Onyx, I don't know if *I* would've been able to keep a clear head. I will be very surprised if both he and Onyx return without a scratch," Jade replied as she swerved around another corner. For a few minutes, she continued driving straight down the smooth, well-kept road. The houses grew larger and larger as they continued deeper into the gated community.

"Wait, stop," Shae said abruptly, straightening up in her seat. Jade pulled to a halt, watching as Shae glanced down at the small piece of paper she held with the address written on it.

"What is it, Shae?" Alex asked as she leaned forward. Ace looked out the window. Across the street from them, men were toiling in the sun. They were working on an enormous house, which was currently just a pale wooden skeleton looming in the sunny afternoon. The construction men were so wrapped up in their work that they either didn't notice the car screeching to a sudden stop or disregarded it. *We can't be the first Mercedes to pass down this way*, Ace thought as she rolled her neck.

Shae looked at the paper with the address on it and then at the construction site. "According to Sly's contact, this is where Caleb Brown supposedly lives."

"You've got to be kidding me," Jade grumbled as she grabbed the paper from Shae. She looked between the construction site and the address before handing the paper back to Shae and leaning back in her seat. Ace could hardly believe her eyes, but it was more because of the size of the clean wooden frame.

"All right, we already know what we're going to find, but might as well confirm it. You three check it out," Jade ordered, taking the lead as she always did. "I'm going to call the mansion. Maybe Sly got the address wrong."

"I don't know. Sly is usually pretty thorough," Alex mentioned as she unbuckled her seatbelt. Ace mirrored her actions and opened the car door, stepping out into the moderately sunny day. The days were noticeably shorter. There were supposed to be flurries next week.

"Never hurts to double-check," she heard Jade's reply, though it was muffled by the car's interior.

~~*~*~*

"Holy shit!"

As he stood amidst the carnage in the gloom of the Obsidian Manor, Ajax had to agree with his youngest brother's exclamation. It summed up exactly what he was thinking. There was blood everywhere, blood and bodies. The lighting was dim, but nothing could conceal the scene before them. The stench of death was heavy in the main hall. The air was warm, most likely from numerous weapons firing. The wind howled through the many broken windows. Ajax had left Malone and Devin outside to investigate the burned out car that had smashed into the side of the manor. He and Nero had entered the Obsidian Manor to investigate the scene inside. Ajax had been expecting to find the bodies of a few guards. What he hadn't expected to find was the aftermath of a slaughter.

"If this is the work of a single experiment . . ." Nero trailed off and shook his head, not needing to say more. Ajax knelt down to examine one of the bodies. He studied the man's weaponry, focusing on the heavy gun strapped to his shoulder. The man had been killed by a single slash to the back of the neck that had severed his spinal cord, as best as Ajax could tell. The eldest Deverell wasn't afraid of much, but this woman scared him. Looking at how young some of the guards were and the indiscriminate way she killed, Ajax began to understand how ruthless Blitz truly was.

The sound of a quiet thump followed by Nero swearing made Ajax look over his shoulder. Nero pushed himself up on his elbow, grimacing. Ajax stood up, carefully making his way to his brother. He slipped in a large puddle of blood pooling under a younger man in a security uniform, but Ajax managed to remain standing. He reached Nero and offered a hand.

"Are you all right?" he asked as Nero took his hand.

"Yeah, just bruised my pride," Nero responded as Ajax helped him up. He made a face of disgust when he saw the blood smeared on his clothes. Ajax's eyes were drawn to another security guard who was holding a firearm. He knelt down and retrieved the gun, pulling out the magazine.

"The clip's half full," Ajax observed as he put the gun

off to the side and placed the back of his hand on the side of the woman's face. "And the body's still warm. I'm not a medical examiner, but I'd estimate this woman has only been dead a couple hours."

"They're all assassins who are armed to the teeth and more than half of them didn't have a chance to empty their guns?" Nero asked, incredulously, as he approached his oldest brother. "There's at least fifteen bodies here."

Ajax nodded, distracted, as he pressed the button in his earpiece that made it crackle to life. "Devin, Malone, have you got anything out there?"

He waited for the response, which came from Devin a few seconds later. "The body's charred, but it looks like she killed him before lighting him up. It smells like she doused the car in gasoline."

Ajax's eyes swept over the bodies on the first floor. He had noticed a few wore grenades and wondered why she hadn't used those. Facing off against well-trained assassin guards was no easy feat and it would be common sense to use whatever weapons she could get her hands on.

"Ajax?" Malone's voice sounded hesitant, which took Ajax by surprise. Malone was probably the most confident of his brothers. Nero glanced over to Ajax when he heard Malone's cautious tone.

"Yes?" Ajax answered.

"I think you should come out here."

"I'll be there in a minute," Ajax replied. "Nero, will you be all right on your own for a few minutes?"

"Yeah," Nero said, making his way for the staircase, slipping once. "I'm going to do a sweep of the second floor, see if there are any stragglers lurking about."

"Watch your back," Ajax called after him. Nero waved dismissively as he started up the stairs.

"I'll send Devin in," Ajax stated.

"Okay."

Nero disappeared down the hall on the second floor and Ajax made his way to the front door. He and Malone had found a security pass on the ground in front of the garage, which unlocked the side door. They had laid a stone in between the front doors to keep one propped open.

As he stepped out onto the front stairs, Ajax briefly closed his eyes and lifted his face to the afternoon sun. The cool air felt wonderful on his flesh. He opened his eyes and looked down the steps. Devin was sitting on the last one, scrolling through his phone. Looking over to the damaged wall of the manor and the wrecked car, Ajax could see Malone standing behind it. He was staring at it, his attention solely on the wreckage.

"Devin, could you go inside and help Nero?" Ajax asked. "He's investigating the second floor."

"Yep," Devin said as he got to his feet, sliding his phone into the back pocket of his pants.

"Be careful. There's not a spot on the floor that isn't covered in blood or gore. It's really easy to slip," Ajax warned as Devin approached. He nodded and passed by Ajax, disappearing inside the manor. Ajax jogged down the few steps and moved to where Malone was standing in front of the car. Wisps of smoke still curled up from it and heat waves shimmered in the air. The smell of burnt flesh still lingered.

If there had been survivors, they had long since vacated the premises and Ajax didn't blame them. The place always had a cold feeling, even before Blitz's visit. Now it just felt dead, uncomfortably so. It had a somber feeling most massacre sites held, but this one didn't command respect. It demanded solitude. The assassins would likely regroup elsewhere. Blitz's attack had probably rattled them and they wouldn't return to a place of defeat.

Ajax moved around the car to where Malone was standing. There was a look of intense focus on Malone's face as he leaned down.

"She shot him," Malone stated, gesturing inside the car. "You can see a little of the blood spatter on the driver's window."

Ajax leaned down and looked at the inside of the car. The body was charred, but the build was similar to Blackjack. Looking down at his right hand, Ajax spotted the assassin's trademark ring. The one containing a drop of blood from one of his many, many victims. He straightened up and moved toward the hood of the car, noticing a hole in the blackened windshield and the spiderweb of cracks spreading out from it.

"The hole is too big to be from a bullet," Malone mentioned, following his older brother. "Whatever she used, it looks like it impaled him. He lost control of the car, crashed into the manor, and she killed him. Afterwards, she lit the car up."

"That's a hell of a lot of overkill," Ajax observed, looking over at his brother. "If she already killed him, why bother burning the car?"

Malone shrugged. "There are two other bodies in the garage, both guards. I haven't been inside. Did she burn any bodies in there?"

Ajax shook his head. "She didn't take any weapons either."

Malone glanced back at the smoking car. "We know she was after him, but this one seems a little more . . . personal than the others. Everyone else was collateral damage, but she took her time with him."

"All her kills have been quite brutal," Ajax pointed out.

"I think there's a reason behind this kind of overkill, but we just can't see it," Malone mentioned, looking over at Ajax. "There's method behind this brutality."

Malone moved away from the car, motioning for Ajax to follow him.

"There's some blood over here by the garage," Malone explained as he led his brother over to the garage. He crouched down beside a decorative shrub and when Ajax crouched opposite him, Malone pointed to the wall between the sectional doors.

"See these few spots here? She sat here and watched him burn," Malone explained, turning his head to indicate her line of sight. Ajax rubbed his chin as he studied the tiny spots of blood.

"So she was wounded at some point, enough to leave a trail," Ajax said. Malone nodded.

"The shotgun on the car in the garage fired two slugs. She might have been hit," he mentioned. "With a slug, there would normally be a larger trail. It looks as though she was probably just grazed."

Ajax stood up and looked back toward the manor. Malone stood as well, rubbing his hands together.

"What are you thinking?" Malone asked.

"She's dangerous, Malone. How are the guardians supposed to keep someone like this in a cell?" Ajax said. Malone followed his brother's gaze across the manor's land.

"You think she should be put down?"

Ajax was quiet for a moment, scratching the back of his head as he pondered his answer. Wind swept through the grounds, the only sound as Malone waited.

"Honestly? I don't know. As a loyal protector, I don't believe in murder, but have we ever encountered anyone like this before?" Ajax rubbed his forehead. "There's just no easy answer in this situation. Not that there ever is, mind you."

Malone looked back at his brother and Ajax shook his head. It seemed as though they were always one step behind this mysterious killer. Ajax didn't want to think about how much more death she would leave in her wake if they couldn't capture her. In his long years, he hadn't encountered anyone as deadly as the mysterious Blitz.

"I'll call the Monroes and tell them what we found," Ajax said, taking his phone out of his jacket pocket. "You, Devin, and Nero do a final sweep. Take pictures of whatever evidence you can. Then we'll get out of here."

Malone nodded and moved toward the mansion while

Ajax selected his address book on the phone's screen and scrolled to the Monroes' number. He put the phone to his ear, patiently waiting for the protector leaders to answer.

~~*~*~*

On an island, the warm sun beamed down on white sandy beaches and the blue-green ocean. Everything was happy and inviting. Even the beautiful songbirds that occasionally flew across the clear blue sky seemed to rejoice in the relatively untouched paradise. The large palm trees waved their long green leaves in the occasional cool breeze drifting by. Almost everyone on the island was polite and had a smile on their face. It was difficult to be depressed or stressed out in the environment.

On the south end of the island, there was an enormous villa surrounded by acres of vibrant green grass. A large brick wall and two enormous curvy white gates kept the islanders and tourists out. The road to get to the huge estate was rarely used. The isolated villa sat atop a cliff, looking out over the island. The architecture of the home was beautiful and spoke of wealth. Some of the island children delighted in scaring each other with stories about a witch living in the huge home. Some of the teenagers even told tales of a silhouette walking about the property in the late hours of the night. Huge red signs on the gate declared the villa to be private property and it was treated accordingly.

Luckily for the team of four assigned to apprehend the villa's owner, the superstitions and legends surrounding the home and road guaranteed the property would be completely empty. Therefore, it was easy to Appear just outside the gates. Sly knew Jet didn't like the idea of her, Alpha, Steve, and Jensen Appearing in broad daylight, but they didn't have the option of playing it safe. As it was, they would probably be lucky to apprehend even one suspect. The mysterious hunter was working at an alarmingly fast rate. Sly would be surprised if the stealthy Blitz hadn't already beaten them to Onyx's isolated dwelling. She had told Jade as much earlier when they were in bed. *You may be right, but we have to try anyway,* Jade had responded before leaning over and kissing her passionately for luck.

Sly glanced over to Jensen who already had his silver handgun out and pointed to the ground. He stood out like a sore thumb in his nice clothing and shoes. She watched as he checked the clip in his gun to make sure it was full. Sly had begged Jet and Lilly not to send Jensen with her, but they had reassured her Jensen would be fine. The man was a ticking time bomb, but in the Monroes' opinion, he was fit enough to go on this mission.

Alpha was standing behind Jensen. Her short black hair was messy as usual and had streaks of purple in it. She wore the tightest dark blue jeans Sly had ever seen, coupled with a T-shirt, the sleeves raggedly ripped off to expose the elaborate bird tattoo on her upper arm. "Bitch" was scrawled across the shirt in large faded letters. The rebel was examining her perfectly sculpted nails, looking about as unbothered as Sly had ever seen her look. She had an iPod in her back pocket and Sly could see the small earbuds in her ears and her head bobbed to whatever she was listening to. Sly stared at her, wondering how she could possibly be so indifferent to the situation.

Steve stood just behind Sly, wearing his usual casual attire of plain jeans and a red T-shirt. He was just as eager as Sly to get this mission over with. Sly wasn't too concerned about him, but Shae had requested she keep an eye on him. Steve was a protector and a capable fighter, but Shae still worried. For over twenty years, his objective had been simple: protect Isis and make sure she didn't find out about her heritage too early. Sly watched as Steve looked up at the brick wall they stood in front of, staring at it for a moment.

"Hey, Sly? Check this out," Steve said. Sly approached

him and looked up at the faded white graffiti on the brick wall. It looked like an enormous skull. The paint was fading and it was impossible to make out the shape unless standing right in front of it.

"That's reassuring," Sly muttered.

"Guess it's a good thing we don't believe in omens," Steve stated with cheerful smile. Sly gave him a sardonic look.

"Is there any reason why you're wasting time looking at graffiti?" Jensen grumbled in a curt tone as he checked the bullets in his backup gun one final time before snapping the clip into place. If he had been on his own, Sly was positive he would have gone gung-ho by now. Jensen was a great warrior and a descendant of one of the greatest protector families, but this assassin had taken away his only surviving family as well as his two lovers. It was enough to drive anyone over the edge. Sly glanced up when a quiet breeze brushed through the long palm leaves shading them from the sun's hot rays.

"Not a lot of people come up the road. Think it's Onyx's handiwork?" Steve asked, ignoring Jensen.

"I doubt it. Onyx wouldn't waste her time drawing on a wall. She never struck me as the artistic type," Sly replied as she took a closer look at the faded symbol. She approached Alpha and tapped her on the shoulder. The rebel pulled out her earbuds.

"Time to move out," Sly said in response to Alpha's look.

"What's up with the skull?" Alpha asked, following Steve's gaze to the wall. Sly crouched down and unzipped the duffle bag they had brought. She looked up at the wall.

"Steve and Alpha will take the back. Jensen, you and I are going in through the front," she stated. She wanted to keep an eye on Jensen and intended to keep him on a short leash. Steve would be fine with Alpha watching his back.

"Fine with me," Jensen muttered as he moved over to one of the large trees surrounding the road and brick wall.

He stuffed the handgun in the back of his dark pants and scaled the tree with impressive ease. When he reached a branch just above the brick wall, he stood on it. He walked across the thick branch until he was just above the wall. Grasping the branch with his hands, he allowed his long legs to drop, dangling just over the property line. He dropped out of their sight, landing with a quiet thud behind the wall. While he was doing that, Sly pulled a thick purple rope from the duffle bag and ran it through her fingers, checking it.

"Jensen, I'm tossing the rope over," she called over to him.

He grunted in response. Sly rolled her eyes and hurled a length of rope over with much more force than was necessary, smiling when she heard a quiet curse on the other side of the wall.

"Got it," his bitter voice called. Sly glanced over at Alpha, offering her the rope. Alpha stepped forward and grabbed it. She approached the rough wall and put a goth-style army boot on the surface. The rebel tightly grasped the rope and scaled the medium-sized wall. Once she reached the top, Alpha let go of the rope and turned around on the thin ledge of the brick wall, lowering her body on the other side. She disappeared from their sight, landing with a soft thud on the other side of the wall.

Sly handed the rope to Steve. Steve put a cross-trainer on the wall and quickly scaled it. Once he disappeared on the other side of the wall, Sly wasted no time climbing the brick wall. The nylon rope trembled in her hand but remained taut. Jensen could easily hold her weight. She soon reached the top of the wall. Sly dropped to the ground, absorbing the impact in her knees as she had done countless times in her forest.

They landed behind shrubbery just as Lilly predicted when she had observed the aerial shots Sly's contact managed to obtain. Sly glanced over the ornamental hedges, noticing the shades were all drawn in the villa. *If I*

Appeared out here for nothing when I could have stayed in bed with two beautiful women, I am going to be pissed, she thought. Sly gestured with one hand for Steve and Alpha to move out.

Steve and Alpha moved to where she directed, remaining hidden behind the trees and shrubs. Sly and Jensen started forward toward the villa. The property had an oddly whimsical look to it due to the amount of landscaping. Sly found herself questioning why the hell Onyx would keep all kinds of plants, due to the amount of cover they provided. There was a short stretch of completely bare land surrounding the large villa, but the hedges still provided cover for any unwanted visitors. Of course, that was only if someone could track her down, which had been quite difficult to do, even for Sly's contacts.

Sly tapped Jensen's shoulder and gestured for him to approach the front door from the right. He nodded his understanding and moved away in that direction. She hoped he would stay in line. It would be anyone's guess whether or not Jensen would be able to keep his cool if they found Onyx. But Sly planned on taking everything one step at a time. Right now, she was only concerned with getting inside the place.

They quickly covered the ground between the hedges and the entrance to the villa's large door. Two short beeps in Sly's earpiece told her Steve and Alpha had reached the back door. She replied by pressing a button in her own earpiece twice, telling them she had reached the front door. One longer beep told them to proceed as planned. She glanced over at Jensen and nodded, indicating everything was going according to plan. She could see sweat beginning to bead on Jensen's skin and could feel the cool liquid on her own body. Though there were cool breezes, it was still quite humid. It didn't concern her. Shape shifters were really only affected by the extremes in temperatures.

Sly and Jensen reached the front porch and put their

backs to the wall next to the door, as one of the security cameras lazily swept over the property. Jensen and Sly both moved in tandem with the monitors, making sure to remain out of sight. Sly looked over to her teammate, nodding. Jensen held up three fingers, lowering one in a countdown. Once he lowered his final finger, both he and Sly spun out from the wall and raised a leg in a powerful front kick. It took two strikes to kick open the door. The frame splintered as the door swung open, jiggling loosely on its hinges. Sly and Jensen entered, keeping their guns drawn and pointed in front of them. The Monroes had lent Sly and Alpha handguns from the mansion's weapons room, fully loaded with a couple spare clips.

Sly glanced around at their surroundings. Everything, from the rare paintings on the walls to the imported tiles on the floor to the diamond chandeliers above them, spoke of wealth. The interior of the villa looked like a castle from some fairy tale told to little girls. It was a bit garish for her taste.

Jensen didn't seem anywhere near as interested as he moved forward to check the rooms. Sly scanned their surroundings again, alert for any sign of movement, then turned her attention back to Jensen. He was kicking open doors with a lot more force than necessary, foolishly giving away their position, probably to everyone on the island.

"Jensen, settle down," Sly hissed as she moved past him to check the next room. He looked over at her and shook his head, muttering something angrily under his breath. He stopped kicking open doors, opting for the quieter method of simply opening them. *Thank the guardians for small blessings,* Sly thought as she moved to check the next room. Jet was definitely going to get another "I told you so" speech from her.

~~*~*~*

Steve and Alpha entered through a window that had

been opened a crack. Alpha managed to yank it open fully, breaking the small gold hinge in the process. She took out a switchblade, opening it with a few deft flicks of her wrist, and cut away the dark screen covering the opening. Closing the knife again, she pulled herself through the window. Steve followed close behind. They were in some kind of library judging from the bookshelves surrounding them. It was an enormous room, as big as the Monroes' study in the mansion. The shades were drawn, so it was cast in a gloomy muted light and was cooler than expected. A white stone fireplace was a few feet in front of them, standing out in stark contrast to the shadows. Two rich red leather chairs sat facing each other in front of the fireplace. The floor was carpeted in some expensive soft material Steve didn't bother trying to identify. It silenced their steps, and that was all he cared about at the moment.

Alpha crept forward confidently, but also exhibited caution. Steve followed close behind her. She opened the door and the room was bathed in bright light, momentarily blinding herself and Steve. Diamond chandeliers hung above them, illuminating the hallway. Alpha moved out into the hall, looking both ways. After a second, she gestured to Steve that it was all right to come out. When he did, the rebel pressed a button on her earpiece. They proceeded toward the back, heading for the kitchen. They stepped inside the enormous room, looking around at the top-of-the-line appliances. There was a quiet humming throughout the room.

"Sly, we're inside and there's no sign of her in the kitchen and the uh," Alpha glanced over to the room on their right, frowning. "Greenroom, I think."

Steve looked over in that direction and noticed a room filled with a multitude of plants. Hidden in one of the spidery-limbed scrawny trees, there was a gray parrot with the most intelligent gold eyes Steve had ever seen. Its red tail feathers stuck out in stark contrast to the surrounding green plant life. The bird bobbed up and down a few times on the branch it clutched between its gray talons, before scooting to the side and disappearing behind a cluster of thick dark green leaves. There were a few oleander plants around the large greenroom. From what he had heard from some of the Monroes' undercover contacts, Onyx had a strange fondness for poison, though she rarely ever used it. She just liked making it.

"Okay, I'll tell him," Alpha said softly before turning to Steve. "Jensen's going upstairs to do a sweep. Sly wants you to meet him up there, sweeping the opposite direction until you do. There's a hidden stairway over here."

"He's not going to shoot me is he?" Steve asked dryly, making sure to keep his voice soft so they wouldn't be overheard. He followed the rebel to the back of the kitchen where there was a doorway.

Alpha smirked and nodded toward the hidden stairwell. "Only one way to find out."

"Yeah," Steve grumbled as he started making his way up the straight red-carpeted stairs. It was a narrow stairway, obviously not meant to be used as the main way upstairs. It was so narrow it was almost claustrophobic. Steve kept his gun pointed at the ground, holding it in a two-handed grip.

"Hey, Steve?" Alpha whispered when he stepped onto the second step, waiting until Steve glanced back at her. "Make sure you see him first."

Steve gave her a sarcastic smile before continuing up the stairs, ignoring the sound of her quiet chuckle.

After ascending the long staircase, he reached a plain teal-colored door. Steve turned the knob, pushing the door open, and immediately pointed his gun forward as he emerged in a small bedroom. The stairwell was some kind of secret passage in or out of the room. Steve glanced left and right, making sure the room was empty, before cautiously continuing forward. There was a white door just in front of him, barely standing out from the powder blue walls. It was odd. Steve always thought Onyx loved the color black. The villa was decorated and painted in every color but black, not at all what they would have expected from the assassin. Everything blended together perfectly and was remarkably classy. Steve reached for the doorknob. He thought he heard a flutter of wings behind him, so he glanced over his shoulder.

With the mercilessness she was infamous for, Onyx smashed an ornamental vase over the protector's head. The dark blue vase shattered into pieces and Steve dropped like a sack of rocks, surrounded by the delicate blue shards. There was a nasty-looking gash on his head and blood lazily crept down his face, dripping onto the carpet. Onyx paid it no heed as she crouched down and plucked the gun from beside his limp hands, admiring it for a second, before looking back to its fallen owner.

"Stevie, that was just *sad*," she taunted the unconscious man, slapping his face lightly before standing up again. "Thanks for the gun, sweetie. I'll make sure it doesn't go to waste."

Onyx pressed her back against the wall and reached out to twist the doorknob. She swung the door open in one quick move, waiting a few seconds before craning her neck to peer out into the hallway. It was empty. She crept out of the small bedroom and closed the door behind her. The assassin moved down the short hallway toward the large main hall on the second floor. Her gait was slow and cautious as she kept the gun pointed in front of her. Any expression had been wiped off her face and her yellow eyes scanned her surroundings for even the smallest movement. Her long hair, which she had recently dyed fire engine red, was tied back tightly to prevent it from falling into her eyes.

As she emerged out into the main second floor hall, Onyx was punched in the face. Reeling from the strike, she was yanked out into the hall and slammed against the wall, causing her to lose her grip on her gun. When she stepped forward, a kick knocked her back against the wall and Onyx looked up, prepared to kill whomever had gotten the drop on her. Her eyes met a familiar blue gaze and she couldn't help but smile. Jensen. She should have known.

"Jensen, darling, you still fight like a human child," she coughed, amusement trickling into her voice as she took him in. He said nothing, but drew his gun. The protector stood stiffly, the gun pointing unwaveringly at her face. She cocked an eyebrow, her own posture relaxed. Onyx raised a leg to rest her foot against the wall as she continued to observe him.

"You seem a bit upset with me," she continued with mocking innocence. Jensen stepped forward and retrieved the gun she had dropped. He kept his own gun pointed at her as he slid the second gun in the holster at his waist. A shot at such close range would completely obliterate her face, but Onyx wasn't concerned. Jensen was an Aldridge and they were nothing if not predictable. It was why they had been so easily slaughtered. Nobility and honor were commendable in theory, but the world demanded one fight dirty in order to survive. It was why protectors would never last.

"Are you going to shoot me, Jensen?" she asked. The price on his pretty little head made her salivate. His corpse would bring in enough for Onyx to buy whatever she desired.

"Give me one reason not to," he got out from behind gritted teeth. Onyx smiled as she dropped her foot and took a step toward him.

"If you kill me, you'll never find the puppet-master," she answered cryptically.

"Stay where you are," Jensen ordered taking a step back.

"Are you scared of me?" she taunted as she continued to approach. Jensen pointed his gun just past her and fired, which made the assassin pause.

"Next one's in your knee," he warned. Onyx smiled

before lashing out with a strong kick, knocking the gun out of his hand. It sailed over the railing and clattered on the ground below. She leapt forward, grabbing one of his arms and spinning into him, jabbing him in the throat with her elbow. He stumbled backward and nearly fell over the railing, gasping for breath.

Jensen recovered and when she came at him again, swung out with a powerful right hook. He succeeded in punching her jaw and she stumbled away from him. Onyx recovered and grasped his arm when he advanced on her. She swung it around so she held him in a joint lock. The assassin applied pressure to his arm, a warning that she could snap it like a twig if she wished and he grunted in pain.

"The first one, well, she didn't see it coming. The second one though. Oh, she died terrified," Onyx said, pausing briefly to press her lips against his ear. "I've never seen someone struggle and whimper so much. Of course, I don't think I'd be ecstatic about drowning in my own blood either."

She let go of his arm and shoved him forward so he crashed into the wall. Jensen turned around, panting. He straightened up, smoothing the front of his nice shirt.

"You know, a couple of my sources have assassin contacts," he began off-handedly. "Word has it that your last job was about five years ago and the target managed to stab you. Heard it left quite a nasty scar."

Onyx narrowed her eyes and gritted her teeth, fury flashing across her eyes. Jensen laughed despite himself.

"Isis stabbed you, huh? Oh, that really had to damage your reputation. Such a young hybrid and she managed to stab you. Good for her."

Onyx charged him. Jensen dodged and struck out with a roundhouse kick, knocking her to the side. He followed up with a leaping knee strike, which slammed her back against another wall. She spun away from him and moved behind a small table. Leaping up onto the smooth surface,

Onyx leapt at him and managed to wrap her legs around his neck. Using her momentum, she pulled him down to the floor. The blow managed to daze the protector and he struggled to breathe when she tightened her thighs about his neck.

In one swift move, Jensen withdrew his combat dagger from its sheath beneath his tailored jacket and sliced her leg. She released him with an angry screech. Jensen didn't give her a chance to recover as he scrambled away and flipped to his feet. Onyx climbed to her feet, putting less weight on her wounded leg, and glared at him. Jensen slowly moved around, pointing the sharp knife at her. He held his other hand a little lower, protecting his midsection.

"Oh Onyx, you're just a knife magnet, aren't you?" he observed, becoming serious again. "It's over. Surrender now."

"Don't celebrate too early, Jenny," Onyx warned before lunging straight at him. Jensen didn't have a chance to react as she tackled him around his midsection and sent them both backward.

When she slammed into him, it felt like Jensen got hit with a wrecking ball. His head struck stair after stair as they toppled down the extravagant winding main staircase. The protector could swear he heard his skull bouncing off each step and he wondered if either of them would survive the fall — not that it really mattered to him either way. They seemed to tumble forever, an undignified tangle of limbs.

The two shape shifters struck the ground and Jensen slid across the floor, crashing into a small table with a blue and white vase in the middle of the circular surface. The table toppled over and Jensen heard something shatter on the floor. He didn't even have the strength to groan at the overwhelming pain that radiated through his body. His ribs felt like they were being pummeled each time he drew a breath and he could feel the warmth of blood crawling down his face. He noticed with some detached interest that his eyes were closed. He could not remember closing them.

Then he heard Onyx laughing a few feet away from him. Jensen forced his eyes open and glared at her. She was sprawled out at the base of the staircase and made no move to get up.

"I'm sorry. I was just remembering the sounds your hybrid lover made as her lungs filled with blood. It sounded so much like your little sister when she was dying," Onyx explained before making gurgling noises in her throat. Jensen closed his eyes in disgust.

"Fuck you," he managed to say.

"You couldn't handle it," Onyx countered.

"As much as I'd like to hear the rest of this *delightful* banter you two have going, we're kind of on a tight schedule."

Both Jensen and Onyx turned their attention to where a familiar sarcastic voice came from. Sly stood in the doorway of another room, gun pointed unwaveringly at the assassin. She looked her usual nonchalant self.

"Thanks for the help, Sly," Jensen mumbled. He started to push himself up using his hands and grimaced in pain.

"You were doing so well on your own. Didn't want to steal your thunder," Sly teased, her attention never moving from Onyx. "You even blink and I will not hesitate to shoot out your kneecaps."

"Former assassin turned protector. Gone soft in your old age, Sly," Onyx commented as Sly approached her. She got to her feet, meeting Sly's gaze. Sly smiled as she examined the assassin.

"I do hope you remember the last time we had some alone time," Sly replied, unaffected by Onyx's attempts to get a rise out of her. "Because you'll remember that I don't hesitate to use force to get what I want."

Onyx rolled her eyes and raised her hands. "I

surrender."

Sly grabbed one of the assassin's wrists, twisted it behind her back, and slammed her against the wall, ignoring Onyx's soft grunt of pain. Sly slipped her handgun back in its holster under her arm and zip-tied Onyx's wrists together. She pressed the button on her earpiece.

"Alpha, I've got Onyx. Jensen's a bit roughed up. Did you find Steve yet?" Sly asked as she shoved Onyx down to sit on the steps. Onyx sneered at her.

"Upstairs now, heading for where he would have come up. There are a lot of rooms up here," Alpha replied. Sly approached Jensen, who had managed to push himself up into a sitting position, leaning heavily on the nearest wall.

"Check in when you find him," Sly told Alpha before calling over her shoulder to Onyx. "If you have created any more work for me, I will be very unhappy. You know what happens when I'm unhappy, Onyx?"

"I'm shaking," Onyx said, bored. Sly turned her attention back to Jensen, crouching down. He looked like hell. One of his arms was wrapped about his middle, possibly indicating some damaged ribs. There was a nasty-looking lump on the left side of his head from where he had banged it going down the stairs and he had also cut his head at some point. Sly maneuvered around him so she could see Onyx out of the corner of her eye.

"Well, Jensen, looks like you're going to be spending some time in the healing wing of the Pearl Castle," Sly commented. Jensen opened his eyes and gave her a dry look.

"Oh joy," he deadpanned. She grinned and stood up, offering him a hand. The protector gladly took it and grunted as she helped him to his feet. He continued to lean against the wall.

"Assassins still talk about the glorious night the Aldridges were slaughtered," Onyx commented. "You know they castrated your father before they beheaded him? Even as he was bleeding out, he pleaded for the life of his family. Like a coward. The head assassin still has his head mounted on the wall of his trophy room, though all the flesh rotted off long ago. It's just a skull now. I won't even go into what they did to your—"

"You don't need your eyes or fingernails to talk, Onyx," Sly warned.

"I found Steve. He seems to be all right, but he's going to have a headache for the next couple days," Alpha's voice came in through her earpiece.

"He's conscious though, right? I really don't feel like dragging a grown shape shifter back, even a scrawny one. I've got my hands full with an assassin," Sly said, glancing over at Jensen. He was making a valiant attempt to ignore Onyx, but Sly could tell it was difficult. She was not going to leave the two alone for fear Jensen would do something stupid in her absence. Both were more than capable of hurting the other. Even though Onyx was cuffed, she was still cunning. Death was her job and Sly was sure she could figure out some way to kill Jensen even without the use of her hands or a weapon. Sly herself still remembered how to snap someone's neck using nothing more than her ankles, an assassin's skill she had learned decades ago.

"He's coming around," Alpha replied and Sly heard a quiet groan on the other end of the earpiece. She scrubbed a hand over her face.

"Isis, that was her name, right? You wall up the corpse yet? Is everyone Jensen ever knew now in the guardian mausoleum? Or is it just his dead family and a couple fuck buddies?" Onyx's voice filtered through Sly's troubled thoughts. She turned around, wondering about the assassin's boldness. Something wasn't right.

Jensen straightened up and started for the assassin. Sly immediately got between the two.

"Jensen, look at me," she ordered and he did.

"Go find Steve and Alpha. Take him back to the Meadows. Alpha and I can handle Onyx."

Jensen held her gaze for a moment before turning and heading for the back of the villa where Steve and Alpha had entered.

"I'll send Alpha down," Jensen growled over his shoulder.

Sly watched him, waiting until Jensen was out of hearing range before turning her attention back to Onyx. She placed her hands on her hips and approached the scowling assassin.

"Tell me something, Onyx," Sly began. "Why do you want us to kill you?"

Onyx didn't respond. Sly hadn't expected her to. She dragged a hand-stitched chair over from where it sat. She sat on it backward, folding her arms over the back of it. The smooth mahogany finish felt nice and cool against her bare arms.

"Taunting is one thing, hitting him where it hurts, I'd expect that from you. But what you're doing is just plain suicidal," Sly continued. "You want us to kill you and I'm rather curious about why."

Onyx remained silent, setting her mouth in a thin tight line. Sly knew she would have to try a different angle to get the assassin to spill. Slowly standing from the chair, she approached Onyx and crouched down in front of her. Sly made sure to maintain just enough distance to ensure she wouldn't get sucker-punched or taken off guard.

"I can be bought, Onyx," Sly murmured, glancing over her shoulder to make sure no one was around. "I act in whatever way is most advantageous to me. All you have to do is make me a reasonable offer."

Onyx rolled her eyes toward Sly. "Bullshit. Your allegiance is to—"

"No one," Sly interrupted, pinning Onyx with her emerald eyes. "I do things that benefit me. If it benefits others, I couldn't care less. The only reason I act as an informant for Jet and Lilly is because so far, their actions have greatly benefited me. If you can put a better offer on the table though . . .”

Sly trailed off, leaving the ball in Onyx's court. Onyx snorted and shook her head, obviously not believing Sly.

“You may have the protectors fooled with your tough-shit indifferent façade and reputation, but you don't fool me,” Onyx replied. “You're the Monroes' little bitch, always at their beck and call. You wouldn't be here otherwise.”

Sly grinned. “Wow, you *really* got in over your head, didn't you? You must have if you're trying to get a rise out of me through cheap shots like that. What happened to all the Western stuff, by the way? I thought the Wild West cowgirl gunslinger was your whole theme, but I haven't seen any sign of it. What's with all the neutral shades and high-end antiques?”

Alpha came down the main hall. “Jensen's with Steve in the Meadows. I told him we'd meet them there. You ready?”

Sly glanced back at Onyx and nodded once. “Yeah, let's get out of here. Onyx was just starting to feel chatty.”

She moved over to Onyx and jerked her to her feet. Suddenly, Sly spun around and looked up at the empty second floor hall. She frowned as her eyes darted back and forth over the emptiness.

“Sly?” Alpha stepped forward and followed Sly's gaze. Sly's attention didn't waver.

“Alpha, still cheap and easy?” Onyx asked with a malicious smile. Alpha laughed sarcastically, but didn't respond. She had dealt with plenty of assassins in her business and prided herself on never stooping to their level.

After a moment, Sly nodded to Alpha. It was time to leave. They had already stayed too long in Onyx's extravagant abode. There was a brilliant shimmering blue light and the three women disappeared from the home.

Up on the second floor, Blitz stumbled out from the side hall where Jensen had originally gotten the jump on

Onyx. She Appeared shortly after the protectors had entered the villa and had just now been able to stand up. Her svelte body was shutting down. She could feel it and knew she only had an hour left, maybe two. That was if she was exceptionally lucky and if she didn't overexert herself. Blitz had barely survived Appearing in the villa and she was uncertain if she could manage it again. Sweat trickled off her face and her skin was pallid, devoid of any kind of color. She looked as if she had just run two marathons back-to-back.

Blitz folded over at the midsection and heaved, vomiting up nothing but blood. She retched for what seemed like hours, but it was only a few minutes. Her whole body was aching when she was able to straighten again. The puddle of regurgitated blood glistened up at her from the pricey carpeting. Blitz closed her eyes and gripped the railing as tightly as she could. Tremors shook her slender frame, but she ignored it. She was determined to finish what she had started.

Her green eyes fluttered open. She had absolutely nothing left to lose. Blitz reached down to her thigh holster and drew her gun. One bullet left, one target remaining. She looked up at the ceiling. The dark-haired woman in the black shirt told the other they were going to the Meadows. Blitz vaguely remembered stories about the place from her days at the Corporation. It was something she had learned about during her lessons. The Meadows was one of the forbidden zones according to the handlers. The few experiments who had the ability to Appear were never to go there. To do so would result in immediate termination.

Blitz closed her eyes again and concentrated on centering herself. She took in the sounds of the island. The calls of the many birds, the lapping of the ocean against the beach, and the sounds of people going about their daily lives allowed her focus her energy once again. Slowly, the violent tremors wracking her body decreased until they were barely noticeable. With a deep breath, Blitz slowly faded out of the villa. Her next destination would be her last.

CHAPTER TEN

Passion sat on her mother's bed in Artemis' private quarters, listening to the shower in the next room. She had let herself in, wanting to get answers to a few questions that had been weighing on her mind. Her slender legs were crossed and in her right arm she held a large worn-looking book. She drummed the fingers of her left hand on the old book's cover. Hearing the water turn off, Passion turned her stormy blue eyes to the closed door.

After a moment, the door opened and Artemis exited the bathroom, tying the sash of her satin robe. She didn't notice Passion sitting on the bed as she made her way over to the bookshelf, running her slender fingers over the bindings. With her free hand, Artemis ran her fingers through her still damp hair.

"Hello, mother," Passion stated. Artemis gasped and jumped backward, her hands grabbing a hold of the edge of her desk.

"Passion!" she exclaimed. "You scared me half to death."

Their frequent arguments almost always started with yelling, but Passion remained quiet and calm as she continued drumming her fingers on the book, the only sound in the room. The younger guardian could see that it was beginning to grate on Artemis' nerves.

"Are you going to tell me why you're here or do you expect me to read your mind?" the older guardian asked as she relaxed her position and crossed her arms over her chest. Passion pursed her lips, her eyes never moving from her mother.

"I went to the library this morning. Electra brought something rather troubling to my attention, but before I go into that, there's something I need to know," Passion began, the coolness never leaving her voice.

"Which would be?" Artemis asked.

"Who was the consort of Chaos? I know he had a lover, a guardian woman, but I can't recall who it was," Passion said. Artemis closed her eyes and rubbed her forehead. Passion had never been one to pay attention during her history lessons. In her much younger years, she found the topic dull. It was one of the many reasons why she clashed with the Muses and they still harbored a grudge about it, Clio in particular.

"His lover was Pyra, eldest daughter of Fira, the second generation leader of the lands of fire. Pyra was the heir to the lands of fire, but was banished for her treachery," Artemis stated. "If you bothered to look at the family trees—"

"So if it is already known Pyra was the consort of Chaos, why is she completely edited out of our sacred texts?" Passion asked, anger lighting up her eyes.

"I don't understand."

Passion approached the desk and dropped the worn volume on it, flipping through the pages. Artemis recognized it as one of the ancient sacred volumes detailing the history of their home and people. The angry rustling of the pages made her wince. Passion was a lover of the arts, but she could be quite cruel to literature when angry.

"Look," Passion said as she found the place she had

been looking for. "There are pages torn out of this volume, which I assume were about Chaos and Pyra. It's not just this book either. I was in the library yesterday. Every single volume that would have mentioned Pyra has pages missing. The family trees have been altered as well. I can't find her name anywhere in our texts or records, at least not the ones I have access to."

"What?" Artemis was in a state of disbelief. She moved forward and studied the book, reverently turning it around so she could better see the ancient text. Her delicate fingers ran gently over the binding where the remnants of the missing pages still resided. She switched on the desk lamp. The clean glow illuminated the book and allowed her to better examine it.

"I remember this tome," Artemis spoke in a quiet voice. "There used to be a portrait of Pyra in it. I often wondered how a fire guardian could look so cold."

Artemis examined the page right after the torn out section as Passion watched her. The page she was examining mentioned the casualties suffered in the Meadows during the war. They were numerous, most of them shape shifters save for one name: Selene. There was a small asterisk next to her name on account of Death making an exception that one time and allowing her to return back to life. It hadn't mattered though. The night guardian had vanished without a trace a few short years later.

"You're on the High Council, mother," Passion pointed out as she sat down on the smooth desktop, her tight red dress riding up a little. "No decision as big as censoring can be passed without your consent, so I want to know why something we're taught as children has been completely erased."

"Passion, I honestly don't know," Artemis protested vehemently. "I *never* would have allowed this. Censoring is against our laws. The High Council would never approve of it."

Artemis turned her attention back to the old book in front of her, ignoring Passion's skeptical look. The yellowish-brown parchment was still strong and thick. The black ink was as clear as it had been the day the words had been penned. Time would never affect this book the way it frequently did books on Earth. The guardians treated their books with as much respect as humans did their religious artifacts. They were precious items not to be misused in any way, shape, or form. Artemis closed the book and turned back to Passion.

"I'll make some inquiries and bring this to the High Council's attention. Is that all?" she asked. Neither of them was aware they had been civil toward each other for a record-setting amount of time.

Passion shook her head. "Some things have been bothering me lately, our censored history being at the top of that list."

"Why not go to Adonia?" Artemis asked as she once again crossed her arms over her chest. Passion raised an eyebrow, deciding to bite her tongue. She had a feeling telling her mother that she was easier to read would not go down well.

"She's busy with Jet and Lilly at the moment," Passion replied simply. "I needed an answer immediately."

"I'll ask her tomorrow, if you like," Artemis offered.

Passion slid off the desk, pausing momentarily as she straightened her dress. "Mother, why has there never been a guardian of war?"

Artemis shrugged. "Nobody is really sure. Perhaps because war is not a natural state."

"But if we truly do have an impact on everything, then surely there should be a guardian in control of wars to make sure they don't get completely out of control," Passion pressed.

Artemis straightened up, crossing her hands in front of her. "You know as well as I that the guardians do not take part in the conflicts of others. We are not at war, it does not affect our home, so we have no need of a war guardian. The protectors are the ones who make sure wars do not spiral completely out of control. We're here to watch over the natural elements and emotions. Now, may I ask where all these questions are coming from?"

"After hearing Roan's story of Grenich and then finding our history books censored, I've begun to wonder if we're as in control and powerful as we seem to believe we are," Passion replied cryptically, an unusual manner for the younger guardian. "I'm going to leave that volume in your hands so you can examine it further."

Passion left the room, closing the door behind her. She paused, wondering where to head to next. She had debated whether or not she should visit Ocean's lands and swim to the bottom of the swamp where Death's lair was located. Death was one of the last original guardians. He was a crotchety man, one of the very few to dwell in the land of the guardian women. Although, after hearing of his new outgoing personality and his plan to relive the decades he felt he missed out on, Passion was unsure what she was more afraid of: finding the same old cranky Death or meeting the new welcoming Death.

Passion began to descend the marble staircase, passing a number of messengers on her way down. Smiling at the ones she recognized, she continued down the stairway. Maybe she should see Roan. After all, if anyone had answers, it would probably be him. He had been much more cooperative the past few years.

Passion paused when she noticed a sudden bright shimmering of light. Someone was Appearing. When she was younger, Passion had been fascinated with the beauty of the light preceding someone Appearing. She loved to sit on the balcony overlooking the main hall of the castle and watch guardians Appear and disappear for hours on end. She even skipped a few lessons just to watch the gorgeous lights, much to Artemis' chagrin. Even now, despite her age, Passion couldn't help but stand and watch when someone was Appearing.

When Sly and Alpha Appeared with Onyx in tow, something inside the guardian of passion snapped. It would be a while before she could remember what happened, and even then, Passion's memory of the incident would be nothing more than a hazy recollection.

~~*~*~*

Sly felt a sense of relief when they Appeared in the castle. Now she could finally wash her hands of this whole mess. Jet and Lilly had everything they needed and she was officially through with this case. She glanced up, smiling when she saw the look of wonder on Alpha's face. It was the rebel leader's first time in the magnificent castle of the Meadows.

"Pretty, huh?" Sly remarked. "A bit over the top, in my humble opinion. Give me my forest any day of the week. I'd just get lost in a place like this."

Alpha nodded distractedly as she took in the sea of pastel colors created by the numerous messengers who moved about, heedless of their presence. The castle was predominantly done in neutral earth tones and pastel shades, but there were splashes of color here and there. The marble was immaculate, as was the rest of the castle. *Messengers don't get anywhere near enough credit*, Sly thought with amusement as she took in the cleanliness of the castle. Despite the pure atmosphere, the castle never lost the comfortable feeling of being home. It was part of the magic associated with guardians. They could make even the most dilapidated shack feel like a comfy little home.

"You people are so goddamn cliché," Onyx mumbled with a shake of her head. Sly grabbed a hold of her ponytail and jerked her head back, causing the assassin to grimace.

"Don't forget: there are numerous body parts that aren't required for speaking," she warned before releasing the assassin's hair. Onyx licked her lips and looked between the two women.

"Are you two still fucking or are my sources no longer up to date? Is Jade still in the picture or did the high and mighty act get to be too much?" she continued trying to goad them.

"How much longer do we have to deal with her?" Alpha groaned, rubbing her eyes.

"Hopefully not too much longer," Sly answered, distracted. She wanted to get Onyx out of the open before anyone spotted them. The last thing she needed was Passion or Electra walking around a corner and seeing the woman who killed Isis. It was a situation Sly preferred to avoid. She turned to Alpha and opened her mouth to request she find Jet. She glimpsed Ajax and his brothers in the hall that led to the healing wing, where Jensen and Steve were undoubtedly sitting around.

Sly heard a primal scream of rage and before she even had a chance to turn her head, she was crashing to the floor along with Onyx. Sly hit the marble and was thrown over Onyx by the force that had tackled them. She smashed into Alpha's legs, sending the rebel leader to the floor as well. Both women let out a grunt of pain when they came into contact with the merciless stone. Sly shook the stars out of her vision first and glanced toward whoever had gotten the jump on her. Passion was straddling Onyx, her hands tightly wrapped about the assassin's throat. Onyx was flapping around weakly like a fish out of water, unable to put up much of a fight with her hands cuffed behind her.

"Well, this was entirely expected," Sly said, sitting and brushing off her hands. She looked up when Ajax bolted off, probably going to get Jet. Sly turned her attention back to Onyx and Passion, briefly wondering if she should do something. Onyx looked over at her, wide-eyed. It was the first time Sly had ever seen the assassin genuinely scared. She smiled and rested her chin on her folded hands when

Onyx let out a strangled gurgling noise.

"What was that, Onyx?" Sly asked, tilting her head a little. "Didn't quite hear you."

The assassin let out another strangled gasp. Sly raised her eyebrows, turning her attention to Passion. The guardian's irises had turned blood red.

"Passion, I don't think Onyx can breathe," Sly observed. Passion didn't seem to hear her as she continued strangling the assassin. Sly looked back to Onyx and spread her hands.

"Shouldn't we do something?" Alpha asked as she got back to her feet, looking between the guardian and Sly.

"Passion, no. Stop," Sly said lethargically, crossing one long leg over the other and examining her nails.

"She deserves to die," Passion replied in a chillingly calm tone, though her voice did tremble a bit. "After what she did, she deserves to die like the animal she is."

Sly looked up at Alpha, shrugging. "She makes a good point. Can't really argue with it."

Alpha approached the guardian, crouching down next to her. "Passion, please listen to me. Do you really want to sink to her level? What right do you have to take her life? Are you the Meadows' executioner?"

"She killed my daughter, that's what gives me the right," Passion snapped, her grip tightening as tears began to creep down her cheeks. Onyx's breath was coming out in strangled little gasps and her lips were beginning to turn a light shade of blue. Alpha looked around for anyone to help her.

"Passion!"

As if materializing out of thin air, Jet was there on Passion's other side. He struggled to disengage her strong grasp, finally breaking her grip on the assassin's throat. Onyx rolled to her side and coughed harshly as she struggled to get her breath back.

Jet pulled Passion away, even as she continued to struggle against him.

"Damn you! Let me go!" she snapped at him.

"Not until you've calmed down," he responded. "You cannot do this!"

"I really think she can," Sly put in, amusement clear in her voice. Jet glared at her.

"Not a good time, Sly," he said. Sly leaned back on her elbows, a small half-grin dancing across her lips. Jet turned his attention back to Passion, spinning her around so he was blocking her view of Onyx.

"Passion, I need to question her. If you want justice for your daughter, you have to let Lilly and I do our job."

"I'm just supposed to let her live?"

"Yes, Passion. I'm afraid you are."

Passion shook her head, tears welling up in her eyes. "It isn't fair. It isn't right."

"No, it's not," Jet agreed. "But you know as well as I do that's life. We have to take the higher road. It's what makes us different from people like Onyx."

Passion stared at him for a beat, shook her head again, and made her way to the staircase, climbing up the steps. Jet nodded to Ajax, who quickly approached.

"Look after her. I'll be in after the interrogation," Jet requested before turning his attention to Sly, Alpha, and Onyx. "You all right, Sly? Alpha?"

"Oh yeah, peachy keen. Thanks to your *excellent* timing, I'm pretty sure I only have a minor concussion," Alpha grumbled as she got to her feet. Sly gave him a thumbs up. Around them, things were beginning to move about again, back on schedule now that the crisis was over.

Jet pulled Onyx to her feet, gripping her arm as she wavered on unsteady legs, still coughing and gagging. Sly stood up and smoothed the front of her pants.

"Was she any trouble?" Jet asked.

Alpha snorted and Sly raised an eyebrow. "Define *trouble*."

"That's what I thought," Jet said as he turned back to Onyx. "Well, lucky for you, we found you before you could disappear. Now, I think it's about time you and I had a little chat. Shall we?"

He shoved Onyx forward, unconcerned that she fell to her knees before rising again. She turned toward him, anger blazing in her yellow eyes.

"I won't tell you a goddamn thing," she hissed. Jet smiled before giving her another rough shove toward the dungeons. The messengers avoided eye contact and scattered out of the way when the assassin was shoved at them. Nobody attempted to hinder Jet as he marched her in the direction of the interrogation rooms.

The two women watched as Jet and Onyx disappeared down a flight of stairs at the far end of the main hall. Alpha brushed herself off, obviously less than happy with the rough treatment.

"Well, that was fun," she commented as she pulled her iPod out of her pocket and checked it for damage. Finding it still in working order, she put the earbuds in her ears and turned her music on. She began to bob her head to the music as she followed Sly to the healing wing to check on Steve and Jensen. Alpha hung a few feet back and slipped a small dark red cell phone out of her left pocket. Alpha glanced up at Sly's back as they approached the doors to the large room. She unlocked the cell phone screen, ignoring the few voice and text messages she had, and selected the icon she needed. With her thumb, she selected the contact she wanted and then typed a brief message. As they entered the healing ward, Alpha pressed *send* and slipped the phone back into her pocket.

~~*~*~*

The two inhabitants of the secluded cabin were wide awake. Sun bathed the entire dwelling in a cheerful glow, illuminating all the furniture and art within the home. The cabin was immaculate because the doctor had been up all night cleaning. Years of working in the Grenich

210

Corporation and the endless daily stress had caused him to develop mild obsessive-compulsive disorder. He discovered cleaning helped keep the nightmares, both sleeping and waking, away. There was not a speck of dust in sight. The doctor cleaned the entire cabin top to bottom every other day. The only room he avoided was Blitz's. Even though she was out, the doctor still respected her personal space. The Corporation had not allowed any kind of privacy. Everything there was monitored by hidden cameras and guards. They went so far as to actually bathe the experiments, even though they were more than capable of doing so on their own. Grenich had always been inventive when it came to degrading shape shifters.

But something was tugging at the doctor's mind, an unknown or unrealized fear. There was something behind her door he had to see, perhaps something that would explain the way she was acting or where she had gone. He paused, looking up and down the hall. Jack was most likely in his own room or in the main room, probably with his nose buried in a book. He allowed the doctor in his room earlier that morning. The notion of privacy still bewildered Jack. The doctor ran a hand over the three days of stubble on his face.

"Sorry about this, Blitz," he murmured to the absent woman. His hand closed around the knob and he turned it. The doctor pushed the door inward and found that all the blinds had been drawn. Not only that, the room was completely bare. It was like the cells at Grenich; just the necessities and nothing else. No art on the walls, no books on the shelves, and the bed had obviously never been touched. Blitz had made the room as sterile and devoid of life as she could. It disturbed the doctor.

Shards of glass on the dresser caught his eye. She had shattered the mirror, probably with her fist. The doctor moved in for a closer look when something on the other side of the light-colored bureau caught his sharp blue eyes. There, in the small wicker garbage basket, was a mess of white tissues. What concerned him though were the red stains that starkly stood out against the white. The doctor grabbed the wastebasket and turned it over, spilling red-stained tissues everywhere. His concern grew as he sorted through them. The blood had first been a few speckles, but it had gradually been turning a darker color with clots. *Guardians have mercy, Blitz. Why didn't you tell me?* he thought. As he remembered the past few weeks, the doctor mentally slapped himself for not seeing it. He was a doctor, how could he not have seen it?

The doctor moved toward the door, his cleaning now forgotten. He stormed out of the room and up the hall to the main entertainment room. Sure enough, Jack was sitting on the couch, back to him, head angled slightly down. He was reading.

"Why didn't you tell me?" the doctor shouted. Jack turned around and looked at him, unbothered by the doctor's sharp tone.

"Pardon?" he asked.

"Why didn't you tell me Blitz was infected with something?" the doctor snapped, unable to keep the anger out of his voice. He was not really upset with Jack. His anger was more frustration at the fact that he had missed indications of Blitz's deteriorating health. The sun continued to beat down upon them from the large bay windows. It was a nice day, but Jack and the doctor didn't notice.

Jack looked straight ahead for a moment. "That would explain the paleness of her skin and the sudden spells of low energy."

"What are her other symptoms?" the doctor demanded. "Has she been vomiting? Seizures? Is blood pouring from every orifice? Help me out here, Jack!"

Jack closed his book and placed it on the coffee table as he straightened up into a sitting position. "There have been a few times when I showered and noticed the faint odor of vomit—"

"When?"

Jack shrugged, his eyes traveling over the woven carpet behind the couch. "Past few weeks, probably since she's been going out hunting."

The doctor began to pace, rubbing his forehead. "So her health has been deteriorating for weeks unbeknownst to either of us? That makes a whole hell of a lot of sense!"

"Doctor, she is an experiment. You know as well as I do that you generally can't tell something's wrong with us until we drop. We were modified to mask all forms of weakness," Jack pointed out softly. "You shouldn't blame yourself."

"She's not dead, Jack! Quit talking like she is!" the doctor snapped, his blue eyes blazing. "Okay, if I were an experiment, where would I go?"

He continued pacing and muttering to himself, wracking his mind for an answer. He could feel Jack's eyes on him, but disregarded the experiment. Blitz could be almost anywhere.

A sudden beeping and vibrating noise brought Jack's attention to the coffee table. The doctor's cell phone sat there. Jack reached forward and grabbed it, ignoring the doctor's quiet mutterings. He unlocked the screen, unbothered that it didn't belong to him. Jack's glowing brown eyes stared back at him in the phone's screen as he scanned the message.

"I know it's a virus developed at the Corporation, probably given to her just before she was extracted. That time frame narrows it down to, oh, just a hundred of the viruses they've created," the doctor continued speaking to himself, not paying attention to Jack rising from the couch and approaching him. "I'm going to have to do a blood test and physical to determine what exactly I'm dealing with. That's assuming I have any time if we manage to find her. I don't even know where to start looking—"

"I do," Jack stated, standing in front of the doctor to halt his pacing. He handed him the cell phone, the screen alight with a text message. The doctor frowned, his face falling as he read the message. *Ah dammit,* he thought. He rubbed the back of his neck, closed his eyes, and turned his face to the ceiling.

"We have to go," the doctor said, defeated. "That's almost certainly where she's headed."

"Think they'll be able to handle it?"

The doctor shrugged. "It's anyone's guess. The protectors are beginning to ask the right questions concerning Grenich, although a part of me wonders if they'll ever be ready for what we know. To tell you the truth, Jack, it might be too soon. If Blitz's life didn't depend on me getting to her, I don't know if I would go."

"She may not even be there," Jack offered.

The doctor shook his head. "You and I both know she'll go wherever her target is. The best we can hope to do is beat her there. Then maybe she'll at least have a chance of pulling through."

Jack glanced around at the secluded cabin. This place had been welcoming, providing an odd sensation of inner warmth he hadn't experienced before. For one of the first times, the doctor could see hesitation in the experiment. Jack's sharp glowing eyes traveled back to the doctor, who was watching him.

"We should go," Jack said. The doctor smiled and nodded once.

"I'll get my bag," he replied grimly. He turned around and walked quietly back to where his own room was. Time was the one thing they needed, and it had almost run out.

~~*~*~*

Jet and Onyx sat across from each other in one of the interrogation rooms in the dungeons. The walls were bare, as was the floor. There was a plain table between them and they each sat in a hard wooden chair. A cold feeling seeped through the plain gray walls. At the top of each wall was a flat strip of clear glass glowing with clean light, illuminating everything within the simple room.

Onyx sat with her back straight, one leg crossed over the other, and her hands folded in front of her. Her dark hair was dyed an artificial red color. Her yellow eyes watched every move the protector made. Her run-in with Passion had left her with five large scratches across her cheek. Her right eye was swelling up and would no doubt be a shiner in the morning.

Jet sat in a similar rigid posture, but his arms were casually crossed over his chest. He had rolled up the sleeves on his blue shirt. His light blue-green eyes watched Onyx, waiting for her to try and bait him. He had heard just about everything Sly had said through her earpiece. He was also curious about the lack of western attire and sudden reckless nature of the assassin.

"I could sit here all day," Onyx remarked, daring him to try and crack her.

"As could I," Jet replied. "So why don't we try to make this easy? Why did you kill her?"

Onyx chuckled, shaking her head once. "Come on, Jet. You're going to start with the most obvious question? The price was right so I killed her, end of story. It's never personal with assassins. I killed her for the same reason I killed your other girls: money. It's what makes the world go round."

"Who ordered the hit?" Jet asked calmly. He knew that Onyx would try and goad him, but she wouldn't succeed. His father and Remington had taught him about the art of interrogation and how to maintain his cool during questioning. Though he found Onyx despicable, Jet had left his personal feelings at the mansion. There was nothing the assassin could say that would get under his skin.

"Sorry babe, client confidentiality," Onyx answered as she leaned back in her chair. She tilted it up on two legs, balancing perfectly.

"What happened to your usual style?" Jet asked, changing the subject. He planned on rotating the questions around until he got all the answers he desired. Jet was patient and prepared to go all night if he had to.

"Routine makes it easy to get caught," Onyx stated with a shrug. Jet's trained eye caught the sudden stiffening in her posture. It happened so fast he almost missed it. She was nervous.

"What do you know about—?"

He was interrupted by the door behind him opening. Jet looked over his shoulder, surprised to see Artemis poke her head in. Her dark hair was still damp, indicating that she had recently showered or gone for a swim.

"Jet, there's something you should see," she said softly. Jet noticed the careful way she chose her words. Artemis was amazingly well-spoken and it was the first time Jet had heard hesitance in her voice.

"Can it wait?" Jet asked. Artemis shook her head and Jet couldn't read her expression. She was purposely not looking in Onyx's direction. Jet knew it was to keep her composure. The assassin across from Jet had murdered her granddaughter and it was only from years of experience that Artemis managed to maintain her composure.

Jet ran his hands over his face. The day was turning out to be quite a long one indeed.

"Better go see what's got the old hag so nervous, Jet," Onyx's taunting voice filtered through his mind as he looked over at her. "I promise to sit here and behave like a good little lapdog."

Both Jet and Artemis looked at Onyx as she smiled and rocked her chair back and forth. Jet rose out of his chair and leaned forward so he was towering over Onyx. He felt a faint sense of satisfaction when he saw she didn't like the change in positions.

"I know you're going to sit here and behave because you really don't a choice now do you?" he stated coldly. "I'll be back momentarily and we will pick up where we left off."

With that, Jet turned and followed Artemis out into the hallway. He closed the door and locked it. He quickly tested the knob, which only turned partway.

"Artemis, what is so important it needs my immediate attention?" Jet asked the guardian. She swallowed as they continued down the hall toward the steps leading out of the dungeons. They walked in a heavy silence that seemed to grow with each step, almost becoming suffocating. The usual sound of the messengers rushing about was absent and it sent a chill down the protector's spine. An uncomfortable feeling grew in the pit of his stomach as icy tendrils of apprehension gripped him. His shirt collar seemed tight and Jet stuck his left index finger in to adjust it.

"Artemis, please tell me what's going on," Jet quietly requested. "Why is it so quiet?"

"See for yourself," Artemis replied as they emerged into the large main hall of the castle. She stepped to the side, allowing Jet to see the two figures that stood in the center of the large main hall. Jet felt incredibly small in the wide open space.

The two men were roughly equal in height and both had their backs to him. One stood slightly behind the other. The man closest to the protector leader was wearing a dark gray shirt and dark blue jeans. He had dark olive-colored skin and dark hair cut incredibly short, almost a crew cut but with just slightly more body. Jet stepped forward, glimpsing Adonia and Lilly over the shoulder of the man who stood in front of the one closest to him. The man wore a plain light blue shirt and tan pants. On his feet were plain blue and gray sneakers. He had brown hair, which was on the lighter side and almost sandy in color.

Jet took another step forward so he was a few steps behind the man closest to him, opening his mouth to ask who the men were. The man in front of Jet went completely rigid. He spun around and before Jet knew what was happening, his feet were kicked out from under him and he was slammed to the hard floor. All the oxygen seemed to leave his body in a rush as his back contacted with the stone. The stranger's hand was locked around his throat, making it almost impossible to breathe. When his sight was clear again, Jet found himself looking up into a pair of unnaturally luminous brown eyes. Distantly, he heard voices, most of them alarmed. He recognized all of them, although he had to be mistaken about one. Perhaps it was a hallucination brought on by oxygen deprivation.

"Jack! Stop!" the familiar voice shouted. "Let him go! That's Jet!"

The glowing brown eyes softened and the man studied Jet's face. The pressure gradually left Jet's throat and he coughed loudly, struggling to get his breath back. He unconsciously massaged his sore neck with one hand, propping himself up with one elbow. Lilly was at his side in an instant, kneeling beside him and looking him over for any injuries.

"Jet, are you all right?" she asked, concern clear in her voice. Jet coughed and nodded, waving to indicate he was fine.

"I'm sorry," the experiment apologized in a mellow tone. Jet stared at him in complete shock, stunned at his strength and speed. He had barely even seen the man move when he had thrown him. He looked like a completely normal shape shifter, aside from the glowing eyes. There was something else about him though, something that was off. Jet immediately thought of the rebel stories about the strange glowing-eyes. The experiment, Jack as the other man had called him, rose to his feet with an effortlessness not even the guardians were capable of. The smooth way Jack moved was like nothing Jet had ever seen before.

Jack held out a hand to Jet. Jet recoiled slightly and stared at the hand as if it would bite him, debating whether or not to take it. With some reluctance, he put his hand in

Jack's and allowed the experiment to help him up. Jet felt the muscles in Jack's hand tense a little but he didn't have time to ponder the strange reaction since the experiment pulled him up so quickly Jet was sure he felt his feet leave the ground for a moment. The strength the man possessed was simply astonishing. When he was on his feet again, Jet took a step back from the experiment. He felt Lilly's gentle hands on his arm as she stood beside him. Jet smoothed the front of his shirt, making sure to keep the strange man in his line of sight.

"I'm sorry, Jet," the other man apologized. "Had I known you were coming up behind us, I would've warned you."

Jet turned stunned eyes to the other man, whom he had almost forgotten about. For a moment, he was sure he was seeing things. The man who stood before him — it couldn't be. He had been dead for over thirty years now. Jet blinked and shook his head, hoping to wake himself up. When he opened his eyes, the man still stood before him. He glanced over to Adonia, who looked quite troubled. Looking to his wife, Jet saw that Lilly wore a similar expression as she turned her eyes to the other man.

"Orion?" Jet asked the only thing he could think at the moment.

~~*~*~*

In the interrogation room, Onyx was becoming incredibly bored. She sat in the seat Jet had occupied, already having slipped out of her handcuffs. She massaged her wrists, which were bright red from the tight cuffs. The older shape shifters had mastered the ability of changing form almost to the point of making it a fine science. Onyx was fairly young, barely over two hundred, but her mentors had schooled her well. At the age of one hundred, she had already mastered the art of changing only certain parts of her body. It was fairly simple to slip out of cuffs when she changed her hands from human form into dog paws.

There was no hope of amusing herself though, aside from changing seats. The room was bare except for the lights, table, and two chairs. Jet had escorted her to the interrogation room and emptied her pockets, handing the contents off to a couple messengers. He was nothing if not thorough. On the rare occasions Onyx had been captured, her enemies usually missed at least one or two smaller weapons.

The assassin groaned and leaned back, her red hair cascading down the back of the chair in a sleek wave. She turned her face to the ceiling and closed her eyes, wondering what the hell the holdup was. Jet was annoying, but at least he gave her something to do.

Behind her closed lids, she felt a strange light on her face. Onyx's eyes snapped open and she lowered the two front legs of the chair to the drab gray ground. They made a hollow thunking noise as they met the stone beneath her. In the corner, there was a silver glow. It was dim and slightly dirty-looking, a sickly sort of light. Onyx frowned as she watched it gradually increase in brightness. She had seen guardians and shape shifters Appear before, but there was usually a bright flash of light before a form took shape. This light was pitiful and incredibly weak. It was also taking a lot longer than Onyx had ever witnessed. Usually Appearing only took a few seconds.

A shadowy form took shape in place of the light, which vanished quickly. Once the person had appeared, she lurched forward and braced herself against the table. Onyx jolted, her entire body going rigid. The stranger's head was down so Onyx only saw the top of her short dark hair. A dripping noise brought the assassin's attention to the immaculate table. Small droplets of blood splattered on the clean surface at a steady rate. Onyx gulped and heard a click in her throat. She knew who it was, even before she saw the skintight catsuit. Onyx glanced at one lithe arm holding the woman steady and her frightened reflection stared back at her from the shiny blackness molded around the willowy limb. A sudden hacking cough brought Onyx's attention back to the woman's face, still turned toward the ground, angled in such a way that Onyx couldn't see her features. More crimson droplets speckled the smooth surface of the table. The woman was breathing strangely. Each breath rattled in her chest. She was sick, probably dying, judging from the amount blood she was hacking up.

As if reading her thoughts, the woman's head slowly rose. Onyx suppressed a shudder when she saw the glowing green eyes, which were as cold as the Arctic. A shimmering silver charm sat at her pale throat. The most frightening thing about the woman was the two thin lines of blood that ran under her eyes and trailed out from the corners like tears. The dark, muddied red liquid slowly crept down her face. The woman paid the blood absolutely no heed.

In a movement faster than any eye could see, Blitz had drawn her gun and pointed it steadily at Onyx's face. Her legs wavered, no longer wanting to support her svelte body, but her arm never shook.

Onyx raised her hands, hoping to placate the experiment. "Whoa, whoa. You really don't want to do that. Okay? I've got connections. Whatever answers you want, about the Corporation or anything else, I can get them. The heads of Grenich, they're the ones you should really be pissed at. I'm just—"

"Their pawn?" Bitz asked in a raspy whisper.

"Well, I wouldn't say pawn exactly," Onyx quickly amended her answer when Blitz's finger tightened around the trigger, "Or you could say pawn, I guess. Look, as much as I hate to admit it, I'm just as much a victim as you are. But, with your ability and my connections, we could take them on. You want revenge, right? So, let's go after the right people. I'm an assassin, you're a modified killing machine, it's a match made in heaven. What do you say?"

Blitz was silent for a moment as she just watched Onyx, her countenance blank. The pain in her body was reaching an agonizing level and she knew her end was very near. Her thoughts were of Jack and the doctor, but she didn't know why. Her vision, completely black and white, seemed a little fuzzy now. Her eyes never moved from Onyx. She noticed the assassin's body tense as she prepared to do something. People never changed and many never learned.

"You should've stayed out of Grenich affairs," she stated quietly. Then she squeezed the trigger.

~~*~*~*

The Meadows was a relatively peaceful place. It resembled a paradise untouched by the modern age. There were no computers in sight or electrical sockets or any other kind of "modern day wonder." They had some technology, but it was kept out of sight for fear it would ruin the peaceful serenity flowing throughout the untainted lands. No guardian had ever or would ever even think of handling a gun. Guns were an evil only protectors had to deal with.

War had not touched the lands for millennia and only Death had to deal with mortality on a regular basis, which was probably one of the reasons he was frequently irritable. Violence, unfortunately, was a part of life. Therefore, guardians were exposed to it early. But they were only aware of the violence that occurred within nature or which affected it in some way. The shape shifters were much more familiar with violence since they lived on Earth. So it was no surprise that there was a wide range of reactions to the sound of a shot emanating from the interrogation room.

In her room, Passion had been reminiscing with Ajax. Aside from Jet and Lilly, the Deverell brothers were some of the closest friends Passion had. When Electra was growing up, they had always been ready and willing to lend a helping hand. Ajax opened his mouth to speak when a strange sound shattered the peacefulness of the Pearl Castle. It wasn't the harsh report of a normal gun. It was a soft noise, an almost metallic sound, which rang through the vents. Passion's eyes went wide and she looked at Ajax. He had risen off the bed and moved to the door, opening it to look out into the empty hallway. That hadn't sounded like any gun he had ever heard before, but it was undeniably a shot.

The dungeons were the closest to the interrogation rooms. Roan had been taking a light nap, unaware of anything happening above him. The sudden sound of the shot caused him to jerk awake. His green eyes were wide as he sat straight up on his cot, looking toward the glass. Immediately leaping to his feet, he stood in front of the glass and tried to see down the hall. He pounded the glass a couple times, calling for Astrea. Roan knew the sound of the weapon. It had been specially made, like all the ones Orion had. He felt a small amount of fear for the first time in his life. Something bad had happened and he couldn't just stand idly by, not if he could be doing something to help. His calls went unheeded as the dungeons went into lockdown.

In the healing rooms, Amethyst had just finished healing Steve and Jensen. Steve was content to just lie back on his bed and relax whereas Jensen was sitting on the edge of his and drumming his fingers. Orion had always complained that Jensen wouldn't be able sit still if his life depended on it. Alpha was straddling a chair backward, listening to her iPod while Sly sat in a similar fashion next to her. Electra sat next to Steve's bed, one hand propping up her head, her feet resting on his bed. The Four had also joined them and were sitting in chairs off to the side, except for Shae, who was sitting on Steve's bed and swinging her legs back and forth. Sly had been filling them in on what had happened, starting from when they first entered Onyx's villa and continuing on until they were all up to speed. Amethyst had been making her way out of the room when the strange metallic sigh reached their ears. All of them, except Alpha, jumped and looked toward the door. Electra was the first to break the silence with a simple question.

"What was that?"

~~*~*~*

Quiet had fallen over the small group in the main hall as Jet struggled to comprehend the fact that another supposedly dead man was standing before him. Orion looked almost exactly like he had the last time Jet had seen him. The protector looked a lot more drawn and had lost a noticeable amount of weight. His once lively eyes now seemed dull and tired, but it was definitely him. Adonia stood behind him, watching Jet. Artemis stood just behind Jet, unsure of what to make of the whole situation. She had been startled by the quickness and efficiency with which Jack moved. Lilly still stood beside her husband, watching the two visitors in the hall. Her mouth was set in a thin line and she had one hand resting on Jet's arm.

"I know you probably have a lot of questions," Orion began.

"Questions? I *probably* have a lot of questions?" Jet asked incredulously, anger creeping into his usually calm voice. "Of all the lunacy I have seen in my life, *this* has to take the cake! Resurrection! Of all the things I really *don't* need at the moment! First Roan and now you? At least with Roan we never actually found a body."

Jet felt Lilly intertwine her fingers with his, giving his hand a gentle squeeze. He realized he was close to shaking with anger.

"Jet, please," Orion pleaded, his voice soft and even. "I promise, I'll tell you everything you want to know but—"

"You better believe you're going to tell me all I want to

know and then some," Jet interrupted, noticing the other man, Jack, was looking around uneasily. He didn't look in awe like most people did when they first visited the Meadows and the beautiful homes of the guardians. The man seemed to be on edge and was doing his best not to show it.

"Look, I don't have time for this," Orion suddenly took on an urgent tone. "Where is Onyx?"

"Why do you want to know?" Jet countered and Jack shook his head.

"Excuse me? Jack, was it?" Lilly suddenly spoke up. "Are you all right?"

Jack turned his glowing brown eyes to her, nodding once. "Yes, ma'am. I am fine."

Jack glanced over to where Artemis stood, between him and the dungeons. She looked away when Jack looked in her direction, doing her best to be polite and not stare. Jet disregarded him for the moment.

"Jet, listen to me. She's in a lot of danger at the moment and she's not the only one. If you want her to live long enough to answer your questions you'll—"

A strange sound suddenly echoed throughout the entrance hall of the large castle. It was soft but had a metallic ring to it. It reminded Jet of the futuristic guns in the awful sci-fi films his son, Cassidy, enjoyed. He felt Lilly's hand tighten on his as she twisted to look behind them at the entrance to the dungeons. Orion's eyes widened and he muttered something under his breath. Adonia stiffened in surprise and Artemis let out a quiet gasp, turning to look behind her where the noise had come from.

Jet glared at Orion one last time before turning on his heel and walking toward the dungeons, ignoring Orion's warnings for him to wait.

"Will you keep an eye on them?" he asked Lilly and she nodded once.

As he passed Artemis, Jet exchanged a look with her.

He was going down to the dungeons alone and wanted the guardians to help his wife keep an eye on their unexpected visitors until he returned. Artemis nodded once in understanding and Jet was again reminded why it was an advantage to be so close to the guardians.

He walked down the hall, ignoring Orion's protests, and entered the door leading down to the dungeons. The large door closed behind him, cutting off Orion's voice. Jet continued down the stairs, swiftly reaching the bottom. He turned right, heading for the interrogation rooms.

"They should really install two-way mirrors," Jet muttered to himself as he fished the key to the room out of his pocket. He paused when he reached the door, straining his ears in the hopes of picking up any noise that would tell him what was going on in there.

Jet bounced the key on his palm as he debated whether or not to call out. He stuck the key in the lock as quietly as he could, cringing at each noise the small key made. When he was trying to be quiet, Jet's hearing always sharpened. Whispers sounded like shouts and something as simple as a key turning in a lock sounded as loud as a gunshot.

The deadbolt slid open and Jet grasped the silver knob, preparing himself for whatever he would see.

The first thing he noticed was the amount of blood splattered across the once spotless room. Judging from the amount and the spray pattern, Jet could tell almost immediately that someone had been shot at close range. His gaze fell to his chair where Onyx's body was slumped. Her head was back, facing toward the ceiling, and the bullet had struck her between the eyes, which were opened and staring blankly. Blood was splattered all over her face, rendering her almost unrecognizable. Jet had seen many gruesome things in his long life, but the sight made his stomach twist. The overwhelming scent of blood filled the room and made it even harder to quell the nauseous feeling. He could hear the soft dripping noise of blood hitting the ground. All thoughts of the mess in front of him left Jet's mind when he saw who stood across the table from him and Onyx's body.

At first, Jet didn't recognize her. It had been five years and she looked so much different than he remembered. Her dark hair was cropped extremely short and dyed black in color. She was even thinner than when she had first come to the mansion. She was clothed in a form-fitting black catsuit and a silver charm hung about her throat.

She was looking down at the floor, wavering a little on her feet. Her skin was unnaturally pale. A gun that looked similar to a Beretta was grasped in her right hand, which was relaxed at her side. One shaking hand held her upright, as she braced herself against the table. *She doesn't know I'm here,* Jet realized. He swallowed and pushed any trepidation to the back of his mind.

"Isis?" he asked gently, just loud enough so she would hear him.

It was as if an electric current suddenly zapped through her body, shocking her to life. Her body jerked to a rigid posture and Jet found himself staring down the barrel of her gun. He saw her green eyes and felt his heart break. They were unnaturally luminous, just like Jack's. Isis had been experimented on. There was no sign of recognition in her eyes, just two trails of blood dribbling down her face in dark crimson streaks. She kept the gun trained right between his eyes, probably exactly as she had killed Onyx.

Jet opened his mouth to say something, hopefully talk her into giving the gun to him, but didn't get a chance.

She pulled the trigger.

~~*~*~*

After eliminating the assassin, Blitz leaned against the table in the room. She closed her eyes and rubbed them, smearing blood beneath her eyes. Exhaustion had seeped into her bones long ago. Her climbing temperature was now exactly 104.9 degrees Fahrenheit, 40.5 degrees

Celsius...

Her mind drifted just as it began to convert her temperature into Kelvin scale. The next thing Blitz was aware of was a soft voice — familiar though she couldn't really place from where — speaking a name she recognized from mythology: *Isis.* She forced her dying body to life, jerking up and pointing the gun at her unwanted company.

A man stood near the assassin's body, looking at her with light-colored eyes. When their eyes met, Blitz read the same kind of sympathy in the stranger's eyes as she had multiple times in the doctor's. It was a strange longing to make everything better even though it was impossible. Her vision was blurry now and everything was in strange gray blobs. The second their eyes met, Blitz pulled the trigger. A hollow click reached her ears; the gun was empty. She dropped it, listening to it clatter on the stone floor. *Oh well,* she thought with her usual detachment. Blitz could have stabbed him with a sai or combat knife, but she just didn't have the energy anymore. He hadn't been on her list anyway.

"The rest is silence," her strange specter whispered softly in her ear, her glow warming Blitz's left side. Blitz swallowed and her vision suddenly went black. She felt herself falling.

CHAPTER ELEVEN

Jet lunged forward the second Isis' legs buckled, just barely preventing her from striking the stone floor. The bright glow of the lights in the room enhanced the unnaturally pallid complexion of her skin. Jet gently ran his hand over her forehead, his concern increasing ten-fold when he felt the heat radiating off her. She was burning up and it was only a matter of time before her temperature reached dangerous levels. *If it hasn't already,* Jet thought as he lifted her willowy form into his arms. One arm was under her knees and the other supported her back. Jet was shocked by how light she was. He turned and moved out of the interrogation room, away from the scene of blood and gore.

As he made his way down the hall that led out of the dungeon, Jet's mind raced. There were so many things to take in: first Orion, and now Isis. Isis, what had happened to her? The woman in his arms was nothing like he remembered. She had been bold but never murderous. *She almost killed me,* Jet realized as his eyes traveled back down to the silver charm that glittered at her throat. The elusive Blitz, she had been the one responsible for so many deaths. Jet shook the dark thoughts out of his mind as he hurried up the stairs toward the main hall of the castle. After she had been taken care of, he would ask the questions that needed answering.

As he entered the main hall, he saw Jack and Orion. Jack's eyes immediately traveled to Isis' limp form and then to Orion, exchanging a look with him. Lilly, Adonia, and Artemis all looked taken off guard when they saw the ailing woman in Jet's arms. The three women moved forward to help.

"Stop! Don't touch her!" Orion's bellowed order stopped everyone in their tracks. Even Jet went rigid at the command. The shape shifter hurried forward and placed a hand on Isis' forehead, a frown twisting his features.

"I need to be shown to an isolated room or cell, preferably with reinforced walls," he said, his attention never moving from Isis. "If you want me to save her, you have to do everything I say without question. I promise once I'm done with her, I will answer all your questions."

Jet exchanged a look with Adonia, clueless about what to do. It was the first time he saw the guardian queen look just as unsure as he felt. Lilly stood beside her husband again and she reached out a hand, running it over Isis' brow.

"Jet, she's burning up," she whispered, alarmed.

"She doesn't have time! I need somewhere isolated with a door that locks from the outside!" Orion snapped. Jet opened his mouth to protest when Isis suddenly began shaking in his arms. The trembling was so violent Jet almost dropped her. Orion stepped forward and took her svelte form out of his arms. Jack moved to his side to help.

"This way, Orion," Adonia finally spoke and gestured toward the dungeons.

"Jack, get my bag," Orion managed to grunt out as he struggled to hold onto the seizing woman. Jack snatched the dark bag that had been sitting unnoticed beside Orion. The experiment swiftly followed Orion and Adonia, disappearing behind the door leading down to the dungeons.

Jet watched as the door softly shut behind them, internally debating whether or not he should follow. He turned to look at Artemis and Lilly. Both women looked as unsettled as Jet felt. He glanced back toward the door Orion, Adonia, Jack, and Isis had disappeared behind and then looked to Artemis and Lilly again.

"Lilly, I need you to tell the Deverell brothers, the Four, and Remington that we're going to have a meeting here in half an hour," Jet said. "I'm going down to have a brief talk with Roan."

He was about to leave but was by stopped Lilly's quiet voice. "Jet?"

Jet turned back from the dungeon, trying to ignore the dark red droplets of blood he knew were from Isis. Artemis stood with her arms crossed over her chest.

"What about Passion and Electra?" Lilly asked. Jet closed his eyes and rubbed the back of his neck. His mind hadn't even had a chance to process the most recent curveball thrown at him, much less how he would break the news to the mother and sister of the apparently resurrected shape shifter. What if they lost her again? A rising fever, seizing, blood flowing from her eyes; none of the symptoms boded well for Isis.

"You two go speak with my daughter and granddaughter," Artemis said, drawing their attention to her. "I shall gather the others."

Jet turned his eyes to Lilly, nodding once.

"We'll tell Passion," Jet said softly, changing his path. Roan could wait, at least until after they got what they needed from Orion. Passion and Electra would need the Monroes more. Lilly offered him a reassuring smile and started for the stairway. Jet paused at the bottom of the long flight of marble steps.

"Artemis," he spoke softly. "There's a mess in interrogation room one. I'll explain later, but please ask a messenger to clean it up."

Artemis nodded and walked away. Jet and Lilly walked up the marble staircase, quickly reaching the third level where the private living quarters were. They turned in the direction of Passion's room and Jet saw Ajax exiting it. Ajax spotted the Monroes and approached with a questioning look.

"Was that a gunshot I heard?" he asked as he stopped in front of them.

"Unfortunately yes," Jet replied with a weary sigh. "Ajax, I've got news of a somewhat disconcerting nature."

"Roan's apparent return from the dead and now gunfire in the Meadows? I doubt I'll ever feel disconcerted again." Ajax attempted to lighten the mood. His humor fell flat. He had never been the comedian of the family — that was Nero's job — but after the past few months, it was difficult to laugh at anything.

"Prepare yourself," Jet replied as he glanced behind Ajax to make sure Passion hadn't snuck up on them.

"Orion's alive and so is Isis." Lilly spoke in her usual quiet tone.

Ajax stared at them, his lower jaw dropping open slightly. Jet ran a hand through his hair, messing it up a little, and looked behind him.

"And that's not all," Jet added. "Isis, she's . . . she's different."

"Different?" Ajax asked as Jet looked off to the side again and swallowed. The protector leader nodded and let out his breath slowly, feeling his wife's gentle hand on his arm.

"She's been experimented on. That was the gunfire you heard. She killed Onyx, shot her in the face. Apparently, she's the mysterious Blitz we've been hearing about," Jet explained as he turned his eyes to Ajax once again. "Could you go to the Healing Rooms and send Electra up to Passion's room? We're hoping to have a meeting in about half an hour to figure out what to do. Artemis is gathering the others."

Ajax nodded, still shell-shocked from the most recent revelations. "Where is my older brother now?"

Jet ran a hand over his face. "Isis is really sick, quite possibly dying. Orion and Jack are caring for her in the dungeons, probably the old section. Nobody is to go in there under any circumstances, okay?"

Ajax looked bewildered. "Who the hell is Jack?"

Jet closed his eyes briefly. "Oh, uh, an experiment Orion came with."

Ajax looked rather confused, but he turned and made his way to the stairs, swiftly disappearing from sight. Jet turned his eyes to Lilly, taking her hands within his. She smiled in a comforting way, gently squeezing his hands.

"Are you ready?" Jet asked and Lilly nodded.

"Are you?" she asked. Truth be told, Jet wasn't entirely sure if he was, but he knew he had to be. He nodded and then turned back, letting out a breath before starting toward Passion's door again.

They reached the door and Lilly knocked. Passion called out an invitation and the two protector leaders exchanged a look before Lilly opened the door.

Well, here goes nothing, Jet thought as he quietly stepped inside the room and shut the door behind him.

~~*~*~*

Adonia showed the two men to one of the older sections of the dungeons. The stone cells had thick iron doors with a small slot for sliding meals through and a square opening toward the top with thick bars. There was only a bed, a small desk and chair, and a few other necessities. Out of the corner of his eye, Orion noticed Jack shudder as they entered the space. The room resembled some of the cells at Grenich. Usually experiments never came out of them.

"Jack, set up my bag on the desk. Bring me the color-coded vials and the blood drawing equipment," Orion called over his shoulder as he gently laid Blitz on the bed. He placed two fingers on the inside of her wrist and looked at the simple watch on his free arm. He timed her pulse. Erratic and thready, it wasn't good. He found the zipper on her catsuit and pulled it down, stripping the tight garment off her hot skin. Jack brought Orion some gauze, which the doctor used to dab away the blood running out of Blitz's eyes.

"Get me a pair of latex gloves, a syringe, and a couple vials so I can draw some blood," Orion muttered. "I'm assuming you know how to test for the Omni viruses?"

Jack brought over the things Orion needed. He watched as the doctor swiftly pulled on the tight gloves, flexing his fingers a few times.

"Shouldn't we check some of the shape shifters? They could've been exposed," Jack mentioned.

Orion shook his head as he grabbed the syringe Jack held, quickly working on Isis' arm. "No. They would've displayed symptoms almost immediately had it been one of the newer strands. This is an older virus, not even double digits. If I had to venture a guess, I'd say—"

He was cut off when Isis began to seize violently. Orion swore as he and Jack turned her onto her side, struggling to hold her on the bed. After a moment, the seizing abated as a trickle of blood dribbled from the corner of her mouth. Orion forced her lips open and pulled a small flashlight out of the back pocket of his pants, shining the small circular light inside her mouth, checking to make sure her throat wasn't swelling shut. He would have given anything for a small tube to see down her esophagus.

"Dammit. The internal damage is probably increasing," he said as he switched off the light and put it back in his pocket. He and Jack gently eased the ailing woman onto her back again. She remained unresponsive.

Jack extended her arm and applied the drab yellow tourniquet as Orion sorted out his small glass collection tubes, each color-coded to identify which strand of the Omni virus was contained in them.

Within a matter of minutes, Orion had drawn the nine samples he needed and placed them in the small rack from his bag. He glanced over at Isis' inner elbow where he had drawn the blood. The small puncture was taking an unusually long time to heal. *But it's healing, which means her regenerative abilities are still working,* he reminded himself as he turned his attention to the rack on the desk. The blood in one vial had begun to turn noticeably darker almost immediately: vial number five. Orion lifted the small glass oval up and looked closer. He had thought that particular virus had been eliminated when the more advanced strands had been tested and proved more effective. *I can barely keep up with their advancements anymore,* he thought grimly as he returned the vial to the rack and turned his attention to his bag on the desk.

"Jack, please dispose of the blood," Orion called over his shoulder as he removed a small ampoule filled with a transparent light blue liquid and held it up to the light. Grabbing another syringe out of his bag, he pulled the protective plastic covering off the thin needle with his teeth and spit it out to the side. He stuck the thin silver needle into the small white circle at the top of the ampoule, slowly pulling the plunger back about halfway. His sharp blue eyes checked the precise measurement before he pulled the needle out of the ampoule. Placing the glass bottle on the desk again, Orion flicked the syringe twice, making sure there were no bubbles in the clear blue liquid. Pressing on the plunger, he squirted a short stream of liquid out of the end of the needle to assure it was working correctly.

Orion approached Isis again, cringing when he saw her body was wracked with small tremors. They were cutting it much closer than he would have liked. He took her limp arm and pressed the needle under her skin, pushing the life-saving medicine into her bloodstream. Almost immediately her tremors ceased. Orion laid her arm down again and glanced over at Jack, who had just finished placing the small vials of blood in a plastic container that held the used samples. Orion would have to dispose of it later. He approached Jack and tossed the used syringe into the plastic container. The experiment quickly sealed it and hurried over to where his bag was, placing it inside.

"I'm going to have to answer their questions now," Orion mumbled, sounding as weary as he felt. "Stay with her. She'll be out for—"

"Probably a little more than five hours," Jack interrupted. Orion smiled thinly. He should have known an experiment would be able to estimate the time an antidote would take to work. He rubbed the back of his neck, glancing at the pallid woman on the bed. There was no doubt in his mind Isis had known about the virus.

"Make sure you aren't in the cell when she wakes up. I have a feeling she isn't going to be happy with either one of us," Orion stated as he turned toward the door.

"Doctor?"

"Please, call me Orion, Jack," Orion replied as he turned back, to which the experiment nodded.

"Orion, how did they know to infect her?" Jack asked. "Why her and not me?"

Orion shrugged. "Either sheer coincidence or he anticipated someone infiltrating the facility. The logical side of me says it's the latter."

Jack nodded again and leaned his weight against the desk. "We should consider adjusting our strategy."

"One crisis at a time, Jack," Orion replied, almost pleading with the experiment. Jack nodded in acquiescence but Orion could tell by the look in his glowing eyes he was not satisfied with the response. Experiments, being flawless soldiers, wanted to be prepared at all times. Every issue had to be solved the instant it came up, quickly and efficiently. Unfortunately, non-experiments didn't operate in this way. It was one of the many reasons why experiments had trouble being around normals for long spans of time.

"They may have questions for you later, but don't worry. It won't be an interrogation or mission debriefing," Orion explained. Jack nodded in understanding. Orion turned back to the open door.

"Doc — Orion," Jack's voice halted his forward progression. "Do you think they'll be able to accept us?"

Orion pinched the bridge of his nose, pondering the question for a moment before turning back to look at Jack again. It was a difficult question. Besides the physical appearance and mannerisms of the experiments, there was also the psychological aspect and their instincts. As much as Orion hated to admit it, they were not ordinary shape shifters. Their detachment and lack of clear emotions was probably unlike anything the shape shifters had ever encountered before. Unlike sociopaths, experiments couldn't really mimic emotions believably. They also had difficulty letting go of knee-jerk reactions, which made them dangerous.

"I believe so, but it'll take some time," Orion replied honestly. Jack frowned as he thought over the doctor's answer. He shrugged and stuck his hands in the pockets of his jeans.

"Ah, Jack. You and Coop give me hope even in the bleakest of situations," Orion said with a small smile. He stepped out of the cell, leaving the door open a crack so the experiment could get out if he needed or wanted to. Jack approached the bed Blitz laid on. He pulled a blanket up so her exposed body was concealed. He knew Orion probably wanted to get her into some looser clothing.

Once he was through covering her up, Jack moved to the desk and hopped up on the smooth surface. He ran his hands over his face before holding them in front of him and examining his palms. He slowly rubbed his fingertips together, focusing on his extraordinary sense of touch. It was only now that he was out of the Corporation that he was able to comprehend just how different experiments truly were. Freedom, as Orion called it, allowed him to see what the world was truly like. Inside the Corporation, experiments were made to believe the world outside was simply another extension of Grenich, a simulation that was controlled by the mysterious head. The one who saw and controlled all.

Jack dropped his hands to his lap, glancing at the door. In his mind, he could vividly see the faces of the normals who saw him without the specially made contact lenses or sunglasses. It was fearful awe, usually the last thing he saw in a target's eyes. He turned his attention back to Blitz and focused on her, not wanting to think of the Corporation anymore. *One crisis at a time,* he repeated the doctor's words in his head.

~~*~*~*

Orion emerged from the stairway to the dungeons into the main hall, surprised to find no one waiting for him. There was a random messenger every now and again, hurrying across the marble floor to deliver something somewhere. Surely Isis' loved ones should be out here, anxiously awaiting an update on her condition.

"Orion."

He glanced up at the sound of Adonia's stern voice, spotting her on the second floor in front of an archway leading to the hall where the main meeting room was. She stared down at him, her eyes guarded. Orion remembered the guardian queen as being particularly compassionate. Leave it to him to bring out her distrustful side. She gestured to the lavish stairway in front of him. He nodded and hurried up the steps. Orion soon reached the queen of the guardian women. Adonia turned and led him down the hall to the main meeting room. He followed compliantly. No words were exchanged between them.

They finally reached a large door, which Adonia

opened and gestured for him to enter. Orion did and a similar stony silence fell over the quiet chatter that had been buzzing about prior to his arrival. He walked to the front of the room, staring at his feet the entire way. The eldest Deverell put his hands on the back of the chair placed at the front and raised his blue eyes to take in the familiar faces, which were all glued to him. He saw his brothers along with Jensen. His brothers looked shocked, but Jensen looked more curious. The members of the Four were there, including his daughter Ace, who looked indifferent. Jet and Lilly, Remington, Steve, Artemis, Passion, Electra, and Adonia wore looks of intense scrutiny. Alpha and Sly stuck to the back, both looking rather intrigued in their typical unbothered way.

"I imagine you want to know about Isis' condition. Physically, she'll be fine. I gave her an injection that will eradicate the virus from her system. She'll be awake in about five hours. None of you is to enter the old section of the dungeons without my permission for reasons I'll explain shortly," Orion stated as he leaned down so his forearms rested on the head of the chair, dropping his head. "Where should I begin?"

"How about at the beginning?" Lilly suggested, her tone stern and unyielding. The protectors wanted the facts and nothing else. Orion nodded, though he wondered where exactly the beginning was. He noticed Passion couldn't sit still, which probably didn't bode well for him.

"Let me start off by saying that what I'm about to tell you is only my account. I'm sure Roan has given you his. While I have a bit more information than him, it is not much. I still have some questions I'm trying to find answers to. I have no doubt you'll have questions for me once I'm through," he began. "But first, let me ask: how much has Roan told you?"

"A vague account of a Corporation called Grenich, which is supposedly the root of all evil, using concepts such as intolerance to shield itself, while experimenting on shape shifters and turning them into weapons," Jet responded. "And it's run by a former guardian who now calls himself Set."

"You know, your typical sci-fi, living weapon sort of tale," Nero chimed in. Orion straightened up and ran his hands over the back of the chair. The material was smooth against his palms.

"All right, I'll tell you everything that has happened that I know about. Please don't interrupt me. Save the multitude of questions for after I'm finished," he said as he lifted one hand to run through his brown hair.

"My story begins a couple years after Jet managed to smuggle Nat and Jensen into the country. A man approached me and offered me a job at a research facility. He claimed they were researching different kinds of serums and antidotes to diseases plaguing mankind. It sounded quite promising to me and I have always had a desire to help humans. I met with this man's boss, a Mr. Russell Carding. He was a pleasant enough fellow, warm and inviting. What made me take the job was his humanistic idealism. He was years ahead of his time or so it seemed. He claimed to have been from a family who had known about shape shifters for centuries and he was working to strengthen our alliance. If you ever meet him, I guarantee you'll be drawn in by his charisma.

"Anyway, long story short, I accepted the job of head physician at one of the main research facilities. I lived underground for a couple years, until I met Cheryl and then we were allowed to live within Corporation borders above ground. Years passed without incident. We made astounding progress and life was good. Looking back on it now, there were many warning signs that should've sent up red flags. When I entered Grenich, I was an optimist and I think that may have been my downfall. I treated so many wounded shape shifters, horribly mangled and all of them at death's door. That was when I first began to suspect something. I realized all my patients were shape shifters and their eyes were always concealed for some reason, either with glasses or lenses. No humans at all.

"My suspicion grew when I started paying closer attention to the psychology of my patients. You've come into contact with an experiment already: Coop. At first glance, they're completely unremarkable, totally normal. However there is always something about them that stands out. The way they move, the way they act, almost everything about them is different often in a subtle way. If you spend an extended amount of time with the ones inside the Corporation, you come to realize their emotions are practically non-existent. Their only concern is their objective, the assignment they're expected to carry out. To Grenich, the race of shape shifters is nothing more than products, animals to be used as they see fit. These experiments are brainwashed to believe things like freedom are mere human fairy tales. They know almost everything, but they are also convinced that Grenich is the world. They believe the heads of Grenich control the planet. The experiments are expected to do as their handlers command or they'll suffer the consequences for their insubordination. Once I figured out what was going on, I already had a wife and young daughter at home."

Orion paused, turning his attention to his daughter. "Ace, at this point, I want you to know how truly sorry I am for how the repercussions affected you."

Ace just scowled and looked away, crossing her arms over her chest. Shae put a hand on her shoulder and looked back to Orion, her expression unreadable. Jet glanced over at Ace before looking back to Orion. He crossed his arms over his chest and waited for him to continue. Orion paused, preparing to go on with his dark tale.

"In the end, I knew I wouldn't be able to live with myself if I just stood by and did nothing. I tried to get Cheryl to leave town with Ace, guardians have mercy I tried. But my wife had the same sense of righteousness as I did. We formed a small resistance comprised of fellow shape shifters who knew of the heinous experimentations going on within the walls of the Corporation. Alice and James worked in security. Alice's lover, Matt, worked in the tech department. We staged a plan to bring down Grenich from the inside. Matt was going to release a computer virus into the servers that would shut down the security systems in the facility while Cheryl and I were going to release the experiments. Alice and James were going to keep the guards off our backs. Everything was meticulously planned and we prepared for every possible scenario. We thought our plan was perfect. We were wrong.

"Carding found out about us somehow, or perhaps one of the heads of the Corporation did. They struck first. Alice and Matt were grabbed in their private quarters. James broke them out later and they made a run for it, but they were recaptured soon after and I haven't heard anything of them since. While this was going on, Carding's favored cleaner was hunting Cheryl and me. The assassin got Cheryl first. He lured her down to my offices, posing as me and he—"

Orion paused and swallowed thickly. He looked down and took a few deep breaths, gathering himself for the next part of the story.

"He slit her throat. Then he waited in my office for me. I always got Cheryl and myself coffee in the cafeteria before we went to work. I got to my office, saw her body, and he slammed the door. The two of us were locked in my office. He had a gun pointed right between my eyes, but he hesitated. He couldn't do it. I guess fratricide is the one thing Roan is incapable of. I baited him, yelled at him, dared him to pull that damn trigger, all to no avail. He questioned whether the surveillance bugs were present in my office — they were not — and then he put the gun away. Roan wanted out of the Corporation and he wasn't going to kill me, realizing I might be his only way to get out. So, I decided to follow through with the only option left to me. With my brother's help, I faked my death.

"I dropped Ace off at a Rebel Lair just outside of town, drove back, and gave Roan the proper drugs that would slow all my body's functions so that I would appear dead for a good amount of time. He paid off one of the morgue workers as well as a truck driver. All the employees were terrified of Roan because he was a Grenich enforcer and cleaner. Once Carding had seen my body and ordered me incinerated, Roan went to the control room and opened the cells where the experiments were kept. A few left their cells, some were even cognizant enough to make a run for it, although only about fifteen or so actually escaped from Corporation grounds. Only two remain free today. This created chaos, during which the morgue worker was somehow able to sneak my body out and put me in the truck. Roan was already aboard. He gave me a shot of adrenaline and we were off. We parted ways a short time after and didn't see each other for years. The next time I saw Roan, he was at death's door. I saved him, knowing he could eventually prove to be useful. We've been in hiding ever since, waiting for the perfect opportunity to bring that damn Corporation down.

"That's my story and now I'll tell you some of the things that I know about Grenich. It has been around for millennia. I can't find an exact date, but I do know they were working with genetics long before the field was 'discovered.' They were working with modern technology during the Renaissance. Roan is correct about the head of the Grenich Corporation being a former guardian, Chaos, or Set as he is now called, but few are aware of this. Nobody knows where he is except for the bosses who run the main facilities, which are located all over the globe. The bosses act as the mouthpieces; so normal you could pass by them on the street and not even spare them a second look. However, they are revenants, servants to Set. Most of them died well over two hundred years ago, but

Set gave them a second life to serve him."

Orion paused, drumming his fingers on the back of the chair he leaned over. "Set wants chaos more than anything and he plans to create this using the Key. You see, Set believes it's his destiny to find the Key, which he believes is the ultimate weapon. From what little I've been able to figure out about the prophecy he's following, the Key will have unmatchable skill and infinite knowledge. Whoever controls it would have power over the world and the ability to enter the Meadows, but it's also a bit of a double-edged sword. The Key can also destroy the wielder if not properly understood.

"Finding the Key is proving to be even more difficult than Set anticipated. Through a process that I don't understand, Set has Carding pick certain experiments out of different groups and inject them with something. This study is called Project Mimic. Of the hundreds who have been subjected to these injections, only three have survived. Two of them were Jack, whom a couple of you have met, and Isis. I have an ally who has access to the facility, or at least he did. I'm not sure if he does anymore. He helped me extract them from the Corporation. They've been staying with me ever since, at my cabin."

Orion paused momentarily before turning his eyes to Jet and Lilly, who were watching him intently. "Grenich is an empire, more powerful than any we've ever encountered and it has been around longer than any of us, most current guardians included. Each day they grow stronger. Each day shape shifters die within the facilities or out on missions. They've been committing atrocities for centuries, right under our noses. It's only a matter of time before Set finds his Key and uses it to wipe us out completely. There are revenants in some of the highest offices in government around the world and just as many in the treasury departments of different countries. There are Grenich laboratories all over the world, filled with experiments. Set already controls the majority of the world's wealth and by my estimates, his army of experiments will be double the size of the world's militaries combined in a little less than ten years."

There was quiet for a few moments as the people in the room tried to absorb Orion's information.

"What about my sister?" Electra asked. "What happened to her and why did you have to care for her in an isolated cell?"

Orion turned his attention over to her. "She's been experimented upon, heavily, due to the possibility of her being the Key. She's not the woman you once knew, hence the need to care for her in an isolated cell. It's both for her protection and for yours. Because of the extreme amount of programming experiments undergo, it's difficult for them to return to the regular world. They can adjust, but they are never the same people they were before. Among other things, there are some reflexes that will always be apparent. For example, a mere touch sets off a knee-jerk reaction. They'll twist your arm behind your back and slam you into the nearest solid surface, all in the blink of an eye. I have yet to have a bone broken by an experiment, but I have had a number of bruises, contusions, sprains, and fractures. Jet has had a firsthand experience with their lightning fast reflexes. Lilly, Adonia, and Artemis witnessed the incident as well."

Jet sighed. "He's right. They're faster than anything I've ever seen before. That strength . . . I got the impression Jack could've torn my head off with his bare hands if he wanted."

"Are you telling me Isis is nothing more than a weapon? I refuse to believe that," Passion stated, sounding quite upset. Orion glanced over at her and shook his head.

"No, they're not machines. They can kill, yes, but once off the medications they're given—"

"You keep saying medications," Jade interrupted, leaning forward. "What exactly do these experimentations entail?"

"Nobody knows for sure, aside from those involved in the processes. I can give you a general overview of what happens. Shape shifters are 'recruited' in one of three ways: some are bought, some are born inside the Corporation, and others are simply taken. The ones brought to the main facility from the outside are heavily sedated to the point where they're totally compliant. They're taken to the showering room where they're de-loused, scrubbed down, and then shaved. The whole goal of the first month is to strip them of their identity. Thirty days, that's all it takes for the Grenich Corporation to convince shape shifters they are objects instead of living beings. The second month is when the majority of the modifications take place. This is where it gets very foggy. A medium-sized group is shackled together and taken to Carding's office. They disappear for a couple months, and when the survivors return, they're completely different. Their eyes glow due to injections of a special bioluminescent concoction, their personalities are gone, their reflexes have been heightened along with their senses, their brains have been precisely lesioned so they can no longer sleep — they meditate instead of sleep — and they possess a vast amount of knowledge. After that 'vacation,' the experiments follow a strict schedule. Any deviation from this schedule results in death. The days are all the same: meditation, injections, training or deployment, shower room, injections, training, dinner, injections, training, turn-in, repeat. Part of their training includes torture sessions, just to test their limits."

"Earlier you said something about groups?" Adonia questioned. Most of the room's occupants were quiet, horrified by the story Orion was recounting.

"Yes, there are many different kinds of experiments. They are stripped of their names their first day inside and given numbers. Most of them are identified by the first numbers in their identification code. For example, Jack and Isis are both seven series. Jack was 7-295 and Isis was

7-299. Coop was part of a series that is no longer created by the Corporation: the Lock series. He can press his fingertip against any lock and his finger will turn into the key needed to unlock it. Coop is also trained in combat and strategy. The Lock series were the top series between 1910 and 1948, but the Corporation wasn't achieving good results with them, so they moved on to a new series with different research goals. Coop was the only one of the line who survived. Carding is under strict orders to keep at least one of every series, just in case it is decided to renew a particular line."

"You still haven't answered my question," Electra growled. Orion glanced at her, rubbing the back of his neck.

"It normally takes a few years for experiments to really grasp that the outside world is real and not a simulation controlled by Grenich. It's a very rewarding thing to experience. However, Isis . . . well, I just don't know how to describe it. She hasn't had that experience. I've given her the antidote to the virus she was suffering from, so physically she should be okay. Psychologically might be another story. I've tried everything to convince her she is free, but she refuses to believe me. She's distant and completely detached from her emotions, but she's also operating under faulty Corporation logic. For example, Isis believes killing a Grenich recruitment team was based purely on self-preservation instincts. She perceived a threat to her well-being, so she eliminated it as quickly and efficiently as she could. She refuses to acknowledge it was an act of revenge, even though her actions suggest otherwise. I don't know whether she can snap herself out of this. We'll just have to wait and see."

"How could you let her get so sick?" Passion asked, not even attempting to hide the accusatory tone in her voice.

"It's incredibly hard to decipher when an experiment is ill. They have to be at death's door before you even realize there's something wrong. When experiments are in the Corporation, they have a strong survival instinct. If there's any silver-lining to this whole mess, it's that Isis seems to be acting contrary to this instinct. She's breaking away from their hold, even if she doesn't realize it yet. Believe me, had I realized her health was deteriorating, I would've acted much, much sooner," Orion replied sincerely. He still felt guilty for not noticing how sick she had been.

Orion didn't miss the scrutinizing looks his brothers were giving him. He knew he was very different from the man they remembered. The Grenich Corporation was poisonous; tainting all who came into contact with it. It could change even the happiest person into a grim shell.

"May I have a glass of water?" Orion inquired to no one in particular. For a moment, nobody moved. Finally, Ajax approached the table where there was a pitcher of water and a few glasses set out. He poured the clear liquid into one of the pristine glasses and slid it over to Orion. The oldest Deverell brother easily caught the glass and drank half of it in one gulp.

"This is a lot to take in," Jensen spoke up as he ran his hands through his short dark hair. Orion noticed he was having trouble sitting still, likely anxious to know how Isis was doing. He had heard the two of them had become somewhat close before Isis' recruitment.

"Does Isis remember us?" Malone asked.

Orion swirled the water in his glass, creating the motion by slowly rotating his wrist. "That's another difficult question to answer. Right now, she probably doesn't. Experiments have superior memories and will be able to place faces with names, but the emotional connection is a lot trickier. The best case scenario is she'll recognize you and she'll remember from where, but she will have difficulty remembering any emotional connection or bonds. Coop and Jack both know that they had lives before Grenich, but they don't remember them in the traditional sense. Coop once told me what little he remembers prior to the Corporation seems like a story he once heard. Isis is willfully blocking any ideas or evidence suggesting there is a world outside Grenich, so she may have more difficulty with memories."

Orion drank the last gulp of water and set the empty glass on the table. He wanted to get back to Isis. He was concerned for her, but he was also tired of remembering all the painful memories of times long past.

"I should probably check on Isis," he began. "When she wakes up, we can discuss visitation—"

"You're not running things, Orion," Jet interrupted, his tone firm.

"I'm the only one who has firsthand experience with experiments," Orion replied a bit tersely. "I know how important Isis is to all of you, believe me I do. I would like nothing more than to let you all crowd in the cell and have a big happy reunion with her, but that's not life. You can hate me as much as you like but you have to accept the fact that the Isis you knew is not in that cell. She's not the woman you remember, and chances are, she never will be. As I was saying, once she wakes up, you can visit with her but you have to be prepared. Now if you'll excuse me, I have to see to my patient."

With that, Orion turned and made his way out of the meeting room. He heard someone following him, most likely Jet and Lilly. Orion turned and watched as the Monroes exited the room. Lilly shut the door behind them. Only muted murmurs escaped from behind the heavy door.

"You and I are not done," Jet warned quietly, glancing to his side when Lilly approached. "You have given us a lot of information to process and if I wasn't sure you knew how to help Isis, I would have had the guardians throw you in the cell next to your brother."

"Yes, Jet," Orion replied. The three stood out in the hall for a moment, silently. Jet finally turned and moved back toward the meeting room, but Lilly remained. Her eyes were studying Orion, searching for something. Orion rubbed the back of his neck as he held her gaze.

"There's a war happening, Lilly. It's only a matter of time before you and Jet will need to act," Orion stated. "Are you ready for that? More importantly, are you prepared for the consequences?"

Lilly raised an eyebrow. "I would ask the same of you. Judging from what you've told us, it would appear you have not been faring well in this fight."

Orion opened his mouth to respond but closed it again, knowing the protector leader was right. The wise former guardian was always very straightforward and had a way of seeing through vague responses. Leave it to her to point out his own failings. Orion hated to admit it, but he was losing the battle against Grenich. He needed help, a lot of it, and he might have lost the trust of potential allies.

Orion turned and continued down the hall, heading for Isis' cell. War was not his area of expertise; it never had been. He was a healer and at the moment, he had a patient who needed him. Orion kept his eyes to the ground as he moved to the main hall, noticing the change in light. Afternoon was quickly coming to a close.

~~*~*~*

Blitz's eyes snapped open as she came to consciousness again. Toward the end of her sickness-induced sleep, memories had played behind her closed lids and she suddenly felt incredibly ill. A warm wet feeling filled the back of her throat and invaded her mouth. Isis rolled onto her side and heaved up bile into a nearby bucket. She hadn't eaten for the last twenty-four hours. To her surprise, she didn't taste any blood. Then again, Blitz was rather shocked to find she was still alive.

When she finished retching, Blitz looked up and observed her surroundings. She was surrounded by stone, a jail cell of some kind from the looks of it. She was wearing some type of soft clothing she didn't recognize. The cell was well lit and she had more than enough room to move around. Blitz tossed the cover off and stood from the bed, her sharp eyes traveling over the walls. She moved silently to the large iron door and pulled on the heavy iron ring. It was locked. There was a small window toward the top of the door with three bars over it. She had already caught a whiff of the doctor's scent on the other side. Isis peered out through the bars.

He was sitting in a chair against the wall opposite the door, reading a book that was approximately three hundred pages long. The binding was unlike any she had seen on Earth and Blitz realized she was still in the Meadows.

"The nausea is from the anti-virus," the doctor said as he turned a page, not looking up at her. "Nasty stuff, packs a punch especially when it's not diluted and given in smaller doses. Then again, most experiments don't deteriorate to the point you—"

"Let me out," Blitz demanded. She needed to do something to keep her mind busy. Something that didn't involve sitting in a cell. He didn't even glance up at her, focusing solely on his book.

"The thing you have to learn about freedom — one of the downsides of it — is there are consequences to your actions," he spoke calmly, turning another page. "You are free to do as you like, but you have to live with the repercussions."

"So you're going to keep me locked up?"

"Not really up to me, but that would be my recommendation. You can't just go on a killing spree when the mood strikes you."

"Your strategy was flawed."

"Life is more than battle strategies. There are different ways to neutralize threats and most of them don't involve killing."

"Then they're ineffective," she replied, smacking the

door. Judging from the thickness, she wouldn't be able to punch her way out. Blitz stood on her tiptoes, trying to see how far down the lock was.

Orion closed his book and rubbed his temple. "Isis—"

"That's not my name."

"It is actually. You just can't remember and won't allow me to explain."

"Explaining asinine things of no consequence is not something I have interest in," Blitz stated as she began to pace the cell. She wanted to get out of the enclosed space. Grabbing one wrist, she wrapped her fingers around it absentmindedly.

"Will you allow me to draw some blood?" Orion asked softly. "Just to make sure the antidote is working?"

"If you get within reaching distance, I'll rip your head off," she snarled. The walls seemed to be closing in as her mind continued buzzing with information, processing every last sight, sound, and smell. Even at Grenich, Blitz had things to do in her cell. Experiments needed to keep busy, serve some purpose.

Orion stared at her. "Well that makes me want to let you out."

Blitz glared at him as she continued pacing the cell. He scratched the back of his head as he approached the cell door.

"I wish there was—"

He was cut off when her hand shot out between the bars and grabbed a hold of his throat. She yanked him forward, slamming his face against the door, and tightened her grip on his throat.

Their eyes locked and in that moment, Blitz thought of killing the doctor. Since he had taken her from Grenich, there had been an unspoken respect between them. Somehow, they intuitively knew each other's boundaries and made sure not to cross them. He provided a sense of "home," a term that was downright alien to her. The thought of harming him had never crossed her mind before.

"Make no mistake, doctor. You cannot keep me captive and you cannot control me. If I wish to leave, I will do so. If I wish to return to the Corporation, I will do so. You can do nothing to stop me."

With a suddenness that took him completely off guard, Blitz shoved Orion backward. He collided with the wall and fell to his knees, grimacing in pain. He closed his eyes and sucked in the oxygen that she had deprived him of, gagging and coughing.

"Isis—"

He spoke with a hesitance she had never heard from him before. She had hurt him, but not physically. Blitz continued to pace the small space, not looking at the doctor. After a moment, she heard him exhale but continued to ignore him.

"I'm not giving up on you yet, Isis," Orion said, making sure to use her actual name. She didn't respond, listening to his footsteps fade down the short hallway. A door opened and closed. He was gone.

~~*~*~*

Jack glanced up at Orion as he exited the hall leading to Blitz's — or rather, Isis'— cell. The stairway to the dungeons led to an open circular room where different doors led to different cellblocks and sections. There were a few windows on the far wall between the doors.

The doctor looked haggard and almost defeated. Jack was sitting on the intricately crafted bench that sat just outside the door to the isolation block. The bench was clean and smooth, as if it had just been made that day. Orion had sent Jack out of the room so he could speak with Isis alone. He had hoped Jack would take the opportunity to explore the castle. Though that could be a potentially dangerous situation, Orion was hoping for Jack to show a little free will. He was still behaving as though

Orion was a handler, doing every last thing he asked without question. It was well and good to be respectful, but Jack was acting more like an obedient dog than a free shape shifter.

"I have to make a call," Orion said tiredly. "Make sure no one goes through that door."

"All right, doctor," Jack said before quickly correcting himself. "Orion."

Orion nodded before walking across the room to the stairs. He made his way up the stairs and disappeared from Jack's sight. Jack leaned back against the wall and stared up at the arched ceiling. A peaceful night had fallen over the Meadows, casting the Pearl Castle in soft velvet shades of dark blue. A million tiny stars twinkled in the indigo sky, like diamonds in the night. Jack was beginning to feel bored and wished he had brought a book or something to keep his mind busy. He had finished *The Count of Monte Cristo* a while back and had started on a novel entitled *Fahrenheit 451*. He liked the quality of the writing, but not the story. It brought back too many memories and made Jack uncomfortable. Still, he couldn't stop reading it. He found it fascinating how normals could see something and be so blind to it at the same time. It was another paradox he couldn't work out.

Light footsteps made his entire body go rigid with pent-up energy. Someone was coming down the steps, a woman shape shifter by the sound of it. The footsteps in question were a little heavier than that of the guardians, something only Jack's unnaturally heightened senses could pick up. He opened his glowing brown eyes and lay flat on his stomach on the bench, instinctively concealing himself.

A woman in a dark purple blouse came down the steps. Her reddish hair was loosely pulled up, held in place by two wooden sticks. She didn't see him as she crossed the circular room and moved over to one of the arched windows, her eyes fixed outside. Jack carefully shifted his position so he could watch her. Since being taken out of the Corporation, Jack had only had limited contact with the normals. Orion had everything delivered to his home through secured channels. Jack couldn't help but be intrigued by their complex world.

He stood from the bench and approached the woman. The experiment was just a few feet behind her when she turned to leave. She let out a yelp of surprise and jumped back, her pulse briefly increasing. Jack took a step back, muttering an apology as he turned his glowing brown eyes to the floor. One of her hands fluttered up to her chest and she closed her eyes in relief. Jack wasn't sure how he had scared her, but he knew it was probably either his silence or his eyes. Orion had explained to Blitz and him how those would be the main things that would take normals off guard.

"You scared me," the woman exhaled, confirming what he already guessed. A small friendly smile touched her otherwise sad expression.

"I apologize," Jack stated. "It was not my intention to frighten you."

The woman looked at him curiously. "You're the other experiment — Jack, right?"

Jack looked up. "Yes, I am."

"I'm Shae," the woman replied, offering one of her slender hands. Jack took the offered hand gently and shook it politely, as the Corporation had taught him to do when approaching high-ranking normals; politicians and the like. He studied her hand for a moment, carefully turning it so he could see her knuckles. They were visibly raw.

"You're hurt," Jack observed as he took in the state of her knuckles. A few were even cracked open and bleeding. Shae lightly disengaged her hand from his, causing Jack to look up at her. She turned her gaze outside.

"Slammed it in a drawer," she said, sounding mildly annoyed. Jack shook his head, looking back at the wounded hand. She attempted to hide it, obviously not enjoying the scrutiny.

"No. From the location and depth of the wound, you had to have struck a solid surface with a closed fist. Microscopic flecks of light blue paint, non-toxic, a fairly recent blend and brand. Judging from the healing rate of the wound, you punched a wall approximately twenty-one point five hours ago," Jack seemed to think aloud as he examined her hand from where he stood.

"What's it to—?" Shae began defensively, pausing and frowning. "Wait a minute, how did you do that?"

Jack looked back to her, confused. "Do what?"

"You figured out the time I hit a wall just by looking at my hand? And how the hell did you deduce that about the paint?" Shae asked as she stared at her hand, flexing her fingers a few times.

Jack shrugged. "My eyesight is heightened enough that I can see the healing progress of skin and estimate about what time the incident occurred. As for the paint, I could smell the microscopic remnants embedded in the knuckles, which indicate you hit it incredibly hard. I'm guessing there's a fairly good sized dent in your wall. Don't worry, the paint remnants will wash away in another day or two."

"But how did you guess the color and blend?"

"Different dyes and pigments are used in different kinds of paints. They all have different scents," Jack explained. He didn't understand how normals could go through the world with such dulled senses.

Shae looked at her knuckles again. Jack was quiet, watching her. She appeared to be upset and he hoped it wasn't because of him. Jack wasn't sure whether or not he had said something wrong. Shae lifted her head and glanced in the direction of the door to the isolated cells.

"Isis is like you, right?" she asked.

"Isis? Oh, Blitz, right," Jack said. He kept forgetting they had names other than the ones they had adopted inside the Corporation. He glanced over his shoulder toward the door to Blitz's cell.

"Blitz?" Shae asked with a hint of amusement.

"Yeah, it was probably on account of the lightning bolt in the cat symbol she wears. It stuck," Jack explained.

"Sounds like the kind of name Isis would take," she laughed. Jack attempted to smile and then thought better of it. He shifted his weight and leaned against the wall near the window. Shae sat on the sill, studying him.

"She's still in there," Jack said, quietly. "I know what Orion told you, but he doesn't want to give false hope. We remember bits and pieces of our old lives eventually. I don't know quite how to explain it, but in some way we still are who we once were."

Shae pulled her leg up, folding it under her. Jack sat on the sill opposite her, keeping his feet down on the ground. He glanced across the land, smelling the air. A part of him wanted to wander outside, check out the perimeter, but he was still nervous to be around so many normals. Jack looked over at Shae when she laughed softly.

"I think you may be the first shape shifter I've ever seen look bored in the Meadows," she chuckled. Jack tilted his head.

"How do normals usually react?"

"Usually? Most of them are probably awestruck, some are even a little intimidated," Shae replied, laughter dancing in her eyes.

"Why?"

Shae laughed again and Jack had no idea how to respond. So he continued to absorb information from his senses. He wasn't good at conversation. Some experiments were, such as the ones who were modified for deep cover missions.

"You're close to Bli — Isis," Jack corrected himself again. Shae chuckled at the slip up, sliding a stray lock of hair behind her ear.

"We're cousins by adoption," she explained, looking to her feet for a moment and swallowing. "I'm one of the few people she could stand growing up."

"I see," Jack said, his gaze moving about their surroundings. He turned his eyes back to Shae, noticing her curious look. She was probably one of the first normals whose immediate reaction wasn't fear when encountering an experiment.

"When are you going to lock us away?" Jack asked. Shae appeared to be puzzled by the question and her brow furrowed a little.

"Lock you away? Who told you that?"

"It's the only sensible action to take. We were modified to kill. We've done the things you fight against. Jet and Lilly need to lock us away to maintain order," Jack explained. "I wanted to know if it would be okay to have a few books in my cell. I need to have something to keep my mind busy."

"Jack, I don't know where you got the idea that you were going to be locked up, but as far as I know, we're not going to imprison you. We don't understand enough about Grenich and the two of you are probably the best chance we have to strike back at the Corporation," Shae reassured him. "You're free, okay? Nobody's going to lock you up in the dungeons or anything like that. We might ask you to help us fight Grenich, but it's entirely up to you whether or not you agree to do so."

Jack looked over at Shae, confused by the reassurance. What she spoke of would surely result in chaos. Jack knew he and Blitz were dangerous, even if not consciously. They had been modified to be perfect soldiers and retained many dangerous instincts. It only made sense to lock them up. It was why experiments were kept on a tight schedule in Grenich and not allowed to roam around.

"I do not understand your actions, but I will help you in whatever way I can," Jack promised quietly.

"I'm sure the Monroes will be very happy to hear that," Shae replied with a small smile. She turned her eyes toward the sky outside again.

"It's a beautiful night," Shae commented. Jack looked

up at the sky and tried to understand the appeal of the serenity of the lands of the guardians. He supposed it was what the normals thought of when they used a term like "peaceful." Jack closed his eyes when a pleasantly cool breeze swept over him.

In the stairway, Orion watched them with a smile. He had returned a few minutes ago and caught the tail end of Jack and Shae's interaction. It was the little moments and interactions that gave Orion a small amount of hope. He glanced out over their heads toward the clear night, watching the moon. Things were bad now — probably would be for a few centuries — but there would always be some good in the world. No matter how tiny it was, it was something. Watching Jack have a regular conversation with Shae reminded Orion the experiments could lead relatively normal lives. They weren't the mindless animals Grenich believed them to be. Orion knew the Corporation would always haunt them, as it would him. Survivors were always changed in some way by the trauma they lived through, but that was to be expected.

Orion moved back up the stairs, letting Jack and Shae have some privacy. His main concern was how to lessen the danger of experiments toward the world. He was not naïve and recognized how dangerous experiments were. Those knee-jerk reactions were of particular concern. He had tried a few ideas with Coop to see if he could lessen them, but had little success. Experiments had to learn their boundaries and how not to cross them. It had taken Coop quite some time to learn the relatively simple lesson. *Living weapons — normals will have a field day with that one,* Orion thought grimly as he stopped in the main hall and sat down on the stairs. He grimaced when he realized he had used the term "normal." At some point, he had begun using the lingo of experiments and hadn't even realized it. His bright blue eyes took in the Pearl Castle, which was cloaked in the dark shades of night. The elaborate windows cast elegant shadows all around the main hall.

Rubbing the back of his neck, Orion closed his eyes. He couldn't worry about the future right now. He had to take things one step at a time, just like he told Jack.

"You have that look about you," a familiar voice observed. Orion looked up and smiled when he saw Ajax standing above him, a steaming dark green mug in each hand. He handed one to Orion before sitting down on the step next to his oldest brother.

"What look would that be?" Orion asked as he inhaled the thin wisps of light gray steam curling up from the dark liquid inside the mug. Coffee, freshly pressed, just the way he liked it. He smiled, touched by the gesture. He and Ajax had always been close. They had very similar personalities and were the most responsible of the Deverell men.

"Like you've got the world on your shoulders," Ajax answered. "You always did have the compulsion to take responsibility for all the ills of the world."

Orion shook his head and looked into his mug. "How could I have been so oblivious for so many years? Mass murder and torture was happening right under my nose and I played an active part in it because I was so damn dense."

"I doubt it was that simple," Ajax responded as he sipped his coffee.

"Ignorance is no excuse," Orion argued stubbornly. Ajax glanced at his older brother and then returned his gaze to the quiet castle. Occasionally they heard the soft footsteps of a messenger hurrying off to some place.

"From what you've told me, this place has been operating since before any of us were even born. Chaos was from the *first* generation of guardians. He's ancient," Ajax stated, pausing to sip his coffee. "If Grenich has been in operation for so long a time, they must know how to hide what they're doing. You can't be held at fault for that. Blaming yourself isn't going to accomplish anything."

Orion was quiet for a moment, sipping his coffee. "I don't know what to do, Ajax."

"Pardon?"

"I don't know what to do about anything. Grenich, the experiments, Isis, all of it. I couldn't say anything before, but . . . I'm in over my head. I don't know how to fix any of this."

Ajax set his mug down, pressing his long hands together in front of him. "Maybe that's because it's too big for any one shape shifter to figure out. You've got help now. We'll put our heads together and figure this out."

"Help," Orion snorted humorlessly. "What I've got is a lot of shape shifters who don't trust me. Not that I blame them."

"Well, you have to admit that rising from the dead is quite a feat," Ajax replied, a little humor bleeding into his tone. "Nero's even got a theory involving cyborgs. But he's always had a fondness for science fiction."

Orion couldn't help but chuckle at that. Nero was nearing one-hundred years old and he still had his moments of childish glee.

"So I'm a cyborg now?" Orion asked.

"That's a compliment coming from Nero," Ajax replied, adding bitterly, "All I get is big ears and big nose."

Orion had been sipping his coffee while Ajax was speaking. He gagged and choked on it when he heard Nero's way of taunting Ajax. His brother didn't look as amused, which made it worse because Ajax had a very entertaining annoyed expression. Orion had to turn away to regain control. For a moment, the two sat in a comfortable silence.

"Tell me, Ajax—" Orion began.

"Wondering why I trust you after all the misery you put everyone through by faking your death," Ajax finished for him, a mischievous glint in his otherwise serious blue eyes. Orion raised an eyebrow.

"I would've put it less bluntly, but you got the gist of my question," he responded as he finished his coffee. Ajax was quiet for a moment, glancing behind them at the enormous floor-to-ceiling window. The moonlight cast the arched shape of the window in the shadows that spilled across the floor near their feet.

"Because when I looked in your eyes, aside from the pain, I saw my older brother. Whom I have missed quite a lot over the years," Ajax finally responded with a small shrug. Orion turned his attention to the silver moonlight on the marble floor.

"Good enough for me," he said quietly. They fell into another comfortable silence, each enjoying the other's company. Outside, the night remained serene. Orion couldn't help but feel it was a fleeting state. If there was one thing he had learned at the Corporation, it was happiness never lasted for very long.

CHAPTER TWELVE

The sun rose on another day in the Meadows and a very different atmosphere touched the peaceful lands. There was still serenity in the air, but now it was tainted with a grim feeling. A week had passed since Orion and Isis' surprise arrival. In that week Isis hadn't shown any signs of recovering psychologically. Physically, she had mostly recovered in less than forty-eight hours after receiving the antidote to the virus that had been afflicting her. Guardian healing no longer worked on her because she had taken life in cold blood, but Isis didn't need it due to her regenerative abilities. She remained in her isolated cell and each day seemed to infuriate her more. She was mostly quiet, passing the hours doing crunches or push-ups. Isis had demanded her own clothes and now wore her tank top and pants made of the same sleek black material as her catsuit. She often paced about when the messenger brought her meals, which she didn't touch until they took a bite first. Whenever Orion attempted to talk to her, she ignored him. She had even kicked the chair in her cell at the door once. It was quite apparent he wasn't her favorite person.

Orion had remained in the Meadows to care for her.

He was still under suspicion, though it seemed highly unlikely he was working as some kind of double agent. The eldest Deverell was a completely different protector than the one most of them remembered. Orion had always been an optimist and an unwavering pacifist. He had always believed everyone was basically good and it was rare to see him without a smile on his face. He had loved life, but that had been before the Corporation. Now his laugh had yet to be heard and his eyes were bloodshot and haunted. He hadn't gotten more than a few hours' sleep since he had arrived and it showed in his drawn scruffy features.

The High Council was called to decide on the fates of the three shape shifters. Aneurin had already questioned Orion about Jack and Isis. Adonia had sat in on the questioning, but it didn't yield any new information.

The morning after the questioning, Adonia, Jet, Lilly, and Artemis sat in Adonia's large office. The gauzy light of the room was somewhat calming, but it did nothing for the heaviness they all felt deep within their hearts. They had been discussing the current situation in the Meadows. Something was niggling at Artemis, but she was waiting for an appropriate time to bring it up. There were currently more important matters that needed to be resolved.

"I don't know what to do," Jet continued on. His normally pleasant voice was rough from lack of sleep. "The rules are very clear about murder, but I don't think we've ever encountered a situation like this before. In fact, I *know* we haven't encountered a situation like this before. The Isis I know, or knew, would never have taken a life in cold blood. But does that person still exist?"

Adonia nodded in agreement. "I understand, Jet. The High Council is also at somewhat of a loss about what to do in this situation. We simply can't overlook that she killed a lot of people. Orion has told us the experimentation involves a certain amount of brainwashing, which should be taken into account. The question that the High Council is most concerned with is if she is dangerous."

"She tried to shoot me in the face," Jet put in. "So I would say the answer is yes. She's pretty damn dangerous."

"I do not disagree that Isis is changed and perhaps dangerous," Lilly began. "However, if we are to believe Orion's story, which I feel is true, it seems cruel to imprison Isis indefinitely. Especially taking into account everything she has been through."

"Well we can't just let her go free, not in the state she's in now," Jet pointed out and Lilly shook her head.

"I was not suggesting that. We need to figure out a solution that protects both us and her."

Adonia rubbed her brow. "Passion is understandably upset about the recent revelations, as is Electra. Nobody really knows what to do about Isis and Orion or Jack for that matter. Based on our limited experiences with these experiments, they've proven to be rather adept at blending in for the most part. Coop certainly had us fooled until he broke through the guardian glass in the dungeons. If not for the glowing eyes and seeing him in action, I'd think Jack was just an average shape shifter."

Jet shook his head. "That's another troubling thing about this whole dilemma. I don't know whether these experiments would be able to fit into society, with those reflexes and reactions. Jack nearly strangled me because I was standing behind him. Two would be a handful, but when we eventually take the fight to Grenich, we'll be releasing who knows how many of these modified shape shifters into the world. Where will they go? The mansion wouldn't be able to house that many shape shifters. The only alternatives I could see would be imprisoning them or letting them loose. I'm not comfortable with either of those options."

Jet leaned forward and rubbed his palms together. "I don't like the odds of this fight. According to Orion, Set has revenants in every government treasury and military. So not only is he in control of the wealth, but also the weapons. Along with who knows how many modified soldiers in laboratories around the world. We're no match for the experiments and we only have two or three on our side. Any way you look at it, we're at a severe disadvantage."

"Protectors have always fought against the odds and emerged victorious," Artemis finally spoke up, resting her chin on the back of one of her hands. "We are focusing too much on what might be instead of focusing on the here and now. You said it yourself Jet: we have a few modified shape shifters on our side. That's something. We also have the Four. You're overlooking the one major advantage we have over Set. We have two experiments who might be the Key. Two of the three possibilities, those are favorable odds."

Both Adonia and Jet looked at her, a bit mystified by her statement, while Lilly just smiled. Artemis tended to be as by-the-book as Aneurin and was often a stickler for the old ways. She glanced from Jet to Adonia with her deep blue eyes, which held the same type of profound wisdom as her mother.

"We all knew something bad was coming," Artemis continued as she lowered her hand, glancing over at Lilly. "The Book of Oracle predicted it and we've all felt it for some time now, the guardians especially. Orion and Roan have given us grim stories about this Grenich Corporation, but when have we ever encountered an easy threat?"

Jet turned his eyes back to Adonia, who sat back. She had a thoughtful expression as she watched her daughter.

"We're going to get through this, I'm certain of that. We need to understand the situation and come up with some sort of plan of action," Artemis continued. "I think that is what we should tell the High Council."

She bowed her head respectfully toward Adonia and then got up, strode out of the room, and closed the door behind her. Artemis saw Passion sitting on the floor outside the door. Her daughter was wearing a long fiery red dress. Her back was straight against the wall and her chin rested on her knees. Her feet poked out from beneath the red hem. Artemis wondered how many times she would have to tell her daughter not to sit on the floor before it finally sank in.

"Eavesdropping is impolite, Passion," Artemis reproached gently. Passion's bright eyes turned up toward her, not angry but determined. They were blue, as they usually were during the autumn and winter seasons.

"How long are you going to keep my daughter locked up like an animal?" Passion asked quietly. "I'll burn this place to the ground before I allow the High Council to charge her like some kind of common criminal."

"I'm sure you would," Artemis agreed, knowing how impulsive her daughter could be. Passion was a very protective mother and Artemis didn't even want to think of the scene she would cause if anyone even thought of confining Isis for any extended amount of time.

Passion scowled and turned her eyes from her mother. "If it's because of Roan, you know, we can't be one-hundred percent sure he's their actual father."

"For the love of all we hold sacred, Passion, would you just stop?" Artemis said, exasperated. "This isn't about Roan and it isn't really even about Isis. We were meeting to discuss where we stand. When Isis recovers, we will decide what to do next."

Passion stretched her legs out in front of her, looking down at her slender hands. Her fingernails were well-kept. Passion normally worked on her nails when nervous or agitated, which she had been all week. She and Electra probably had the best cared for fingernails and toenails in all of the Meadows. The younger guardian looked down the hall, biting her lip which was beginning to tremble. Artemis turned, heading the opposite way to the stairs leading up to the living quarters.

"She's not getting better," Passion's voice halted Artemis. For a moment, the older guardian stood silent, contemplating what to say to her daughter.

"She will. She has inherited your strength," Artemis finally responded before continuing on her way, turning into another hall and out of Passion's sight.

Passion stared after her mother for a moment or two. She turned her attention back to the opposite wall and slid a smooth dark blue ball from where she had been hiding it behind her back. The guardian examined the ball for a moment and then threw it at the wall. It bounced on the floor, hit the wall, and sprang back into her slender hand. Passion bounced it again, the repetitive motion soothing her frayed nerves.

~~*~*~*

Jensen woke up, mentally cursing at the painful crick in his neck. For the past week, he had slept on the bench in the circular room with the doors leading to different sections of the dungeons. He was wearing the same clothes he had worn the night before: a dark jacket, a nice shirt, and dark pants that matched his jacket. Jensen hadn't even bothered to take off his shoes, which were currently propped up on the thin armrest of the bench. His wrinkled jacket was bunched up under his head, serving as a makeshift pillow. Normally, wrinkled clothing drove him up the wall. He ironed everything he wore and abhorred looking anything other than completely put-together. The protector groaned when he felt the familiar sensation of sharp needles on the soles of his feet, which were numb. Running a long hand over his face, Jensen winced at the sandpapery stubble covering his jaw. He hadn't shaved in a couple days.

"You are uncomfortable," a soft voice came from the side.

"Gah!" Jensen exclaimed as he jolted up and whacked his head against the smooth wall behind him. His voice bounced off the high walls of the empty room. The experiment who had come with Orion, Jack, was sitting on the sill of one of the large windows. The sunlight illuminated him, creating a gold aura about him. Jensen rubbed the back of his sore head, scowling. It was near impossible to catch Jensen off guard, but he hadn't encountered many experiments.

"Son of a—! You scared the hell out of me," he grumbled irritably.

"I apologize," Jack said.

"It's fine," Jensen muttered as he looked down at his hand. "I thought you were elsewhere. Sleeping or something."

"No, I've mostly stayed around here," Jack replied as he glanced out the window. "I don't sleep."

"Right, because of all the . . ." Jensen gestured vaguely about his head. Jack watched his action and looked a little puzzled. Jensen dropped his hand back to the bench. He realized it was a little tactless to ask such a blunt question, but it was quite early in the morning and he was annoyed at being surprised.

"I'm assuming your gestures are referring to the experimentation. You are correct," Jack answered after a moment, unbothered by Jensen's bluntness. "An army that sleeps is an army that loses, as the handlers frequently tell us."

Jensen stared at the odd man. "That bodes well for us."

Jack studied him and Jensen shifted his weight, uncomfortable by the curious look in the glowing brown eyes. Telepathy was a gift unique to a few guardians, but Jack's piercing gaze made Jensen wonder. The small movement sent pain racing up his spinal column and he made a mental note to sleep on the floor or at least get some kind of pillow. Jack pulled one leg up and rested his back against the stone frame of the window.

"You are the last Aldridge?" Jack asked, resting a wrist on his folded knee.

"That's me," Jensen said. He still hadn't been to the

guardian mausoleum. He didn't think he could handle any more grief, though he knew he had to go eventually.

"The last, but you are not alone," Jack observed. Jensen frowned at the odd statement. Something suddenly occurred to him, a question he wanted to ask but didn't know how to bring up. Jensen leaned forward and pressed his long hands together, looking up at Jack.

"Was Grenich behind the murder of my family? The Deverells helped me hunt down most of the assassins who carried out the hit, but …"

"I do not know for certain. Experiments are not informed of missions they do not actively participate in. From a strategic standpoint, it would make sense," Jack answered, hopping down from the windowsill. "The Aldridges were important allies to the Monroes and invaluable to the guardians. I know the head of Grenich had a personal vendetta against them, though I do not know the motivation behind it. Their demise caused more damage than even you are aware. You survived, the last of the Aldridge bloodline, so you are important."

Jensen swallowed and looked off to the side. He had a feeling that was how Jack would answer. Destroying an ancient line of protectors had probably been advantageous to Set. It robbed Jet and Lilly of important and valuable allies. He closed his eyes and pressed his hands against his face. His life had always been extremely dangerous. Jensen had accepted long ago that someone would always be trying to kill him and would probably eventually succeed. He had a feeling he was a lot less worried about Grenich than the other shape shifters. It was just one more danger to him, one more threat to his life.

"You are attached to Blitz?"

Jensen opened his eyes and looked back at the experiment, surprised by the question. It sounded more like a statement than a query. From what Orion had told them, Jensen theorized experiments never outright asked anything. One had to pay close attention to their voice to distinguish one tone from another.

"The others are also concerned, but you are here every night," Jack pointed out.

"Yes, I do care about her," Jensen replied, with quiet conviction. He had only known Isis a few short weeks before she had been killed, or so they had thought. After Bryn, he had sworn to himself he would never enter into a relationship again. After her death, sex became mechanical for him. Whenever he needed it, he would indulge in it with a partner, a simple transaction with no-strings attached. With Isis however, he had gotten a strange feeling. Being with her, it felt right.

"Last night, Shae told me of your search for her," Jack mentioned. He was the very picture of laid-back and Jensen had a hard time believing the shape shifter was actually dangerous. To him, Jack and Coop didn't seem extraordinary. Aside from their eyes, it was only when they moved, or fought, that it became apparent they were anything but normal.

Jensen stood up and stretched his back, listening to the various pops as he took on a normal posture. "Orion told me you both usually wear some kind of lenses to hide your glowing eyes. Why aren't you wearing them?"

Jack gave a half shrug. "Pointless. Everyone here already knows about experiments. Do my eyes make you uncomfortable?"

"It's a bit hard to get used to," Jensen responded honestly.

"I can imagine," Jack stated, unbothered by the answer. "If it were up to me, I'd have the process reversed. Glowing eyes are a severe disadvantage in the field. Even when we shift into animals, our eyes maintain a slight glow."

Jensen rubbed the back of his neck, feeling guilty and a little uncomfortable. He coughed and glanced over at the door to the cellblock, wishing for it to open and interrupt what had become a rather awkward exchange. Jensen was fidgeting and he knew it, but he needed to move to prevent himself from going mad waiting in the rotunda. Jack was completely still, but his stoicism was partly because of the harsh lessons that had been drilled into his skull during his years at the Grenich Corporation. No unnecessary movement, every action must have a purpose, and so on and so forth.

"I've read just about everything on psychology," Jack stated, drawing Jensen's attention back to him. "According to your books and philosophies, it is difficult to recover from trauma. I believe it will be even more difficult for us because we have to forever carry the brands and trademarks of the Corporation, as well as the memories that were taken from us."

The experiment went quiet for a moment and then looked over at Jensen. "But experiments are nothing if not resilient. Blitz is tough. She will recover."

Jensen couldn't help but chuckle a little. He had no doubt Isis would eventually recover, but it was reassuring to hear an experiment say it. If he truly was a superior creature, Jack would have a better idea than he would.

Jack's glowing eyes turned back to the lands of the Meadows. Jensen opened his mouth to say something more, but was interrupted when the door to the cellblock finally opened. Jensen immediately straightened up, adjusting the cuffs on his shirtsleeves as he waited for Orion to exit. The haggard man stepped out into the room and glanced over at Jack. He was drenched and looked irritated as he tried to shake the excess water off his hands.

"She wasn't thirsty. Thankfully they heeded my advice about not giving her access to glass. If they hadn't, I'm fairly certain I would be missing an eye," Orion grumbled, wiping some of the water off his face. He paused and looked over at Jensen. "Guardians have mercy, tell me you didn't sleep on the bench *again*."

"Come now, Orion. If you keep talking like that, I'll start to think you don't care very much for me," Jensen teased with a grin.

"Jensen, I find it hard to believe that you would think anyone didn't like you," Orion replied as he rubbed his eyes with his thumb and his index finger. "Out of curiosity, do you have any casual clothes? Anything that isn't tailored?"

"What's wrong with this?" Jensen looked down at his clothing, his face scrunching. "It's in need of ironing, I grant you, but—"

"Guardians, you are *exactly* the same," Orion stated in disbelief.

"And it's this clever banter that I have missed so much since you bit the dust," Jensen responded with a wicked grin. Orion gave him a sarcastic smile and waited for the question he knew was next. It was the same routine every morning.

"How is Isis?" Jensen asked, his tone softer.

"Same as she was yesterday, same as she will probably be tomorrow," Orion replied, sighing when Jensen continued to look expectantly at him. "She's still trapped in Grenich and I don't know if she's going to snap out of it."

"What kind of substandard doctoring is that?" Jensen asked, smirking briefly before sobering again. "Can I see her?"

Orion dropped down onto the bench Jensen had been sleeping on. "I wouldn't. She's quite angry at the moment."

"Well then, I'm off to the kitchens," Jensen stated, sticking his hands in his pockets. "I'll be back later."

Jensen strode off toward the stairs. Jack approached Orion and sat down next to him. For a while, the two sat in silence.

"They sleep a lot, like you," Jack commented.

Orion nodded. "Yes, Jack. We normals need our sleep to function."

"Sleeping is probably more pleasant than meditating,"

Jack mentioned. Orion shook his head, not looking at the experiment but rather at the floor in front of them.

"Trust me, it really isn't."

Jack looked over at him. "Are you still suffering from nightmares?"

"When don't I?" Orion replied as he glanced at Jack. His healthy olive complexion told Orion that Jack had been wandering outside a little, which was encouraging. He could tell the experiment was quite bored in such a stable environment though. There wasn't much for an experiment to do in the Meadows.

"You should sleep more," Jack stated. "You're no good to Blitz exhausted."

"Perhaps, but I'm beginning to wonder if anyone . . ." Orion trailed off, causing Jack to look at him. His blue eyes lit up as he got to his feet.

"Oh my god, I may have an idea," Orion stated, before turning and hurrying for the stairs, pulling his cell phone out of his pocket. Jack tilted his head as he watched the doctor go.

As Orion exited the stairs leading down to the dungeons, he nearly ran into Electra. Her dark blue shirt made her green eyes stand out. She was finishing a small slice of toast, likely her breakfast. The moment she saw Orion, suspicion clouded her eyes. He smiled politely at her and nodded in greeting. Orion hadn't had much of a chance to speak with his other niece or anyone else for that matter. He did know of Electra's suspicion toward strangers, especially those she believed posed any kind of threat to her family. On the second level, Orion could hear a ball being bounced against a wall.

"Would she like some breakfast?" Electra's sudden question pulled Orion out of his thoughts. He rolled the cell phone in his hand a couple times as he looked to her. Messengers continued to rush around them, a sea of pastel.

"Would who — oh! No, I doubt she'd eat right now.

Maybe in an hour or so," Orion said gently. "If you'll excuse me, I have to make a call."

Electra studied him for a moment. "What's with you?"

"I may have a solution that will snap your sister out of this state," Orion paused for a moment, his brow creasing as he thought something over. "I don't suppose you'd be willing to help me."

"How?" Electra asked, her tone not losing its suspicious edge.

"Would you be able to make sure no one entered the dungeons for maybe two or three hours?" Orion asked. Electra arched an eyebrow, crossing her arms over her chest.

"Why?"

"Electra, please. I don't have a lot of time and neither does Isis," Orion pleaded.

Electra was quiet for a moment. "All right, I'll try. But don't expect any miracles."

"Thank you," Orion said as he continued on his way. Electra watched him leave. The sound of the bouncing ball had stopped. Hopefully Adonia and the Monroes had finished discussing what to do about their current situation, namely Isis and Orion. Everything was nightmarish. The wild tales of conspiracies and secret empires were only supposed to happen in stories, certainly not in reality. And they still had yet to explain the censored sacred texts.

The sound of a ball once again softly bouncing off the wall drew Electra out of her racing thoughts. She made her way toward the dungeons where her sister was.

~~*~*~*

Blitz worked on the chair in her cell. She had managed to break off one leg and was now focusing on another. If she had a decent weapon, it would be easy to force someone to open the cell door. She had already tried

Appearing, but it proved to be futile. There was some kind of force field around the cell. The guardians were intelligent and knew how to keep their prisoners confined. She would have to get out of the block and to do that, Blitz needed to use force. She was mostly recovered from the strong antidote, but the medicine had wreaked havoc with her system and muddled her senses slightly. Blitz could have attempted an escape earlier, but she wanted her health to improve a little more. The time had also let her observe patterns and behaviors, which allowed her to figure out an escape plan.

Blitz broke the second leg free of the chair. They were primitive, as most improvised weapons were, but they would do. She froze when she heard the door to the cellblock open. It was too early for a meal. Was the doctor back already? She crouched down when she heard the door to her cell unlock and the heavy door creaked open just a crack. Blitz attempted to crane her neck to see more, but could only see a sliver of the stone wall across from the door.

Blitz cautiously stood and approached the opening. She saw no one, but there was a faint scent outside the cell, indicating someone was out there. Blitz tightened her grip on the chair legs she held and used one to push open the heavy door even further. She stepped out of the cell, twisting around when she heard the click of an expanding baton.

A stranger stood there, holding the narrow weapon. He was clean-shaven with dark brown hair and stood an even six feet. Wearing a plain green shirt and dark blue jeans, he could have been mistaken for an average ordinary shape shifter. Except for his stormy blue eyes, which glowed like fire in the night. He was a Grenich experiment. Blitz got into a ready position, holding the chair legs aloft.

"I know telling you I have no interest in fighting would not matter," the man said. Blitz frowned and started backing up, toward the door. The man moved forward and

Blitz stiffened.

"I don't want to fight, but I can't let you leave. Not yet," the man continued as he took another few steps forward.

"Get in my way and I will see it as an aggressive act," Blitz warned as she continued backing up. The man suddenly sped forward. She swung out with one chair leg and he twisted, barely able to parry the blow. Blitz swung at his head with the second chair leg and he ducked under it, spinning away and striking out with the baton. He succeeded in hitting her leg, forcing her down on one knee.

As she leapt up and away from him, he positioned himself between her and the door. Blitz moved at him again, striking at the man with the chair legs. He could barely keep up with the speed of her blows. She managed to clip his ribs with one chair leg and followed through with an elbow strike, knocking him back against the door.

A reverse roundhouse kick caught her by surprise and knocked her into the wall. Blitz spun around, raising her sticks and blocking another strike with the baton. She leapt up and attempted to kick his head, but he arched back and narrowly avoided her foot. He stumbled a few steps. Both of them were panting a little.

"What series are you?" Blitz asked as she blocked another thrust, countering with a swing at his ribs. She pushed the advantage when he dodged and was able to knock him against an empty cell door.

"One long since obsolete," the man answered. "I'm the last of my line."

"You are outmatched," she pointed out. He swung the baton down, managing to clip her wrists. He swung it up again, knocking her under the chin. Blitz stumbled backward, losing her grip on the sticks, and crashed into the stone wall.

"The newer series are always a little too arrogant for their own good," the man stated. He swung the baton again. She ducked under the swing and executed a leaping reverse roundhouse, which struck him between the shoulders. The man collided with the wall, losing his own grip on his baton.

"I know of no such flaw," Blitz said. She lunged forward when he spun around and pinned him to the wall with her foot. He grabbed her leg and shoved her away. She stumbled back, recovered, and struck out with a cross punch. He pushed her arm away as the punch went past his face. Blitz retaliated with an elbow strike to the face. He reeled back a few steps, blood flowing from a split lip, but recovered and landed a reverse kick to the small of her back. She fell to her knees, looked over her shoulder, and struck out with a strong back kick to his gut. The man doubled over and she quickly got to her feet, grabbing his shoulders and leaping up with her knee raised. The blow caused him to stagger back a little, but nowhere near as much as he would have if he had been a normal.

Blitz kicked high, aiming for his head again. He caught her foot but she leapt up and twisted her body around so that she struck the side of his face with her free foot. They both dropped to the cold stone floor. She instantly grabbed his arm, wrapped her legs around it, and held him in a tight joint lock. With his free hand, the man withdrew a combat knife and pressed it against her thigh. Cutting her femoral artery wouldn't kill her, but since her regenerative ability was still a little sluggish, it would slow her down for at least an hour. Enough time for him to either finish her off or toss her back in the cell. For a moment, they just lay there.

"Truce?" he asked and Blitz watched him suspiciously.

"Count of three, we each let go," the man offered after another moment. She looked at the knife and then back at him, nodding once.

"One ... two ... three."

Blitz let him go and scooted back. He sat up and rotated his arm a couple times. The man put the knife back in the sheath hidden behind his back. He crawled over to the wall and sat with his back against it. For a moment, Blitz studied him, waiting to see if he would attempt another attack.

"I know you from somewhere," she mentioned, keeping her distance. The man looked familiar, but not enough for her to get within stabbing distance. He looked over at her.

"But you don't remember from where, right?" he asked.

"It is of little consequence. I recognize many people, it is of no matter to me," she replied. He let out a huff of breath, which might have been a laugh, and nodded. The man seemed almost amused by her response, which was peculiar for an experiment.

"My name is Coop. We met before Grenich 'recruited' you," Coop explained, ignoring her as his gaze traveled elsewhere. "You might also remember me from some of your 'lessons' from the Corporation. Let me guess what they said about me: killer, thief, traitor, danger, spy, turncoat, double agent. Please correct me if I'm wrong."

Blitz didn't say anything. He was correct: the Corporation had drilled those lessons into their minds. Coop, one of the escapees, last of the Lock series who posed a serious threat to the Corporation. In the past, many had been deployed to bring him back, but he had somehow eluded all of them. The heads of Grenich grew tired of trying to recover him and instead ordered him to be eliminated on sight.

"Don't suppose you would consider relaxing for a minute. I'm not going to attack you," Coop stated. She continued to watch him, suspiciously, her body still tense and prepared for a fight.

"Didn't think so," Coop said, leaning his head back and closing his eyes. "I remember my first couple years outside the Corporation. I was suspicious of everything. My senses went into overdrive. Every last noise had to be analyzed until identified. I didn't know if I wanted to hide from Grenich or return to it. Neither scenario was particularly appealing."

Coop opened his eyes and looked over at her, almost smiling. Blitz continued to watch his every move. He was between her and the door and he was obviously a capable fighter. She was trying figure out a strategy to get out of there.

"I'll make a deal with you. I came here to show you something and you obviously want to leave. You allow me to show you what I want to and then I'll let you go on your way. Deal?" he asked. She was quiet for a moment, her features remaining blank.

"I come with you to see whatever and then I can go? Even if I desire to kill?" Blitz asked.

"Well, I hope you won't do that. I can't guarantee you won't be caught again, either by the Corporation or the protectors. But for me, I'll leave you alone," Coop responded.

"Fine," she agreed as she straightened up again. Coop got to his feet and led her out into the rotunda. He held out his large hand and Blitz reluctantly took it. Almost immediately, their surroundings disappeared in a bright flash of light. The circular room melted into a forest with trees reaching as far as she could see, which wasn't very far ahead of her. The natural air and sweet scent of wilderness immediately filled Blitz's lungs. Once their surroundings became vivid and real, Coop released her hand. She looked around, confused.

Coop noticed her puzzlement. "Very few experiments can Appear. It's a skill the Corporation can neither teach nor control."

"Grenich controls everything," Blitz responded automatically.

"No, they don't," Coop replied. "And I can prove it."

He started off down a dirt bike path, gesturing for her to follow. She did, focusing on their surroundings. The dirt, small rocks, and twigs made almost no noise beneath their feet. The sky was overcast above them and in the distance, she could hear a very faint rumble of thunder. There were some birds still singing in the trees. A nice breeze had kicked up.

Coop led her out into a small clearing. Bright green grass covered the dirt and a few trees were spread out sporadically. For the most part, it was just open space. Wild-flowers added splashes of color, purples and whites mostly. Blitz stepped out in front of Coop, who leaned against a large oak on the edge of the clearing.

"This is how you prove the Corporation doesn't control everything?" she asked after a moment. She didn't look at him though. Her eyes were drawn by all the different shades of green. It seemed as though every tree and every plant had its own unique combination of colors. Every shade was a little different from the others, even the vast amount of green. Another cool breeze rustled through the leaves on the trees. Blitz closed her eyes and inhaled the clean scent of dew, vegetation, and tree bark.

"When's it going to rain?" Coop asked, pulling her out of the tranquility of the forest. She turned to look back at him, tilting her head a little.

"What?" Blitz asked softly.

He crossed one leg over the other, resting his elbow on the lower branch of the tree. "When is it going to rain and for how long? If Grenich controls the planet, then they must've ingrained the knowledge of when each individual storm is going to take place. After all, we have to be prepared for everything. Now both of us know it is going to rain, judging from the current weather conditions and environmental indicators, but I want an exact time and duration."

Blitz looked up to the clouds, back to Coop, and then up at the clouds again. True, it was going to rain, but she found that she was unable give him an answer. She remained silent for a long while.

"I don't know," she admitted. The sky opened up. Small cool droplets of water drizzled down to splash lightly on her smooth face. It beaded on her clothing and skin, dripping off her to the ground.

As the rain began to intensify, she had a fleeting moment in which everything became shockingly clear. She saw it all and the sight overwhelmed her for a short time. As quickly as it had come, it was gone but the feeling of liberty remained. Blitz ran a hand through her short hair and closed her eyes, feeling the rain for what felt like the very first time. The Grenich Corporation didn't own her, they never had. It was a façade they created to control her, but now she saw through it. She looked around and her vision seemed clear for the first time in a while.

"You see, Isis," she heard Coop's quiet voice behind her. "They make you believe that they control everything, but it's a lie. Out here, they control nothing."

Isis nodded as she let the rain run down her flawless face. She had been numb to everything for too long, but now she was awake.

~~*~*~*

Orion was pacing the marble floor of the castle, antsier than he had been in a while. He was completely unaware of his younger brothers watching his every move. *It's going to work, it's going to work, just calm down,* he thought until the words became one repeating mantra.

"I think his head's going to explode," Nero spoke up. "Any takers?"

"You're wrong. He's going to wear a hole in the floor first," Devin replied with a shake of his head. Their bantering and Orion's pacing were interrupted by a shimmering light that appeared in the middle of the castle, directly in front of Orion. Within a few seconds, two people stood there. Isis was dripping wet and smelled of rain with the sweet hint of trees. Raindrops still shimmered in her short dark hair.

Coop stood behind her, dressed in lighter shades. Nowhere near as dark as the black she wore. Both of them stood at attention, backs straight and gazes unwavering.

For his part, Orion was completely speechless. Isis was still an experiment, but something about her was different. She was awake. Raindrops continued to roll off her in small droplets, splashing lightly on the floor. She regarded him for a moment, studying him. As usual, her expression betrayed no emotion or thought.

"Isis," he said. Her glowing eyes were a bright blue color and seemed to pierce right through him.

She remained quiet for a moment before softly stating, "We can't hide anymore."

Orion frowned. "Pardon?"

"Hiding and remaining on the defensive is an ineffective strategy," Isis explained. "If you truly desire to bring down Grenich, we must strike at them. We don't have the numbers for a full on assault, but we can use guerilla tactics. Jack, Coop, and I can help the protectors. The first thing we must do is figure out how to liberate the experiments in the main facilities."

"Isis, it's going to take some time," Orion began. "We will dismantle Grenich, but we have to make sure we're prepared for what they throw at us."

Isis shook her head, sprinkling more drops of rain on the floor. "If we liberate the experiments in the main facilities, we'll have the resources we need to cripple Grenich. Once we accomplish that, then we can focus on destroying Set and his allies."

She sidestepped him. His quiet voice stopped her.

"You are underestimating the necromancers," Orion warned. "You're not talking about a recruitment team. We're talking about people in the highest corridors of power around the world. If we move too soon, they will destroy us. Don't forget, Isis, you and Jack are valuable to Set. He won't stop hunting you."

Isis tilted her head a little, not turning to face him. "Good, it means he'll get sloppy. Set started this war and we're going to finish it. If I have to take his empire apart brick-by-brick, so be it."

And then she was gone, back to her cell to await sentencing.

CHAPTER THIRTEEN

Roan lay on his back in his cell, looking at the ceiling in sheer boredom. A sudden chill caused a shiver to go through his lean body and he frowned. He knew something big was coming. The former assassin had already been told by Jet and Lilly of Isis' return and the subsequent slaughter of Onyx. The thought of one of his daughters being subjected to Grenich experimentation turned his stomach. Roan had known that the Grenich higher ups would probably target her. The cost of a job at Grenich was usually one of the employee's children. They made it sound like some big moral decision — your child could end war and save the lives of countless people. The truth was the Corporation ran on greed just like everything else in the world. Since Electra was unobtainable, Isis would be the target by default.

Roan turned his head when he saw movement out of the corner of his eye. Orion's only daughter, Ace, stood before his cell. Her eyes were almost exactly like Orion's. Most of her looks were from her father, which added to her more masculine appearance. Like her father, Ace tended to have a serious expression, which was quite unusual for rebels. Roan groaned and swung his legs off the bed so that he was sitting up.

"What is it, Ace?" he asked.

"Isis is out of her rage, but now she's determined to bring Grenich down," Ace responded. Roan shrugged and spread his hands. *Yeah, and …?*

"Hasn't that been our goal all along?" he asked when Ace didn't go on, trying to keep the sarcasm out of his voice. He wouldn't be difficult with his niece. That was something Roan saved for his older brother. The former assassin watched as she stuck her hands in the pockets of her baggy jeans, rocking back and forth on her feet. Roan could see she preferred more masculine attire and had a more masculine stance.

"Yeah, but she's an experiment now. When they're determined, they don't stop until the job is done or they're dead. Attacking Grenich is suicide, but that's exactly what Isis is going to do," Ace replied. "Orion still doesn't know as much as he'd like. There are still too many questions surrounding the Key, not to mention we're not even one-hundred percent clear on exactly where the heads of the Corporation are or even how many there are. Hell, we don't even know who some of them are."

Roan smiled at her uneasiness. *Ah to be young,* he thought.

"Orion and the Monroes are going to have to start taking risks if they want to get anything accomplished. At least they have a couple of experiments with them. Trust me, Ace, that's something," Roan stated as he got up off the bed and approached the glass. "Speaking of which, do the Monroes know about the part you and Alpha played in Orion's 'master plan'?"

Ace smiled a little as she shook her head and crossed her arms over her chest.

"Nah. I don't think they'll ever realize that we played any part," Ace stated. "Until we reveal it to them, if we ever do. Are the two of you ever going to tell the Monroes everything? Seems kinda cruel to keep allies in the dark."

Roan shook his head. "I've been straightforward for my part, as much as I can be. They know pretty much everything I do concerning Grenich. The important stuff anyway. This is one of those scenarios we'll have to improvise as we go along. The protectors will probably find out a lot of it on their own. In any case, revealing is not a pressing matter. Finding out everything there is to know about Set and his allies is our main concern. You're going to need Jack and Isis to do that."

"Yeah, yeah," Ace replied dismissively.

Roan smacking the glass causing Ace to jump, startled. The sound echoed like a shot down the empty hallway, shattering the peace that existed even in the dungeons.

"Don't be flippant about this, Ace. And don't let your guard down, not even for a second. Grenich probably already knows everything about us, meaning we're going into this at a severe disadvantage no matter what we do. I wouldn't be surprised if Set even knew that Orion and I are still among the living. They will not hesitate to kill you if they have even the slightest inkling you know where their runaways are. Jack and Isis — they aren't like Coop. They're ten times more important and a more valuable commodity to Grenich," Roan advised firmly, his gaze intense as he stared at Ace. "They'll never stop hunting them or the ones who shelter them, always remember that."

"I know, because Jack or Isis might be the Key, right?" Ace responded, obviously still spooked by Roan's sudden outburst. Roan merely nodded, his dark green eyes imploring Ace to take the matter seriously. Ace glanced down the hall leading from Roan's cell.

"I better get going, seeing as how I kinda snuck in," she said.

Roan nodded down the hall. "Then make sure you aren't seen when you sneak back out."

He watched as Ace jogged down the hall, grateful he had been updated on the current situation. The inexplicable chill hit him again. He moved across the floor of his cell and stretched his lean body out on the bed again. Roan frequently wondered if the guardians knew just how comfortable their prisoners were. He closed his eyes. There were so many thoughts racing about his sharp mind.

"Watch out for them, Roan. Few know the darkness as you do."

Roan sat bolt upright when he heard an alluring mysterious feminine voice. His wide eyes darted nervously about his cell. There was no one there. He stood up and approached the glass. Nobody in the hallway either. He hadn't recognized the hypnotic voice and he was quite sure he hadn't imagined it. It was too clear, almost as if the speaker had been sitting right beside him, whispering in his ear. His pale features seemed to lose what little color they had and for one of the first times in his life, Roan was genuinely unnerved.

After a moment, the former assassin moved back to his cot. He didn't turn his back to the glass wall of his cell and paid close attention to his peripheral vision, as well as to what was in front of him. When his right leg met resistance, Roan folded his body down to a sitting position on the bed. He lay down and rolled onto his back, putting his hands behind his head.

~~*~*~*

"So, I don't know what your room was like in our old cabin. It's been *at least* several decades since I've been there."

Isis was only half-listening to Orion's youngest brother, Nero, prattle on. She was taking in the dusky surroundings of the mansion. It was evening and only the soft glow of a few scattered electric sconces lit up the large hallway. It had the odd feeling that Orion referred to as warm, very similar to the cabin. "Home-like" and "comfortable" was how the normals described it. Her heightened senses were absorbing information, which her busy mind then processed.

A few days had passed and the guardians finally allowed the experiments to go to the mansion. She and Jack had listened to the whole debate in the main council room, unbeknownst to the parties involved. They hadn't really meant to. Orion told them to stay out in the hall and they had. Their heightened hearing had been able to pick up the debate that took place behind the heavy doors. It was as clear to them as if the thick doors had been opened. The guardians, namely the leader of the guardian men, wanted them put in the dungeons. In his view, they were dangerous and unpredictable. *Orion has told us they were modified for one thing and only one thing: war. They were created to kill and that is what they are motivated to do. And let us not forget one of them is likely the actual Key and could very well be the instrument of our destruction,* he had vehemently argued. Isis and Jack had exchanged a look, knowing they should feel something at that statement. They hadn't felt anything other than agreement. His point was valid. They were more puzzled when the protectors and guardians arguing for them had leapt to their defense. They didn't understand their reasoning, which seemed quite flawed.

In the end, the High Council had voted on their side. They decided the experiments probably had a crucial part to play in the events that were to take place and the protectors needed to know exactly what they would be up against. Another war, another fight, more violence, more blood: it was nothing new to them. It was what they had been modified to do. There were a few conditions, though. They were to be with someone at all times, be it Jet, Lilly, the Four, or another protector who was trusted by the guardians. They were also not to venture outside without concealing their glowing eyes. And they were under no circumstances to fight in plain view of the public unless it was a matter of life or death and there were no other nonviolent options available. Should either one of them break the conditions, the guardians would have no choice but to put them in the dungeons.

"I tell ya, you're probably the lightest packing person in the world," Nero's voice pulled her out of her thoughts and she glanced over at him as he adjusted the strap of the black duffle bag over his shoulder. "I mean honestly, did you pack air or something? This bag weighs nothing."

"I do not require very much," Isis said almost to herself as she looked up at a portrait. The painted eyes of the well-dressed woman followed her down the hall, as did the gentle eyes of the brown and white horse behind her.

"I see," Nero said, coughing uncomfortably. She glanced at him before turning her attention to their surroundings again. Orion had told her many of the shape shifters would try to engage her in conversation and it would take them a while to adjust to how much she had changed. Nero was probably searching for some sign of the woman she used to be.

"So, what do you want me to call you? Isis or Blitz or another alias you favor?" he attempted conversation again.

"Call me what you like. It is of no matter to me," she replied simply. Isis was still getting used to these people. They were all very different, unique as Orion termed it. All of them carried memories of a person who no longer existed, a woman who once had her face. Each time they spoke with her, there was a small amount of grief hidden in their tone. This was especially true of Passion and Electra. Isis already preferred the mansion to the Meadows. It was a little closer to what she was used to. There were more things to keep her occupied. The Meadows was too serene. Like Jack, she had begun to get bored.

Isis took off her sunglasses to reveal her glowing green eyes and adjusted the matching black bag she carried. Jack and Orion were somewhere on the third floor, each one moving into his new room. They had packed up earlier, which didn't take long since none of them had very many personal effects. They just Appeared in the mansion. Orion was hesitant about letting the experiments go on their own to their rooms, but he allowed it. They had much to learn about being independent and they couldn't if he was always sheltering them.

Isis continued to follow Nero down the hall. They passed an ornate mirror made of silver. She glanced up at the reflective surface and jumped backward, hitting the smooth mahogany wall. In the mirror was her specter, smiling with a knowing look in her blue eyes. A bright aura still shone around her, highlighting her flowing dark brown hair. Isis swallowed as the spirit continued to stare at her, briefly raising a finger to her rose-colored lips.

"As harbingers preceding still the fates and prologue to the omen coming on," she whispered, her form gradually becoming gauzy and indistinct.

"Isis?"

Isis turned her head sharply toward her uncle, who was looking between her and the mirror. There was a curious expression on his face as he studied her, puzzled. She turned her eyes to the mirror, but saw only her own reflection. Nero's was also visible off to the side, but there was no sign of the ghost.

Isis looked to Nero, then back to the mirror, and finally shook her head. "Some after effects of the virus."

Nero stared at her, mystified, and then studied the mirror. She watched as he ran the tips of his fingers through his dark hair, straightening it and preening like many normals tended to do. Isis swallowed and adjusted the gloves on her hands, waiting for Nero to open the door they had stopped at. She had already deduced it was her room since she noticed Nero reaching out for the handle when she had spotted the ghost in the mirror.

"Oh-kay," Nero said as he finished playing with his hair in the mirror. He crossed the hall to where she waited by the door, flinching when he noticed her body tense up. Isis noticed his reaction as she patiently waited for Nero to open the door. Orion's usual gloom-and-doom lecture made the normals jumpy. It was difficult enough with her reflexes and heightened senses, but now that the normals were nervous, it made her feel more on edge. Nero opened the door and stepped inside, momentarily disappearing from her sight.

"This is your room," Nero's voice came from inside the cool room.

Isis stepped in and glanced around at the large, dark room. She was keenly aware of Nero watching her, but disregarded him. She turned her head toward him when he dropped the first duffle bag onto the large bed.

"So, would you like the grand tour?" he asked in a chipper tone.

"It is unnecessary. I can find my way around," Isis responded, turning her eyes back to the room. "It will give me something to do."

"Yeah, gotta keep that super brain working," Nero chuckled at his own joke, rubbing the back of his neck. "Um, oh! Your old clothes are in the drawers and the wardrobe, if you want. We didn't move or get rid of anything. We shape shifters have packrat tendencies."

"I have my own clothing," she replied, still looking around the room. Isis would look through the things later on. It would offer valuable information on the woman everyone remembered.

"You burned candles here once," she mentioned as she ran a hand delicately over the light wood of the dresser. "Ordinary wax, nothing scented. The drapes are drawn and the faint scent of lilies is in the air. All indicators of mourning."

Nero swallowed, glancing toward the windows. "Yeah but now you're back, so yay. Fiesta time."

Isis glanced at him again as she continued to nimbly make her way around the room.

"Your words and conflicting emotions are confusing" she pointed out. "I am not the woman you remember, the one you grieved, and that makes you sad."

"Is that really what you think?" Nero asked as she approached the bed. She could not identify the tone of his voice. It was a mix of hurt and uncertainty.

She paused, studying him. "It is logical. The evidence supports my conclusion."

Nero shook his head. "I can't speak for everyone, but I'm pretty sure nobody cares any less about you just because you've changed a little."

Isis watched him for a moment. He was an odd normal, but she found him amusing, like a small dog. The youngest Deverell was lighthearted and seemed to have the same desire as his older brother: the desire to make everything better.

"Okay, a lot," Nero amended. "But it doesn't matter, you're still Isis. And we love you for it. You may be different but it will never change who you are on the inside."

"No, my organs are the same except for the regenerative abilities," she agreed.

"Metaphor and humor, two things we're definitely going to need to work on," she heard him mutter under his breath. Isis focused on the bed, her sharpened sight picking out an imprint that was most likely invisible to the normals' eyes. Her nostrils twitched as she picked up another faint scent.

"Don't suppose you're the hugging type," Nero said as he rocked on his heels. Isis straightened up immediately, staring at him warily. He put his hands up in a gesture of surrender, a smile playing over his features, and she relaxed a little but still watched him suspiciously. She didn't like the idea of being constricted in any way and physical displays of affection were something she had no interest in.

"Guess I'll take that as a no," he said, chuckling. She glanced back to the bed and then to him. Her ears picked up the deep rumbling of thunder in the distance.

"He's been in here a lot during the past couple days," Isis said quietly as her eyes danced briefly over the ceiling.

"Who?"

Her head tilted. "Jensen. I can just pick up his scent."

"Going heavy on the aftershave again, is he?" Nero said. From his tone, Isis could tell it was an attempt at levity. She still didn't know the proper way to respond to humor. The Corporation never believed comedy to be all that important and so experiments almost never encountered it.

Isis shook her head, raising an eyebrow as she looked at him with a sidelong glance. "He doesn't wear aftershave, unlike you."

Nero snorted and spread his hands. "Hey, it's a special occasion. I wanted to go the whole nine yards for one of my favorite nieces."

He searched her face for some kind of reaction, his shoulders slumping a little when he found none. Isis turned her attention back to the bed, keeping him in her field of vision.

"His scent is subtle," she continued after a moment, trailing her fingers over the smooth sheets. "He uses different brands of soap, deodorant, and shaving products, but they are all imported. All high-end products."

"Yeah, Jensen is very particular about his brands. Loves that pricey imported stuff," Nero confirmed, sounding impressed. "You got all that from sniffing the room?"

She shrugged. "Perfect weapons need superior senses. You never know when you're going to need them."

Isis watched him as he began to fidget, something he often did. Nero straightened the already straight sleeve of his dark blue shirt, sighed, and brushed his hands over the rough denim of his jeans. Isis crossed one leg over the other, interlacing her fingers on her knees.

"You are having difficulty putting words to a thought," she observed.

"Yeah, I am," Nero admitted, swallowing. "He —

Jensen — he nearly went insane when you di-went away. We didn't see him again for five years."

Isis turned her attention back to the window. The faint scent was causing tingling all over her body, as if a mild electric charge were traveling through her bones. She closed her eyes and exhaled softly, trying to will the odd sensation away.

"I think he loves you," Nero explained. "He tries to claim otherwise, but Jensen really is a romantic. I mean, he can be a cocky bastard and doesn't always make a great first impression. The first time the two of you met, you *definitely* didn't get along. But you both saw through each other's prickly demeanors and you just . . . worked. You two made a good pair."

"Guardians and shape shifters aren't allowed to engage in romantic relationships," Isis stated. "It's a strictly platonic alliance, according to the sacred laws of the guardians."

Nero shrugged. "Eh, you've never been a huge fan of rules. Neither is he."

"I was an anarchist?" she asked, puzzled. A protector anarchist was something she had never encountered before and it didn't make sense. The two were contradictory. Nero smiled and laughed softly.

"Believing some archaic rules and laws are unfair and unjust doesn't make you an anarchist. It makes you really fucking cool," he explained, winking at her conspiratorially. Isis blinked a couple times, trying to understand his answer. Rules and laws were to be followed, not questioned.

"I'm sure Orion's already had Jet and Lilly let you see the blueprints of this place so you know where everything is," Nero said, nodding when she did. "Okay, you're all set. I know you don't sleep so feel free to roam about the mansion. I don't know whether or not you can go outside on your own, being under house arrest and all."

"I'm allowed to walk the grounds of the property, but

not beyond them. Not without a protector escort," Isis responded as she watched him make his way to the door. Nero opened it and pausing, looking over his shoulder at her.

"Well, good night," he said, stepping out and closing the door behind him. Isis listened as his footsteps faded down the hall. She moved over to the balcony door and pushed the curtain aside, observing the night. After a moment, Isis turned away from the window, made her way across the room and opened the door. If she didn't find something to do, she would go mad. Her mind needed to be occupied with something. Experiments weren't built to be sedentary.

~~*~*~*

"So what do you think she can do?"

Both Jade and Shae glanced over to Alex at the sudden question. The kitchen staff had left a few hours ago, leaving the room dark and empty. Even the cold steel appliances around them seemed to be asleep, worn out after a full day of working. Jade was sitting at a small table against the far wall, flipping through a paper, only half-interested in the tiny dark print. The dim amber light from the small sconce on the wall beside her barely provided enough light to make out the words. Alex was leaning against a counter across from the long wooden island where meats and vegetables were chopped. Shae was sitting on another counter next to one of the sinks, tossing a bright green tennis ball up and down from hand to hand.

"What do you mean?" Jade asked. Shae looked back to Alex, her repetitive tossing over for the moment. Alex shrugged, though her eyes were alight with interest.

"What can an experiment do exactly?" she clarified. "Obviously she's been modified and trained for combat. But what discipline?"

"All of them, like Orion said," Shae responded. "Jack

mentioned they know how to use every weapon, including those that are no longer used, and every fighting style. They use whatever is advantageous in the situation they're in."

Jade turned another page in her paper. Shae glanced over at the digital clock above the kitchen's doorway. It was a little after midnight. Alex started drumming her fingers on the counter, obviously not finished with the conversation.

"Think Isis is going to make an appearance tonight?" Alex asked after a minute. Jade closed her paper and neatly folded it, her dark eyes regarding Alex.

"She'll come around when she feels like it," Shae replied, as she leaned over and flipped on the bright light over the sink. The round light above the sink spilled a wide circle of light about the kitchen. Both Jade and Alex glanced over at the click of the light switch being flipped on.

"Why are you suddenly so fascinated with Isis anyway?" Jade questioned, her attention turning back to Alex. She crossed her arms over her chest and leaned back against the wall.

Alex shrugged, hopping up on the counter. "Just worried about our teammate."

"Bullshit," Jade stated, her eyebrows furrowing a little as her features became scrutinizing. "That's not the whole reason, not by a long shot. I know you, Alex."

Alex hooked her thumbs in the pockets of her jeans, squaring her shoulders. Shae turned her attention to Alex, rolling the soft green ball in her hand.

"If Jack and Isis are what Orion claims them to be, do you know what that means?" Alex asked, unable to hide the excitement in her voice.

"That we have a hell of a problem to deal with," Shae suggested dryly. "One that's probably going to end with the apocalypse and our horrible demises, lots of blood and screaming and all that fun stuff."

Alex and Jade both gave Shae a sardonic look. She held up her pale hands in the light. Her thin fingers, with perfectly manicured fingernails, held the ball tightly in her right hand.

"Resurrection, genetic modification even after birth. Genetics period. Regenerative abilities. Enhanced brain power in terms of memory and recall. Who knows what else? And," Alex paused and glanced over her shoulder to make sure no one was listening. "If we really are up against an empire run by a guardian turned necromancer, I'm thinking it's not such a bad thing to have a couple living weapons on our side."

Jade ran her hands over her face, muttering. "Guardians have mercy."

"She's not a toy, Alex," Shae grumbled.

"I wasn't suggesting she was," Alex protested.

"A weapon is actually a tool, not a toy," a quiet voice came from the doorway, startling the three of them.

It was as if a ghost had spoken. None of them could see a body to go with the soft voice. Then Isis emerged from the darkness beside the open door. The shadows slowly melted away from her as she stepped into the light. Her gait was stealthy and smooth. Her sleek black clothes didn't even rustle. She stopped at the head of the counter, trailing the tips of her fingers over the smooth green marble surface before lightly resting them on it. Her glowing green eyes were turned down to the counter, but Alex had a feeling she already knew their exact positions. She glanced at Jade and Shae, a nervous questioning look in her eyes. She was wondering whether or not she should apologize.

"Are you settled?" Jade asked. Isis nodded once. Shae put the ball down on the counter she was sitting on. Isis glanced in Shae's direction, her eyes fixing on the ball for a split second before turning back to the protector.

"Would you like to go out tomorrow?" Shae asked, a bit hesitantly. Isis studied her.

"I am still acclimating to my new surroundings. Perhaps in a few days," she answered, her gaze wandering around the dark kitchen.

"So, Isis," Alex began, wanting desperately to keep the quiet at bay. The dark was eerie enough on its own. She waited until Isis looked at her to continue. "The wiry build is for maximum agility and speed, correct?"

Shae and Jade both glared at Alex with disapproving looks. Isis, however, merely shrugged.

"From what I understand, I've always been built like this. But the answer to your question is yes. Most experiments, especially those of the seven series, have wiry frames for optimal movement. However, there are many different lines of experiments, each with its own individual purposes and objectives," she answered.

Alex nodded and reached for a shiny red and gold apple in the fruit bowl behind her. "And how quick are you?"

In one smooth fast move, faster than the naked eye could see, Isis hurled a small combat knife. The three only saw a flash of silver and the weapon was embedded in the center of the apple that Alex had just picked up. All three women jumped, startled at the quiet whisper of the sharp blade piercing the apple's flesh.

Alex let out a yelp as she dropped the apple in shock. It fell to the tiles with a dull thud. She looked back to Isis, unnerved and also in awe. It was a remarkably perfect aim. The knife had pierced the apple exactly in the middle so that neither the hilt nor blade touched any part of Alex's hand. Isis remained still as stone, staring at the speared apple on the floor. After a moment, she moved over to the apple, crouched down and picked it up. She easily pulled the small knife out of the red and gold flesh and handed the fruit to Alex. Alex swallowed as she took the apple.

"You're afraid of me," Isis observed as she grabbed a towel that was hanging out of one of the wooden cabinets and wiped off the blade of the knife, placing it in a small sheath at her hip. "It is understandable, but I can assure you that you needn't be. In time, you will become accustomed to experiments."

Isis glanced at each of them again and then made her way across the kitchen tiles, melting back into the murky shadows coating the mansion. Jade grabbed her newspaper, rolled it up, and threw it at Alex.

"Hey!" Alex yelped in surprise and she turned to look at Jade and Shae. "What the hell was that for?"

"You just had to ask her," Jade hissed.

Alex's jaw dropped open. "I was curious. Besides, the last time I checked, sheltering wasn't all that great an approach when dealing with trauma survivors."

Jade opened her mouth to argue, but Shae interrupted her. "Sorry, Jade. But I agree with Alex on this."

Jade turned stunned eyes to Shae. "I'm sorry?"

Shae shrugged. "We shouldn't treat her any differently. She's still Isis. The only way she's going to heal is if life goes on as it always has. If she finds comfort in her abilities, then I say we let her demonstrate and practice whenever and however she wants as long as she doesn't hurt anyone or attract any unwanted attention. Isis is right; we have to get used to her. I'm pretty sure the reverse is true too."

Jade ran a hand through her thick black hair. "I get what you're saying, but that's not the safest way to look at the situation."

"What's your answer? Lock her up and throw away the key?" Shae asked shortly. Alex ran a hand through her sleek hair, sensing an argument brewing. Shae was overprotective of her cousin and it blinded her to certain realties.

"You know that's not what I was suggesting," Jade replied calmly. "Let's just take things one step at a time and try not to instigate any reflexes."

"I can do that," Alex agreed.

Shae nodded and turned her gaze to the windows

behind her. Lightning lit up the sky with an electric blue hue.

"Storm's coming," she commented. Even as she spoke, raindrops began to softly patter on the clean panes of glass. Jade and Alex looked at the window with half-interest. After a moment, Jade stood up out of her chair and stretched.

"It's late. I'm calling it a night," she said. "See you both in the morning."

Shae and Alex nodded and watched her go. It had been a long day and weariness had seeped into their bones. The remaining two left the kitchen shortly after Jade, heading to their rooms and a much welcomed dreamless sleep.

~~*~*~*

Shortly after two in the morning, Jensen made his way down to the first floor of the mansion. His shoes quietly clicked on the rough green tiles as he wandered about aimlessly. He hadn't been able to sleep and decided to wander the long halls of the mansion. The protector frowned when he heard the soft crackle of a fire. A short way down the main hall, amber light danced out from one of the rooms. Jensen continued on his way, relieved to be able to focus his mind on something else. He had considered showing Isis to her room, a job that ultimately fell to Nero. He ran a hand over his face. His feelings hadn't changed and when he looked at Isis, Jensen didn't see a cold-blooded killer. All he saw was the feisty and occasionally infuriating woman he had made love with.

Jensen reached the main library and saw it was dimly lit from a fire in the hearth. Outside, a thunderstorm softly continued. The rain slapping against the glass almost drowned out the crackling of the fire. Thunder rumbled quietly, seeming to lack the energy to make the loud bangs that were so startling, even when they were expected. His eyes traveled to the elegant dark red sofa sitting in front of the fireplace. On the end furthest from the door sat Isis, one arm resting on the armrest. Her glowing eyes seemed to be mesmerized by the bright flames before her. They were a sparkling emerald green. She didn't look at him, but Jensen knew she was aware of his presence. He cleared his throat and she slowly turned her gaze to him.

"Apologies. I didn't know anyone else was awake," Jensen said as he turned to continue on his way.

"I don't sleep," her quiet voice stopped him and he turned back to her. She watched him for a moment before turning her gaze back to the fire. "What is your excuse?"

Jensen couldn't help but smile at the question, which was reminiscent of one of the first conversations they'd had. He leaned his shoulder against the wooden doorframe.

"Couldn't sleep," he replied, choosing to remain vague. She nodded once, the warm light illuminating her lovely features. Jensen watched her for a few moments, wondering what to say. She saved him the trouble.

"You can sit if you desire," she said, her voice barely above a whisper. "I am not actively seeking solitude and I am no threat to you."

Jensen stepped into the room, approaching the sofa. "The thought never crossed my mind."

Isis glanced over at him. Behind them, thunder rumbled in the stormy night. The rain continued to flow down the glass. The atmosphere remained pleasantly warm and cozy. Jensen sat on the opposite end of the couch and ran his fingers over the smooth fabric of the sofa.

"I always liked this furniture. It's among my favorites in the mansion," he mentioned. "I think it's from my brief time as a thief. Old habits die hard."

Isis spread her slender fingers over the armrest. "Late nineteenth century Baroque style, walnut and silk damask. You could probably get a good sum for it."

Jensen chuckled. "Good eye."

She turned her attention to him. "Partly. An

encyclopedic memory allows me to accurately price most things. Grenich believes it advantageous to have barracks full of personal cat burglars."

"So you're a soldier and a thief?" he asked, amused.

"I'm a bit of everything," Isis answered, turning her attention back to the fire. A large knot of wood popped, sending sparks spraying up toward the chimney. The black steel grate in front of the fireplace prevented any sparks of flame from escaping the firebox. Jensen smoothed the already smooth fabric of his pants.

"I owe you an apology."

Isis looked over at him and if she was puzzled, she didn't look it. He crossed one hand over the other on his lap.

"I should have recognized you at the hacienda," Jensen began. "I should have stopped you. My own desire for revenge put you in danger."

She shook her head, turning her gaze back to the fire. "You did not. I had already decided to kill the people on that list. Had you attempted to stop me, I would have killed you."

It was chilling how simply she said it. She was stating a fact, not musing out loud. Jensen looked over at her, studying her for a moment.

Isis turned her intense gaze to him. "I didn't see it then, when we first encountered each other outside the hacienda. Your manner around me, the bits of information I've gathered from others. We were lovers, back before Grenich recruited me."

She went quiet again, turning her eyes back to the fire. Jensen continued to watch her, patiently waiting for her to speak again. The flickering amber light seemed to enhance her beauty, but it also highlighted her shadows. Jensen didn't care. She was different, but she was still Isis. That would never change.

"I don't remember it, my life before the Corporation. I don't know if I ever will or if I want to, but I do feel a connection to you," she continued. "I don't know how else to describe it and I'm not sure I understand it entirely."

Jensen didn't say anything for a moment, just regarding her with his bright blue eyes. He carefully approached her and sat next to her, so close their long legs were almost touching. Isis looked over at him, her eyes meeting his. He placed a strong warm hand on her face, sadly noting how every muscle in her body seemed to go rigid at the simple touch. Jensen leaned forward and laid his lips upon hers in a gentle but intimate kiss.

Her thin rose-colored lips were just as warm and soft as he remembered them. Jensen felt her hand hesitantly cover his. She was incredibly cautious, but he had expected that. They remained locked in the simple loving kiss for a few brief moments before Jensen finally pulled back and looked at her, resting his forehead against hers.

Jensen stood, looking years younger than he had when he first entered the room. He smiled at her and Isis saw affection clearly reflected in his eyes. There was something about the way he acted around her, the way he seemed comfortable and unafraid, that made her feel more like an individual instead of a weapon off an assembly line. Coop had told her out in the forest that this would happen. Through her family and loved ones, she would relearn what it meant to be an individual. She could forget all the bad that Grenich put in her and by doing so, she would discover how to use her skills against them.

Isis watched Jensen leave, listening to his footsteps vanish down the hall. He was heading to bed. She turned her attention back to the fire, which was dying down. Behind her, the storm was also beginning to let up. The shadows of the deep night remained, hiding the moon and stars. Isis stood up and approached the large window, staring out at the inky darkness and imagining what lay beyond it.

She turned away from the window, approached the

fireplace, and watched the flames gradually die and extinguish. When the room was dark again, lit only occasionally by a streak of lightning, Isis left the room to wander the halls. Her mind was racing with thoughts and sensations. Now that she was free, everything seemed so vibrant and alive. But she wouldn't allow herself to enjoy everything to its fullest just yet. Orion and Jack needed her help with their new allies.

They had an empire to dismantle.

CHAPTER FOURTEEN

Jet didn't sleep the night Isis returned to the mansion. When the sun rose the next morning, Lilly was curled up next to him, sleeping peacefully as she always did. Jet, however, lay on his back. His blue-green eyes were focused on the dark blue ceiling above them. He hadn't even realized the entire night had passed until he felt the sun on his face. Jet slid out of bed, careful not to wake his beloved wife. He paused at the side of the bed and put his feet into his slippers, which happened to be in the shape of dark green frogs. They had been a gift from his youngest daughter, Hunter, years back. She had gotten her mother a pair of rabbits. Both sets of slippers were worn with age. Jet looked down into the half-lidded, dark eyes of the frogs. Some of the paint had chipped away on the right eye of the frog on his left foot. The frogs had a lazy look of contentment on their faces, as if they enjoyed keeping the protector leader's feet warm.

Jet looked toward the bed when Lilly sighed in her sleep and turned over, slipping her slender hands under the pillow. He turned and continued on his original intended path, exiting the room and closing the door behind him. The new morning light was just beginning to brighten the dusky sky and nobody but Jet was in the halls. *Well, except for the experiments,* he thought. Jet glanced over his shoulder, wondering if he would see one of them, but the hall was empty behind him.

He continued on his way, heading for the kitchen. Jet enjoyed this part of the day because he was the only one around. He could walk to the kitchen, brew a cup of coffee, and grab the paper Remington always brought in before going on his daily jog. Remington was usually the first one up and out, but only by a few minutes. Jet and Lilly were usually the last ones to turn in for the evening. He figured it somehow evened out.

When he was halfway to the kitchen, Jet paused and frowned. He could distinctly smell coffee brewing in the kitchen. Remington didn't drink coffee, only tea. Jet doubted he had ever even used the coffee machine. So who else was around this early? He wondered if maybe one of his children had come home early with a hangover. Jet stepped into the kitchen, almost dreading the mess he'd find.

"Oh," he said when he saw who had made the coffee. "It's you."

Orion sat in the same seat Jade had occupied the previous evening. A dark red mug was held firmly in his hand, steam wafting out of the top. Orion looked over at Jet when he entered the kitchen.

"You were expecting someone else?" Orion asked as he turned his attention back outside the window. Jet approached the small table where he sat and took the seat across from him, blocking his view of the window. Orion's bright blue eyes regarded him, waiting for the protector leader to speak. Something caught his eye and he looked down to the floor, frowning.

"Jet," Orion began, puzzled. "What are you wearing on your feet?"

Jet looked down at his slippers. "They're frogs."

Orion raised his eyebrows as he returned his eyes to

Jet. "I see."

"I'm actually glad you're here. There are a few things that I need you to clear up for me," Jet began. "Some loose ends have been bothering me."

"All right," Orion said as he put his mug down and crossed his arms over each other. He kept his eyes on Jet. The morning was awash with a bright golden light, chasing away the last remnants of night. The kitchen would soon be alive with activity. At the moment, though, it was just the two men in the large quiet room. A strong wind blew through the trees on the property, stripping off even more leaves.

"How did you know Isis was in the Corporation?" Jet asked, his tone wary.

Orion shrugged. "Like I told you before, I have my sources."

"Do these 'sources' have names?"

Orion shook his head. "I'm not at liberty to divulge that information. It would endanger their lives and I will not do that."

Jet leaned forward. "You want to tell me how you and Roan just happened to know about Isis? The last time I checked, her heritage was unknown on Earth. Even I didn't know a good portion of her personal information."

Orion smiled a little, the golden light of dawn brightening the kitchen even more. "Again, I can't tell you where I get my information from. But don't you find it a little funny how Isis wound up just a hop, skip, and a jump away from the mansion?"

"I don't know. Coincidence maybe," Jet replied as he tilted his chair back. Orion chuckled as he picked up his coffee mug again.

"When you become aware of the Grenich Corporation's true modus operandi, you learn that coincidences are usually anything but," Orion stated before sipping his warm coffee. Jet looked at him, perplexed.

"What does that mean?" Jet asked.

Orion looked up at him again. "It means things usually happen for a reason, whether we realize it or not. Is there anything else troubling you?"

Jet paused, thinking over how to ask his next question. Orion saved him the trouble as he put the mug down again. It made a soft clinking noise as it contacted the hard green surface of the table.

"You want to know how a woman who died can be up and about without so much as a scar," he stated as he raised his eyes to Jet's again. Jet nodded.

"There's another line of experiment in the Corporation, frequently referred to as the blood-givers. They have special blood. It's loaded with stem cells, among other things." Orion looked off to the side and shook his head. "I'm not sure what is in it exactly, but whatever it is, it is powerful. Something the necromancers created long ago. One transfusion and all wounds are healed. Blood from the younger ones can even restart a heart for up to thirty-three hours after it has ceased beating. The blood may do more, but that's all I was told about it."

Orion looked back to Jet. The older shape shifter stood up and brought his mug to the sink, pouring out the remaining contents. He rinsed the mug out and placed it in the dishwasher, frowning as he closed the door. Orion rested his weight against the counter.

"There are so many aspects of life that are connected, so many supposed coincidences. I doubt we'll ever truly realize just how connected we really are," Orion said, thinking out loud. "For as long as I've been fighting Grenich, I've had this strange feeling I wasn't the first to do so. This fight goes back further than any of us."

Jet looked over at him, his morning routine long since forgotten. Listening to Orion, he was a little unnerved by how viable the older shape shifter's "feeling" seemed. After a moment, Orion shook himself out of his musing. He glanced over at Jet and smiled a little.

"Ignore me," Orion said quietly. "I've been deprived of

sleep for too long. I'm guessing we have another long day ahead of us."

Jet nodded, distracted, as he watched Orion exit the kitchen. He turned his attention outside to the dawn-kissed lands. Autumn was gradually turning to winter. Soon there would be frost on the ground and the leaves would all be gone, leaving only bare branches. Jet stood up and approached the counter where a hot pot of coffee still sat. He moved over to the wooden cabinets, opening one and retrieving his old dark blue mug. Jet seemed to be moving in a daze as he poured himself a cup of coffee, adding the usual small amount of cream and sugar, and then proceeded down the brightly lit hallway toward the study. The sunlight bathed the room where he and Lilly did most of their work, but Jet hardly noticed it as he sat down in front of the computer. His mind was racing with a million questions, questions that might forever go unanswered.

The sudden ringing of the office phone jerked him out of his thoughts and caused him to jump. Jet cursed under his breath as the coffee sloshed out of the mug, burning his hand. He grabbed a couple blank sheets of paper from the printer and placed them on the tidy desk. Jet laid the mug down on the papers and examined his hand, wincing when he saw the angry shade of red on his skin from the scalding coffee. The phone chirped pleasantly again, bringing Jet's focus back to it. He lifted it from the cradle and was suddenly overcome with a feeling of cold. It was like ice raced through the phone into his bones. He shuddered and cleared his throat as he brought the phone to his ear.

"Jet Monroe speaking," he answered.

"Jet," a warm, boisterous masculine voice boomed through the earpiece. "It's so good to finally speak to one of the infamous protector leaders."

"I'm sorry, who's calling?" Jet asked, as he tried to place the voice. Somehow he knew he wouldn't be able to. He didn't know the caller, who was acting otherwise. A low chuckle traveled over the line, strangely menacing despite being an amused and friendly laugh.

"Of course, forgive me. I have heard so much about you, I feel we already know one another," the man continued after a moment. "My name is Russell Carding. And I believe you have something that belongs to my employer."

For a moment, Jet couldn't even comprehend he was speaking to the man Orion had told him about. The very same man who had overseen whatever had been done to Isis. The right hand of Set, a man allegedly committing countless atrocities on a daily basis, was speaking to him over the telephone. The ridiculousness of the situation almost made Jet laugh.

"Jet, are you still there?" there was genuine concern in the man's voice.

"I don't know what you're talking about," Jet finally managed to respond, wishing Lilly were with him.

Carding let out a long-suffering sigh, which was followed by the sound of papers being shuffled. "Two seven series, identification numbers 295 and 299, you probably know them as Jack and, of course, Isis. I'm assuming you already know of my boss, yes? Now, Set already knows Orion's alive. He knows Roan's alive. And he knows that you are in possession of two of his more successful products. I'm afraid he needs them back, Jet."

"They're not products," Jet growled, sick to even use the word in association with two individuals. "They're shape shifters with names and rights—"

"Is that what you truly believe?" Carding interrupted. "Surely by now you've seen some of what they're capable of, what they are. Jet, you've got two time bombs under your roof. They're not puppies you can hit with a rolled up newspaper when they chew on the furniture. They're deadlier than you realize and they need to be kept in a controlled environment."

"You mean a cage?" Jet asked with mock pleasantness,

sitting back in his chair. "Or do you prefer the term 'jail cell'?"

"Jet, my employers are trying to save you a lot of pain and heartache. You may think otherwise, but we are not on opposite sides. At least we needn't be. Set and Pyra merely want to avoid the tragedy that will inevitably ensue should you unwisely allow your emotions to dictate your actions, like the good Dr. Deverell has done. Think about your lovely wife and co-leader upstairs, sleeping soundly," Carding's voice took on a strangely hypnotic quality.

"I don't respond to fear mongering and neither does she," Jet replied tersely, not liking how much this man seemed to know. "And if you threaten my family again, you will regret it Mr. Carding."

Carding was quiet for a moment. "I didn't want to resort to this, but you leave me no choice. One way or another, I'm going to retrieve my employer's products and bring them back to where they belong. I know he would prefer we settle this matter like civilized men, but I get the impression that's not going to happen and I am authorized to use force if necessary. Jet, I want you to understand what those two experiments are capable of. Imagine a world without war, pain, terrorism, violence, or even disease. A perfect utopia. It *is* achievable. Unfortunately, curing the world's ills requires sacrifice. It is an unfortunate and nasty business, what I do, but it is a necessary evil. A few shape shifters sacrificed to achieve a perfect world hardly seems like much to ask."

"What you're talking about is impossible," Jet stated. "And if the price of achieving it is by doing business with men like you, who do the things that you do, then I would prefer to live in a flawed world."

"Your father didn't see it like that, neither did his father before him," Carding replied softly. From his tone of voice, Jet could almost see the serpentine smile crossing his face.

"My father has been gone longer than you've been

alive," Jet replied calmly, keeping his anger in check. Carding was obviously trying to provoke such a response and Jet refused to give it to him.

"Come now, Jet. You know I'm not human," Carding said, then laughed raucously and audibly slapped his knee. "Oh my friend, you are *very* funny."

Jet cringed at the sound of the man's laugh, which was giving him a headache. He leaned forward.

"So you're a revenant then," he said.

"I am a humble and loyal servant of Set and Pyra," Carding stated, his friendly tone never wavering. Jet racked his mind as he tried to think of what he knew about revenants. It wasn't much.

"Enough with mirth," Carding continued after a moment, reverting to a business manner with frightening ease and speed. "If you do not hand over the experiments willingly, then Set will consider that a hostile act and will have to retrieve his products through force. You do not want to go to war with him. Jet, believe me when I tell you it is within his power to decimate your entire race. The last shape shifter who tried to stand against him ... well, I'm sure you remember what happened to the Aldridge line. Not many shape shifters left from that once prospering family now, are there? You have to ask yourself: are two experiments really worth that?"

Jet decided that he'd had enough of the conversation. He leaned forward and slammed the phone back down in its cradle. Leaning back in his seat, Jet closed his eyes, the chill gradually leaving his body. He spun his chair around so he was looking out the window. Around him, the mansion was just beginning to wake up. Jet could hear the sounds of its occupants going about their daily routines, not a care in the world outside of their responsibilities.

His eyes were drawn to a smaller tree just outside the window. All of its leaves were gone. All except for one single dried leaf in the exact middle, already brown. Autumn had ended and winter was arriving.

~~*~*~*

Deep in the depths of a Grenich laboratory, Set sat on a couch. Stretched out on the smooth cream-colored fabric, her head in his lap, was Pyra. Her eyes were closed, but she was fully awake. Set ran his fingers through her curly gold hair, his other arm resting on the arm of the couch. Resting his feet on the glass table in front of the couch, Set's dark eyes were fixed on the wall across the room. He wore his more youthful appearance — his guardian persona.

A quick knock drew his attention to the door. Pyra turned her head in his lap.

"Enter," Set called. An older-looking security guard opened the door and Tracy entered, carrying a small folded bit of paper.

"Ah Tracy," Set greeted. "It is good to see you again."

"Sir," Tracy said respectfully, bowing her head. "Mr. Carding just got off the phone with Jet."

She handed Set the bit of paper and Pyra looked up at him, wrapping a golden curl around one finger. She pursed her bright red lips as her dark brown eyes skimmed the small blue print.

"Well," Set said, folding the paper again. "This is most disappointing, but not unexpected. The Monroe family has always possessed more morality than wisdom, always guided by their emotions."

He held the paper out and Pyra snapped her fingers. The paper disintegrated in a flash of flame and smoke. Set smiled and stroked her hair again.

"Is there something else you wanted, Tracy?" he asked, his eyes on Pyra.

"No, sir," she said, shifting her weight.

"Your revenant is lying," Pyra observed, playing with one of the straps of her red dress. Set smiled, looking up at Tracy.

"The lady is astute," he said, snapping his fingers. Pyra sat up, allowing Set to stand. She sat on the couch, spreading her long arms across the back. Set held his hands behind his back as he approached Tracy, circling her once. He looked at her with appraising eyes. She kept her gaze ahead, knowing better than to look him directly in the eye.

"You're wondering why I didn't allow you to capture the seven series. You probably wish to inquire about the wisdom of such a move," Set observed, moving to the small table.

"I would never question your judgment, sir," Tracy responded.

"It is all right. The two seven series are Key possibilities and now they're with the protectors," Set explained. "While it is not the ideal situation, it is one that could prove beneficial to us. You're making the same mistake the protectors are and assuming the experiments are regular shape shifters."

"Which they are not," Pyra added, smirking.

"A bored experiment is a time bomb," Set continued. "One need look no further than 7-299's actions on the outside."

"She killed the recruitment team that captured and retrieved her," Tracy said.

"That she did, saved me a lot of trouble," Set said, glancing at the floor. "There are two seven series in the mansion, absorbing valuable information about the protectors and guardians, even the Meadows. Information that will be quite advantageous for me when I get the Key."

Tracy looked over at him. "But sir, how will you retrieve them?"

Set touched the delicate petals of the yellow tulips on the table. They immediately withered and died, shriveling up into dry husks.

"We wait for the inevitable to happen," he explained,

looking over his shoulder at Tracy. "You see, my dear, one of two scenarios is going to happen. Experiments are not meant to live for extended periods outside of Corporation walls. The Monroes' sentimentality will be their undoing and, by extension, the guardians' as well. Though 7-299 may wear a familiar face, her mind and motivation is no longer the same. Either the experiments will kill an innocent on their own accord or we'll force them to do it. The protectors will turn on them and by extension the Monroes."

Set returned to the couch, sitting beside Pyra. She was bouncing a ball of fire from hand to hand.

"Darling, there is one thing you are not thinking of," Pyra pointed out, extinguishing the ball of flame. "The seven series that killed the recruitment team, she could turn her rage on the facility she was stolen from."

Set laughed. "That would actually be entertaining to watch, but experiments are not suicidal. To attempt an attack on a Grenich laboratory with mere protectors as back up? She would never take such a risk. There is nothing to gain from it and the experiments know that. Still, it never hurts to be prepared. Tracy, please go down to security and tell them I wish for all facilities to remain on high alert until further notice. Increase the number of guards, check security systems, and make sure every vulnerability is accounted for and remedied."

"Right away, sir."

Tracy turned and opened the door, disappearing down the hall. Set leaned back on the couch and Pyra rested her head against his shoulder.

"Our allies will amass in the next couple months," Set mentioned. "I've sent out a few of the newer series to neutralize those who were sluggish to respond."

"I still wish those two seven series were back in the facility," Pyra mentioned. "One possibility out of three is not favorable odds."

Set shushed her. "I told you before, 7-299 did us a huge

favor by killing the recruitment team and she will be instrumental in destroying the protectors. She belongs to us, no matter what Dr. Deverell believes. The two seven series will return to us, one way or another."

To Be Continued

ACKNOWLEDGMENTS

Thank you so much to my friends and family, who are continually supportive of me. Thank you to my parents for their endless patience, love, and support. Thank you to my brother, Michael, and Mom for being great proofreaders. Thank you to my amazing godmother, Leandra Torres (Aunt Punkey), a woman who I very much admire and who is always there with an encouraging word.

Thank you to my amazing editor, Rose Anne Roper. Thank you to my cover artist, Najla Qamber. Thank you to my always awesome beta reader, Taia Hartman.

Thank you so much to Crimson Fox/Snowy Wings Publishing for helping me achieve a dream and providing support, as well as helping immensely with marketing. I must give a very special thank you to my good friend, Lyssa Chiavari, who invited me to join Snowy Wings and for being one of the absolute best people in the world. It is truly an honor to know you and call you a friend.

Thank you so much to all the wonderful professors in my life, who have taught me and continue to teach me to this day. Thank you so much, Alex and Jess Hall for your continued knowledge of all things concerning mythology. It is an honor to know you both. Thank you, Marco Benassi and Alexander Bolyanatz, for never giving up on me and providing advice when needed. Thank you Ángela Rebellón (the best ASL teacher there is). Thank you to all the professors and teachers who I've thanked in previous novels. If you enjoyed this novel, it is thanks to them. Any success I've experienced is thanks in large part to the dedicated professors and teachers I've had the privilege to learn from.

Thank you so much to all the incredible asexual artists who I have met through Asexual Artists. Thank you to my dear friends, Joel Cornah, Darcie Little Badger, and T. Hueston. You put such beautiful art into the world and it inspires me so very much. I love you all.

Thank you so much to my family and friends for providing me with the support I need to continue on the rocky path that is writing. Thank you, Billy Payne, for coming to my first reading and making the experience a lot less terrifying. Thank you Robyn Byrd, Emily Kittell-Queller (extra special thanks to you and your housemates for being a safe haven on the holidays), Julie Denninger-Greensly, Ryan Prior, Leigh Hellman, and anyone else who I'm forgetting (and will undoubtedly feel just awful about later). Your love, kind words, encouragement, and support make a world of difference in my life.

A special thank you to Becca (who gave me the most wonderful compliment a writer can ever hope to hear) and Susan Sandahl, who continue to be active on my author page and are some of the most awesome people I've ever had the pleasure of meeting. You're both my favorite readers and I apologize for the ridiculously long wait.
Again, I must thank all my readers. Thank you for your kind words and gestures. Thank you for getting lost in the crazy world I created. Thank you for continuing to be so generous with your time. I cannot begin to express my gratitude to you all. You continue to humble me and I hope this book lived up to your expectations. Thank you all, so very, very much.

ABOUT THE AUTHOR

Lauren Jankowski, an openly aromantic asexual feminist activist and author from Illinois, has been an avid reader and a genre feminist for most of her life. She holds a degree in Women and Genders Studies from Beloit College. In 2015, she founded "Asexual Artists," a Tumblr and WordPress site dedicated to highlighting the contributions of asexual identifying individuals to the arts.

She has been writing fiction since high school, when she noticed a lack of strong women in the popular genre books. When she's not writing or researching, she enjoys reading (particularly anything relating to ancient myths) or playing with her pets. She participates in activism for asexual visibility and feminist causes. She hopes to bring more strong heroines to literature, including badass asexual women.

Her ongoing fantasy series is *The Shape Shifter Chronicles*, which is published through Crimson Fox Publishing.

www.ingramcontent.com/pod-product-compliance
Lightning Source LLC
Chambersburg PA
CBHW030536190726
48283CB00006B/1940